Praise for

THE
ALICE
NETWORK

"Both funny and heartbreaking, this epic journey of two courageous women is an unforgettable tale of little-known wartime glory and sacrifice. Quinn knocks it out of the park with this spectacular book!"
—Stephanie Dray, *New York Times* bestselling author of *America's First Daughter*

"*The Alice Network,* which hinges on the unsung valor of female espionage agents in the Great War, perfectly balances a propulsive plot, faultlessly observed period detail, and a cast of characters so vividly drawn that I half expected to blink and see them standing in front of me. This is historical fiction at its best—thrilling, affecting, revelatory."
—Jennifer Robson, international bestselling author of *Moonlight over Paris*

"*The Alice Network* has history, suspense, romance and women kicking butt. I couldn't put it down."
—*NPR Books*

THE ALICE
NETWORK

By Kate Quinn

THE ALICE NETWORK
THE HUNTRESS
THE ROSE CODE

The Empress of Rome Series
LADY OF THE ETERNAL CITY
THE THREE FATES (novella)
EMPRESS OF THE SEVEN HILLS
DAUGHTERS OF ROME
MISTRESS OF ROME

The Borgia Chronicles
THE LION AND THE ROSE
THE SERPENT AND THE PEARL

Collaborative Works
A DAY OF FIRE: A NOVEL OF POMPEII
A YEAR OF RAVENS: A NOVEL OF BOUDICA'S REBELLION
A SONG OF WAR: A NOVEL OF TROY
RIBBONS OF SCARLET:
A NOVEL OF THE FRENCH REVOLUTION'S WOMEN

THE ALICE
NETWORK

A NOVEL

KATE QUINN

wm

WILLIAM MORROW
An Imprint of HarperCollins*Publishers*

Excerpt from *The Diamond Eye* Copyright © 2022 by Kate Quinn.

THE ALICE NETWORK. Copyright © 2017 by Paul Wehmeyer Productions LLC. All rights reserved. Printed in Lithuania. No part of this book may be used or reproduced in any manner whatsoever without written permission except in the case of brief quotations embodied in critical articles and reviews. For information, address HarperCollins Publishers, 195 Broadway, New York, NY 10007.

First William Morrow mass market printing: February 2022
First William Morrow paperback printing: June 2017

Print Edition ISBN: 978-0-06-321524-5
Digital Edition ISBN: 978-0-06-265420-5

Cover design by Elsie Lyons
Cover photographs © Malgorzata Maj/Arcangel (woman); © Stephen MulcaheyArcangel (warplanes); © David & Myrtille/Arcangel (car); © Shutterstock
Map by Nick Springer. Map copyright © Springer Cartographics

William Morrow and HarperCollins are registered trademarks of HarperCollins Publishers in the United States of America and other countries.

22 23 24 25 26   SB   10 9 8 7 6 5 4 3 2 1

To my mother
The first reader, the first critic, the first fan
This is for you

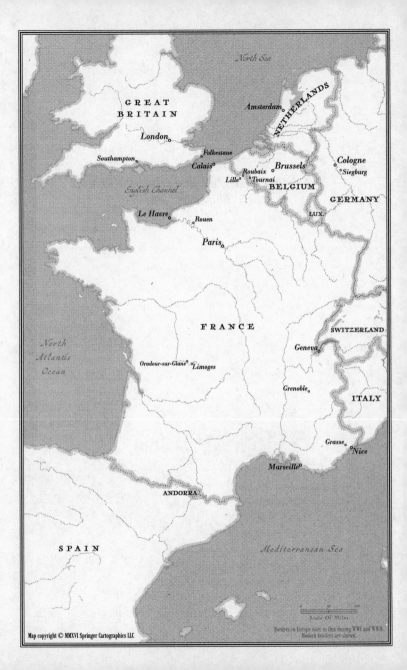

North Sea

GREAT
BRITAIN

Amsterdam

NETHERLANDS

London

Southampton

Folkestone

Calais

Cologne

Brussels

Siegburg

Roubaix

Lille   Tournai

BELGIUM

GERMANY

English Channel

LUX.

Le Havre   Rouen

Paris

FRANCE

SWITZERLAND

Geneva

North
Atlantic
Ocean

Oradour-sur-Glane   Limoges

Grenoble

ITALY

Grasse   Nice

Marseille

ANDORRA

SPAIN

Mediterranean Sea

Scale Of Miles

Map copyright © MMXVI Springer Cartographics LLC

Borders in Europe were in flux during WWI and WWII.
Modern borders are shown.

PART 1

CHAPTER 1
CHARLIE

May 1947
Southampton

The first person I met in England was a hallucination. I brought her with me, onboard the serene ocean liner that had carried my numb, grief-haunted self from New York to Southampton.

I was sitting opposite my mother at a wicker table among the potted palms in the Dolphin Hotel, trying to ignore what my eyes were telling me. The blond girl by the front desk wasn't who I thought she was. I *knew* she wasn't who I thought she was. She was just an English girl waiting beside her family's luggage, someone I'd never seen before—but that didn't stop my mind from telling me she was someone else. I averted my eyes, looking instead at the three English boys at the next table, who were busy trying to get out of tipping their waitress. "Five percent tip or ten?" a boy in a university tie was saying, waving the bill, and his friends laughed. "I only tip if they're pretty. She had skinny legs . . ."

I glowered at them, but my mother was oblivious. "So cold and wet for May, *mon Dieu!*" She unfolded her napkin: a feminine flurry of lavender-scented skirts among the heaps of our baggage. Quite a contrast to me, all rumpled and cross. "Put your shoulders back, *chérie.*" She'd lived in New York since she married my father, but she still sprinkled her phrases with French. "Do stop slouching."

"I can't slouch in this getup." I was crammed into a waist cincher like a band of iron, not that I needed one because I was built like a twig, but my froth of skirts wouldn't hang right without it, so band of iron it was. That Dior, may he and his New Look rot in hell. My mother always dressed right at the crest of any new fashion, and she was built for the latest styles: tall, tiny waisted, voluptuously curved, a confection in her full-skirted traveling suit. I had a frilly traveling suit too, but I was drowning in all that fabric. Nineteen forty-seven was hell for little bony girls like me who couldn't wear the New Look. Then again, 1947 was hell for any girl who would rather work calculus problems than read *Vogue*, any girl who would rather listen to Edith Piaf than Artie Shaw, and any girl with an empty ring finger but a rounding belly.

I, Charlie St. Clair, was officially three for three. That was the other reason my mother wanted me in a waist cincher. I was only three months gone, but she wasn't taking any chances that my shape might announce what a whore she'd brought into the world.

I stole a glance across the hotel court. The blond girl was still there, and my mind was still trying to tell me she was someone she wasn't. I looked away again with a hard blink as our waitress approached with a smile. "Will you be staying for the full tea, madam?" She did have bony legs, and as she bustled away with our order, the boys at the next table were still complaining about leaving her a tip. "Five shillings each for tea. Just leave a tuppence . . ."

Our tea arrived soon in a clatter of flowered china. My mother smiled her thanks. "More milk, please. *C'est bon!*" Though it wasn't all that *bon,* really. Hard little scones and dry tea sandwiches and no sugar; there was still rationing in England even though V-E Day had been two years ago, and the menu of even a sumptuous hotel still showed the ration-set price of no more than five shillings per diner. The hangover of war was still visible here in a way you didn't see in New York. There were still soldiers in uniforms drifting through the hotel court, flirting with the maids, and an hour ago when I'd disembarked the ocean liner, I'd noticed the shelled look of the houses on the wharf, like gaping teeth in a pretty smile. My first look at England, and from dockside wharf to hotel court it all looked gray and exhausted from the war, still shocked to the bone. Just like me.

I reached into the pocket of my heather gray jacket, touching the piece of paper that had lived there for the past month whether I was in a traveling suit or pajamas, but I didn't know what to do with it. What *could* I do with it? I didn't know, but it still seemed heavier than the baby I was carrying. I couldn't feel that at all, or manage to have a single clear emotion about it. I wasn't sick in the mornings, or craving split pea soup with peanut butter, or feeling any of the other things you were supposed to feel when you were knocked up. I was just numb. I couldn't believe in this baby, because it had changed nothing. Only my whole life.

The boys rose from the next table, tossing a few pennies down. I could see the waitress coming back with milk, walking as if her feet hurt, and I looked up at the three English boys as they turned away. "Excuse me," I said, and waited until they turned back. "Five shillings each for tea—a bill of fifteen shillings gives a total five percent tip of ninepence. Ten percent tip would be a shilling and sixpence."

They looked startled. I was used to that look. No one thought girls could do figures at all, much less in their heads, even *easy* figures like this. But I'd been a math major at Bennington—numbers made sense to me; they were orderly and rational and easy to figure out, unlike people—and there wasn't a bill anywhere I couldn't tot up faster than an adding machine could do it for me. "Ninepence, or one and six," I repeated wearily for the staring boys. "Be gentlemen. Leave the one and six."

"Charlotte," my mother hissed as the boys left with sour looks. "That was very impolite."

"Why? I said 'Excuse me.'"

"Not everyone tips. And you should not have inserted yourself that way. No one likes pushy girls."

Or girls who major in math, or girls who get knocked up, or— But I let the words go unspoken, too tired to fight. We'd been six days crossing the Atlantic in a single stateroom, longer than expected because of rough seas, and those six days had passed in a series of tense squabbles lapsing into even more uncomfortable civility. Everything underlain by my shame-filled silences, her incandescent silent rage. It was why we'd seized the opportunity to get off the boat for a single night—if we didn't get out of that close-confined stateroom, we were going to fly at each other.

"Your mother's always ready to fly at someone." My French cousin Rose had said that years ago, when

Maman had subjected us to a ten-minute tirade for listening to Edith Piaf. *That's not music for little girls, it's indecent!*

Well, I'd done something a lot more indecent now than listen to French jazz. All I could do was turn my emotions away until I stopped feeling them, fend people off with a sharp-jutted chin tilted at an angle that said, *I don't care.* It worked well enough on rude boys who didn't tip their waitress, but my mother could get behind that shell anytime she liked.

She was chattering away now, complaining about our passage. "—knew we should have taken the later boat. That would have brought us direct to Calais without this silly roundabout stop in England."

I remained silent. One night in Southampton and then tomorrow straight on to Calais, where a train would take us to Switzerland. There was a clinic in Vevey where my mother had scheduled me for a certain discreet appointment. *Be grateful, Charlie,* I told myself for the thousandth time. *She didn't have to come with you at all.* I could have been packed off to Switzerland with my father's secretary or some other indifferent paid handler. My mother didn't have to miss her usual vacation in Palm Beach just to bring me to my appointment herself. *She's here with you. She's trying.* I could appreciate that even in my stew of fogged, angry shame. It wasn't as if she was wrong to be so furious with me, to think I was a troublemaking slut. That's what girls were, if they got themselves in the fix I was in. I'd better get used to the label.

Maman was still talking, determinedly cheerful. "I thought we'd go to Paris after your Appointment." Every time she said it, I heard the capital letter. "Get you some proper clothes, *ma p'tite.* Do something with your hair."

What she was really saying was, *You'll come back to school in the fall with a chic new look, and no one will know about your Little Problem.* "I really don't see that equation balancing out, *Maman.*"

"What on earth do you mean?"

I sighed. "One college sophomore minus one small encumbrance, divided by six months' passage of time, multiplied by ten Paris frocks and a new haircut will not magically equal one restored reputation."

"Life is not a math problem, Charlotte."

If it was, I'd have been a lot better at it. I'd often wished I could work out people as easily as I did arithmetic: simply break them down to their common denominators and solve. Numbers didn't lie; there was always an answer, and the answer was either right or it was wrong. Simple. But nothing in life was simple, and there was no answer here to solve for. There was just the mess that was Charlie St. Clair, sitting at a table with her mother, with whom she had *no* common denominators.

Maman sipped her weak tea, smiling bright, hating me. "I shall inquire as to whether our rooms are ready. Don't slouch! And do keep your case close by; you've got your grandmother's pearls in there."

She floated off toward the long marble counter and the bustling clerks, and I reached for my traveling case—square and battered; there had been no time to order me smart new luggage. I had half a pack of Gauloises tucked under the flat box with my pearls (only my mother would insist I pack pearls for a Swiss clinic). I'd happily leave the baggage *and* the pearls to get stolen if I could just step outside for a good smoke. My cousin Rose and I tried our first cigarette at the respective ages of thirteen and eleven, snitching a pack from my older brother and disappearing up a tree to try some grown-up vice. "Do I look like Bette Davis?" Rose had asked, trying to exhale smoke through her nose. I nearly fell out of the tree, laughing and coughing together after my single puff, and she stuck her tongue out at me. "Silly Charlie!" Rose was the only one to call me Charlie instead of Charlotte, giving it a soft French lilt. *Shar-lee,* emphasis on both syllables.

It was Rose, of course, who I saw gazing at me across the hotel court now. And it *wasn't* Rose, it was just an English girl slouching beside a pile of luggage, but my brain stubbornly told me I was seeing my cousin: thirteen, blond, peach pretty. That was how old she'd been the last summer I saw her, sitting in that tree with her first cigarette.

She'd be older by now, twenty-one to my nineteen . . .

If she was still alive.

"Rose," I whispered, knowing I should look away, but not doing it. "Oh, Rose."

In my imagination, she gave an impish smile and a toss of her chin to the street outside. *Go.*

"Go where?" I said aloud. But I already knew. I thrust my hand into my pocket and felt the scrap of paper I'd been carrying for a month. It had been stiff and crinkly, but time had worn it soft and pliable. That piece of paper bore an address. I could—

Don't be stupid. My conscience had a sharp, condemning voice that stung like a paper cut. *You know you're not going anywhere but upstairs.* There was a hotel room waiting for me with crisp sheets, a room I wouldn't have to share with my mother's brittle fury. A balcony where I could smoke in peace. Another boat to catch tomorrow, and then the Appointment, as my parents euphemistically referred to it. The Appointment, which would take care of my Little Problem, and then things would be All Right.

Or I could admit that nothing was All Right, and

nothing would be All Right. And I could just go, right now, down the path that started here in England.

You planned for this, Rose whispered. *You know you did.* And I had. Even in my passive, blunted misery of the last few weeks, I'd pushed for the boat that would take my mother and me the roundabout way through England, not the later passage that would have borne us right to France. I'd pushed for it without letting myself think about *why* I was pushing for it: because I had an English address in my pocket, and now, without an ocean in the way, all I lacked was the guts to go there.

The unknown English girl who wasn't Rose had gone now, headed for the hotel stairs behind a bellboy laden with luggage. I looked at the empty place where Rose had been. I touched the scrap of paper in my pocket. Little jagged pieces of feeling poked me through my numbness. Fear? Hope? Resolve?

One scribbled address plus one dash of resolve multiplied to the power of ten. Work the equation, Charlie.

Break it down.

Solve for X.

Now or never.

I took a deep breath. I pulled out the scrap of paper, and with it came a crumpled pound note. Recklessly, I slapped it down on the table next to mine where the braying boys had left their measly tip, and I walked out of the hotel court clutching my traveling case and my French cigarettes. Straight out through the wide doors of the hotel, where I asked the doorman, "Excuse me, but can you direct me to the train station?"

Not the wisest idea I've ever had: strange city, girl on her own. I'd spent the last few weeks in such a daze from my endless bad luck—the Little Problem, the screaming in French from my mother, the icy silence from my father—I'd been willing to go anywhere I was led. Straight off a cliff I'd march, blank and obedient, and not wonder or care why I was falling till I was halfway down. I'd been halfway down the hole my life had become, turning endlessly in the air. But now I'd grabbed a handhold.

Granted, it was a handhold in the shape of a hallucination, a vision I'd been seeing on and off for months as my mind insisted on painting Rose's face on every blond girl who passed me by. It had frightened me badly the first time, not because I thought Rose was a ghost, but because I thought I was going crazy. Maybe I *was* crazy, but I wasn't seeing ghosts. Because no matter what my parents said, I didn't entirely believe Rose was dead.

I held on to that hope as I hurried down the street toward the train station on the high cork soles of my impractical shoes ("always high heels for a girl as short as you, *ma chère,* or you'll never look like anything but a little girl"). I pushed through the crowds, the rough, swaggering laborers headed toward the docks, the smartly dressed shopgirls, the soldiers lingering on street corners. I hurried until I was short of breath, and I let that hope bloom, rising through me with a pain that made my eyes burn.

Go back, the sharp voice of conscience scolded. *You can still go back.* Back to a hotel room, to my mother making all the decisions, to my insulating cotton-wool fog. But I kept hurrying. I heard the hoot of a train, took in the smell of cinders and billows of steam. Southampton Terminus. Hordes of passengers were disembarking, men in fedoras, children red faced and fretful, women lifting crumpled newspapers over their waved hair to protect it from the faint drizzle. When had it started to drizzle? I could feel my dark hair flattening under the brim of the green hat my mother had chosen for me, the one that made me look like a leprechaun. I pushed on, running into the station.

A train conductor was crying out something. A departure in ten more minutes, direct to London.

I looked again at the piece of paper clenched in my hand. *10 Hampson Street, Pimlico, London. Evelyn Gardiner.*

Whoever the hell that was.

My mother would already be looking for me at the Dolphin, launching imperious monologues at the hotel clerks. But I didn't really care. I was just seventy-five miles from *10 Hampson Street, Pimlico, London*, and there was a train standing right in front of me.

"Five minutes!" the conductor bawled. Passengers scurried aboard, hoisting their luggage.

If you don't go now, you never *will,* I thought.

So I bought a ticket and climbed onto the train, and just like that I was gone into the smoke.

As afternoon dropped toward evening, the train car turned cold. I shrugged into my old black raincoat for warmth, sharing my compartment with a gray-haired woman and her three sniffling grandchildren. The grandmother gave my ring-less, glove-less hand a disapproving glance, as if wanting to know what kind of girl was traveling to London on her own. Surely girls traveled on trains all the time, given wartime necessities—but she clearly didn't approve of *me*.

"I'm pregnant," I told her the third time she tutted at me. "Do you want to change seats now?" She stiffened and got off at the next stop, dragging her grandchildren with her even as they whined, "Nana, we're not supposed to get off till—" I set my chin at the *I don't care* angle, meeting her final disapproving glance, and then sagged back into my seat as the door banged and left me alone. I pressed my hands to my flushed cheeks, giddy and confused and hopeful and guilty. So many emotions that I was nearly drowning, missing my numb shell. What on earth was wrong with me?

Running off into England with an address and a name, my sharp inner voice said. *What do you think you can do? You're such a helpless mess, how are you supposed to help anyone else?*

I winced. *I'm not helpless.*

Yes, you are. The last time you tried to help anyone, look what happened.

"And now I'm trying again," I said aloud to the empty compartment. Helpless mess or not, I was *here.*

Night had fallen by the time I staggered, weary and starving, off the train in London. I trudged out into the streets, and the city rolled out in front of me in one huge dark smoky mass; in the distance I saw the outline of the great clock tower over Westminster. I stood there a moment as cars splashed past, wondering how London would have looked just a few years ago when this fog would have been scythed by Spitfires and Messerschmitts, and then I shook out of my reverie. I had no idea where 10 Hampson Street might be, and only a few coins left in my pocketbook. As I hailed a cab, I prayed it would be enough. I really didn't relish having to yank a pearl off my grandmother's necklace just to pay for a taxi ride. *Maybe I shouldn't have left that waitress a whole pound . . .* But I wasn't sorry.

The driver took me to what he said was Pimlico and dumped me at a line of tall row houses. It had started to rain in earnest. I looked around for my hallucination, but there was no flash of blond hair. Just a dark street, the spitting rain, the worn steps of number 10 climbing to a dingy peeling door. I hoisted my case, clambered up, and banged the knocker before my courage deserted me.

No answer. I banged again. The rain was falling harder, and despair rose in me like a wave. I pounded and pounded until my fist ached, until I saw the minute twitch of the curtain beside the door.

"I know someone's in there!" I wrenched the door handle, blinded by rain. "Let me *in*!"

To my surprise the handle turned, and I flew inside, falling at last off my impractical shoes. I hit the floor of the dark hallway on my knees, tearing my stockings, and then the door banged shut and I heard the click of a pistol being cocked.

Her voice was low, graveled, slurred, ferocious. "Who are you, and what the bloody fuck are you doing in my house?"

The streetlamps sent a blurry light through the curtains, half-illuminating the dark hallway. I could see a tall gaunt figure, a straggle of hair, the fiery end of a lit cigarette. The gleam of light off a pistol barrel, pointing straight at me.

I should have been terrified, recoiling from the shock and the gun and the language. But fury had swept aside the last piece of my feel-nothing fog, and I gathered my legs under me to stand, torn stocking snagging. "I'm looking for Evelyn Gardiner."

"I don't care who you're looking for. If you don't tell me why I've got a damned Yank breaking into my house, I'll shoot you. I'm old and I'm drunk, but this is a Luger nine-millimeter P08 in excellent condition. Drunk or sober I can take the back of your skull out at this range."

"I'm Charlie St. Clair." Pushing the wet hair out of

my eyes. "My cousin Rose Fournier went missing in France during the war, and *you* might know how to find her."

Abruptly the electric wall lamp switched on. I blinked in the rush of harsh light. Standing over me was a tall gaunt woman in a faded print dress, her graying hair straggling around a time-ravaged face. She could have been fifty, or she could have been seventy. She had the Luger in one hand and a lit cigarette in the other; she kept the pistol steadily trained on my forehead as she raised the cigarette to her lips and took a long drag. Bile rose in my throat as I saw her hands. Good God, what had happened to her *hands*?

"I'm Eve Gardiner," she said at last. "And I don't know anything about this cousin of yours."

"You might," I said desperately. "You might—if you'll just talk to me."

"That's your plan, little Yank?" Her hooded storm-gray eyes surveyed me like a contemptuous bird of prey. "Burst into my house at nightfall, no plan, and I'm betting no money, on the chance I'd know something about your m-missing friend?"

"Yes." Faced with her gun and her scorn I couldn't explain *why*, why the chance to find Rose had turned suddenly all-consuming in my wrecked life. I couldn't explain this strange savage desperation, or why I had let it drive me here. I could only state the truth: "I had to come."

"Well." Eve Gardiner lowered her pistol. "I suppose you'll want t-tea."

"Yes, tea would be—"

"I don't have any." She turned and made her way back down the dark hall, walking long-strided and careless. Her bare feet looked like an eagle's claws. She weaved a little as she walked, the Luger swinging freely at her side, and I saw she still had a finger through the trigger. *Crazy,* I thought. *The old cow is crazy.*

And her hands—they were monstrous knobbed lumps, every knuckle misshapen and grotesque. They looked more like lobster claws than hands.

"Keep up," she said without turning, and I scurried after her. She struck a door open and flicked on a light, and I saw a cold sitting room—a mess of a place, grate unlit, drapes drawn so no chink of light could come in off the street, old newspapers and dirty tea mugs lying everywhere.

"Mrs. Gardiner—"

"Miss." She flung herself down in a shabby armchair overlooking the whole messy room, tossing her pistol down on the table beside it. I winced, but the thing didn't go off. "And you can call me Eve. You've f-forced your way into my house, so that's a level of intimacy I'm already disliking you for. What's a name?"

"I didn't mean to force my way—"

"Yes, you did. You want something, and you want it badly. What is it?"

I struggled out of my wet raincoat and sat down on a hassock, suddenly uncertain where to start. I'd been so focused on *getting* here, I hadn't thought how exactly I should begin. *Two girls times eleven summers, divided by one ocean and one war . . .*

"G-get on with it." Eve seemed to have a faint stutter, but I couldn't tell if it was drink or some other impediment. She reached for a crystal decanter sitting beside the pistol, unstoppering it with some clumsy maneuvering of her mangled fingers, and I smelled whiskey. "I've got limited hours of sobriety left, so I suggest you don't waste them."

I sighed. Not just a crazy old bat, but a *drunk* old bat.

With a name like *Evelyn Gardiner*, I'd been picturing someone with privet hedges and a rolled bun, not a decanter of whiskey and a loaded pistol. "Would you mind if I smoked?"

She tilted her bony shoulder in a shrug, and as I hauled out my Gauloises, she hunted for a glass. Nothing in arm's length, so she sloshed a measure of amber liquid into a flowered teacup. *God,* I thought as I lit my cigarette, half fascinated and half appalled. *Who are you?*

"It's rude to stare," she said, staring back at me just as frankly. "Christ, all that ruffly stuff you've got on—is that what women are wearing these days?"

"Don't you ever get out?" I asked before I could stop myself.

"Not much."

"It's the New Look. Modeled after the latest from Paris."

"It looks b-bloody uncomfortable."

"It is." I took a grim drag on my cigarette. "All right. I'm Charlie St. Clair, well, Charlotte, just arrived from New York—" My mother, what would she be thinking right now? She'd be furious and frantic and ready to scalp me. But I thrust that aside. "My father's American, but my mother's French. Before the war we spent summers in France, with my French cousins. They lived in Paris, and had a summer house outside Rouen."

"Your childhood sounds like a Degas picnic." Eve took a slug of her whiskey. "Make this m-more interesting, or I'm going to drink a lot faster."

It *was* like a Degas painting. I could close my eyes and those summers blurred into one long hazy season: the narrow twisting streets, the old copies of *Le Figaro* lying about the big rambling summer house with its stuffed attics and worn sofas, the haze of greenery with the sun filtering through and lighting up all the dust motes.

"My cousin Rose Fournier—" I felt tears prick my eyes. "She's my first cousin, but she's like my older sister. She's two years ahead of me, but she never shut me out. We shared everything, told each other everything."

Two little girls in grass-stained summer dresses, playing tag and climbing trees and waging furious battle against our combined brothers. Then two older girls, Rose with the beginning of a bosom and me still scrape kneed and gangly, both of us warbling along with jazz records and sharing a giggly crush on Errol Flynn. Rose the daring one with one outlandish scheme after another, me the devoted shadow she shielded like a lioness when her schemes got us into trouble. Her voice came at me, so suddenly it was like she was standing in the room: "Charlie, hide in my room and I'll stitch your dress up before your mother sees that rip. I shouldn't have taken you climbing over those rocks—"

"Please don't cry," Eve Gardiner said. "I cannot stand crying women."

"I can't either." I hadn't cried a drop in weeks, I'd been too numb, but now my eyes burned. I blinked fiercely. "The last time I saw Rose was the summer of '39. Everyone was worried about Germany—well, except us. Rose was thirteen and I was eleven; we just wanted to sneak out to the movies every afternoon, and that seemed a lot more important than anything happening in Germany. Poland got invaded right after I went back to the States. My parents wanted Rose's family to come to America, but they kept dithering—" Rose's mother, convinced she was too delicate to travel. "Before they could make the arrangements, France fell."

Eve took another sip of whiskey, her hooded eyes unblinking. I took another steadying drag on my cigarette.

"I got letters," I said. "Rose's father was important, an industrialist—he had connections, so the family could get word out now and then. Rose sounded cheerful. Kept talking about when we'd see each other again. But we had the news, everybody knew what was happening there: swastikas flying over Paris, people getting carted off in trucks and never seen again. I'd write her begging to know if she was really all right, and she always said she was, but . . ." In the spring of '43, we'd traded photographs since it had been so long since we'd seen each other—Rose had been seventeen and so pretty, striking a pin-up pose and grinning at the camera. I had the photograph in my pocketbook now, worn and soft at the edges.

"Rose's last letter talked about a boy she'd been seeing on the sly. She said there had been *much excitement.*" I took a shaky breath. "That was early in '43. I heard nothing from Rose after that, nothing from any of her family."

Eve watched me, her ravaged face like a mask. I couldn't tell if she pitied me, had contempt for me, or didn't care at all.

My cigarette was almost down to the nub. I took a last deep drag, and stubbed it out in a tea saucer already overflowing with ash. "I knew it didn't mean anything, Rose not writing. Wartime mail is hell. We just had to wait for the war to be over, and then the letters would start getting through. But the war ended, and—nothing."

More silence. It was harder than I'd thought it would be, saying all this. "We made inquiries. It took forever, but we got some answers. My French uncle had died in '44, shot while trying to get black-market medicine for my aunt. Rose's two brothers died in late '43, a bomb. My aunt's still alive—my mother wanted her to come live with us, but she wouldn't, just walled herself up in the house outside Rouen. And Rose—"

I swallowed. Rose sauntering ahead of me through the green haze of trees. Rose cursing in French, yanking a brush through her unruly curls. Rose at that Provençal café, on the happiest day of my whole life . . .

"Rose vanished. She left her family in '43. I don't even know *why*. My father put out inquiries, but Rose's trail after the spring of '44 came to a dead end. Nothing."

"A lot of dead ends in that war," Eve said, and I was surprised to hear her gravelly voice after speaking myself for so long. "Lots of people disappeared. You surely don't think she's still alive? It's been two years since the bloody w-war ended."

I gritted my teeth. My parents had long concluded Rose must be dead, lost in the chaos of war, and the odds were they were right, but— "We don't know for sure."

Eve rolled her eyes. "Don't tell me you'd have f-*felt* it if she died."

"You don't have to believe me. Just help me."

"Why? What the hell has all this got to do with m-me?"

"Because my father's last inquiry was to London, seeing if Rose might have emigrated here from France. There was a bureau helping to locate refugees." I took a deep breath. "You worked there."

"In '45 and '46." Eve tipped more whiskey into her flowered teacup. "I was fired last Christmas."

"Why?"

"Maybe because I came to work sloshed. Maybe because I told my supervisor she was a spiteful old cunt."

I couldn't help recoiling. I'd never in my life heard anyone swear like Eve Gardiner, much less a woman.

"So—" She swirled her whiskey. "I'm guessing the

file on your cousin crossed my desk? I d-don't remember. As I said, I came to work sloshed a fair amount."

I'd never seen a woman drink like this either. My mother's drink was sherry, two tiny glasses at most. Eve was knocking straight whiskey back like water, and her voice was starting to slur. Maybe the faint stammer *was* just drink.

"I got a copy of the report on Rose," I said desperately before I lost her for good, either to disinterest or whiskey. "It had your signature. That's how I got your name. I telephoned pretending I was your niece from America. They gave me your address. I was going to write you, but—" Well, my Little Problem had seeded itself in my belly right about then. "Are you sure you don't remember if there were any other findings on Rose? It could be—"

"Look, girl. I cannot help you."

"—anything! She was out of Paris by '43, the following spring she went to Limoges. We got that much from her mother—"

"I said, I can't help you."

"You have to!" I was on my feet, but I didn't remember standing. Desperation was building in my middle, a solid ball far denser than the insubstantial shadow that was my baby. "You have to help! I am not *leaving* without help!" I'd never shouted at an adult in my life, but I was shouting now. "Rose Fournier, she was in Limoges, seventeen years old—"

Eve was on her feet too, far taller than I, jabbing one of her unspeakable fingers into my breastbone, her voice deadly quiet. "Do not shriek at me in my own house."

"—she'd be twenty-one now, she's blond and beautiful and funny—"

"I don't care if she was Saint Joan of Arc, she's not my business and neither are you!"

"—she was working at a restaurant called Le Lethe owned by a Monsieur René, and after that no one knows—"

Something happened to Eve's face then. Nothing in it moved, but something still *happened*. It was like something moving at the bottom of a deep lake, sending the very faintest surge to the surface. Not even a ripple—but you still knew something was moving down there. She looked at me, and her eyes glittered.

"What?" My chest was heaving as though I'd run a mile, my cheeks hot with emotion and my ribs pressing against the iron grip of my waist cincher.

"Le Lethe," she said softly. "I know that name. Who did you s-say owned the restaurant?"

I scrambled for my traveling case, pushing aside the spare clothes, seeking the pocket in the liner. Two folded sheets of paper; I handed them over.

Eve looked at the short-form report on top, her own name across the bottom. "There's nothing here about the restaurant's name."

"I found that out later—look at the second page, my notes. I telephoned the bureau hoping to talk to you, but you were gone by then. I talked the clerk into hunting down the original tip in their files; it gave the name Le Lethe, owned by a Monsieur René, no last name. It was hopelessly garbled, so maybe that's why it wasn't typed into the report. But I assumed if you *signed* that report, you'd have seen the original tip."

"I didn't. If I had, I wouldn't have s-signed off." Eve looked at the second page, and kept looking. "Le Lethe . . . that's a name I know."

Hope was such a painful thing, far more painful than rage. "How?"

Eve turned and scrabbled for the whiskey bottle again. She sloshed more into her teacup and drank it all down. She filled the cup again, and then she stood there with her eyes staring past me at nothing.

"Get out of my house."

"But—"

"Sleep here if you haven't anywhere else to g-g-g—to go. But you'd better be gone by morning, Yank."

"But—but you know something." She picked up her pistol and moved past me. I grabbed her bony arm. "Please—"

Eve's maimed hand whipped up faster than I could follow it, and for the second time that night I had a gun pointed at me. I recoiled, but she advanced half a step and pressed the barrel right between my eyes. The cold circle of it made my skin tingle.

"You crazy old cow," I whispered.

"Yes," she rasped. "And I will shoot you if you are not gone when I wake up."

She moved off unsteadily, out of the sitting room and down the uncarpeted hall.

CHAPTER 2
EVE

May 1915
London

Opportunity walked into Eve Gardiner's life dressed in tweed.

She was late for work that morning, but her employer didn't notice when she slipped through the law office doors ten minutes after nine. Sir Francis Galborough rarely noticed anything outside his racing pages, Eve knew. "Here are your files, m'dear," he said as she came in.

She took the stack in slim unmarked hands: a tall girl with nut-brown hair, soft skinned, deceptively doe eyed. "Yes, s-s-sir." *S* was a hard letter to get out; only two stops on it was good.

"And Captain Cameron here has a letter for you to type in French. You should see her rattle away in Frog,"

Sir Francis said, addressing the lanky soldier sitting across his desk. "She's a gem, Miss Gardiner is. Half French! Can't speak a word of Frog myself."

"Nor I." The Captain smiled, fiddling with his pipe. "Entirely over my head. Thank you for the loan of your girl, Francis."

"No trouble, no trouble!"

No one asked Eve if it was any trouble. Why should they? File girls, after all, were a kind of office furniture, more mobile than an umbrella fern, but just as deaf and dumb.

You're lucky to have this job, Eve reminded herself. If not for the war, a post in a barrister's office like this would have gone to some young man with better recommendations and brilliantined hair. *You are lucky.* Very lucky, in fact. Eve had easy work, addressing envelopes and filing papers and typing the occasional letter in French; she supported herself in relative comfort; and if the wartime shortage of sugar and cream and fresh fruit was starting to pall, well, it was a fair exchange for safety. She could so easily have been stuck in northern France starving under German occupation. London was frightened, walking about now with its eyes trained on the sky, looking for zeppelins—but Lorraine, where Eve had grown up, was a sea of mud and bones, as Eve knew from the newspapers she devoured. She was lucky to be here, safe away from it.

Very lucky.

Eve took the letter silently from Captain Cameron, who had been quite a regular visitor to this office lately. He wore rumpled tweeds rather than a khaki uniform, but the straight spine and the soldierly stride shouted his rank better than any bank of ribbons. Captain Cameron, perhaps thirty-five, a hint of a Scottish lilt in his voice, but otherwise so entirely English, so utterly lanky and graying and rumpled he could have appeared in a Conan Doyle serial as the Quintessential British Gentleman. Eve wanted to ask, "Do you have to smoke a pipe? Do you have to wear tweed? Must you be *that* much of a cliché?"

The captain leaned back in his chair, nodding as she moved toward the door. "I'll wait for the letter, Miss Gardiner."

"Yes, s-sir," Eve murmured again, backing out.

"You're late," Miss Gregson greeted her in the file room, sniffing. The oldest of the file girls, inclined to boss the rest, and Eve promptly turned on a wide-eyed look of incomprehension. She loathed her own looks—the soft, smooth face she saw looking out of her mirror had a kind of blank unformed prettiness, nothing memorable about it except a general impression of youth that had people thinking she was still sixteen or seventeen—but her appearance served in good stead when she was in trouble. All her life, Eve had been able to open her wide-spaced eyes and blink her lashes into a perfect breeze of innocent confusion, and slide away from consequences. Miss Gregson gave an exasperated little sigh, bustling away, and later Eve caught her whispering to the other file girl. "I sometimes wonder if that half-French girl is a bit simple."

"Well"—a whisper and a shrug replied—"you've heard her talk, haven't you?"

Eve folded her hands around each other, giving two sharp, precise squeezes to stop them from forming fists, then bent her attention to Captain Cameron's letter, translating it into impeccable French. It was why she'd been hired, her pure French and her pure English. Native of both countries, at home in neither.

There was a kind of violent boredom about that day, at least as Eve remembered it later. Typing, filing, eating her wrapped sandwich at midday. Trudging through the streets at sunset, getting her skirt splashed by a passing cab. The boardinghouse in Pimlico, smelling of Lifebuoy soap and stale fried liver. Smiling dutifully at one of the other boarders, a young nurse who had just got herself engaged to a lieutenant, and sat flashing her tiny diamond chip over the supper table. "You should come work at the hospital, Eve. That's where you find a husband, not a file room!"

"I don't m-much care about finding a husband." That earned her blank looks from the nurse and the landlady and the other two boarders. *Why so surprised?* Eve thought. *I don't want a husband, I don't want babies, I don't want a parlor rug and a wedding band. I want—*

"You're not one of those *suffragettes*, are you?" Eve's landlady said, spoon paused in midair.

"No." Eve didn't want to check a box on a ballot. There was a war on; she wanted to *fight*. Prove that stuttering Eve Gardiner could serve her country as capably as any of the straight-tongued thousands who had dismissed her throughout her entire life as an idiot. But no amount of suffragette bricks through windows would ever get Eve to the front, even in a support role as a VAD or an ambulance driver, because she had been turned down for both posts on account of her stammer. She pushed back her plate, excusing herself, and went upstairs to her single neat room with its rickety bureau and narrow bed.

She was taking down her hair when a *mrow* sounded at the door, and Eve smiled as she let in the landlady's cat. "Saved you a bit of l-liver," she said, fishing out the scrap she'd taken from her plate and wrapped in a napkin, and the cat purred and arched. He was kept strictly as a mouser, subsisting on a sparse diet of kitchen crumbs and whatever he could kill, but he'd spotted Eve as a soft touch and had fattened up on her supper scraps. "I wish I were a cat," Eve said, lifting the tabby onto her lap. "Cats don't have to sp-sp—have to speak except in fairy tales. Or maybe I should just wish to be a man." Because if she were a man, she could at least *hit* anyone who mentioned her stuttering tongue, not smile at them with polite forbearance.

The tabby purred. Eve stroked him. "Might as well wish for the m-m-moon."

A knock sounded an hour later—Eve's landlady, so tight-lipped her mouth had almost disappeared. "You have a caller," she said accusingly. "A *gentleman* caller."

Eve set the protesting tabby aside. "At this hour?"

"Don't give me those innocent eyes, miss. No male admirers to visit in the evenings, that is my rule. Especially soldiers. So I informed the gentleman, but he insists it is urgent. I have put him in the parlor, and you may have tea, but I expect you to leave the door *ajar.*"

"A soldier?" Eve's puzzlement increased.

"A Captain Cameron. I find it most irregular that an army captain would seek you out, at home and in evening hours!"

Eve agreed, rolling up her loosened nut-brown hair and sliding her jacket over her high-necked blouse again as if she were going to the office. A certain kind of gentleman looked at any shopgirl, or file girl—any woman who *worked*—and saw her as entirely available. *If he's here to make advances, I will slap his face. Whether he reports me to Sir Francis and gets me fired or not.*

"Good evening." Eve struck open the door of the parlor, deciding on formality. "I am most surprised to see you, C-C-C—" Her right hand clutched into a fist, and she managed to get it out. "C—Captain. May I be of ass—assistance?" She held her head high, refusing to let the embarrassment color her cheeks.

To her astonishment, Captain Cameron replied in French. "Shall we switch languages? I've heard you speaking French to the other girls, and you stammer much less."

Eve stared at this consummate Englishman, lounging in the stiff parlor chair with his trousered legs loosely crossed, a faint smile showing under his small clipped mustache. He didn't speak French. She'd heard him say so, just this morning.

"Bien sûr," she replied. *"Continuez en français, s'il vous plaît."*

He went on in French. "Your eavesdropping landlady hovering in the hall will be going mad."

Eve sat, arranging her blue serge skirts, and leaned forward for the flowered teapot. "How do you take your tea?"

"Milk, two sugars. Tell me, Miss Gardiner, how good is your German?"

Eve glanced up sharply. She'd left that skill off her list of qualifications when she was looking for a post— 1915 wasn't a good time to admit to speaking the language of the enemy. "I d-don't speak German," she said, passing him his cup.

"Mmm." He regarded her over the teacup. Eve folded her hands in her lap and regarded him back with sweet blankness.

"That's quite a face you have," the Captain said. "Nothing going on behind it, nothing to show, anyway. And I'm good with faces, Miss Gardiner. It's mostly in the tiny muscles around the eyes that people give themselves away. You've got yours mostly under control."

Eve stretched her eyes wide again, lashes fanning in

innocent perplexity. "I'm afraid I don't know what you mean."

"Will you permit a few questions, Miss Gardiner? Nothing beyond the bounds of propriety, I assure you."

He hadn't leaned forward and tried to stroke her knee yet, at least. "Of course, C-C-Captain."

He sat back. "I know you are an orphan—Sir Francis mentioned it—but would you tell me something of your parents?"

"My father was English. He went to Lorraine to work in a French bank; he met my mother there."

"She was French? Doubtless that explains the purity of your accent."

"Yes." *And how would you know if my accent is pure?*

"I would think a girl of Lorraine would speak German as well. It's not far from the border."

Eve cast her lashes down. "I did not learn it."

"You really are a rather good liar, Miss Gardiner. I would not like to play cards with you."

"A lady does not play c-cards." Every nerve she had sang in warning, but Eve was quite relaxed. She always relaxed when she sensed danger. That moment in the reeds, hunting ducks, before squeezing off a shot: finger on the trigger, the bird freezing, a bullet about to fly— her heartbeat always slowed at that moment into utter placidity. It slowed now, as she tilted her head at the captain. "You were asking about my parents? My father lived and worked in Nancy; my mother kept house."

"And you?"

"I went to school, home for tea every afternoon. My mother taught me French and embroidery, and my father taught me English and duck hunting."

"How very civilized."

Eve smiled sweetly, remembering the roaring behind the lace curtains, the coarse slurs and vicious arguments. She might have learned to put on gentility, but she'd come from something far less refined: the constant shrieking and throwing of china, her father roaring at her mother for frittering away money, her mother sniping at her father for being seen with yet another barmaid. The kind of home where a child learned quickly to slide unseen around the edges of rooms, to vanish like a shadow in a black night at the first rumble on the domestic horizon. To listen to everything, weigh everything, all the while remaining unnoticed. "Yes, it was a very instructive childhood."

"Forgive me for asking . . . your stammer, have you always had it?"

"As a child, it was a trifle more p-p-p—more pronounced." Her tongue had always hitched and tripped. The one thing about her that wasn't smooth and unobtrusive.

"You must have had good teachers, to help you overcome it."

Teachers? They'd seen her get so hung up on words that she was red faced and close to tears, but they'd only moved on to someone else who could answer the question more quickly. Most of them thought her simpleminded as well as hitch tongued; they could barely be bothered to shoo the other children away when they circled around her taunting, "Say your name, say it! G-g-g-g-g-gardiner—" Sometimes the teachers joined in the laughter.

No. Eve had beaten her stutter into submission with sheer savage will, reading poetry out loud line by faltering line in her bedroom, hammering on the consonants that stuck until they unspooled and came free. She remembered taking ten minutes to limp her way through Baudelaire's *Les Fleurs du mal* introduction—and French was her *easier* language. Baudelaire had said he'd written *Les Fleurs du mal* with rage and patience; Eve understood that perfectly.

"Your parents," Captain Cameron continued. "Where are they now?"

"My father died in 1912, of a heart b-blockage." It was a kind of blockage, getting stuck in the heart with a butcher knife wielded by a cuckolded husband. "My mother didn't like the rumbling from Germany, and decided to bring me to London." To escape the scandal, not the Boche. "She died of influenza last year, God rest her soul." Bitter, vulgar, and haranguing to the end, flinging teacups at Eve and swearing.

"God rest her soul," the captain echoed with a piety Eve didn't buy for one moment as genuine. "And now we have you. Evelyn Gardiner, orphan, with her pure French and pure English—you're sure about the German?—working in an office for my friend Sir Francis Galborough, presumably passing time until she marries. A pretty girl, but she tends to slide from notice. Shyness, perhaps?"

The tabby wound his way through the open door with an inquiring meow. Eve called him up to her lap. "Captain Cameron," she said with the smile that made her look sixteen, tickling the tabby under the chin, "are you trying to seduce me?"

She'd succeeded in shocking him. He sat back, coloring in embarrassment. "Miss Gardiner—I would not dream—"

"Then what are you doing here?" she asked directly.

"I am here to evaluate you." He crossed his ankles, recovering his aplomb. "I've had my eye on you for a number of weeks, ever since I first walked into my friend's office pretending to speak no French. May I speak plainly?"

"Have we not been speaking plainly already?"

"I don't believe you ever speak plainly, Miss Gardiner. I've heard you murmuring evasions at your fellow file girls, to get out of the work you consider boring. I heard you tell a bold-faced lie when they asked why you were late this morning. Something about a cabdriver who delayed you with his unwanted attentions—you're never flustered, you go about cool as cream, but you faked fluster beautifully. You weren't late because of an amorous cabdriver; you were staring at a recruitment poster outside the office door for a good ten minutes. I timed it, looking down from the window."

It was Eve's turn to sit back and blush. She *had* been staring at the poster: it had showed a line of stalwart-looking Tommies, soldierly and identical, with a blank space in the middle. *There is still a space in the line for YOU!* the headline above it blared. *WILL YOU FILL IT?* And Eve had stood there bitterly, thinking, *No.* Because the lettering inside that blank space in the line of soldiers said in smaller script, *This space is reserved for a fit man!* So, no, Eve could never fill it, even though she was twenty-two and entirely fit.

The tabby in her lap protested, feeling her fingers tighten through his fur.

"So, Miss Gardiner," Captain Cameron said. "Can I get a straight answer out of you if I ask a question?"

Don't count on it, Eve thought. She lied and evaded as easily as she breathed; it was what she'd had to do all her life. Lying, lying, lying, with a face like a daisy. Eve couldn't remember the last time she'd been completely straight with anyone. Lies were easier than the hard and turbulent truth.

"I am thirty-two," the captain said. He looked older, his face lined and worn. "Too old to fight in this war.

I have a different job to do. Our skies are under attack from German zeppelins, Miss Gardiner, our seas by German U-boats. We are under attack every day."

Eve nodded fiercely. Two weeks ago the *Lusitania* was sunk—for days, her fellow boarders dabbed at their eyes. Eve had devoured the newspaper accounts dry-eyed, enraged.

"To stave off further such attacks, we need people," Captain Cameron went on. "It is my job to find people with certain skills—the ability to speak French and German, for example. The ability to lie. Outward innocence. Inward courage. To find them and put them to work, ferreting out what the Boches have planned for us. I think you show potential, Miss Gardiner. So, let me ask: do you wish to stand for England?"

The question hit Eve in a hammer blow. She exhaled shakily, setting the cat aside, and answered without thinking. "Yes." Whatever he meant by *stand for England*, the answer was yes.

"Why?"

She began to pull together something pat and expected about the vile Fritzes, about doing her bit for the boys in the trenches. She let the lie go, slowly. "I want to prove myself capable, to everyone who ever thought me simpleminded or weak because I cannot speak straight. I want to f-f-f—I want to f-f-f-f—"

She hung on the word so badly her cheeks heated dully, but he didn't rush to finish her sentence in that way that most people did, the way that filled her with fury. He just sat quietly until she slammed a fist against her skirted knee and the word broke free. She spit it out through clenched teeth, with enough vehemence to startle the cat out of the room.

"I want to *fight*."

"Do you?"

"*Yes.*" Three straight answers in a row; for Eve it was a record. She sat under his thoughtful gaze, shaking, close to tears.

"So, I ask for the fourth time, and there won't be a fifth. Do you speak German?"

"*Wie ein Einheimischer.*" Like a native.

"Excellent." Captain Cecil Aylmer Cameron rose. "Evelyn Gardiner, would you be interested in entering the Crown's service as a spy?"

CHAPTER 3
CHARLIE

May 1947

had vague nightmares of gunshots going off in whiskey glasses, blond girls disappearing behind train cars, a voice whispering, "Le Lethe." And then there was a man's voice saying, "Who are you, lass?"

I peeled my gummy eyelids open with a groan. I'd gone to sleep on the broken-down old sofa in the sitting room, not daring to wander about the house looking for a bed when that crazy woman was on the loose with a Luger. I'd unhooked myself from my fluffy traveling suit, curled up under a threadbare knitted throw, and gone to sleep in my slip—and now it was apparently morning. A shaft of sunlight showed through a chink in the heavy curtains, and someone was staring at me from the door: a dark-haired man in a worn old jacket, resting his elbow up against the doorjamb.

"Who are you?" I asked, still half stupefied from sleep.

"I asked first." His voice was deep, with a hint of a Scots burr to the vowels. "I've never known Gardiner to have visitors."

"She's not up, is she?" I threw a frantic look behind him. "She threatened to shoot me if I was still here when she got up—"

"Sounds like her," the Scotsman commented.

I wanted to start rummaging for my clothes, but I wasn't standing up in my slip in front of a strange man. "I've got to get out of here—"

And go where? Rose whispered, and the thought made my head pound. I didn't know where to go from here; all I'd had was a scrap of paper with Eve's name. What was left? My eyes burned.

"Don't bother scrambling," the Scotsman said. "If Gardiner was right smashed last night, she likely won't remember a thing." He turned, shrugging out of his jacket. "I'll make tea."

"Who are you?" I started to say, but the door swung shut. After a moment's hesitation I tossed the blanket aside, my bare arms prickling in the cold. I looked at the mass of my crumpled traveling suit and wrinkled my nose. I had one more dress in my case, but it was just as fluffy and cinched and uncomfortable. So I slipped into an old sweater and a worn pair of dungarees my mother hated, and padded off in bare feet searching for the kitchen. I hadn't eaten in twenty-four hours, and the roar of my stomach was fast overcoming everything else, even my fear of Eve's pistol.

The kitchen was surprisingly clean and bright. The teakettle had been put on, and the table laid. The Scotsman had tossed his worn jacket over a chair, and stood in equally worn shirtsleeves. "Who *are* you?" I asked, unable to help my own curiosity.

"Finn Kilgore." He took down a pan. "Gardiner's man of all work. Help yourself to tea."

Curious, that he called her just "Gardiner" as though she were a man. "Man of all work?" I wondered, collecting a chipped mug from beside the sink. Aside from the kitchen it didn't seem like much work was done around this house.

He rummaged in the icebox and came out with eggs, bacon, mushrooms, half a loaf of bread. "Did you got a good gander at her hands?"

". . . yes." The tea was strong and dark, just the way I liked it.

"How much do you think she can do with hands like that?"

I gave a little bark of a laugh. "From what I saw last night, she can cock a pistol and uncork the whiskey just fine."

"She manages those two things. For the rest, she hires me. I run her errands. I collect her post. I drive her when she goes out. I cook a wee bit. Though she won't let me tidy up anything more than the kitchen." He added rashers of bacon to the pan one by one. He was tall, rangy, moving with a casual loose-jointed grace. Perhaps twenty-nine or thirty, with a dark sheen of stubble in need of a razor, and rumpled dark hair that came to his collar and badly needed a barber. "What are you doing here, miss?"

I hesitated. My mother would have said it was highly improper for a man of all work to be asking questions of a guest. But I wasn't much of a guest, and he had more right to be in this kitchen than I did. "Charlie St. Clair," I said, and as I sipped my tea I gave him an edited version of why I'd landed on Eve's doorstep (and her couch).

Without things like the screaming and the pistol pressed between my eyes. Not for the first time, I wondered just how my life had turned so thoroughly upside-down in barely twenty-four hours.

Because you followed a ghost all the way from Southampton, Rose whispered. *Because you are a little bit crazy.*

Not crazy, I shot back. *I want to save you. That doesn't make me crazy.*

You want to save everyone, Charlie my love. Me, James, every stray dog you ever saw in the street when we were little—

James. I flinched, and the nasty inner voice of my conscience whispered, *Didn't do such a good job of saving him, did you?*

I cut that thought off before the inevitable surge of guilt hit, and waited for Eve's man to ask questions because my story was, frankly, bizarre. But he stood silent over the pan, adding mushrooms and a can of beans. I'd never seen a man cook before; my father never so much as spread butter on toast. That was for my mother and me to do. But the Scotsman stood there stirring beans and crisping bacon perfectly deftly, not seeming to mind when the grease leaped out and sizzled on his forearms.

"How long have you worked for Eve, Mr. Kilgore?"

"Four months." He started slicing the half loaf of bread.

"And before that?"

His knife hesitated. "Royal Artillery, 63rd Anti-Tank Regiment."

"And then to work for Eve; that's a switch." I wondered why he'd paused. Maybe he was ashamed, going from soldiering against Nazis to doing housework for a pistol-wielding madwoman. "How is she . . ."

I trailed off, unsure where my question was going.

How was she to work for? How did she *get* this way? "How did she injure her hands?" I asked finally.

"She's never told me." He cracked eggs into the pan one by one. My stomach rumbled. "But I could take a guess."

"What would you guess?"

"That she had every joint of every finger systematically smashed."

I shivered. "What kind of accident could do that?"

Finn Kilgore looked me in the eye for the first time. He had dark eyes under straight black brows, both watchful and remote. "Who says it was an accident?"

I wrapped my (whole, unbroken) fingers around my mug. The tea suddenly seemed cold.

"English breakfast." He lifted the hot pan off the stove, setting it next to the sliced bread. "I've got a leaky pipe to look at, but help yourself. Just leave plenty for Gardiner. She'll come down with a foul headache, and a one-pan breakfast is the best hangover cure in the Isles. Eat it all, and she really will shoot you."

He sloped out without another glance. I took a plate and went to the sizzling pan, mouth watering. But as I stared into the delicious mess of eggs and bacon, beans and mushrooms, my stomach suddenly revolted. I clapped a hand over my mouth and turned away from the stove before I vomited all over the best hangover cure in the Isles.

I knew what this was, even if I'd never experienced it before. I was still starving, but my stomach was rolling and heaving so hard I couldn't have taken a bite if I'd had Eve's Luger pointed at my head again. This was morning sickness. For the first time, my Little Problem had decided to make itself known.

I felt sick, in more ways than a rolling stomach. My breath came short and my palms started to sweat. The

Little Problem was three months along, but it had never seemed like more than a vague idea—I couldn't feel it, couldn't imagine it, couldn't see any signs of it. It was just something that had barreled down the center of my life like a train. After my parents got involved it was simply a problem to be x'ed out like a bad equation. One Little Problem plus one trip to Swizerland equaled zero, zero, zero. Very simple.

But now it felt like a lot more than a Little Problem, and not simple at all.

"What am I going to do?" I said quietly. It was the first time I'd thought about that question in a long time. Not what was I going to do about Rose, or my parents, or going back to school—but what was I going to do about *me*?

I don't know how long I stood there before an acerbic voice broke my statue pose. "The American invasion is still here, I see."

I turned. Eve stood in the doorway in the same print housedress she'd worn last night, her graying hair loose and wild, and her eyes bloodshot. I braced myself, but maybe Mr. Kilgore was right about her forgetting her threats of the previous night, because she seemed less interested in me than in massaging her own temples.

"I've got the Four Horsemen of the apocalypse going hammer and tongs in my skull," she said, "and my mouth tastes like a urinal in Chepstow. Tell me that goddamn Scotsman made b-breakfast."

I waved my hand, stomach still rolling sickly. "The one-pan miracle."

"Bless him." Eve fished a fork out of a drawer and began eating straight out of the pan. "So, you've met Finn. He's a dish, isn't he? If I weren't older than dirt and ugly as sin, I'd climb that like a French alp."

I pushed away from the stove. "I shouldn't have come

here. I'm sorry I forced my way in. I'll just go—" What? Crawl back to my mother, face her fury, take the boat for my Appointment? What else was there? I felt the cotton-thick surge of numbness creeping back over me. I wanted to put my head on Rose's shoulder and close my eyes; I wanted to curl over a toilet and vomit my insides out. I felt so sick, and so helpless.

Eve mopped up a glob of egg yolk with a hunk of bread. "Sit d-down, Yank."

That raspy voice had authority, stammer or not. I sat.

She swiped her fingers on a dish towel, reached into the pocket of her dress, and fished out a cigarette. She lit up with a long, slow drag. "First fag of the day," she said, exhaling. "Always tastes the best. Almost makes up for the bloody hangover. What was your cousin's n-n-name again?"

"Rose." My heart began to pound. "Rose Fournier. She—"

"Tell me something," Eve interrupted. "Girls like you have rich mummies and daddies. Why aren't your parents beating the bushes for their little lost lamb of a niece?"

"They tried. They made inquiries." Even when I was angry with my parents, I knew they'd tried their best. "After two years of nothing, my father said Rose surely must be dead."

"Sounds like a smart man, your father."

He was. And as a lawyer specializing in international law, he'd known the channels and byways through which to conduct his overseas inquiries. He'd done what he could, but when no one had gotten so much as a telegram from Rose—even me, the one she loved best of our whole family—my father had drawn the logical conclusion: that she was dead. I'd been trying to get used to that idea, trying to convince myself. At least until six months ago.

"My big brother came home from Tarawa with only half a leg, and six months ago he shot himself." I heard my own voice crack. James and I had never been close when little; I'd just been the younger sister he could bully. But once he grew out of the hair-pulling stage, the teasing gentled; he joked about putting a scare into any boy who came to date me, and I teased him about his terrible haircut once he joined the marines. He was my *brother*; I loved him and my parents thought he hung the moon. And then he was dead, and right around that time Rose started to step out of my memory and into my field of vision. Every little girl running past turned into Rose at six or eight or eleven; every blonde saun- tering ahead of me across a campus green became the older Rose, tall and just beginning to curve . . . A dozen times a day my heart knocked and then crashed as my memory played merciless tricks.

"I know it's probably hopeless." I looked Eve in the eye, willing her to understand. "I know my cousin is probably . . . I know what the odds are. Believe me, I could calculate them out to the last decimal. But I have to try. I have to follow every trail to the end, no matter how small. If there's even the faintest possibility she's still out there—"

I choked up again before I could finish it. I'd lost my brother to this war. If there was even the smallest chance of getting Rose back from oblivion, I had to pursue it.

"Help me," I repeated to Eve. "Please. If I don't look for her, no one else will."

Eve exhaled slowly. "And she worked at a restaurant called Le Lethe—where?"

"Limoges."

"Mmm. Owned by?"

"A Monsieur René something. I made some more telephone calls, but no one could find a surname."

Her lips thinned. And for a few moments she just stared at nothing, those horrendous fingers curling and flexing, curling and flexing at her side. At last she looked at me, her eyes impenetrable as flat glass. "I might be able to help you after all."

ve's telephone call did not seem to be going well. I could only hear half of the conversation as she shouted into the receiver, pacing up and down the bare hall with her cigarette flicking back and forth like the tail of an enraged cat, but half the conversation was enough to get the gist. "I don't care what it costs to put a call through to France, you desk-bound secretarial cow, just put me through."

"Who are you trying to reach?" I asked for the third time, but she ignored me like she had the first two, and kept on haranguing the operator.

"Oh, stop *ma'am*ing me before you choke on it and put the call through to the major . . ."

I could still hear her through the panels of the front door as I slipped out of the house. The gray wetness of yesterday had disappeared; London had dressed up today in blue skies and scudding clouds and bright sunshine. I shaded my eyes against the sun, looking for the shape I thought I'd seen on the corner through last night's taxi window—there. One of those bright red phone boxes so iconically English it looked faintly ridiculous. I aimed for it, stomach rolling again. I'd forced some dry toast down after Eve began her telephone call to this mysterious major, and that had calmed the queasy pangs of my

Little Problem, but this was a different kind of sickness. I had a telephone call of my own to make, and I didn't think it would be any easier than Eve's.

A wrangle with the operator, and then another wrangle with the desk clerk at the Dolphin Hotel in Southampton, giving my name. And then: "Charlotte? *'Allo, 'allo?*"

I pulled the receiver away from my ear and stared at it, suddenly irked. My mother never answered the telephone that way unless there was someone around to hear her. You'd think that with her knocked-up daughter doing an overnight bolt into London, she'd be worrying about something other than impressing the Dolphin's desk clerk.

The receiver was still squawking. I put it back to my ear. "Hello, *Maman*," I said briskly. "I haven't been kidnapped, and I'm clearly not dead. I'm in London, perfectly safe."

"*Ma petite,* have you gone mad? Disappearing like that, the fright you gave me!" A little sniff and then a murmured *merci*; clearly the desk clerk had offered her a handkerchief to dab her eyes. I doubted very much that her eye makeup ran. Catty of me, perhaps, but I couldn't help it. "Tell me where you are in London, Charlotte. At once."

"No," I said, and something expanded in my stomach besides the nausea. "I'm sorry, but no."

"Don't be absurd. You have to come home."

"I will," I said. "When I've found out once and for all what happened to Rose."

"*Rose?* What in—"

"I'll telephone again soon, I promise." And I replaced the receiver.

Finn Kilgore turned to look at me as I came back

through Eve's front door and then the kitchen. "Hand me a dish towel, miss?" He gestured with his chin, up to his elbows scrubbing the breakfast pan. That made me stare again. My father thought dirty coffee cups miraculously cleaned themselves.

"She's on another call," Finn said, nodding toward the hall as he took the towel. "Tried to get through to some English officer in France, but he's on holiday. Now she's shouting down the telephone at a woman, I don't ken who."

I hesitated. "Mr. Kilgore, you said you were Eve's driver. Could you—could you possibly take me somewhere? I don't know London well enough to walk, and I don't have the fare for a cab."

I thought he'd object, considering he didn't know me from Uncle Sam, but he shrugged, scrubbing his hands dry. "I'll pull the car up."

I looked down at my old dungarees and sweater. "I'll need to change."

By the time I was ready, Finn was standing in the open doorway, tapping his boot as he stared out at the street. He looked back over one lean shoulder as he heard the clack of my heels, and not just one but both of those straight black brows rose. I didn't mistake it for admiration. The ensemble was the only clean change of clothes I had in my traveling case, and it made me look like a china shepherdess: a fluffy white skirt over layers and layers of crinoline; pink hat with a half veil; spotless gloves; and a tight pink jacket that would have molded to every curve, if I'd had a single curve to mold to. I lifted my chin and flicked the silly veil down over my eyes. "It's one of the international banks," I said, and handed him an address. "Thank you."

"Lasses in that many petticoats don't usually bother thanking the driver," Finn advised, holding the door open so I could walk under his arm and outside. Even in heels, I cleared his elbow without needing to duck.

Eve's voice came from the end of the hall as I reached to close the door. "You bat-blind bloody French cow, don't you dare hang up on me . . ."

I hesitated, wanting to ask her why she was helping me. She'd been dead set against it last night. But I didn't press for details yet, for all that I wanted to shake her bony shoulders till she coughed up what she knew. I didn't dare anger her or put her off, because she knew *something*. Of that I was certain.

So I left her to it and followed Finn outside. The car surprised me: a dark blue convertible with the top pulled up, old, but buffed shiny as a new dime. "Nice wheels. Eve's?"

"Mine." The car didn't match his disreputable stubble and patched elbows.

"What is it, a Bentley?" My father had a Ford, but he liked English cars, and he was always pointing them out whenever we came to Europe.

"A Lagonda LG6." Finn opened the door for me. "Hop in, miss."

I smiled as he took his seat behind the wheel and reached for the gearshift half buried in my spreading skirts. It was rather nice to be among strangers who didn't know my soiled recent history. I liked looking into someone's eyes and seeing myself reflected as someone who deserved a respectful *miss*. All I'd seen when I looked into my parents' eyes the past few weeks was *whore—disappointment—failure*.

You are *a failure*, my nasty inner voice whispered, but I pushed it away, hard.

London went by in a blur; gray, cobblestoned, still showing rubble, cracked roofs, and bites taken out of seemingly whole walls. All from the war, and yet it was

1947. I remember my father exhaling contentedly over the newspapers after V-E Day, saying, "Excellent, now it can all go back to the way it was." As if roofs and buildings and shattered windows just leaped back into wholeness the day after peace was declared.

Finn negotiated the Lagonda through a street so badly holed it looked like a piece of Swiss cheese, and a thought made me look at him curiously. "Why does Eve even need a car? With gas as short as it is, wouldn't it be easier to get around by tram?"

"She doesn't do well with trams."

"Why?"

"I don't know. Trams, confined spaces, crowds—they set her off. She nearly blew up like a grenade last time she took a tram. Shouting and throwing elbows at all those housewives with their shopping."

I shook my head, wondering, and with a rumble the Lagonda pulled up before the imposing marble-fronted bank that was my destination. My face must have betrayed my nervousness because Finn said rather gently, "Want an escort, miss?"

I did, but a lurking Scotsman who needed a shave wasn't going to make me look any more respectable, so I shook my head as I swung out of the car. "Thank you."

I tried to summon some of my mother's effortless sashay as I crossed the polished marble floor inside the bank. I gave my name and my business, and soon I was being shown into the office of a grandfatherly type in houndstooth check. He glanced up from a chart on which he was scribbling figures. "May I be of assistance, young lady?"

"I hope so, sir." I smiled, marshaled a little small talk. "What's that you're working on?" Indicating his chart and its column of numbers.

"Percentages, figures. Quite dull." He rose, indicating a chair. "Do sit down."

"Thank you." I sat, took a breath under my half veil. "I would like to withdraw some money, please."

My American grandmother had settled a trust fund on me when she died. Not massive, but a good bit, and I'd been conscientiously adding to it since I was fourteen and got my first summer job in my father's office. I'd never touched the account; I had an allowance for college and that was all I needed. I normally left the passbook tucked into my dresser drawer under my unmentionables, but I'd tossed it into my traveling case at the last minute when packing for the ocean liner. That same part of me that had packed Eve's address, and the report about Rose's last whereabouts. Not laying plans, exactly, but listening to the little voice that whispered, *You might need these, if you get up the nerve to do what you really want to do . . .*

I was glad I'd listened to that voice and included the passbook, because I was flat out of cash. I had no idea why Eve had decided to help me, but I didn't think it was from goodness of heart. I'd cross her palm with silver if that was what it took, and the palm of anyone else who might lead me to Rose, but for that I needed the silver. So I presented my passbook and identification, and smiled at the banker.

Within ten minutes, I was holding that smile in place only by sheer force of will. "I don't understand," I said for at least the fourth time. "You have proof of my name and age, and there are clearly sufficient funds in the account. So why—"

"Parting with such a large sum, young lady, is not generally done. Such accounts are held to be in trust for your future."

"But it's not just in trust for my future. My own savings are in there—"

"Perhaps if we could speak with your father?"

"He is in New York. And it's not such a large amount—"

The banker interrupted me again. "A telephone number for your father's office will suffice. If we might speak to him, to gain his consent—"

I interrupted him this time. "You don't need my father's consent. It's my name on the account. It was arranged that I would have access to it when I turned eighteen, and I'm *nineteen*." Pushing my cards at him again. "You don't need anyone's consent but mine."

The banker shifted a bit in his leather chair, but the grandfatherly expression never wavered. "I assure you that something can be arranged if we can just speak with your father."

My teeth gritted as if they had fused. "I would like to make a withdrawal of—"

"I'm sorry, young lady."

I stared at his watch chain and his plump hands, the light shining through the thin spot in his hair. He wasn't even looking at me anymore; he'd pulled his chart back and was scribbling more figures on it and crossing them out again.

It was petty of me, but I reached across the table, slid the chart out from under his hand, and gave the columns of numbers a looking over. Before he could bristle, I took a pencil stub from the edge of the desk, crossed out his figures, and wrote down the correct ones. "You were off by a quarter of a percent," I said, sliding the sheet back. "That's why your balance was coming out wrong. Run it through an adding machine just to be certain, though. Since I clearly can't be trusted with money."

His smile slipped. I stood, chin raised to the highest

I don't care setting on the dial, and stormed out into the sunshine. My own money. Not just money I'd inherited but money I'd *earned,* and I couldn't get five cents of it for myself unless I had my father in tow. It was so utterly unfair my teeth were still grinding, but I couldn't say I was completely surprised.

That was why I had a backup plan.

Finn looked up as I hurled myself back into the front seat, shutting about half my skirt in the door. "You look somewhat disreputable, if you'll forgive me for saying so," I said, reopening the door and yanking the rest of my crinoline in. "Are you actually disreputable, Mr. Kilgore, or do you just hate to shave?"

He folded the battered paperback he'd been reading. "Bit of both."

"Good. I need a pawnshop. Someplace that won't ask too many questions if a girl has something to sell."

He stared a moment, then moved the Lagonda back into the noisy London traffic.

My American grandmother had left me some money in a trust fund. My French grandmother had had a spectacular double strand of pearls, and before she died she'd had them divided into two single-strand necklaces: "One each, for *petite Charlotte* and *la belle Rose*! I should give them to my daughters, but *mon dieu*, how pinch-mouthed your mothers both turned out," she'd said with her usual French candor, making us giggle guiltily. "So you two wear them instead when you get married, *mes fleurs*, and think of me."

I thought of her, reaching into my purse and fingering the luscious strand of pearls. My little French grandmother, dead long before she ever saw a swastika waving over her beloved Paris, thank God. *Pardonnez-moi, Grand-mère,* I thought. *I've got no choice.* I couldn't get at my savings, but I could get at my pearls. Because my mother had been quite serious about dragging me to Paris after my Appointment, getting new clothes and making calls on old friends and making it clear we were in Europe for *social reasons,* nothing scandalous. Hence, pearls. I let myself have one more look at them, the great milky beads with the single square-cut emerald that served as a clasp, and then I stalked into the pawnbroker's shop where Finn had pulled up, laid the pearls down on the counter with a clatter, and said, "What can you offer me?"

The pawnbroker's eyes flickered, but he said smoothly, "You'll have to wait, miss. I'm finishing up some important orders."

"Usual trick," Finn murmured, having unexpectedly followed me in this time. "Get you impatient so you'll settle for what he offers. You'll be here a spell."

I jutted out my chin. "I'll sit here all day."

"I may just go check on Gardiner; the house isn't far from here. You won't scarper on me, miss?"

"You don't have to call me *miss,* you know." Even if I rather liked it, the formality seemed silly. "It's not like you're escorting me around Buckingham Palace."

He tilted a shoulder and loped out. "Yes, miss," he said just as the door closed. I shook my head, then sat down in an uncomfortable chair with my grandmother's pearls looped through my fingers, and it was a good thirty minutes before the pawnbroker turned his attention and his jeweler's glass to me. "I'm afraid you've been duped, young lady," he said with a sigh. "Glass pearls. Good glass, but just glass. I could give you a few pounds, I suppose—"

"Try again." I knew down to the dime what my necklace was insured for. Mentally I converted dollars to pounds, added 10 percent, and named my sum.

"Do you have some provenance? Perhaps a bill of

sale?" His glass flashed at me, and I could see his fingers twitch toward the emerald clasp. I twitched the
strand back and we kept haggling. Another half hour
eked grimly by, and he wasn't budging, and my voice
rose despite myself.

"I will go somewhere *else*," I snarled finally, but he
just smiled, bland.

"You won't get a better offer, miss. Not without provenance. Now, if you had your father with you, or your
husband—someone to give assurances that you had permission to dispose of them . . ."

That again. All the way across the Atlantic, and I
was still on my father's strings. I turned my head toward the window to hide my rage, and saw the flash of
Rose's blond head in the passing throng outside. A moment later, I saw it was just a scurrying schoolgirl. *Oh,
Rosie,* I thought miserably, staring after the girl anyway.
*You left your family and went to Limoges; how in God's
name did you* do *it? No one lets girls do anything at all.*
Not spend our own money, sell our own things, or plan
our own lives.

I was girding myself for a helpless argument when
the shop door banged open, and a woman's voice car-
oled, "Charlotte, what on earth—lord, gel, I told you to
wait for me. I suppose you knew it would break my poor
old heart parting with my b-baubles, and thought you'd
spare me?"

I stared. Eve Gardiner came sweeping through the
shop, beaming like I was the apple of her eye. She had
on the same print housedress she'd worn this morning,
wrinkled and threadbare, but she had stockings and a
pair of respectable pumps; her gnarled hands were hidden by darned kid gloves, and she'd tucked her straggling hair up under a vast, once-stylish hat with half
an osprey pinned to the crown. She looked, to my utter

astonishment, like a lady. An eccentric lady, maybe, but a lady.

Leaning discreetly in the doorway with his arms folded across his chest, Finn gave an almost invisible smile.

"Oh, I shall be sorry to part with these," Eve sighed, patting my pearls like a dog and turning an aloof smile on the pawnbroker. "South Sea pearls, you know, from my d-dearly departed husband." A handkerchief dabbed to her eye, and it was all I could do to keep my chin from hitting the floor. "And the emerald, that's from India! Came from Cawnpore, *far* back in my family, my dear grandfather under Q-Q—under Queen Victoria. Blowing up sepoys, and good riddance to the little brown devils." Her voice dripped Mayfair elegance. "Now, examine that luster under your glass again, and let's hear your real price, my good man."

His eyes were flicking over her meticulously mended gloves, the wobbling osprey. The picture of threadbare gentility; an English lady on hard times, come to pawn her jewels. "Some provenance, madam? Some proof of—"

"Yes, yes, I've got it here somewhere." Eve thumped an enormous handbag onto the counter, sending the jeweler's glass scattering. "There—no, that's not it. My eyeglasses, Charlotte—"

"In your bag, Grandmother," I weighed in, finally managing to squeeze some words past my astonishment.

"I thought you had them. Do check that bag. No, hold this. Is this it? No, that's the bill for that Chinese shawl, let me see . . . Provenance, it must be here . . ."

Pieces of paper cascaded over the pawnbroker's counter. Eve plucked through each one like a magpie, chattering in that immaculate drawl like she'd just tripped out from tea with the queen, fumbling for nonexistent eyeglasses, holding each scrap of paper pain-stakingly against the light. "Charlotte, do check your bag again, I am *positive* you have my eyeglasses—"

"Ma'am," the pawnbroker said, clearing his throat as another set of customers came in. Eve took no notice, braying away like a dowager in an Austen novel. "Lud, sir, don't fuss at me. This is it, yes—no, well, it's in here somewhere—" Her osprey wobbled dangerously, shed-ding a little shower of feathers that smelled like moth-balls. The pawnbroker tried to move to the next set of customers, but she rapped him on the knuckles with his own glass. "Don't wander off on me, my good man, we're not finished with our business! Charlotte, dear, read this for me, my old eyes . . ." The customers who'd walked in stood there for a while, then finally wandered back out.

I stood there like a bit player in a movie as the pawn-broker finally gave a little moue of impatience. "Never mind, madam. Provenance is not required—I am not so little a gentleman that I cannot take the word of so obvious a lady."

"Good," Eve said. "Let's hear your price."

They wrangled for a while, but I knew who was go-ing to win. A moment later the defeated pawnbroker was counting a great many crisp banknotes into my hand, and my pearls disappeared behind his counter; we turned to see Finn holding the door with a grin that only showed around his eyes. "My lady?" he said, straight-faced, and Eve swept through like an old duchess, os-prey bobbing.

"Ah," she said as the shop doors closed behind us, and the Mayfair drawl was utterly gone from her voice. "I enjoyed that."

She looked entirely different from the drunk old bat of last night, with her teacup of whiskey and her Luger.

For that matter, she looked entirely different from the hungover crone of this morning. She looked sober, crisp, savagely entertained, her gray eyes sparkling and her bony shoulders shedding the age and the aura of threadbare gentlewoman as though it was an inconvenient shawl.

"How did you do that?" I demanded, still clutching my handful of notes.

Eve Gardiner tugged off a glove, revealing that monstrosity of a hand again, and tugged her ever-present cigarettes out of her bag. "People are stupid. Stick a halfway d-decent story and a random bit of paper under their nose, and with plenty of self-possession one can always get through."

She sounded like she was quoting someone. "Always?" I parried.

"No." The sparkle disappeared from her eye. "Not always. But this wasn't m-much of a risk. That pompous arse knew he was getting a b-bargain. I just made him want to shovel me out of the shop a little faster."

I wondered why her stammer came and went the way it did. She'd conducted that charade in the shop as smooth and cool as cream. And *why* had she gone through with that charade in the first place? I studied her as she held her cigarette out to Finn and he struck a match for her. "You don't like me," I said at last.

"No," she said, and gave me that hooded glance again, like an eagle looking down from her aerie. An amused glance, but I saw no liking there at all, no softness.

I didn't care. She might not like me, but she spoke to me like an equal, not a child or a slut. "So why did you help me in there?" I asked, matching her bluntness. "Why are you helping me at all?"

"How about money?" She looked at my fistful of

notes, and named a chunk of it that made me gasp. "I c-can take you to someone who might know something about that cousin of yours, but I'm not doing it for free."

I narrowed my eyes, wishing I didn't feel so short, tucked as I was between the tall Scotsman and the tall Englishwoman. "You don't get a penny till you tell me who you were calling this morning."

"An English officer currently stationed in Bordeaux," she said without hesitation. "We go back thirty years, he and I, but he's on holiday. So I tried another old acquaintance, a woman who knows a thing or two. I asked her about a restaurant called Le Lethe, and the man who ran it, and she hung up on me." A snort. "The bitch knows something. If we go talk to her in person, I'll g-get it out of her. And if we can't get it out of her, I can certainly get it out of my English officer once he's back from duck hunting in Le Marche. So, is that worth a few quid to you?"

She was asking for a lot more than just a few quid, but I let that go. "Why did your interest prick up when I mentioned Monsieur René?" I shot back instead. "How can you know him when we don't even have a last name? Or was it the restaurant's name that hooked you?"

Eve smiled through a haze of smoke. "Fuck off, Yank," she said sweetly.

No stammering on *that*. It wasn't a word I'd ever heard a woman say before Eve Gardiner. Finn looked at the sky, carefully blank faced.

"All right," I said. And counted banknotes one by one into her hand.

"That's only half what I asked."

"You'll get the rest after we talk to your friends," I said just as sweetly. "Or else you'd probably go on a bender and leave me high and dry."

"Probably," Eve agreed. But I wondered, despite my own words. She wanted something more than my money. I was sure of it.

"So, where do we find this old friend of yours, the woman?" I asked as we all squashed into the Lagonda convertible, Finn behind the wheel, Eve in the middle with her arm slung carelessly around his shoulder, me squashed up against the door stuffing the rest of the banknotes into my pocketbook. "Where are we going?"

"Folkestone." Eve reached to stub her cigarette out in the dashboard, but Finn snatched it from her and tossed it out the window, glaring. "After Folkestone—France."

CHAPTER 4
EVE

May 1915

France. That was where Eve would be going to work as a spy. *A spy,* she thought experimentally, probing the thought the way a child probed the hole left by a missing tooth. Her stomach fluttered, part in nerves and part in excitement. *I am to be a spy in France.*

But before France, Folkestone.

"You think I can pluck you out of a file room and drop you straight into enemy territory?" Captain Cameron said on the train, carrying Eve's stuffed carpetbag for her. It was just a day after he'd recruited her over a pot of tea in that boardinghouse parlor—she'd have gone with him that night in the clothes she stood up in, hang propriety, but the captain insisted on collecting her very properly the following afternoon, giving her his arm to the station as though they were off on holiday. The only one to see Eve off was the tabby cat, whom she had kissed on the nose and whispered to, *Look to Mrs. Fitz next door; I made her promise to feed you extra scraps while I'm gone.*

"Should anyone ask," Captain Cameron said as they settled into their empty compartment, "I am a fond uncle taking my favorite niece to Folkestone for the sun." He closed the doors firmly, making sure they had the compartment to themselves, and did another check for eavesdroppers.

Eve tilted her head, surveying his lean face and rumpled tweeds. "Rather young to be my uncle, aren't you?"

"You are twenty-two and look sixteen; I am thirty-two and look forty-five. I am your uncle, Edward. That's to be our cover, now and in future."

His real name, she had learned, was Cecil Aylmer Cameron. Prep schools, Royal Military Academy, a stint serving in Edinburgh which must have added the faint Scottish mist to his English voice—Eve knew his public credentials now, listed meticulously when she accepted his offer. The private credentials would be given only as necessary in this very private business . . . And now she had the first of them: a code name. "Uncle Edward it is." Another flutter rippled through Eve's stomach. "What will my c-code name be?" She'd read Kipling and Childers and Conan Doyle—even in silly books like *The Scarlet Pimpernel*, spies had code names, disguises.

"You'll find out."

"Where will I be g-g—where will I be going in France?" She no longer minded stuttering in front of him.

"Wait and see. Training first." He smiled, the lines about his eyes crinkling. "Careful, Miss Gardiner. Your excitement is showing."

Eve smoothed her face into porcelain innocence.

"Better."

Folkestone. A sleepy coastal town, before the war. Now a bustling port, ferries crammed with refugees arriving every day, more French and Belgian voices heard on the docks than English. Captain Cameron didn't speak until they were out of the busy station and heading down the boardwalk in some measure of privacy. "Folkestone is the first stop from Vlissingen in the Netherlands," he said, setting their pace to keep well out of earshot of the other strolling couples. "Part of my job is to see that the refugees are interviewed before they are allowed farther into Britain."

"Looking for people like me?"

"And those like you who work for the *other* side."

"How many have you f-found of each?"

"Six of one, half a dozen of the other."

"Are there many women?" Eve wanted to know. "Among the—the recruits?" What did one call them? Apprentice spies? Spies-in-training? It all sounded absurd. Part of Eve still couldn't believe this was happening at all. "I never thought women would be considered for such a role," she said honestly. Captain Cameron (*Uncle Edward*) seemed able to hook the truth out of her in odd ways. He must be a marvel in an interrogation, she thought. He slipped information out of you so gently, you were hardly aware it crossed your lips.

"On the contrary," the captain said. "I like to recruit women. They frequently have the ability to pass unnoticed where a man would be suspected and stopped. I recruited a Frenchwoman, some months ago"—he gave a sudden, fond smile as if at a particularly good memory—"who now manages a network covering more than a hundred sources, and makes it look simple. Her reports on artillery positions come so quickly and accurately, we can see them bombed in a matter of days.

Quite remarkable. She's the best we have, male *or* female."

Eve's sense of competition stirred hungrily. *I will be the best.*

He hailed a cab—"Number 8, the Parade." A shabby little place, not much different from the boardinghouse where Eve had lived, and a boardinghouse was probably what this address passed for if neighbors proved curious. But when the captain ushered Eve inside and she came to stand on the faded parlor rug, it wasn't a starchy old maid with a pinched mouth who greeted her, but a tall major in full uniform.

He gave Eve a dubious look, fingering the waxed points of an impressive mustache. "Very young," he disapproved, looking her up and down.

"Give her a chance," Captain Cameron said mildly. "Miss Evelyn Gardiner, meet Major George Allenton. I leave you in his hands."

Eve experienced a moment's fear, seeing Cameron's tweedy back disappear, but she banished it. *I must not fear anything*, she reminded herself. *Or I will fail.*

The major looked unenthusiastic. Eve guessed he did not share Captain Cameron's preference for female recruits. "The first room on the second floor is yours. Report back here in fifteen minutes." And as easily as that, the secret world opened.

The Folkestone course lasted two weeks. Two weeks in stuffy low-ceilinged rooms with windows sealed against the May warmth. Rooms full of students who did not look like spies, learning strange and sinister things from men who did not look like soldiers.

Despite Captain Cameron's recruiting preference, Eve found herself the only woman. The instructors overlooked her, eyes going to the men in the room before they let Eve answer anything, but that didn't trouble her because it gave her time to evaluate her classmates. Just four of them, and how different they were from each other. That was the thing that struck Eve most. Any recruiting poster for the fighting troops showed you a line of identical Tommies, stalwart and sturdy, faceless in their similarity. That was the ideal soldier: a line, a regiment, a battalion of strong men all exactly alike. But a recruitment poster for spies, she realized, would merely show you a line of people, all different, who did not look like spies.

There was a burly Belgian with a graying beard; two Frenchmen, one with a Lyonnais accent and the other with a limp; and a slender English boy burning with such incandescent hatred for the Huns that he almost glowed. *He won't be any good,* Eve judged. *No self-control*—and she wasn't sure about the limping Frenchman either; his hands balled into fists whenever he encountered the least frustration. The whole *course* was an exercise in frustration, fiddly skills to be learned with infinite patience: the picking of locks, the writing of codes, and the learning of ciphers. The various types of invisible ink, how it could be made and how it could be read. How to read and draw maps, how to conceal messages—the list went on and on. The Belgian swore softly when they learned how to compile reports on the smallest possible scraps of rice paper, because his huge fists were like hams. But Eve quickly mastered the system of tiny letters, each no bigger than a comma on a typewriter. And her instructor, a lean Cockney who had barely looked at her since she arrived, smiled at her work and began to watch her more closely.

Just a fortnight, and Eve wondered how much it was possible to change in two weeks. Or was it not change, but becoming what she already was? She felt like she was being burned, sloughing away every extraneous layer, every scrap of ballast from mind or body that could possibly weigh her down. Each morning she woke with alacrity, tossing the covers aside and springing from bed, her mind one long hungry scream for what the day had to offer. She manipulated her fingers around those tiny scraps of paper, those deft manipulations that would persuade a lock to give up its secrets, and she thrilled with more sheer, fierce pleasure the first time she sensed a lock's tumblers click than she had ever felt when a man tried to kiss her.

I was made for this, she thought. *I am Evelyn Gardiner, and this is where I belong.*

Captain Cameron came to see her at the end of the first week. "How's my pupil?" he asked, strolling unannounced into the stuffy, makeshift classroom.

"Very well, Uncle Edward," Eve said demurely.

His eyes laughed. "What's that you're practicing?"

"Hiding messages." How to swiftly slit a seam on her cuff and poke in a tiny rolled message, and how to quickly pluck it back out. It took speed and deft fingers, but Eve had both.

The captain leaned against the edge of the table. He was in uniform today, the first time she'd seen him in khaki, and it suited him. "How many places can you hide a message, in what you're wearing now?"

"Cuffs, hems, fingertips of a glove," Eve recited. "Pinned into the hair, of course. Rolled around the inside band of a ring, or inside the heel of a s-shoe—"

"Mmm, better forget that last one. I hear the Fritzes have caught on to the shoe-heel trick."

Eve nodded, filing that away. She unrolled her tiny blank message and began swiftly threading it through the hem of her handkerchief instead.

"Your classmates are taking target practice," the captain observed. "Why not you?"

"Major Allenton did not think it necessary." *Can't see a woman ever being in a position to fire a pistol* had been his words, and so Eve was left behind while her classmates tramped off to the targets with borrowed Webleys. Only three classmates now—the slender English boy had been deemed unfit, and left weeping and swearing. *Go join the Tommies if you want to fight Germans*, Eve thought, not without sympathy.

"I think you *should* learn to fire a pistol, Miss Gardiner."

"Isn't that g-going against the major's orders?" Cameron and Allenton didn't like each other; Eve had seen that on the first day.

Cameron merely said, "Come with me."

He didn't take Eve to the range, but to a deserted stretch of beach, far down from the bustle of the docks. He set off toward the water, shoulder-slinging a knapsack that clinked with every step, and Eve followed, her boots sinking into the sand and the wind tugging at her neatly rolled hair. The morning was hot, and Eve wished she could take off her jacket, but this tramping off alone to an isolated beach with a man who most certainly wasn't her uncle was already improper enough. *Miss Gregson and the rest of the file girls would all think me no better than I should be.* Then Eve pushed that thought aside and stripped down to her shirtwaist, reasoning that she wouldn't get far as a spy if she thought too much about propriety.

The captain found a driftwood log, unpacked a series of empty bottles from his clinking knapsack, and lined them up on the log. "This will do. Step ten paces back."

"Shouldn't I be able to shoot from farther than that?" Eve objected, dropping her jacket on a patch of sea grass.

"If you're taking aim at a man, odds are it's up

close." Captain Cameron paced off the distance, then took his pistol from its holster. "This is a Luger nine-millimeter P08—"

Eve wrinkled her nose. "A German p-pistol?"

"Don't sneer, Miss Gardiner, it's far more accurate and reliable than our English ones. Our lads get the Webley Mk IV; that's what your classmates are training with, and they might as well not bother because you need weeks to get good with a Webley, the way they jump on firing. With a Luger, you'll be hitting your targets with just a few hours of practice."

Briskly, Captain Cameron broke the pistol apart, named the parts, and had Eve assemble and reassemble it until she lost her clumsiness. When she caught the trick of it and saw her hands moving with deft speed, she thrilled with the same liquid excitement she'd been feeling ever since she arrived, whenever she managed to decipher a map or decrypt a message. *More,* she thought. *Give me more.*

Cameron had her load and unload, and Eve could tell he was waiting to see if she'd beg to shoot and not just fiddle with the pistol's parts. *He wants to see if I have patience.* She pushed a wind-whipped lock of hair back behind one ear and took the instruction mutely. *I can wait all day, Captain.*

"There." At last, he pointed at the first of the bottles lined up on the driftwood log. "You have seven shots. Sight down the barrel, so. It doesn't kick like a Webley, but there's still recoil." He tapped a finger to her shoulder, her chin, her knuckles, correcting her stance. No attempts to make this intimate—Eve remembered the French boys in Nancy whenever she appeared on a duck hunt. *Let me show you how to aim that!* And then they'd start wrapping their arms around her.

The captain nodded, stepping back. The stiff salt

breeze tugged at his short hair and ruffled the slate blue of the Channel water behind him. "Fire."

She emptied out her seven shots, the reports reverberating around the empty beach, and didn't hit a single bottle. Disappointment stabbed, but she knew better than to show it. She just reloaded.

"Why do you want this, Miss Gardiner?" the captain asked, and nodded for her to fire again.

"I want to do my part." She didn't stutter at all. "Is that so strange? Last summer when the war began, every young man in England was burning to join the fight, make something of himself. Did anyone ask them why?" She lifted the Luger, squeezing off another seven shots carefully spaced. Clipped one of the bottles this time, sending a chip of glass flying, but didn't shatter it. Another stab of disappointment. *But someday, I will be the best,* she vowed. *Better even than your prize recruit in Lille, whoever she is.*

The captain's voice continued. "Do you hate the Fritzes?"

"They weren't far from Nancy, where I grew up." Eve began to reload. "I didn't hate them then. But they invaded France, tore it to pieces, took everything g-g-good about it for themselves." Snapping the last bullet in. "What gives them the right?"

"Nothing." He studied her. "But I think it's less patriotism with you than the urge to prove yourself capable."

"Yes," she admitted, and it felt good. That *was* what she wanted above all. Wanted it so badly it hurt.

"Relax your grip a touch. You're pulling the trigger rather than squeezing it, and it's throwing your aim to the right."

On her second shot a bottle exploded. Eve grinned.

"Don't think of this as a game." The captain looked down at her. "I see so many young men on fire to beat the German swine. That's all right for the rank and file; they'll lose that illusion the first week in the trenches and no harm done to anything but their innocence. But spies cannot be *on fire* for anything. Spies who think it a game will get themselves killed, and likely their fellows as well. The Germans are clever and they are ruthless, regardless of anything you have heard about the stupid Boches, and from the moment you set foot in France they will be determined to catch you. As a woman, you might not be stood up against a wall and shot, as happened to a boy of nineteen I sent to Roubaix last month. But you could be shoveled off to rot in some German prison, starving slowly among the rats, and no one could help you—not even me. Do you understand, Evelyn Gardiner?"

Another test, Eve thought, her heart beating hard. Fail, and she'd get nowhere near France. Fail, and she went home to a rented room and filing letters. *No.*

But what was the right answer?

Captain Cameron waited, eyes steady on hers.

"I never thought this was a game," Eve said at last. "I don't play g-games. Games are for children, and I may look sixteen, but I have *never* been a child." She began to load the pistol again. "I can't promise I won't fail, but it won't be because I think it's all a lark."

She returned his gaze fiercely, heart still thumping. *Was that the right answer?* She had no idea. But it was the only one she had. "You will be sent into German-occupied Lille," Captain Cameron said at last, and Eve's knees nearly buckled in relief. "But you go to Le Havre first, to meet your contact. Your name will be Marguerite Le François. Learn to respond to that name as if it were your own."

Marguerite Le François. In English it would translate to something like "Daisy French," and Eve smiled. A perfect name for an innocent girl, a girl to be ignored and talked over. Just a harmless little daisy, lurking fresh-faced in the grass.

Captain Cameron smiled back. "I thought it would suit." He pointed at the row of bottles, just six left—he had lean, tanned hands, and Eve saw the gold flash of a wedding ring on the left. "Again."

"Bien sûr, Oncle Édouard."

By the end of the afternoon all the bottles were smashed. With a few more days of practice under his tutelage, she could pick off seven bottles in seven shots.

"Making a great deal of time for you, Cameron is," Major Allenton observed one afternoon when Eve came back to class after practice. He hadn't bothered speaking to Eve since her arrival, but now he gave her a speculative glance. "Be careful there, m'dear."

"I can't imagine what you m-mean." Eve settled back down behind her desk, first to arrive for a practice session on code breaking. "The captain is a perfect gentleman."

"Well, not *perfect,* perhaps. There was that nasty business that sent him to prison for three years."

Eve nearly fell out of her seat. Cameron, with his gentlemanly voice lilting its faint hint of Scotland and his impeccable public school grammar, the mild gaze and lanky grace. *Prison?*

The major fingered his waxed mustache, clearly waiting for her to press for juicy details. Eve straightened her skirts and kept silent. "Fraud," he said at last, satisfaction evident to be dishing on a subordinate. "If you're curious. His wife tried to claim her pearl necklace had been stolen, which made it insurance fraud and a very dodgy business. He took the blame for her, but who knows what really happened?" The major looked rather pleased at Eve's expression. "Don't suppose he told you about the prison sentence, eh?" A wink. "Or the wife."

"Neither," Eve said frostily, "is any of my b-business. And since he was reinstated to His Majesty's army in a position of trust, then it is not my p-p—my place to q-question his authority."

"Wouldn't call it a position of *trust*, m'dear. War makes for strange bedfellows; we need all hands on deck, even the soiled ones. Cameron got his pardon and his reinstatement, but that doesn't mean I'd want any girl of mine off walking the beach alone with him. Once a man's been behind bars, well . . ."

Eve imagined Cameron's long hands loading the Luger for her. She could not imagine those hands thieving anything. "W-w-will that be all, sir?" She was aching to know more, of course, but she'd be hanged before she asked this spiteful walrus with his ridiculous mustache for another word. The major wandered off, clearly disappointed, and Eve eyed Cameron covertly the following day. But she didn't ask him anything, because everyone in Folkestone had secrets. And on the day the training course ended, he tucked the Luger into her neatly packed carpetbag as a gift, and said, "You leave for France in the morning."

PART II

PART II

CHAPTER 5
CHARLIE

May 1947

don't know how long the Channel crossing took. Time stretched on forever when you spent it vomiting.

"Don't shut your eyes." Finn Kilgore's Scottish burr sounded behind me as I clung grimly to the railing. "Makes your stomach worse if you can't see which direction the swells are coming from."

I screwed my eyes shut tighter. "Please don't say that word."

"What word?"

"Swells."

"Just look at the horizon and—"

"Too late," I groaned, and leaned over the railing. I had nothing left to bring up, but my stomach turned itself inside out anyway. Out of the corner of my eye I could see a pair of Frenchmen in dapper suits wrinkling their noses and edging farther down the deck. A stiff gust of wind whipped across the deck, and my dark green hat with its horrid rolled brim went cartwheeling away. "Let it go," I gasped between heaves as Finn made a swipe over the rail. "I hate that hat!"

He smiled, reaching to gather my whipping hair and hold it out of my face as I retched one final time. I'd been hideously embarrassed the first time I vomited in front of him, but now I was too ill for humiliation. "That's a delicate stomach you've got for a Yank," he observed. "Judging from their hot dogs and their coffee, I thought Americans didn't get sick at anything."

I straightened, probably looking as green as an old can of peas. "Please don't say hot dogs."

He dropped my hair. "As you wish."

We were standing at the opposite end of the boat from Eve, because she'd found my misery enormously amusing, and I'd had to retreat before I killed her. Eventually Finn had joined me. He must have gotten tired of her swearing and her smoke fumes, though it was hard to imagine they were worse than my endless nausea.

He leaned back on his elbows against the rail, tipping his head back to look at the boat's squat upper deck. "Where do we go once we get to Le Havre, miss?"

"Eve says the woman we need to talk to is in Roubaix, so we may as well go there before Limoges. But I was thinking . . ." I trailed off.

"Thinking what?"

"Rouen first?" It came out as too much of a question, and I kicked myself for that. I didn't have to ask permission for where we went next; this was my quest, though that was far too grandiose a word. My mission? My obsession? Well, whatever you called it, my money was funding everything so I was the one in charge. Finn and Eve seemed to take that for granted, something I couldn't help but enjoy after so many weeks of feeling like a leaf on the surface of a whirlpool. "We'll go to Rouen," I said firmly. "My aunt left Paris and moved to the summer house for good after the war. Rose's mother. She wasn't very forthcoming in her letters, but if I turn up on her doorstep surely she'll talk to me."

I thought of my French aunt with her endless rattling handbag full of pill boxes for all the illnesses she was convinced she was dying of, and I wanted to seize hold of her bony arms and shake her till she coughed up the answers I wanted. *Why did Rose leave home in '43? What happened to your daughter?*

I looked across the deck and saw the eight-year-old Rose, wiry and freckled, skipping along the rail. She smiled at me, and then I saw she wasn't Rose at all. She didn't even have Rose's blond hair. I watched the child run back to her mother at the bow, and still my imagination tried to tell me it was Rose's fair plaits bouncing against that narrow back, not a stranger's brown ones.

"Rouen," I repeated. "We'll stay the night in Le Havre, then drive in the morning. We could get there tonight if we could take the train . . ." Eve had flatly refused to consider anything but car travel, and so I'd had to fork over a good sum to have Finn's Lagonda lifted ponderously up into the boat by crane. Like we were British lords off for a Continental motoring jaunt with a champagne picnic. For what it cost to bring the car— and because of the car, we had to take the slower boat to Le Havre rather than Boulogne—I could have ferried *six* people to France and back. "Couldn't that cow buck up and suffer a train ride?" I grumbled.

"I don't ken she could," Finn said.

I glanced at my unpredictable ally at the other end of the deck. On the car journey she'd been by turns insulting or silent, refusing to get out of the car when we reached Folkestone, and Finn had to escort me out to

buy tickets for the Channel crossing. When we came
back to the Lagonda she'd disappeared, and after going
up and down in the car we found her standing outside
a shabby row house marked number 8 on the Parade—
just standing there, scowling. "Still wonder where that
skinny English boy went," she'd said apropos of nothing. "The one b-booted out of the course. Did he join
the boys in the trenches, get himself blown up? Lucky
bastard."

"What course?" I'd asked, exasperated, but she just
gave her harsh bark of a laugh and said, "Haven't we got
a boat to catch?"

And now she was sitting at the far corner of the deck
in a shabby coat, hatless, smoking an unending chain
of cigarettes and looking unexpectedly fragile. "My
brother always sat like that," I said. "With his back in a
corner. When he came back from Tarawa, anyway. He
got drunk one night and told me he wasn't comfortable
anymore unless he could see all the lines of fire." A
lump rose in my throat as I remembered James's broad
handsome face, not really handsome anymore under the
blur of drink and the pasted-on smile, because his eyes
were so empty . . .

"A lot of soldiers do that," Finn said, neutral.

"I know." Swallowing down the lump. "It wasn't just
my brother—I used to see it when the soldiers came into
the coffee shop where I worked." I caught Finn's look
of surprise. "What, you think the rich little American's
never had a job?"

That was clearly exactly what he'd thought.

"My father thought his children should know the
value of a dollar. I started working at his office when I
was fourteen." A law firm specializing in international
law, French and German heard on the telephone lines
as much as English. I'd started out watering the plants

and making the coffee, but soon I was filing papers, organizing my father's notes, even balancing his account books once it became clear I could do it faster and more neatly than his secretary. "And then when I went to Bennington," I continued, "and my mother wasn't there to forbid me, I got a job at a coffee shop. That's where I'd see the soldiers come in."

Finn looked bemused. "Why work if you didn't have to?"

"I like being useful. Anything to get me out of white gloves and cotillion. You can watch people in a café, make up stories about them. That one over there is a Nazi spy, that one over there is an actress on her way to a Broadway audition. Besides, I'm good with numbers, so I'm useful in a shop—making change in my head, keeping the register. I was a math major in school."

How my mother's brows had furrowed when she heard I'd signed up for calculus and algebra at Bennington. "I know you like that sort of thing, *ma chère*—I don't know how I'll keep my checkbook balanced with you away in Vermont!—but don't make too much of it on dates. Don't do that thing you do, where you add up all the menu prices in your head to see if you can do it faster than the waiter. Boys don't like that sort of thing."

Maybe that was why I'd taken the coffee shop job once I got to Bennington. My small rebellion against the litany I'd heard all my life about what was proper, what was suitable, what boys liked. My mother sent me to college to find a husband, but I was looking for something else. Some other path besides the one picked out for me—traveling, working, who knew what. I hadn't had it figured out yet, but then the Little Problem came along and shot my mother's plans *and* mine all to pieces.

"Making change for cups of coffee." Finn cracked a smile. "That's a bonny way to spend a war."

"Not my fault I was too young to be a nurse." I hesitated, but asked anyway. My stomach was still rolling, and the conversation helped keep my mind off it. "What about your war?" Because everyone's war was different. Mine was algebra homework, going on the odd date, and waiting every single day for letters from Rose and James. My parents' war was Victory Gardens and scrap metal drives and my mother fretting about having to put makeup on her legs instead of stockings. And my poor brother's war . . . Well, he wouldn't say what it was, but it made him swallow a shotgun. "What was your war like?" I asked Eve's driver again, blinking James's face away before it made my throat tighten. "You said you were in the Anti-Tank Regiment."

"I didn't get wounded. Had a braw time of it, pure dead brilliant." Finn was mocking something, but I didn't think it was me. I wanted to ask, but his face had closed off and I couldn't bring myself to pry further. I hardly knew him, after all—he was Eve's man of all work, the Scotsman who made breakfast. I didn't know if he liked me at all, or was just being polite.

I wanted him to like me. Not just him—Eve too, much as she both baffled and annoyed me. In their company, I had a fresh slate. To them I was Charlie St. Clair, spearhead of the world's most unlikely search party. Not Charlie St. Clair, complete disgrace and all-around tramp.

Eventually Finn wandered off, and my stomach began churning again. I passed the rest of the journey staring at the horizon and swallowing hard. At last the cry went up—*Le Havre!*—and I was the first one down to the docks, lugging my traveling case, so glad to be on firm ground that I could have kissed it. It took me a moment to register the scenery around me.

Le Havre showed even more signs of the war

than London. The harbor had been bombed flat, I remembered—the *storm of iron and fire*, they called it. There was still so much rubble, so many missing buildings. More than that, there was a general gray dispiritedness here, a tiredness in the crowds around me. The Londoners I'd encountered seemed to carry themselves with a certain grim humor, as if to say, *You still can't get cream with your scones, but we never did get invaded, eh?*

France, despite all the giddiness I'd read about in the papers—General de Gaulle marching down the boulevards of Paris in triumph, the delirious screaming crowds—just looked exhausted.

By the time Eve and Finn had joined me, I had shoved my sudden melancholy away and was fingering the wad of francs I'd acquired in Folkestone. ("Dear, does your father know you're changing this much money?") Finn deposited Eve and her dilapidated luggage, then moved off swiftly down the dock to make certain the disembarking crane did not dent his precious Lagonda. "We'll need a hotel," I said absently, recounting my francs and staving off a sudden wave of weariness. "Do you know of somewhere cheap?"

"There's no shortage of *cheap* in a waterfront city." Eve looked at me in amusement. "Want to bunk with Finn? Two rooms are cheaper than three."

"No, thank you," I said coldly.

"What prudes Americans are," she chuckled. We stood in silence until the dark blue Lagonda at last rounded the corner purring.

"How did he ever get a car like that?" I wondered, thinking of Finn's threadbare shirt.

"Probably did something illegal," Eve said carelessly.

I blinked. "Are you joking?"

"No. You think he works for a bad-tempered bitch

like me for fun? Nobody else was about to give him a job. I probably shouldn't have either, but I have a weakness for good-looking men with Scottish accents and prison terms."

I nearly fell off my high heels. "*What?*"

"Haven't you figured it out?" She cocked an eyebrow. "Finn's an ex-convict."

CHAPTER 6
EVE

June 1915

Marguerite Le François came in out of the rain and sat down at an isolated corner table in a café in Le Havre: a respectable girl, hatted and gloved, timidly asking the waiter in her northern-accented French for a lemonade. If you looked in Marguerite's pocketbook you would find all her identity cards in immaculate order: she was born in Roubaix, she had work papers, she was seventeen. Just what else Marguerite was, Eve wasn't sure yet—the identity was filmy, not yet fleshed out with the details that would make it real. When Captain Cameron—Uncle Edward—put Eve on the boat from Folkestone, all he'd given her was the immaculate packet of false papers; a respectable if threadbare traveling suit and a battered case full of more respectable, threadbare clothes; and a destination. "In Le Havre," he said on the dock, "you will meet your contact. She will tell you what you need to know, going forward."

"Is she your shining star?" Eve couldn't help ask. "Your best agent?"

"Yes." Cameron had smiled, eyes crinkling at the corners. Out of his immaculate khaki uniform and back into his anonymous tweeds. "I can think of no one better to prepare you."

"I will be just as good." Eve held his eyes fiercely. "I will make you p-proud."

"You all make me proud," Cameron said. "The moment a recruit accepts an assignment, I am proud. Because this isn't just a dangerous job, it's dirty and distasteful. Not very sporting, really, to listen at doors and open a man's mail—even an enemy's. No one really thinks gentlemen should do such things, even in a time of war. Much less gentlewomen."

"Rubbish," Eve said tartly, and Cameron laughed.

"Consummate rubbish. Still, the kind of work we do isn't much respected, even among those who rely on our reports. There's no acclaim to be had, no fame, no praise. Just danger." He tweaked her drab little hat to a better angle over her neatly rolled hair. "So, never fear that you have failed to make me proud, Miss Gardiner."

"Mademoiselle Le François," Eve reminded him.

"Quite." His smile faded then. "Be careful."

"*Bien sûr.* What is her name, this woman in Le Havre? Your shining star, who I am going to replace?"

"Alice," the captain said in amusement. "Alice Dubois. Not her real name, of course. And if you can best her, you will end the war in six months."

He'd stood for a long time on the dock, watching Eve's boat recede into the choppy surf. She gazed steadily back until the tweedy figure disappeared. She felt a twinge to see him gone—the first person ever to have faith in her, to believe she could be something more, not to mention her last contact with everything left behind. But excitement soon won over loneliness. Eve Gardiner had left England; Marguerite Le François had arrived in Le Havre. And she waited, sipping lemonade and concealing a curiosity that could fairly be called ravenous, for the mysterious *Alice.*

The café was crowded. Sour-faced waiters squeezed past with dirty plates and bottles of wine, customers came in from the street shaking off their rainy umbrellas. Eve scrutinized every woman in sight. A stout matron with a brisk manner had the heavy anonymity and the competent air of a master organizer of spies . . . Or perhaps the raw-boned young woman who leaned her bicycle outside and then had to stop in the doorway to clean her spectacles. She might be concealing eyes like a hawk that had read German plans by the dozen . . .

"Ma chère Marguerite!" a woman's voice shrieked, and Eve's head jerked around at the name she'd trained herself like a puppy to respond to. She had the impression of a hat bearing down on her—not just any hat, but a hat the size of a wagon wheel covered with pink organza and silk roses—and then the hat's owner enveloped her in a cloud of lily-of-the-valley scent and kissed her soundly on both cheeks.

"Chérie, look at you! How is dear *Oncle Édouard*?"

It was the phrase she was told she would hear first, but all Eve could do was stare. *This is the organizer of the Lille network?*

The little Frenchwoman was perhaps thirty-five, bird boned, hardly up to Eve's chin. She wore a dashing suit in a violent shade of lilac, topped by the mountainous pink hat. Shopping bags piled up around her as she settled chattering behind the table, switching from rapid French into equally rapid English. In this part of France,

English voices were common thanks to soldiers and nurses on leave from the front. "*Mon Dieu,* this rain! My hat is sure to be ruined. Perhaps it *should* be ruined. I couldn't decide if it was utterly ghastly or utterly magical, so of course there was nothing to do but buy it." She extracted a few pearl hat pins and hurled the hat to the spare chair, revealing blond hair rolled into a pompadour. "I always buy a morally questionable hat whenever I come through this area. I can't take them back north with me, of course. Wear a nice hat, and a German sentry will just confiscate it for his latest whore. So in Lille I go about in last year's serge and a dismal little boater, and anything fashionable gets abandoned as soon as I return. I must have left morally questionable hats all over France. Brandy," she said to the waiter appearing at her elbow, and unleashed a ravishing smile as he reared back. "It's been an absolute pisser of a day," she said frankly. "So make it a double brandy, *monsieur,* and never mind looking sour. So—" She turned back to Eve, sitting silent and rather wide-eyed through this introductory monologue, and looked her up and down, suddenly all business. "*Merde.* Uncle Edward sends me babies from the cradle now?"

"I'm twenty-two," Eve said with a touch of frost. No fluffy Parisienne who matched pink with purple was going to make her feel like an infant. "Mademoiselle Dubois—"

"Stop right there."

Eve froze, looking around the rackety café. "Is someone listening?"

"No, no, we're safe. If anyone understands English, which I doubt, we're in the corner of a room too full of noise for anyone to hear a useful word. No, I meant stop calling me that horrid name." An extravagant shudder.

"*Alice Dubois.* What sin did I commit to earn a name like that? I shall have to ask my confessor. *Alice Dubois* sounds like a skinny schoolmistress with a face like a bin. Call me Lili. It's not my real name either, but at least it has some dash. I gave Uncle Edward hell until he started using it too. I think he likes it, because he started giving flower names to the rest of his 'nieces,' like Violette—you'll meet her soon; she'll hate you, but she hates everybody—and now you: Marguerite, the little daisy. We're his garden, and he fusses over us like an old maid with a watering can." Alice/Lili had been speaking with her head close to Eve's so their conversation would be inaudible, but she still broke off the instant the waiter approached with her brandy. "*Merci!*" she beamed, ignoring his disapproving look.

Eve had never in her life seen a well-bred woman drink spirits, except perhaps medicinally, but she kept silent, rotating her glass of lemonade. Captain Cameron warned her against thinking of this work as a game, but his prize agent seemed to consider everything a joke. *Or does she?* Under the breezy chatter, Lili showed an instinctive caution: her words paused the moment anyone brushed even remotely close to their table, although her voice was already so low Eve had to bend confidentially near to catch every word. They looked like two women sharing a cozy secret—which of course they were.

Lili didn't seem to mind Eve's scrutiny. She scrutinized right back, her deep-set eyes almost liquid in their movement. "Twenty-two years old?" she repeated. "I'd never believe it."

"And that's why my papers say I'm seventeen." Eve opened her eyes to their widest, fanning her lashes in sweet confusion, and Lili gave a laugh of sheer merriment, clapping her hands.

"Maybe our mutual uncle is a genius after all. What a morsel you are, *chérie*—fresh from the schoolroom and dumb as a daisy, I'd swear it!"

Eve lowered her lids demurely. "M-m-most kind."

"Yes, Uncle Edward said you had a hitching tongue," Lili said frankly. "I imagine that's hell in normal life, but it will stand you in good stead now. People talk around women, and they talk even more around girls, and they'll chatter like geese around a girl who seems half witted. I advise you to play it up like mad. Let's order baguettes! You won't be getting good bread in Lille. All the good white flour goes to the Boches, so whenever I come south I gorge on good bread and fashionable hats. I love this city!"

And as Lili slugged back the rest of her brandy and called for baguettes and jam, Eve began to smile. "Uncle Edward said you'd have details for me." She was hungrier for information than for bread.

"You are a straight-to-business sort, aren't you?" Lili pecked at the first baguette, eating in darting bites like a neat little bird. "You will be going to a restaurant in Lille, very fashionable. The kind of place where they'd never serve a large brandy to a lady in a morally questionable hat." Lili rattled her empty glass. "To have another, *oui* or *non*? *Oui*, of course. If one has the luxury of sleeping safe in the night to come, one should always have more brandy." She raised a finger to the waiter three tables away, pointing to her snifter, and he looked positively pinched. "The restaurant is called Le Lethe," she resumed, lowering her voice even further. "The German *Kommandant* eats there at least twice a week, and half the officers in the region flock after him, considering Le Lethe's cooks get half the black-market food in Lille. There was a waiter who worked there, clever fellow, used to pass me information. *Mon Dieu*, the kind of things he overheard when those officers were deep in their *schnapps*! I wanted someone to put in his place when he was caught, and *voilà*: Uncle Edward tells me he's plucked a perfect little daisy for me."

"Caught?" Eve asked.

"Stealing supplies." Lili shook her head. "He had good ears, but no sense. Stealing chickens and sugar and flour from the people you spy on, *merde*, what an idiot. Of course he was shoved into the nearest back alley and shot."

Eve's stomach churned, and she put down her baguette. *Shot.* How very real it was all becoming—so much more real in this steaming little café than on the sunny beach in Folkestone.

Lili gave a one-sided smile. "You're feeling sick, I know. It's quite natural. So I'll eat your baguette. You really should try to thin down a bit before we let you go to your interview, anyway. You look a bit too healthy to have come from Roubaix. Everyone in the north looks like a rake handle. Look at me, a bag of bones with skin like an ashtray."

Eve had already noted the marks of exhaustion under Lili's eyes, and now she saw the pallor of that thin face despite its smiles. *Will I look like that in a few months?* Eve wondered, and shoved her baguette over to Lili's plate. "Interview?" she prompted.

"For the job at Le Lethe. The owner has let it be known he will consider hiring waitresses instead of waiters. Normally he'd faint dead away before allowing a woman to serve in his establishment, but waiters are one thing he can't get on the black market. War makes men harder to find than white flour, even for a damned profiteer like René Bordelon. Who, I should warn you, is a beast. He'd turn his own mother in to the Germans for a profit, not that he has a mother. The devil probably shit him out after a night's drinking with Judas." Lili polished off the last crumbs of Eve's baguette. "You'll need to persuade Monsieur Bordelon to hire you. He's clever, so don't go thinking it will be simple."

Eve nodded as the identity of Marguerite Le François took firmer shape. A little country girl, wide-eyed, not too bright, not too educated, but deft and quiet and graceful enough to serve *boeuf en daube* and oysters *en brochette* without drawing attention to herself.

"Once you're hired—*if* you're hired—you'll pass anything you hear to me." Lili fished in her handbag and pulled out a silver cigarette case. "I'll see it gets to Uncle Edward."

"How?" Eve asked, trying not to stare as Lili struck a match. *Only common women smoke,* Eve's mother had always decreed, but Lili could not be branded *common* despite her violent pink hat and her brandy.

"That's courier business," Lili said vaguely. "*My* job. I can be any number of people and go any number of places, whereas that hitching tongue would get you recognized if you tried. So we will play to your strengths."

Eve didn't bother being offended. It was the truth, after all. She imagined Lili sashaying through armed checkpoints, chattering up a storm, and smiled. "I think your job is more d-d-dangerous than mine."

"Oh, *pffft.* I manage. With any paper one sticks under their nose and plenty of self-possession, one can get through. Especially a woman. Sometimes I take an armload of parcels and bags and drop every single one as I try to find my identity cards, chatting all the while, and they wave me through out of sheer irritation." Lili exhaled a long stream of smoke. "To tell the truth, much of this special work we do is quite boring. I think that's why women are good at it. Our lives are already boring. We jump at Uncle Edward's offer because we can't stand the thought of working in a file room anymore, or teaching a class full of runny-nosed children their letters. Then we discover this job is deadly dull as well, but at least there's the enlivening thought that someone might put a Luger to the back of our necks. It's still better than shooting *ourselves*, which we know we're going to do if we have to type one more letter or pound one more Latin verb into a child's ivory skull."

Eve wondered if Lili was a schoolmistress before the war. She wondered how Captain Cameron recruited Lili, but she knew no one would tell her. No real names, no backgrounds, not unless necessary. "Uncle Edward says you're his best," she remarked instead.

Lili let out another peal of laughter. "What a romantic that man is! Saint George in tweed; I do adore him. Far too honorable for this business."

Eve agreed, prison sentence or no. She kept turning that mystery over in idle moments—Cameron, imprisoned for *fraud*?—but it didn't really make a difference. Whatever his background, she trusted him, and clearly so did Lili.

"Come along now." Lili stubbed out her cigarette. "You should meet Violette Lameron. She calls herself my lieutenant, though if we had proper ranks I'd be able to scold her rather than having her constantly scolding me. I think it's because she used to be a nurse—which you need to know, by the way, in case you ever have an injury to be patched up. She might have decided she'd rather be shot than roll another bandage for the Red Cross, but she still knows what to do if she sees broken bones or spurting wounds, and she'll see you to right if you ever get yourself hurt. Though you won't enjoy the process. God help me, how that woman can nag!" Affectionately. "The habit of nagging, let me assure you, goes with a nurse no matter *what* she does."

Lili clapped the massive pink hat back over her blond hair, collected her packages, and shepherded Eve into the streets of Le Havre. It was warm despite the rain, and rosy-faced mothers herded their children back toward home as cab horses splashed through the puddles. No one here, Eve observed, had Lili's thinness or her exhausted grainy look, and maybe Lili was thinking the same thing because she unfurled her umbrella with a vicious snap, saying, "I hate this city."

"You said you l-loved it."

"I love it *and* I hate it. Le Havre, Paris. I love their baguettes and their hats, but *merde,* the people have no idea what is happening in the north. None at all." That mobile face was still for an instant. "Lille is overrun by beasts, and here they sniff if you want a brandy and a smoke to get through a pisser of a day."

"Lili," Eve asked impulsively. "Are you ever afraid?"

Lili turned, rain dripping off the edge of her umbrella in a silver curtain between her and Eve. "Yes, just like everybody else. But only after the danger is done— before that, fear is an indulgence." She slid her hand through Eve's elbow. "Welcome to the Alice Network."

CHAPTER 7
CHARLIE

May 1947

Summertime, almost exactly ten years ago. I'd been nine and Rose eleven when our families went on a drive through Provence . . . and ended up leaving us at a roadside café for nearly six hours.

An accident, of course. Two cars, one with the adults and one trundling behind with the children and the nanny. A stop at a café overlooking a vineyard of budding grapes, our parents looking for lavatories and postcards, Rose and me following the smell of fresh-baked bread to the kitchen, our brothers roughhousing . . . and somehow when everyone loaded back up, the nanny thought we'd climbed into the car with our parents and our parents thought we were with the nanny, and everyone drove off without us.

It was the only time I'd ever seen Rose scared, and I couldn't understand it. We weren't in any danger; the plump and motherly Provençal cook had made a great fuss over us once she discovered what had happened. "Don't worry, *mesdemoiselles*! It won't be twenty minutes before your mothers are back." Soon we were settled at a table of our own under a striped awning overlooking the vineyard, with glasses of cold lemonade and thick sandwiches of goat cheese and prosciutto.

"They'll be back soon," I said, munching. As far as I was concerned, this was much better than sitting hot and cramped in the Renault's backseat, getting admonished by the nanny and pinched by our brothers.

But Rose just stared down the road, not smiling. "Maybe they won't come back," she said. "My mother doesn't like me."

"Yes, she does."

"Not now I'm getting, you know. Older." Rose looked down at herself. Even at eleven she was starting to sprout a bust. "*Maman* doesn't like it. She feels old."

"Because you're going to grow up even prettier than her. I won't grow up pretty enough for mine." I sighed, but the gloom didn't last long. The day was too beautiful, and the smiling cook had just laid down a plate of piping-hot *madeleines*.

"Why is it always about being *pretty* with us?" Rose exclaimed, still glaring over the stunning view of vines and sky.

"Don't you like being pretty? I wish I were."

"Well, of course I like it. But when people meet our brothers, they don't just comment on their looks, they ask, 'How do you do in school?' or 'Do you play football?' No one ever does that with us."

"Girls don't play football."

"You know what I mean." Rose looked stormy. "Our parents would never have left the *boys* behind. Boys always come first."

"So?" That was just the way things were, not something to resent or even think about very much. My parents laughed indulgently whenever James pulled my hair, or dunked me in the stream until I was crying. Boys got to do whatever they wanted, and girls got to sit around looking pretty. I wasn't very pretty, but my parents still seemed to have lofty plans for me: white gloves, a proper school, and becoming a Lovely Bride someday. *Maman* had already told me that if I was lucky, I'd be engaged by the time I was twenty, just like her.

Rose sat twisting the end of her blond braid. "I don't want to *just* be pretty when I grow up. I want to do something different. Write a book. Swim the Channel. Go on safari and shoot a lion—"

"Or just stay here forever." The smells of wild lavender and rosemary on the summer breeze, the warmth of the sun overhead, the sound of happy French babble from other diners, the goat cheese and crusty bread delicious on my tongue—this little café seemed just like heaven as far as I was concerned.

"We're not staying here forever!" Rose looked worried again. "Don't say that."

"I was just joking. You don't really think they'd *leave* us here, do you?"

"No." I could see her trying to be rational, the big girl of eleven who knew so much more than me. But then she whispered, as if she couldn't help it, "What if they don't come back?"

I think I realized then why Rose was such a friend to me. She was two years older, she could have brushed me off as a little pest, yet she always welcomed my tagging along. Sitting in that heavenly café, I saw it: her brothers had their own games, her mother resented her just a little, her father was always working. Except for these

summers when I came to visit and became her loyal
shadow, she was lonely.

I was only nine. I couldn't put any of this into words,
or even understand it as well as I did later. But I had
some muddled idea, seeing her fight the fear that her
parents wouldn't bother coming back for her, and I
squeezed her hand. "Even if they don't come back, I'm
here," I'd said. "I won't leave you."

"Miss?"

I blinked, coming back from summer of '37 to
May of '47. Memory had dragged me down so strongly,
it was a shock to look over and see Finn's dark eyes and
tousled hair instead of eleven-year-old Rose's blond plait
and baby blues.

"We've arrived," he said. "This is the address you
gave me."

I shivered. The car had stopped. I looked out at the
gravel drive leading up to the rambling house where I'd
spent every summer of my life up until Germany invaded France: my aunt and uncle's house outside Rouen.
Yet somehow I was still seeing that café in Provence
where two little girls had spent nearly six hours before
their parents realized the mistake at the next stop three
hours down the road, turned around, and raced back.
Those six hours were magic: Rose and I stuffed with
goat cheese and *madeleines*, playing tag among the
grapevines, bundling into aprons to help the friendly
cook wash the mugs, feeling very grown-up when she
allowed us a small glass of watered-down *rosé* apiece.
Sleepily watching the sun come down over the vineyard,
heads on each other's shoulders. Feeling a little disappointed to leave, once our frantically worried parents
arrived with breathless hugs and apologies. The best

day Rose and I ever had. The best day of my life, really, because of the simplest equation in the world: Rose plus me equaled happiness.

I won't leave you, I'd promised. But I had, and now she was gone.

"You all right?" Finn asked. That dark gaze of his didn't miss much.

"Fine," I said, slipping out of the car. "Stay here with Eve." She was dozing in the backseat, the sound of snores rising against the summertime buzz of the cicadas. It had been a long afternoon's drive after a night in Le Havre at a cheap hotel. First a late start because of course Eve was hungover, and then the hours of jolting along rutted French roads, stopping every hour or so for me to get out and throw up. I made excuses about motion sickness, but really it was the Little Problem. Or maybe it was just the thought of what was coming that made me queasy. I looked at the house again, and the shuttered windows looked like dead eyes.

"Go on, then." Finn pulled a tattered issue of *The Autocar* from under his seat, leaning an elbow on the window to read. "When you get back, we'll head into Rouen and find a hotel."

"Thank you." I turned my back on the gleaming blue Lagonda and headed up the drive.

No one answered my knock. I knocked again. It took so long, I was ready to start peering in windows. But at last I heard shuffling footsteps inside, and the door creaked open.

"*Tante Jeanne,*" I began, before the sight of her froze me. My French aunt had always been slender, scented, blond like Rose. An invalid, but the Greta Garbo kind, all pretty lace bed jackets and a delicate cough. The woman before me was horribly thin, gray haired, dressed in a soiled sweater and a drab skirt. I could have passed her on the street and not recognized her—and from her blank look, she didn't know me either.

I swallowed. "*Tante,* it's Charlotte—your niece. I've come to ask you about Rose."

She didn't offer me tea or biscuits, just sank into an old divan and regarded me blankly. I perched on the edge of a frayed armchair opposite. *She lost everything,* I thought, looking at the prematurely aged face in front of me. *Widowed . . . two sons dead . . . Rose gone.* I didn't know how Tante Jeanne was even standing. I knew she'd loved my cousin, no matter what childish doubts Rose had carried.

"I'm so sorry, *Tante,*" I began. "For—for everything."

She trailed a fingertip over the coffee table, leaving a mark in the dust. Dust lay everywhere like a mantle in the darkened room. "War."

Such a small, hopeless syllable to cover so much loss. Tears pricked my eyes, and I laced my gloved fingers together. "*Tante,* there's nothing to be done about *oncle,* or Jules or Pierre . . . But there's Rose. I know it's a slim chance, but she might be—"

Alive. Eve had mocked me for hoping, but I had to hope. I might be a failure at a lot of things, but I was good at hope.

"What do you think I know? She was in Limoges when I last heard from her," my aunt stated as though that were the end of it. "She left off writing at least three years ago. Mid '44, I suppose."

"Why did she leave here?" I asked, trying to see a spark, a gleam—anything—in my aunt's eyes. "Why?"

My aunt's voice was low and bitter. "Because she was a little troublemaker with no morals. No morals at all."

The bottom fell out of my stomach. "W-what?"

Tante Jeanne shrugged.

"No." I shook my head. "No, you don't just *say* that and then shrug."

"That girl went wild. Nazis all over Paris, and she wouldn't keep her head down. First it was sneaking out to listen to God knows what kind of speeches, those clubs where fools talk violence, coming home at all hours of the night. The rows she used to have with her father—the Germans wanted lists of all the socialists and Jews working for his company; what was he supposed to do, refuse? The things Rose shouted at him . . ."

I stared at my aunt, blood thundering in my ears.

She continued in her flat voice. "First she was putting pamphlets on cars, then it was breaking windows. She'd probably have gone on to blowing things up and getting herself shot if it hadn't been for the boy."

I remembered Rose's last letter to me. She was giddy about a boy she was seeing on the sly . . . "What boy?"

"Étienne something. Just nineteen, a bookshop clerk. A nobody. She brought him to meet us once. They glowed when they looked at each other, you could tell they were—" A disapproving huff. "Well, *that* was another row."

I shook my head, numb to my fingertips. "Why didn't you tell us any of this? When my father was making inquiries?"

"I did tell him. I suppose he thought it wasn't suitable for your ears."

I swallowed. "What happened then?"

"Rose's boy got caught with the Resistance. They shipped him off, who knows where. Half of Paris was disappearing overnight. Rose probably would have too—she'd already nearly been arrested for kicking a Brownshirt on the Rue de Rivoli, so we brought her back here to Rouen. But . . ."

"What?" I nearly screamed. "*What?*"

"What do you think?" My aunt's lips pursed like she'd bitten a lemon. "Rose was pregnant."

don't remember how I got to the beech tree outside the house. I just found myself leaning up against the rough bark, breath coming in hitching gasps. I was terrified to look up at the tree branch above my head, fearing I'd imagine two little girls side by side. This had been our tree, our refuge from our bullying brothers back in the days before James grew older and kinder. Rose and me, sitting on that branch now over my head, feet swinging, like we'd sat in that Provençal café. Never alone, as long as we had each other.

Rose. Oh, Rose . . .

"I want to do something different." And she'd had it in her—of course she'd be striding through the Paris nights breaking windows and kicking Brownshirts. I should have known Rose would get involved with the Resistance. But she'd gotten caught in the oldest trap there is, just like me. Rose wasn't going to write a book or swim the Channel or do anything *different*—because once you're pregnant, you're finished.

I'd wanted to save my cousin, but no one could save her from this. I was stuck in the same trap. Helpless.

I let out a single harsh sob, so loud it startled me. Had she sat out here all alone on our tree branch the night she told her parents? After her mother advised her to take a hot bath and have a stiff gin and then see if she could *dance it loose*? After her father shouted and shouted, saying she'd brought shame on the family forever? Tante Jeanne had told me all of that as I sat staring.

My father didn't shout at me when I told him. My mother did all the shouting; he just sat there gazing at me. When I left the room he turned his head away and just said disbelievingly, "Whore."

I'd forgotten that.

I wondered if they'd called Rose a whore too.

I slammed my fists into the beech tree, wishing I could cry, wishing I could wrap myself in my old insulating numbness. But the tears were tied up tight inside me in a huge ugly knot, and stabs of fury and pain cut me too deep for numbness. So I just hit the tree until my knuckles were stinging through my gloves.

My eyes were hot and burning when I finally turned away. My aunt stood watching from the back door, frail and hunched. "Tell me the rest," I said, and she did, her voice flat. My uncle had sent Rose to a little town outside Limoges to give birth away from anyone she knew. She didn't write when the baby was born, told them nothing about it, and they didn't ask. Four months later, Rose sent a brief note saying she was going to work in Limoges, and would pay her parents back for every franc they'd spent on her confinement. Money had come, and two more sets of letters had been exchanged: announcement of first her father's death and then her brothers', and Rose's awkward tear-splotched condolences. No, Tante Jeanne couldn't remember Rose's address; she hadn't saved the letters or the envelopes—and after mid '44, no more had come. "I don't know if she's still in Limoges," my aunt said, and paused. "I asked her to come back, you know. Rose's father would never hear of it while he was alive, but after he . . . well, I asked. She never answered me."

I didn't ask if Rose's baby had been included in that offer of hospitality. I was trembling too hard.

"Are you staying the night?" Tante Jeanne sounded mournful. "It gets very lonely here."

Whose fault is that? I wanted to lash out. *You're the*

one who threw Rose away like trash. You should have left her in that café in Provence. The words burned at my lips, aching to come out, but I bit them down. My aunt was so thin a breeze could blow her away, finally looking like the invalid she'd always claimed she was. A husband and two sons dead. She'd lost so much.

Be kind.

I didn't want to be kind, but at least I managed not to say the things I was thinking. I just said stiffly, "No, *Tante,* I can't stay. I have to go to Roubaix."

Tante Jeanne sighed. "Well, then."

I couldn't make myself hug her. I couldn't bear it. I jerked out a stiff good-bye and moved unsteadily across the weedy lawn, back to the dark blue shape of the Lagonda.

Finn looked up from *The Autocar*'s tattered pages. I don't know what expression he saw on my face, but he sprang out of the car. "Miss?"

"Why'd you go to prison?" I heard myself ask.

"Stole a bearskin hat off a Buckingham Palace guard," he said with no expression. "Are you all right?"

"You're lying about the hat."

"Yes. Get in the car."

I moved toward the convertible, but tripped in the graveled path. Finn caught me around the waist before I could fall, lifted me up and helped me into the front seat.

Eve was awake, regarding me with those hooded eagle eyes of hers. "Well?"

I rubbed my hot cheek with a cold hand as Finn slid back behind the wheel. "I found out why Rose left. Because—because she was pregnant."

The silence was deafening.

"Well," Eve said at last, aiming a deliberate glance at my stomach. "Unless I miss my guess, so are you."

CHAPTER 8
EVE

June 1915

Eve was brought up short not by any of Lille's various horrors—and there were certainly horrors—but by a poster. It was tacked outside a church, flapping in the breeze, and it said in both French and German:

> ANY CIVILIAN, INCLUDING THE CIVILIAN STAFF OF
> THE FRENCH GOVERNMENT, WHO HELPS TROOPS
> WHO ARE ENEMIES OF GERMANY, OR WHO ACTS IN
> A WAY INJURIOUS TO GERMANY AND HER ALLIES,
> WILL BE PUNISHED BY DEATH.

"Oh, those." Lili sounded matter-of-fact. "They went up late last year. I don't think anyone really believed them at first. Then in January a woman was shot for harboring two French soldiers, and that drove the point home nicely."

Eve remembered the recruitment poster she'd lingered in front of in London, watched all the while by Captain Cameron. The stalwart Tommies, the blank space in the middle: *There is still a space in the line for YOU! WILL YOU FILL IT?*

Well, she'd filled it. And now she was standing in front of a poster that promised to kill her if she was caught, and it had all become very, very real. More real than Captain Cameron's promise on a windy Folkestone beach that the Boches did not shoot women.

Eve looked into Lili's sunken eyes in the mobile smiling face. "We're in the m-m-mouth of the beast now, aren't we?"

"Yes." Lili put her arm through Eve's, moving her away from the flapping poster. She looked very different here than she did in Le Havre: no outrageous hat or elaborate pompadour. She stood neat and subdued in a plain serge suit, her gloves mended and re-mended, a bag over her arm. Her papers, giving yet another false name, proclaimed her to be a seamstress, and her bag carried reels of thread and needles. It also carried a set of maps sewn into the lining—maps marked with target points. Thank goodness Eve didn't learn that until *after* they passed the checkpoints into Lille. She nearly fainted when Lili chuckled, "The Fritzes would have been pleased to find that lot! I've marked out all their new artillery positions for bombing."

"You were m-m-making jokes with the German sentries as they were g-going over your papers, and all the while you had *that* in your bag?"

"*Oui*," Lili said serenely, and Eve stared at her in a mix of admiration and horror. She knew right then that her boasting to Captain Cameron about how she would surpass his prize agent was destined to be unfulfilled, because nobody, ever, would beat Lili when it came to sheer nerve. Eve both wondered if her superior was a little mad, and admired her violently.

So, clearly, did Violette Lameron, who greeted them both in a dismal rented room somewhere off the Grand Place. Violette was sturdy and glowering, with neatly knotted hair and plain round spectacles; she hugged Lili with visible relief even while scolding her. "You should have let me fetch the new girl. You make too many crossings, you're going to get noticed!"

"*Tais-toi,* you worrier!" Lili switched into English, as she'd already told Eve they were to do when alone. Far better to spin a story about how they spoke English, if they were overheard, she explained, than to be understood discussing things like secret messages and British codes in French. Lili's English was flawless, but she salted it with casual French curses. "Now, we need to get Marguerite up to date before you and I head to the border to get the reports out." She smiled at Violette. "Our new friend is splendidly dumb faced and she's going to be brilliant, but she needs work."

In Folkestone Eve's training had been formalized: the instructors, the row of desks, the uniforms and flags. This training was quite different. It happened in a damp little room with a narrow bed and a single washstand and a crack running through the ceiling, where everything smelled musty from the unending needle-fine rain falling outside. A room chosen not for its comfort but its proof against eavesdropping, since on one side the building was insulated by the thick stone wall of a chapel, on the other side by a derelict and abandoned apartment building, and above them by an empty attic. A room where three women sat with mugs of an unappetizing drink made of walnut leaves boiled with licorice, because the Germans had confiscated all the coffee, talking matter-of-factly about unspeakable things.

"A German officer walks toward you on the street," Violette began after the door and window were checked and sealed. She looked grim compared to Lili's jauntiness; if her superior refused to be serious, she was clearly carrying the grimness for two. "What do you do?"

"Let him pass, don't look at him—"

"Wrong. Salute. If you don't, you risk a fine, and three days' arrest." Violette looked at Lili. "Do they teach them *anything* in Folkestone?"

Eve bristled. "They teach us plenty—"

"We'll get her ready," Lili reassured her lieutenant. "A German asks to see your papers, then starts to grope you. What do you do?"

"Nothing?" Eve guessed.

"No. Smile, because if you can't fake a smidge of willingness, you will likely get slapped and then possibly searched. A German asks why you have your hands in your pockets, what do you do?"

"T-take them out as quickly as—"

"No. You don't put your hands in your pockets ever, because the Huns will think you are reaching for a knife and they will bayonet you."

Eve smiled uneasily. "Surely not—"

Violette's hand cracked across her cheek, making a sound like a rifle shot. "You think we exaggerate? It happened to a boy of fourteen last week!"

Eve's hand flew to her stinging face. Her eyes turned to Lili, sitting with her little hands wrapped around her mug. "What?" Lili said. "You think we're here to be your friends? We're here to train you, little daisy."

Anger flared through Eve—more than anger, betrayal. Lili had been so warm and welcoming in Le Havre; now everything was wrong-footed. "I've already been trained."

Violette rolled her eyes. "I say send her back. This one is useless."

Eve opened her mouth to snap back, but Lili laid a finger over her lips. "Marguerite," she said, and her voice was matter-of-fact. "You don't have any idea what it is like here. Neither does Uncle Edward. He gave you the training that would *get* you here, but Violette and I have to give you the training that will make you *useful* here—and keep you alive. We have just a few days to do it. If you don't learn, you're nothing but a liability."

Her gaze was steady and unapologetic. She could have been a factory foreman delivering a brisk lecture to a new worker, and Eve's cheeks burned with embarrassment. She let out a slow breath, unclenched her jaw, and managed to nod. "Salute all German officers. Do not object to being groped. Keep my hands out of m-m-m—out of my pockets. What else?"

They drilled her, over and over. Encounter drills: *What do you do if—?* Quick-hide drills: *If they happen upon you before you've hidden a report, what do you do to distract and delay?* And they tutored her about the new rules of life in Lille.

"Trust nothing in the newspapers or bulletins. If it's in print, it's a lie," Lili decreed.

"Carry your identity cards at all times, but hide your pistol." Violette had a Luger of her own which she handled with casual authority. "Civilians aren't supposed to have weapons."

"Steer clear of the German officers. They think they can have any of the women they want, with or without their consent—"

"—and once that happens, a good many people in Lille will despise you for a collaborator and say you flopped on your back just to get favors."

"You'll live here, in this room. Before now we've used

it as a bolt-hole for quick overnights, but now you'll *live* here, so the door outside will need a posted notice with your name and your age in case a roll is called—"

"—no gatherings of more than ten people allowed—"

"How does anyone l-live like this?" Eve wondered on the second day, finally earning enough grudging approval to venture the occasional question.

"Life is shit here," Lili said. "It will likely go on being shit until we drive the Germans out."

"When will I report to you? If I l-l-learn anything."

"We come through regularly, Violette and I." Lili grinned at her lieutenant. "We'll continue to bunk here with you when we need to stay the night in town. But we're on the move so much between all my drops, you'll be alone more often than not."

Violette looked at Eve with an utter lack of enthusiasm. "I hope you're up to it."

"*Salope!*" Lili tugged Violette's taut bun. "Don't be such a bitch!"

German-run Lille was a horrible place, Eve soon saw. Before the war it must have been a fine, bright, bustling city—church spires piercing the sky, pigeons fluttering about the Grand Place, streetlamps casting circles of warm yellow light in the dusk. Now the city was dulled and wretched, every face downcast and pinched with hunger. They weren't far from the trenches and soldiers and the real action of war—the boom of guns in the distance rolled like low thunder, and occasionally a biplane droned overhead like a poisonous wasp. The Huns had held Lille since last fall, thoroughly entrenched: the boulevards sported new street signs with German names, German boots rang confidently on the cobbles, and German chatter resounded loudly in every public place. The only pink well-fed faces were German, and that alone was enough to push Eve very quickly from a rather impersonal dislike of The Enemy to utter, burning hatred.

"Don't get too much fire in your eye," Lili advised, helping Eve dress for her interview. A neat, drab skirt and shirtwaist, but it was more than just the clothes. Lili was dulling Eve's skin with a few strategic dabs of chalk and soot, downplaying the healthy color in her cheeks. "You need to look downcast and beaten, little daisy. That's what the Germans want to see. Fire in the eye will get you looked at."

"D-downcast," Eve repeated grimly. "*Oui.*"

Violette looked her over, round glasses flashing. "Her hair gleams."

They dulled it with a little dirt. Eve rose, putting on her darned gloves. "I am a country g-girl newly come from Roubaix," she recited. "Desperate for work, badly educated. Neat, deft, a little s-s-stupid."

"You look stupid," Violette said matter-of-factly, and Eve glared. She didn't much like Violette, but there was no doubt she excelled at her job. Evelyn Gardiner was gone; the room's single badly polished mirror reflected dull-skinned, hungry-looking Marguerite Le François.

Eve looked at Marguerite, and performer's anxiety stabbed her like any actress preparing to step onstage. "What if I f-f—what if I fail? What if Le Lethe's owner doesn't hire me?"

"Then we send you home." Lili wasn't unkind, merely blunt. "Because we can't use you anywhere else, little daisy. So go lie your head off, try to get hired, and try *not* to get shot."

f René Bordelon was a beast, he had a very elegant den. That was Eve's first thought as she waited in Le Lethe.

Six girls, Eve included, had assembled among the

linen-draped tables and dark paneling, waiting to be interviewed. There had been two more, but they admitted when asked by the *maître d'* that they spoke German, and were dismissed at once. "No one working here is to have any fluency in the language of our patrons, who require the utmost privacy in the places where they converse freely." Eve wondered how the people of Lille could avoid learning German if enemy occupation continued for long, but did not advance the question, merely stating her own firm lie that no, she did not understand a word of German beyond *nein* or *ja,* and was waved to a seat to wait.

Le Lethe was an oasis of elegance in drab, downtrodden Lille: the crystal chandeliers gave off a muted glitter, the deep wine red carpet swallowed all footfalls, and the cloths on the tables—spaced perfectly for privacy—were spotless as snow. The front window was distinctively bow shaped and gold scrolled, and overlooked the river Deûle. Eve could see why the Germans came to dine here. It was a civilized place to relax after a long day of stamping on your conquered populace.

The air wasn't civilized at the moment, however. It was tense and savage as the six girls eyed one another, wondering which two would be chosen and which four would go home. Working here meant the difference between eating and not eating—Eve had been in Lille for only a few days, but she already knew what a razor's edge that was to live on. A month here, and she would be ashy skinned like Violette. Two months here, and her cheekbones would jut out like Lili's.

Good, she thought. *Hunger will keep you sharp.*

One by one, the girls were led upstairs. Eve waited, clutching her pocketbook, allowing herself to look nervous, not allowing herself to worry about being hired. She *would* be hired, and that was all there was to it. She was not going to be sent home a failure before even getting a chance to prove herself a success.

"Mademoiselle Le François, Monsieur Bordelon will see you."

She was led up quiet carpeted stairs to a door of sturdy polished oak. Apparently, René Bordelon lived in a spacious apartment above his restaurant. The door opened to reveal a private study, and it was obscene.

That was the word Eve found as she took it in. Obscene but also beautiful, with a gilt clock upon an ebony mantelpiece, an Aubusson rug, and armchairs of deep mahogany leather. Satinwood bookcases were filled with leather-bound volumes, decorative Tiffany glass, and a small marble bust of a man's bowed head. The room with its walls hung in jade green silk whispered of money and taste, luxury and self-indulgence. And with the terrible conquered world that was Lille visible through the spotless muslin drapes, such opulence was obscene.

Eve despised that study and its owner before a word was spoken.

"Mademoiselle Le François," René Bordelon said. "Please sit."

He indicated the second of the deep armchairs. He reclined in his own with boneless elegance, trousers creased to a razor's edge, snowy shirt and immaculate waistcoat fitted with Parisian precision. He was perhaps forty, lean limbed and tall, hair graying at the temples and swept back from a thin inscrutable face. If Captain Cameron reminded Eve of the consummate Englishman, then René Bordelon was surely the consummate Frenchman.

And yet downstairs every night, he apparently played gracious host to the Germans.

"You seem very young." M. Bordelon surveyed her

as she settled on the edge of her chair. "You are from Roubaix?"

"Yes, *monsieur*." Violette, who grew up in that tiny town, had armed Eve with pertinent details if necessary.

"Why did you not stay there? Lille is a large place for an orphan of"—glancing at her papers—"seventeen."

"There is no work. I thought I might find a job in L-L-Lille." Eve drew her knees close together, gripping her pocketbook, letting herself look swamped and lost in all this luxury. Marguerite Le François would never have seen a gilt clock or a ten-book leather-bound set of Rousseau and Diderot, so she gaped, wide-eyed.

"You may think that to work in a restaurant is simple. The laying of silver, the removal of plates. It is not." His voice did not flex up and down like normal voices. It was a voice made of metal, slightly chilling. "I require perfection, *mademoiselle*. In the food that comes from my kitchens, in the servers who convey it to table, in the atmosphere in which it is eaten. I create civilization here—peace in a time of war. A place to forget, for a while, that there *is* war. Hence the name Le Lethe."

Eve opened her eyes to their widest and most doelike. "*Monsieur,* I don't know what that m-m-means."

She expected a smile, a patronizing glance, even irritation, but he just studied her.

"I have w-worked in a café before, *monsieur*." Eve rushed on as if nervous. "I am d-deft and q-q-quick. I l-learn fast. I work hard. I only want t-t-t-t-t-t—"

She hung up badly on the word. For the past few weeks she hadn't noticed her own stammer much—perhaps because she did most of her talking with Captain Cameron and Lili, who had the gift of not noticing it either—but now a random syllable stuck behind her teeth and wouldn't come out, and René Bordelon sat and watched her struggle. Like Captain Cameron, he didn't rush to finish her sentence for her. Unlike Captain Cameron, Eve didn't think that was out of courtesy.

Eve Gardiner would have balled her fist and pounded her own thigh in sheer, stubborn fury until the word came loose. Marguerite Le François just stuttered into red-faced silence, looking so mortified she could sink through the sumptuously carpeted floor.

"You stammer," M. Bordelon said. "But I doubt you are stupid, *mademoiselle*. A halting tongue does not necessarily mean a halting brain."

Eve's life would be considerably easier if all people thought this way, but not *now,* for the love of God. *It would be far better if he assumed I was an idiot*, she thought, and for the first time her nerves prickled. He *should* think her stupid. It wasn't just the stammer—she'd been layering Marguerite for him in precise strokes ever since she walked through the door. If he wasn't buying the easy camouflage her stutter gave her, she was going to need a different shield. She veiled her eyes with her lashes, pulling confusion around her like a blanket. *"Monsieur?"*

"Look at me."

She swallowed, looking up to meet his gaze. He had eyes of no particular color, and he seemed to have no need to blink.

"Do you think me a collaborator? A profiteer?"

Yes. "It's war, *monsieur*," Eve replied. "We all do what we must."

"Yes, we do. Will you do what you must, and serve the Germans? Our invaders? Our conquerors?"

He was baiting her, and Eve froze. She had no doubt at all that if he saw fire in her eye—as Lili put it—then her chance was gone. He wouldn't hire a girl he thought might spit in the Germans' *boeuf bourguignon*. But what was the right answer?

"Do not lie to me," he said. "I am very good at scenting lies, *mademoiselle*. Will you find it hard to serve my German patrons, and serve them with a smile?"

No was a lie too absurd to even attempt. *Yes* was an honesty she couldn't afford.

"I find it h-h-hard not to eat," she said at last, playing up the stammer just a little. "I don't have t-t-time for other hardships, *monsieur*. Just that one. Because if you do not hire me, I will not find w-work elsewhere. No one will hire a girl with a s-s-s-stammer." This *was* the truth. Eve thought back to her days in London and how hard it was to find that silly filing room job, because jobs that didn't require easy speech were rare. She remembered the frustration of that job search, and let M. Bordelon see her bitterness. "I cannot answer a telephone or give directions in a shop, not w-w-with a stumbling tongue. But I can move plates and lay silver in s-s-silence, *monsieur*, and I can do it to *perfection*."

She gave him the doe eyes again, all desperate, hungry, humiliated youth. He steepled his fingertips—extraordinarily long fingers, no wedding ring—and looked at her. "How remiss I've been," he said at last. "If you're hungry, I shall feed you."

He spoke as carelessly as if speaking of putting milk down for a stray cat. Surely he hadn't offered refreshment to all the girls? *It is not good if he singles me out,* Eve thought, but he'd already rung the bell and was now speaking with a waiter who came from the restaurant below. A few murmured words; the waiter departed and then returned with a plate. Piping-hot toast; and Eve could see that it was good white bread of the kind almost impossible to locate in Lille now, with butter—real butter—spread thick and profligate. Eve wasn't so hungry yet that she could be transfixed by the sight of toast, but Marguerite was, and Eve let her hand tremble as she lifted a triangle of bread to her lips. He sat waiting to see if she'd wolf it down, and she bit off a ladylike corner. Marguerite couldn't be such a country stick as Eve had planned; René Bordelon clearly wanted something more polished in his waitresses. Eve chewed her toast, swallowed, took another bite. Strawberry jam clearly made with real sugar, and she thought of the boiled beetroot Lili used as a sweetener.

"There are advantages to working for me," M. Bordelon said at last. "Scraps from the kitchen are divided nightly among the staff. Exemptions from the curfew are issued to all my workers. I have never had a woman serving in my establishment, but as it is inevitable, I assure you that you will not be expected to . . . *entertain* the clientele. That kind of thing lowers the tone of a restaurant." The distaste in his voice was clear. "I am a civilized man, Mademoiselle Le François, and the officers who eat under my roof are expected to behave like civilized men."

"Yes," Eve murmured.

"However," he added disinterestedly, "if you steal from me—food supplies, silver, or so much as a swallow of wine—then I will hand you over to the Germans. And you will see that they are not always civilized."

"I understand, *monsieur.*"

"Good. You start tomorrow. You will be trained by my second, beginning at eight in the morning."

He did not raise the matter of pay. He knew she would take whatever wage he offered; all of them would. Eve swallowed the last bite of toast, ladylike but hurrying because no one in this city would leave buttered toast unfinished on the plate, and bobbed a curtsy before scurrying out of the study.

"Well?" Violette looked up from the tiny rice-paper message she sat inscribing as Eve tumbled back into the musty room.

Eve nearly whooped in triumph, but she didn't want to look like a giddy little girl, so she nodded matter-of-factly. "I was hired. Where's Lili?"

"Off to get a report from one of her railway contacts. Then she'll head to the border." Violette shook her head. "How she manages not to get shot, I don't know. Those border searchlights would show a flea cowering on the floor of hell, but she always slips through."

Until the day she doesn't, Eve couldn't help but think as she unhooked her boots. But it wasn't profitable to dwell on the ways they could all be caught. *Do as Lili said: be afraid, but only afterward. Before that, it's an indulgence.*

And now that she was out of sight from René Bordelon and his elegantly manicured hands and his eyes that didn't blink, Eve *did* feel fear, humming along her skin like a poisoned breeze. She let out a long breath.

"Getting the shakes already?" Violette raised her eyebrows, light reflecting off her round glasses. Glasses like that must be useful, Eve thought—all she had to do was tilt her head against the light, and her eyes were cloaked. "Wait till you pass a bad checkpoint or have to talk your way past a sentry."

"René Bordelon." Eve lay back on the hard pallet, folding her arms under her head. "What do you know about him?"

"He's a filthy collaborator." Violette bent back over her work. "What else is there to know?"

Do not lie to me, his metallic voice whispered. *I am very good at scenting lies,* mademoiselle.

"I think," Eve said slowly, and the thrum of fear increased just a tick, "that it will be very difficult to spy under his nose."

CHAPTER 9
CHARLIE

May 1947

"No," Eve said. "I hate Lille and we are not staying one bloody night inside those walls."

"Not much choice," Finn said mildly, straightening from the Lagonda's innards. "By the time I get her purring again, it'll be time to stop."

"Not in fucking Lille. We can push on through to Roubaix in the dark."

I'd had just about enough of Eve in the last twenty-four hours. "We stop in Lille."

She glared. "What, because the bun in your oven is acting up again?"

I glared right back. "No, because I'm the one paying for the hotel."

Eve called me something even more unprintable than her usual obscenities, and began stalking up and down the side of the road. *What a day*, I thought as Finn went on fiddling patiently inside the Lagonda. A wretched near-sleepless night in a cheap hotel in Rouen, filled with vague unhappy dreams of Rose disappearing down endless corridors to the accompaniment of her mother's hissed "Whore . . ." A long awkward drive this morning, Eve commenting caustically every time I had to throw up, and Finn not commenting at all, which was somehow worse.

Whore, my aunt whispered from my nightmares, and I couldn't stop from flinching. I had so enjoyed the fresh start I'd made on this journey, savoring the fact that no one in this car knew what I was or what kind of cloud I traveled under. Well, that clean slate was an illusion; Charlie St. Clair *was* a whore, and now everyone here knew it, thanks to that tactless old bat Eve and her flapping mouth.

On the outskirts of Lille, the Lagonda started issuing steam from under its gleaming hood and Finn pulled over and fetched a tool kit from the rear. "Can you get her limping again?" I asked after he announced we had grease on the valves or water in the engine or baby giraffes in the gearshift for all I knew. "At least enough to get us into Lille?"

He was wiping his hands off on a blackened rag as Eve kept stalking about cursing. "If we go slow."

I nodded without meeting his gaze. I'd barely been able to look him in the eye since my Little Problem had been unveiled. I could brazen things out more with Eve—if she was rude, I could pull my cynical shell back around myself and just be ruder. But Finn didn't say a word, and I couldn't out-silent him at the game of let's see who says less. All I could do was pretend not to care.

We piled back into the Lagonda and headed out at a snail's pace. Lille seemed like a pretty enough city with its row houses, the touches of Flemish brick on French stone whispering of the city's closeness to Belgium, and the gracious expanse of the Grand Place. It had been sieged in the war, but clearly not bombed into rubble. There was more cheer here than I'd seen in Le Havre, more spring in the step of the people I saw bustling past with their shopping or their little terriers. Yet Eve grew more and more gray faced the deeper we got into the city.

"'*Any civilian*,'" she said, clearly quoting something, "'*including the civilian staff of the French government, who helps troops who are enemies of Germany, or who acts in a way injurious to Germany and her allies, will be punished by death.*'"

I shook my head. "Nazis . . ."

"That wasn't the Nazis." Eve looked out the window again, face a stony mask. The Lagonda passed a café with a striped awning and street-side tables set out to overlook the Deûle, and I looked at it wistfully, remembering the Provençal café where Rose and I had spent our enchanted afternoon. I wondered if any place on earth had ever made me happier. There was a waitress about my age working in this café, carrying baguettes and a carafe of wine, and I envied her. No Little Problem for her, just freckles on her nose and a red-checked apron and the smell of good baked bread.

Eve's voice, fierce and cold, broke my thoughts. "They should have burned the entire building to the ground after he was gone, and sowed the earth with salt. They should have run the waters of the real Lethe through it and made everyone forget." She was staring at the same pretty little café, with its distinctive bowfront window scrolled in gold.

"Gardiner?" Finn looked over his shoulder. Eve's voice might be fierce but she looked shrunken and frail, her warped fingers twined through each other as if to keep them from shaking. I exchanged puzzled glances with Finn, too baffled to remember I was avoiding his eyes.

"We need to get to a hotel," he said quietly. "Now."

He pulled up at the first *auberge* we found, and rented three rooms. The clerk totaled our room rates wrong and then when I pointed out his error, suddenly couldn't understand my Americanized French. Finally Eve leaned over the counter and fired off a fluent northern-accented burst that surprised me and had the clerk adjusting his rates in a hurry. "I didn't know you spoke French so well," I said, and she just shrugged and slapped a room key into each of our hands.

"Better than you, Yank. Good night."

I glanced at the sky outside. Just twilight, and none of us had eaten. "Don't you want supper?"

"I'm taking a liquid supper." Eve gave a pat to her satchel. I heard the clink of her flask inside. "I'm going to get sloshed to the gills, but if you wait for me to sleep it off tomorrow morning I will bloody well *end* you. We'd better be up and into that car by dawn, because I want out of this evil pit of a city and I will walk if I have to."

She disappeared into her rented room, and I was just as quick to vanish into mine. I had no desire to be left alone in the hallway with Finn.

Supper was a cheap packet of sandwiches eaten on my narrow bed. I washed out my underclothes and blouse in the small sink, thinking that I'd need more clothes soon, and finally steeled myself to head downstairs to use the hotel's telephone. I had no intention of telling my mother where I was going, in case she turned up with the police in tow—I *was* still underage—but I didn't want her worrying that I wasn't safe. Yet the clerk at the Dolphin told me she'd checked out. I left a message anyway, hung up uneasily, and went back upstairs, fighting sudden exhaustion. All I'd done was sit in a car all day, but I was more tired than I'd ever been in my life. These strange waves of tiredness had been hitting me for weeks now, surely another sign of the Little Problem.

I shoved away any thought of the L.P. as I came back to my room. Roubaix tomorrow. Part of me didn't even want to go—Eve still insisted there was someone she had to talk to, a woman who might know something, but thanks to my aunt I already knew something. I knew Rose had been sent to a little town farther south to have her baby, and I knew she'd left afterward to find work in nearby Limoges. Limoges was where I wanted to go, not Roubaix and whatever dubious contact Eve thought she had.

I sat down on the edge of the bed, and let it rise in my chest: hope. As horrible as that hour with Tante Jeanne had been, she'd given me that hope. Because as much as I struggled to convince myself there was a chance Rose could be alive, part of me had gone on thinking my parents were right, that she must be dead. Because the girl I loved like a sister—the girl who feared loneliness— would have found her way back to us by now.

But if her entire family had rejected her, shipped her off to have her bastard, and then wiped their hands clean . . . Well, I knew Rose. She was proud and full of fire. She wouldn't *ever* walk back into the house in Rouen after the way her parents had thrown her out of it.

I could even understand her not writing *me* about her dilemma. Why should she? I'd just been a little girl when we last met, someone to protect, not confide ugly things to. And shame could get to be a habit. I wasn't sure I could have borne to write her about my Little Problem, even if I'd had an address. Face-to-face I could have cried it into her shoulder, but putting these things on paper meant you had to unpack your own disgrace in ugly black and white.

If she was alive, she might be living in Limoges now. Perhaps she had her child with her. *A boy or a girl*? I thought, and heard myself laugh tremulously. Rose with a baby. I looked down at my own stomach, flat and innocuous, alternately making me tired or nauseated, and my eyes blurred. "Oh, Rosie," I whispered. "How did we mess up this badly?"

Well, *I* had messed up. Rose had found love, in the shape of a French bookshop clerk who had joined the Resistance. That sounded like the kind of boy Rose would like. I wondered if her Étienne had been dark or fair, if he'd given his coloring to the baby. I wondered where he'd been taken after his arrest, if he was alive at all. Probably not. So many people disappeared and died, we were only starting to understand the horrifying scope of the losses. Rose's boy was probably gone; if she was alive then she was alone. Left behind, as she'd been at the Provençal café.

Not for long, Rose. I'm coming for you, I swear. I hadn't been able to save my brother, but I could still save her.

"And then maybe I'll know what to do about you," I told my stomach. I didn't want it, had no clue what to do about it. But the sickness of the last few days had brought home with painful clarity that just plain *ignoring* it was no longer an option.

The French night lay full and soft and warm outside my window. I crawled into bed, lids dropping. I wasn't even aware I'd dropped off to sleep until a scream split the night.

That scream clawed me upright and out of bed. I was

on my feet, heart galloping and mouth dry, and the terrible howl just went on and on. A woman's scream, full of terror and agony, and I bolted out of my room.

Finn erupted into the hallway at the same moment, barefoot and bare armed. "What *is* that?" I gasped as other doors farther down the hall started to creak open. Finn didn't answer, just went straight to the door between ours, the one showing a line of yellow light underneath. The scream came from inside. "Gardiner!" He rattled the handle. The scream cut off as though a knife had sliced through a taut throat. I heard the unmistakable click of the Luger being cocked.

"Gardiner, I'm coming in." Finn jammed his shoulder against the door and shoved hard. The cheap bolt tore away from the wall with a sound of screeching nails, and light poured into the hall. Eve towered tall, gray-streaked hair streaming loose, her eyes two haunted sightless pits—and as she saw Finn in the doorway with me behind him, she raised the Luger and fired.

I screamed, dropping to the floor in a ball—but the hammer clicked on an empty chamber. Finn tore the Luger out of Eve's hand, and she spat an obscenity and went for his eyes. He tossed the pistol on the bed, catching her gaunt wrists in both hands. As his eyes found mine, I saw in astonishment that he was quite calm.

"Find the night clerk and tell him everything is fine before someone summons the police," he said, holding Eve hard. She was spitting curses in both French and German. "We don't want to find a new hotel in the middle of the night."

"But—" I couldn't look away from the pistol on the bed. *She fired on us.* My arms, I realized, were wrapped tight around the Little Problem.

"Tell him she had a nightmare." Finn looked down

at Eve. She had stopped cursing, her breath coming in harsh, shallow bursts. Her eyes gazed blindly at the wall. Wherever she was, it wasn't here.

I heard a peevish burst of French behind me, and looked around to see the *auberge's* owner, shrill and sleepy. "*Pardonnez-moi,*" I said, quickly closing the door between her and the strange tableau. "*Ma grand-mère, elle a des cauchemars . . .*"

I poured honey in my slangy American French until all indignation subsided, helped along by a handful of francs. At last the owner trailed off back to his own room, and I dared poke my head around the door again.

Finn had settled Eve, not in her bed but in the farthest corner—the one with the clearest view of the door and window. He'd dragged a chair aside so she could huddle against the wall, and dropped a blanket over her shoulders. He was hunkered down on his heels beside her, talking softly, moving slowly as he laid the whiskey flask in her lap.

She muttered something, a name. It sounded like *René,* and my skin prickled.

"René isna here," Finn soothed.

"The beast is me," she whispered.

"I know." Finn offered her the Luger butt first.

"Are you crazy?" I whispered, but he made a demurring gesture at me behind his back. Eve never looked up. She was quiet now, but she still stared into nothing, her eyes jerking back and forth from the window to the doorway. Her warped fingers wrapped again around the pistol, and Finn released it.

He rose and padded barefoot toward me. I backed into the hall and he followed, gently tugging the door closed and letting out a long breath.

"Why did you give her that gun back?" I whispered. "If it had been loaded, one of us might be dead!"

"Who do you think took the bullets out in the first place?" He looked down at me. "I do it every night. She curses me a fair amount, but considering she nearly shot my ear off the first evening I came to work for her, she doesn't have much of an argument."

"Nearly shot your *ear* off?"

Finn looked at the door. "She'll be all right now till morning."

"How often does she do this?"

"Now and then. Something sets her off—she gets caught in a big crowd and panics, or hears some scaffolding collapse and thinks it's an explosion. You can't predict it."

I realized my arms were still wrapped around my midsection. I could hardly think of the Little Problem as anything but, well, a problem—but my arms had flown to shield it as soon as I saw Eve's gun. I dropped my hands, vibrating all over. I hadn't felt so alive—alive over every shaky muscle, every prickling inch of skin, every hair standing on end—in a very long time. "I need a drink."

"Me too."

I followed Finn back to his room, which was not at all proper since I was halfway to naked in the nylon slip I'd been using for a nightgown. But I shut out the nasty, knowing voice in my head and closed the door as Finn switched on a lamp and fished inside his satchel. He offered me a flask, much smaller than Eve's. "No glasses, sorry."

No more *miss* now, of course. I shrugged, not expecting any different. I knew perfectly well what kind of equation was writing itself here. "Who needs a glass?" I bolted down a swallow of whiskey, relishing the fire. "All right, let's hear it. *René.* Eve does know that name. If it's the same one from the report, who Rose worked for—"

"I wouldn't know. Only that she says that name a lot in these moods."

"Why didn't you *tell* me that?"

"Because I work for her." He took a swallow from the flask. "Not you."

"You two are quite a pair," I snorted. "Both barbed-wire knots made out of secrets."

"And for good reasons."

I thought back to Eve's haunted whisper when she'd quoted that bit about how death awaited the enemies of Germany. Something about her said 'combatant' to me. I'd seen my brother come back from war, marking the changes in him with worried, loving eyes, and James wasn't the only ex-soldier I'd observed. I'd danced with them at mixers, talked to them at parties, made a habit of observing them because I'd hoped I could see something that would help me help James. I'd failed in that; nothing I'd ever done had helped James, and even now I hated myself for it—but still, I knew what a combatant looked like, and Eve showed all the signs. "Will she be all right tomorrow?" James wouldn't even leave his room the morning after episodes like this.

"Probably." Finn leaned on the sill of the open window and looked down at the row of streetlights, taking another thoughtful swallow of whiskey. "She usually goes on the next day like nothing happened."

I wanted to keep probing, but the whole thorny matter of Eve and her secrets made my head ache. I let it go for now, wandering over to join Finn at the windowsill. It was what came next in the equation, after all: girl plus boy, multiply by whiskey. Now add proximity. "So we'll be in Roubaix tomorrow, if the car doesn't break down again." My shoulder brushed his.

He passed me the flask. "I can keep her ticking."

"You're pretty handy with that toolbox. Where'd you learn?" *Prison?* Curiosity was consuming me.

"I've been in and out of garages since I was a wee one. Playing with wrenches in the cradle."

I took another swig. "Could I take a turn driving the Lagonda tomorrow, or is she a one-man car?"

"You drive?" He glanced at me with the same surprise he'd shown when I said I'd had a job. "I figured your family kept a chauffeur."

"We aren't Vanderbilts, Finn. Of course I can drive. My brother taught me." A sweet, painful memory: James had escaped a big family barbecue by dragging me off in his Packard and giving me a driving lesson. "I think he really did it because he wanted to get away from our noisy relatives. But he was a good teacher." He'd ruffled my hair, saying, *You drive home, you're the expert now*—and after I pulled up in a proud swish of tires, we lingered awhile before rejoining the family hubbub. I'd asked James if he would be my date to the next formal dance. *I won't get a real date, James, and we can sit on the sidelines making fun of all the sorority girls.* He smiled sideways and said, *I'd like that, sis.* I'd gone in thinking that for once I'd helped him when he was in one of his moods.

Not three weeks later he shot himself.

I blinked that away, painfully.

"Maybe I'll let you get behind the wheel someday." Finn looked down his lean shoulder at me, light gleaming off his dark hair. "You'll have to be patient with her. She's a persnickety sort of lady, after all. A bit cranky, needs special handling. But she'll always come through."

"Don't go all Scottish and metaphorical." I took another swig from the flask and gave it back, my fingers brushing his. "It's past two in the morning."

He smiled, looking back over the nighttime lights. I waited for him to move closer. But he just drained his whiskey, and moved to sit on the wall bench.

My sharp inner voice was still saying nasty things. Before it got any louder, I went to finish the equation: boy plus girl, multiplied by whiskey and proximity, equaled . . . Taking the flask out of Finn's hand, I climbed into his lap and kissed him. I tasted whiskey on his soft mouth, felt the roughness of his unshaven jaw. Then he broke away. "What are you doing?"

"What do you think I'm doing?" I wound my arms around his neck. "I'm offering to sleep with you."

His dark eyes went over me deliberately. I tilted a shoulder, nonchalant, and let the strap of my slip slide down my arm. His hands skimmed my bare knees on either side of him, then slid over the nylon hem rather than under it, up to my waist and holding me firm as I tried to lean forward for another kiss.

"Well," he said. "It's turning out to be quite the night for surprises."

"Is it?" I felt his hands through the thin silky nylon, big and very warm on either side of my waist. "I've been thinking about this all day." Ever since I'd seen him strip down to his shirtsleeves to work on the Lagonda. He had much better arms than most college boys, who usually ran lanky or doughy.

Finn's voice sounded a little hoarse, but very level. "What's a nice girl like you doing jumping into bed with an ex-convict?"

"You know I'm not a nice girl. Eve cleared that up. Besides, it's not like you're taking me to cotillion," I added bluntly. "You're not meeting my parents. It's just a screw."

His eyebrows went up.

"Though I do wonder what you did," I added in all

honesty, trailing one finger around the back of his neck. "To get yourself tossed in prison."

"I stole a swan from Kew Gardens." He still had a firm grip around my waist, holding me away from him.

"Liar."

"I nicked a diamond tiara from the crown jewels in the Tower of London."

"Still a liar."

His eyes looked black and bottomless in the dim light. "Why ask me, then?"

"I like hearing you lie." I wound my arms around his neck again, sliding my fingers into his soft hair. "Why are we still talking?" Most boys were all hands the minute the lights went out; why wasn't Finn? As soon as Eve made it clear what kind of girl I really was, I'd assumed he would leave off the respectful air and try to get me in the sack. That was what I was used to. I could either shove him off or go along, and I'd already decided to go along. But I wasn't used to making the advances. I might not be pretty, but I was available—that was usually enough to get a man's hands reaching for my clothes without any help from me.

But Finn didn't move, just kept looking at me. His eyes went to my waistline and he said, "Haven't you got a lad? A fiancé?"

"Do you see a ring?"

"Who was it, then?"

"Harry S. Truman," I said.

"Now who's the liar."

The air was thick and warm. I moved my hips, and I could sense him responding. I knew what he wanted. Why wasn't he taking it? "Why do you care who knocked me up?" I whispered, moving some more. "*You* can't knock me up now, and that's what counts. I'm a safe lay."

"That's ugly," he said quietly.

"But it's true."

He pulled me closer then, his face very near mine, and my skin thrummed. "Why exactly are you climbing all over me?"

Whore. The word echoed in my head, in my mother's voice or maybe my aunt's. I flinched, turned it into a shrug. "I'm a tramp," I said, flippant. "Everyone knows tramps sleep around. And you're kind of a dish. So why not?"

He smiled, a real smile instead of the little corner flick of his mouth that I was used to seeing. "Charlie lass," he said, and I had time to think how much I liked my name in his soft Scottish burr, "you need a better reason than that."

He lifted me off his lap like a doll, setting me back on my feet. He rose and went to the door, opening it wide, and I felt a slow crimson flush sweep down my neck. "Good night, miss. Sleep well."

CHAPTER 10
EVE

June 1915

E ve made her debut two nights later as both a spy and as an employee of Le Lethe. Of the two, the second was more exhausting: René Bordelon required nothing short of perfection, and two days' training wasn't much time to achieve perfection. Eve achieved it. Failure, after all, was not an option. She took her new employer's rules into her bones as he repeated them in his metallic voice just before his two newly hired waitresses began their first shift.

A dark dress, neat hair. "You are not to be noticed; you are a shadow." Light feet, small steps. "I expect you to glide in all your movements. My guests are not to have their conversation disturbed." Silence at all times; no whispering or speaking to the patrons. "You are not required to memorize wine lists or take orders. You bring plates to tables and clear them away." Pour wine with the arm in a graceful curve. "Everything in Le Lethe is graceful, even that which passes unnoticed."

And the last rule, the most important one: "Violate the rules, and you will be dismissed. There are many hungry girls in Lille eager to take your place."

Le Lethe came to life in the evening, an unnatural patch of light and warmth and music in a city that went dark at sundown. Eve, standing in her dark dress in her appointed corner, was reminded of the legend of vampires. In Lille, the French went to bed at sundown because even if there were no curfew, there was little paraffin or coal to keep a room lit. Only the Germans came out at night, like the undead, to celebrate their undisputed rule. They came to Le Lethe, uniforms gleaming, medals polished, voices loud, and René Bordelon greeted them in an exquisitely tailored dinner jacket, his smile unforced. Like Renfield, Eve thought, from Bram Stoker's tale: a human turned base and craven in the service of the nightwalkers.

You are being fanciful, she told herself. *Turn your ears on and your mind off.*

She moved through the supper hours like a graceful automaton, soundlessly clearing plates, brushing off crumbs, refilling empty glasses. One would never know there is a war at all: there were endless candles, every table had white rolls and real butter, every glass brimmed. Half the black-market food in Lille must flow through here, because the Germans clearly liked to eat well. "The food," whispered the other waitress, a broad-hipped young widow with two babies at home. "It's torture just looking at it!" Her throat moved as she carried a plate back to the kitchens—there was *leftover food* on it, in a city where the French scraped their plates of every crumb. A puddle of *béchamel* sauce, a dozen bites of veal . . . Eve's stomach growled too, but she shot the other girl a warning look.

"Not so much as a nibble." Glancing behind them at M. Bordelon, circling the room like a well-tailored shark. "Not a bite until end of shift, you know th-th-that." At the end of the night, all leftovers from the kitchens were pooled and divided among the staff. Anyone here would be happy to tattle if a fellow employee sneaked food before the equitable division was made, because everyone was hungry. Eve cynically admired such a system: M. Bordelon successfully invented a reward that both kept his employees honest and encouraged them to spy on one another.

But if the staff were all tense and unfriendly, the patrons were worse. How easy it was to hate the Germans when you saw up close how much they wasted. Kommandant Hoffman and General von Heinrich came to dine three times during Eve's first week, calling for champagne and roast quail to celebrate the latest German victories, roaring with laughter amid a cluster of aides. M. Bordelon was always invited to join them for after-supper brandy, sitting with indolently crossed legs, passing cigars out of a monogrammed silver case. Eve strained to listen, but couldn't linger too obviously as she refilled the water tumblers, and anyway they weren't talking of battle plans or gun emplacements, but of the girls they'd taken as mistresses, comparing their finer physical points and arguing over whether the general's girl was a natural blonde or not.

Then on the fourth evening, Kommandant Hoffman ordered brandy and Eve ghosted out with the decanter. "—bombed," he was saying in German to his aides, "but the new battery of artillery will be in place in four days. As to placement . . ."

Eve's heart slowed in a shaft of diamond-bright excitement. She collected the *Kommandant*'s snifter and filled it as slowly as she dared, letting the liquor bloom as he went over the new placement for the artillery. Her hands, she noticed, were not trembling at all. She replaced the glass, silently begging for an excuse to linger. One of the aides answered her prayer, snapping his fingers for brandy even as he replied with a question about the new guns' capabilities. Eve turned to take his glass, and saw M. Bordelon's eyes on her from the next table where he was glad-handing a German captain and a pair of lieutenants. Her hand gripped the glass tighter, and she wondered in a sudden panic if she'd let her understanding of the *Kommandant*'s words show on her face. If he suspected that Marguerite Le François spoke German . . .

He doesn't, Eve told herself, ironing her features out to perfect blankness and remembering to curve her arm in a graceful arc as she poured. Her employer nodded approval, the *Kommandant* nodded dismissal, and Eve glided back to her alcove with a face smooth as cream and an earful of gold: the precise new locations for the new German artillery around Lille.

She spent the rest of her shift feverishly reciting the information to herself, the numbers, the names, the capabilities, praying she would forget nothing. Rushing home, she transcribed it all onto a slip of thin rice paper in the tiny letters she'd learned at Folkestone, rolled the slip around a hairpin, slid the pin through the knot of her hair, and sagged in relief. Lili arrived the following night on her usual Lille pickup, and it was with a certain ceremony—like the presentation of a victory laurel— that Eve bowed her head, plucked the pin from her hair, and offered it to the leader of the Alice Network.

Lili read the message and crowed aloud, slinging an

arm about Eve's neck and kissing her soundly on both cheeks. "*Mon dieu*, I knew you'd be good."

If the grim Violette were here with her round glasses and her dour disapproval, Eve would try to hide her giddiness, but in the face of Lili's glee she let out the laughter she'd been suppressing since last night.

Lili squinted at the tiny roll of paper. "Transcribing this for my overall report is going to kill my eyes! Next time just code it quickly for me."

"I spent four hours doing th-that," Eve said, crestfallen.

"The new ones always put about six times the effort they should into the first message." Lili laughed, patting her cheek. "Don't look so downcast, it's good work! I'll pass it to Uncle Edward, and that new battery will be bombed by next Thursday."

"Thursday? You can get a position b-b-b—a position bombed so quickly?"

"*Bien sûr.* I have the fastest network in France." Lili wrapped the message back around the hairpin and slid it into her own blond pompadour. "And *you* are going to be a great asset, little daisy. I can feel it."

Her mobile face shone with such unabashed glee that she lit up the drab little room like a border-crossing spotlight, and Eve found herself grinning. She did it; she put her training to use; she accomplished her duty. She was a *spy.*

Lili seemed to sense Eve's inner rush of triumph, because she laughed again as she flopped into the room's only chair. "It's too, too enjoyable, isn't it?" she said as though confessing a naughty secret. "It shouldn't be, perhaps. It's very serious business, serving *la belle France* against her enemies, but it is also such *fun.* There is no job that gives satisfaction like spying. Mothers will tell you children are the most satisfying of all vocations, but *merde*," Lili said frankly, "they're too dulled by never-ending routine to know better. I will take the risk of bullets over the certainty of soiled nappies any day."

"Do you know what I loved?" Eve confessed. "Walking away from that table of uniformed beasts, leaving them to their brandy and their cigars, not one of them knowing . . ." She was so happy she didn't stutter at all, and when she stopped to think about that later, it surprised her.

"*Pffft* to the Germans," Lili said, and began unrolling a scrap of old petticoat on the table. "Come, let me teach you my method for transcribing map positions. It's a simple grid pattern, much more efficient for communicating placement . . ."

That drab little room turned more golden than Le Lethe lit by a hundred candles. They stayed up far too late after finishing the map transcription, Lili sharing a little pilfered brandy and telling stories—"I once got a set of stolen dispatches past a nosy guard by putting them at the bottom of a cake box. You should have seen Uncle Edward's face as I handed him a dispatch case covered in frosting!"

"Brag about me when you give him my report," Eve begged. "I want to make him proud."

Lili tilted her head, looking mischievous. "Little daisy, are you in love?"

"A bit," Eve admitted. "He has a beautiful voice . . ." And he saw that she had the potential to be *here*, to do *this*. Yes, she would find it very hard not to fall a little bit in love with Captain Cameron.

"*Merde*," Lili laughed. "I could easily develop a *tendresse* for him myself. Never fear, I shall brag you up to him shamelessly. You might see him at some point, you know—he passes through German-held territory occasionally, doing something fearfully secret. If he does, promise me you'll do your best to tear all that tweed off him."

"Lili!" Eve rocked, helpless with laughter. She couldn't remember when she'd last laughed so much. "He's married!"

"Why should that stop you? His wife is a bitch who never visited him in prison."

So Lili knew about the prison term. "I thought we were supposed to keep backgrounds secret unless necessary—"

"Everyone already knows Uncle Edward's background; it was in all the newspapers so it can hardly be kept secret. He took his wife's punishment, and to my knowledge she never visited." Eve couldn't repress a little huff of indignation, and Lili smiled. "I say set your cap for him. If your conscience troubles you over a little thing like adultery, give it ten minutes in the confessional and a few Paternosters."

"You kn-know, we Protestants believe in *feeling* our guilt and not just paying it off with a few routine prayers."

"This is why the English are too guilty to make good lovers," Lili declared. "Except in times of war, since war gives even the English an excuse to enjoy themselves. When life could end at any moment on the point of a German bayonet, never allow middle-class morality to get in the way of a good romp with a married ex-convict in tweed."

"I am not hearing this," Eve giggled, clapping her hands to her ears, and the rest of the night slid away on laughter and victory. Eve was still smiling the next day when she woke up to find Lili already gone and the little rice-paper message with her, leaving behind the scrap of petticoat with a scrawled *Go back to work and remember—don't get cocky! Will call in five days.*

Five days, Eve thought, putting on her dark dress and taking herself out toward Le Lethe. *I will have more information for her.* She was serenely confident of that. She'd done it once, and she'd do it again.

Perhaps she *was* a bit cocky, thinking of Lili's approval and a smile in a tweedy Englishman's eyes, when she let herself through the side door into Le Lethe. To be met by the lounging figure of René Bordelon, and the sound of his inflectionless voice saying, "Tell me, Mademoiselle Le François, where are you really from?"

Eve froze. Not outwardly—outside, she was quick to sweep off her hat, fold her gloved hands, let a puzzled expression cross her face. The natural reactions of innocence, quickly deployed. But inside she sank from effervescent lightness to a block of ice in the space of a heartbeat.

"*Monsieur?*" she said.

René Bordelon turned back toward the stairs that led to his private apartments. "Come."

Back into that obscenity of a study, the windows curtained to shut out the wartime grimness of Lille and the lamps lit with such a lavish waste of paraffin during the daytime that it was a slap in the face. Eve came to stand before the soft leather chair where she won this job not quite a week ago, and stilled herself like an animal in the brush waiting for a hunter to pass. *What does he know? What* can *he know?*

He knows nothing, she told herself. *Because Marguerite Le François knows nothing.*

He sat, steepling those very long fingers and regarding her, unblinking. Eve held on to her expression of puzzled innocence. "Is t-there some trouble with my work, *m-m-monsieur*?" she asked at last when it became clear he was waiting for her to break the silence.

"On the contrary," he responded. "Your work is excellent. You do not have to be told twice how a thing is done, and you have a certain natural grace. The other girl clods. I have decided to replace her."

So why am I the one being scrutinized? Eve wondered even as chagrin panged her for broad-hipped Amélie with her two children at home.

"You have pleased me very much, except in one thing." He still hadn't blinked. "I believe you may have lied to me about where you are from."

No, Eve thought. He couldn't possibly suspect she was half English. Her French was perfect.

"Where did you say you were from?"

He knows.

He knows nothing.

"Roubaix," Eve said. "I have my p-papers here." She offered her identity cards, grateful to give her hands and eyes something to do besides meet that unmoving stare.

"I know what your papers say." He didn't look at the cards. "They say that Marguerite Duval Le François is from Roubaix. But you are not."

She schooled her face. "Yes, I am."

"Lie."

That rocked her. Eve hadn't been caught in a lie in a very long time. Perhaps he read her surprise, veiled as it was, because he gave a smile completely lacking in warmth.

"I told you I was good at this, *mademoiselle*. You wish to know how I caught you? You do not speak the French of this region. Your French hails from Lorraine, unless I miss my guess. I travel there frequently to buy wines for my restaurant cellars, and I know the local accent as well as I do the local vintages. So—why do your papers say Roubaix when your vowels say, perhaps, Tomblaine?"

What a good ear he had. Tomblaine was just across
the river from Nancy where Eve grew up. She hesitated,
Captain Cameron's voice coming into her mind, low
and calm with its faint hint of Scotland. *It is best, when
forced to lie, to tell as much of the truth as possible.*
Words from her training, one of those afternoons when
he'd taken her to the lonely beach to shoot bottles.

René Bordelon sat waiting for truth.

"Nancy," Eve whispered. "That is w-where I was
b-b-b-b—"

"Born?"

"Yes, *m-m-m-m—*"

He cut her off with a wave of his hand. "Then
why lie?"

A true answer backed by a false reason—Eve hoped
it would be convincing, because she couldn't think of
anything else. "Nancy is close to G-G-G-Germany,"
she rushed to say, as though embarrassed. "Everyone in
France thinks we're t-t-t-t-traitors, siding with the Germans. Coming to L-L-Lille, I knew I'd be hated if . . .
I knew I wouldn't find w-w-ork. I wouldn't eat. So I
l-l-l—so I lied."

"Where did you get false papers?"

"I d-didn't. I just p-p-paid the clerk to put down a different town. He was sorry for m-me."

Her employer leaned back, fingertips tapping. "Tell
me about Nancy."

Eve was glad she hadn't tried to lie again, give him
some different town. Nancy she knew like the back of
her hand, in far more detail than those memorized facts
about Roubaix. She listed streets, landmarks, churches,
each one a memory from her own childhood. Her
tongue hung up so badly her cheeks flamed scarlet, but
she stammered on, making her voice soft and her eyes
wide.

But the words must have rung true, because he cut her off midsentence. "You clearly know Nancy well."

Eve didn't have time to exhale before he continued, cocking his narrow head.

"Being so close to the German border, there is considerable mixing in the populace in that region. Tell me, *mademoiselle*, do you speak German? Lie to me again, and I will assuredly fire you."

Eve turned to ice again, all the way to the core. He had refused to even consider employing any girl fluent in German. The promise of Le Lethe as an oasis of privacy for German patrons probably guaranteed the best part of its profits. His eyes bored sharp as scalpels, devouring all of her: every movement, every twitch of muscle, every flick of expression.

Lie, Eve, she thought harshly. *The best lie of your life.*

She looked directly into her employer's eyes, straight and guileless, and said without a single hitch, "No, *monsieur*. My father hated them. He would not allow their language to be spoken in his house."

Another long moment of silence, the gilt clock ticking, and it nearly killed Eve. But she held his gaze steady.

"Do you hate them?" he asked. "The Germans?"

She didn't dare risk another lie so close to the last. She hedged instead, looking down at her lap and letting her lips tremble. "When they send half their *b-b-boeuf en croûte* back uneaten," she said tiredly, "yes—I f-find it hard not to hate them. B-but I am too tired for much hatred, *monsieur*. I have to get along in this world, or I w-w-won't live to see the end of this war."

He laughed softly. "Not a popular view to have, is it? I view matters in much the same way, *mademoiselle*. Only I do not just aspire to *get along*." He spread his elegant hands at the beautiful study. "I will prosper."

Eve had no doubt at all that he would. Put profit above

all else—country, family, God—and there wasn't much left to stop you getting it.

"Tell me, Marguerite Le François." René Bordelon sounded almost playful. Eve didn't relax for a second. "Don't you wish to prosper? To do more than merely survive?"

"I'm just a g-girl, *monsieur.* My ambitions are very modest." She lifted her eyes to his, wide and desperate. "Please—will you tell anyone I am from N-N-Nancy? If it's found out I come from that region—"

"I can imagine. People in Lille are"—his eyes narrowed, complicit—"passionate in their patriotism. They might be unkind. Your secret is safe with me."

He was a man who liked secrets, Eve sensed. When *he* was their keeper.

"T-t-thank you, *monsieur.*" Eve seized his hands and gave them a brief clumsy squeeze, bending her head low and biting the inside of her cheek until tears sprang to her eyes. This was a man who appreciated abject gratitude as much as secrets. "Thank you."

She dropped his hands before he could be exasperated at being touched by an employee, then stepped back and smoothed her skirts. His remark came suddenly and in German.

"How graceful you are, even in fear."

She straightened, meeting his eyes, and he devoured her expression, looking for the slightest twinge of understanding. She gave a slow, uncomprehending blink. *"Monsieur?"*

"Nothing." He smiled at last, and somehow Eve had the impression of a finger being eased off a trigger. "You may go."

Her nails had carved deep crescents in her palms by the time she made it down to the restaurant floor, but she consciously uncurled her fists before drawing blood. Because René Bordelon would notice. Oh, yes, he would.

You dodged a bullet, she thought as her shift began, and expected to feel sick now that the danger was past. But her insides stayed stone-cold. Because the danger wasn't past—as long as she had to work, and spy, under the gaze of her observant employer, she would be in danger. Eve had always been such a good liar; for the first time in her life she wondered if she was good enough.

There is no time for fear, she told herself. *It is an indulgence. Turn your ears on and your mind off.*

And she went to work.

CHAPTER 11
CHARLIE

May 1947

W ell, well." Eve raised her eyebrows as I climbed into the backseat of the Lagonda rather than the front beside Finn. "Don't want to share the air with the convict all of a sudden?"

"Don't want you sitting behind me," I retorted. "You *did* try to shoot me last night."

Eve squinted, her eyes bloodshot in the early morning light. "Clearly, I missed. Let's get the hell out of this city and on to bloody Roubaix."

Finn was right in his prediction: Eve was haggard and gray, moving stiffly as an old woman when she climbed into the car, but she said nothing about last night's episode with the Luger. Finn did some tinkering under the hood, murmuring in a Scots burr that got thicker and croonier the more obstinate the Lagonda's innards got— "You cannie aud heap, quit your stalling"—and finally he climbed in, adjusting the various dials and timing for start-up. "We'll be taking it slow," he said as we pulled away from the hotel in a rumble of gears. I turned my head and stared out the window. *Take it slow,* that certainly wasn't Charlie St. Clair's way. Forget about slow, just slug the whiskey, climb on a thirty-year-old Scotsman, and ask for a screw.

I don't care what he thinks of me, I told myself. *I don't care.* But humiliation still choked my throat.

Whore, came the whisper from my nasty inner voice, and I flinched. Maybe I didn't need Finn and Eve for the rest of this journey. Eve had someone in Roubaix who might be able to tell us about the restaurant where Rose had worked in Limoges—after that, would Eve even want to stay with me? She didn't seem to like me. I could pay her what I owed and send her staggering home with her Luger and her ex-convict driver, and I could board a train like a civilized person and take myself to Limoges to look for Rose. Subtract one Scot and one armed-and-dangerous Englishwoman from this equation, and I could conduct my insane quest by my insane self, unhampered by my even more demonstrably insane traveling companions.

"Today," I said aloud, and Finn looked at me over his shoulder. "We need to get to Roubaix today." The sooner the better.

Of course, the day that I couldn't stand the car or the company anymore had turned into a beautiful day for a drive: all bright May sunshine and scudding clouds. It was a short distance to Roubaix, and no one objected when Finn took the Lagonda's top down—even the Little Problem had decided it didn't mind the car's motion so much, so for once I didn't spend the drive vomiting. I rested my chin on my arms, watching fields go by and wondering why the landscape seemed familiar, until something clicked. Another motoring trip, Rose's family and mine, a couple of years after the time we got left behind at the Provençal café. We'd driven past Lille into the countryside, and after a solemn day of touring churches and old monuments, Rose had rolled back the rug in our hotel room and taught me the Lindy Hop. "Come on, Charlie, let your feet *go*—" Moving so fast her curls bounced; tall and bosomy at thirteen, confessing afterward that she'd already had her first kiss. "Georges, the gardener's boy. It was horrible. Tongue, tongue, and more tongue!"

I must have smiled at the memory, because Eve said, "Glad s-someone likes this region."

"You don't?" I tilted my head back at the sun. "Who wouldn't rather be out here than looking at the rubble in London or Le Havre?"

"*'I'd sooner while alive invite the crows to drain the blood from my filthy carcass,'*" Eve said, and added at my blink, "It's a quote, you ignorant Yank. Baudelaire. A poem called '*Le M-Mort Joyeux.*'"

"The Joyful Corpse?" I translated, wrinkling my nose. "Ugh."

"Bit creepy," Finn agreed from behind the wheel.

"Quite," Eve agreed. "So of course it was one of his favorites."

"Whose?" I asked, but naturally she didn't answer me. Did she have to be cryptic when she wasn't being profane? It was like traveling with a whiskey-drinking sphinx. Finn caught me rolling my eyes and smiled, and I looked out at the rolling fields again.

Soon enough, Roubaix appeared on the horizon. A smaller place than Lille, dustier, quieter. A fine city hall, the spires of a Gothic-looking church passing as we chugged through. Eve passed Finn a scribbled address, and eventually we pulled up on a narrow cobbled curb before what looked like an antiques shop.

"The woman you need to speak with is here?" I asked, mystified. "Who *is* she?"

Eve swung out of the car, flinging her cigarette into the gutter with an expert flick of her maimed fingers. "Just someone who loathes me."

"Everyone loathes you," I couldn't help pointing out.

"This one more than usual. C-come or don't, as you like."

She set off into the shop without a backward glance. I piled out after her as Finn cocked an elbow out the rolled-down window and began flipping through *The Autocar* again. Heart thumping, I followed Eve into the dim coolness of the shop.

It was a cramped and cozy little place. Tall mahogany cabinets lined the walls, a long counter made a barrier across the back, and everywhere I saw the porcelain gleam of china. Meissen urns, Spode tea sets, Sevres shepherdesses, and who knew what else. Behind the counter a woman in black updated an account book with a pencil stub, looking up at the sound of our entrance.

She was a sturdy woman about Eve's age, with perfectly round spectacles and dark hair rolled into a neat bun. Like Eve, she had the graven lines of someone who'd lived hard. "May I help you, *mesdames*?"

"That depends," said Eve. "You look well, Violette Lameron."

That was a new name to me. I looked at the woman behind the counter, and her expression never changed. She tilted her head slowly until the lenses of her round glasses flared back the light.

Eve gave a one-note bark of laughter. "That old trick of yours, hiding your eyes! Christ, I'd forgotten that."

Violette or whoever she was spoke evenly. "I haven't heard that name in a long time. Who are you?"

"I'm a graying wreck and time hasn't been kind, but think back." Eve made a circling gesture over her own face. "Doe-eyed little thing? You never liked me, but then again, you never liked anyone except *her*."

"Who?" I whispered, more mystified by the minute—but this time, I saw the other woman's face ripple. She leaned forward over the counter despite herself, peering not into Eve's face but through it, as though the lines of time were just a mask. I saw the blood drain out of the other woman's face, leaving her skin starkly pale against her high black collar.

"Get out," she said. "Get out of my shop."

Jesus, I thought. What had we gotten ourselves into now?

"Collecting teacups, Violette?" Eve looked around the shelves of porcelain. "Seems a bit tame for you. Collecting the heads of your enemies, maybe . . . but then you'd have come after me."

"You're here now, so you must want me to kill you." Violette's lips barely moved. "You cowardly weak-kneed bitch."

I recoiled as if I'd been slapped. But those two battle-axes just stood there with the counter between them, calm as if they were discussing china spoons. Such different women, one tall and gaunt and wrecked, the other sturdy and neat and respectable. But they faced each other erect and granite hard as pillars, and hatred boiled off them in black waves like smoke. I stood dry-mouthed and poisoned in its presence.

Who are you? I thought. *Either of you?*

"One question." Eve's cynical amusement was gone; she looked as deadly serious now as I'd ever seen her.

"One question, and I'm gone. I'd have asked it over the telephone, but you hung up on me."

"You'll get nothing from me." The woman sliced her words off like shards of glass. "Because unlike you, I'm not a yellow-bellied whore with loose lips."

I expected Eve to fly at her. She'd leveled a Luger at my head just for calling her a crazy old cow. But she stood there taking the insults like she was standing in front of a shooting target taking bullets, braced, her jaw set. "One question."

Violette spat in her face.

I gasped, taking a half step forward, but I might as well not have been there for all the attention the two women paid me. Eve stood a moment with spittle trickling down her cheek, and then she peeled off her glove and deliberately wiped her face. Violette watched, spectacles glittering, and I took another step. This was not the way I'd seen women quarrel—vicious cat-claw digs, the vivisection of gossip that flowed through a sorority house. This was the kind of feud that led to pistols at dawn.

Why can't anything be simple? I thought in panic.

Eve dropped the glove to the floor and slammed her bare hand on the counter with a sound like a rifle shot, and I watched Violette's eyes fasten with sick recognition on the other woman's ruined fingers.

"Did René Bordelon die in 1917?" Eve asked, low-voiced. "Yes or no—either way, I walk out."

My hackles rose. *René*, we kept coming back to that name. In the report on Rose. In Eve's nightmares. Now here. *Who is he, who is he—*

Violette was still gazing at Eve's hand. "I forgot about those fingers of yours."

"At the time, you told me I deserved it."

Cool contempt crossed Violette's face. "Your stammer's certainly better. Does whiskey do that for you? You smell like a drunk."

"Whiskey or rage are both fine cures for stammering, and I'm belly-full of both," Eve snarled. "René Bordelon, you sour cunt. What happened to him?"

"How should I know?" Violette shrugged. "You and I left France at the same time, and he was still prospering in those days. Still running Le Lethe."

Le Lethe—the restaurant where Rose had worked. But that had been in *Limoges*, not Lille, I thought confusedly. And I was looking for information about 1944, not the first war. I opened my mouth to say so, then closed it again. I didn't want to step between the two women and their dueling eyes.

Eve's eagle-gray gaze never shifted. "After the war, you returned to Lille for a while. Cameron told me that—"

Cameron now? How many new players had just been pushed onto the stage in this drama? I wanted to shriek, but I kept silent, staring at Eve as though I could yank the answers out of her with a hook. *Stop asking questions and start spitting answers, dammit.*

"—and Cameron also told me René Bordelon died in 1917, shot by Lille citizens for being a filthy collaborator."

"He *was* a filthy collaborator," Violette stated. "But nobody shot him—I'd have heard if they had. There would have been dancing in the streets if he'd died the way he deserved. No, I was told the bastard packed up and ran as soon as the Germans retreated, because he knew a bullet in the back was the best he could expect. No one saw him again in Lille, that's for sure. But he was alive in 1918 at least. That man always was a survivor." Violette gave an unpleasant smile. "So if Cameron told you differently, he sold you a lie. And you were always so proud of your ability to sniff out lies."

None of this meant anything to me, but I saw Eve's proud spine sag. Her ruined hands gripped the counter's edge. Before I knew I was moving, I put an arm around her waist, fearing she'd fall. I half-expected her to slap me away with a caustic remark, but her eyes were squeezed shut. "That liar," she whispered, and wisps of her graying hair flew as she shook her head. "That damned, tweed-hearted *liar*."

"And now"—Violette plucked off her spectacles and gave them a polish—"you can get out of my shop."

"Give her a moment," I snapped. Eve might irk me to the point of madness sometimes, but I wasn't letting any nearsighted shopkeeper tear her to pieces when she looked so shocked and fragile.

"I'm not giving her thirty more seconds, much less a moment," the woman said, looking at me for the first time. She reached under the counter, and came up with a Luger just like Eve's. "I know how to use it, little girl. Get that bitch out of here if you have to drag her by the feet."

"What is it with you old cows and your guns?" I shouted, but Eve straightened, her face a ghastly curdled mask.

"We're done here," she said quietly, and made for the door. I collected her fallen glove and followed, heart hammering.

Violette's voice came from behind me. "Do you dream, Eve?"

Eve halted, not turning. Her shoulders were straight and stiff. "Every night."

"I hope she chokes you," Violette said. "Every night, I hope she chokes the life out of you."

But it sounded like Violette was the one choking

as we left. The door closed behind us on the strangled sound of a sob before I could ask who *she* could possibly be.

'm sorry," Eve said from out of nowhere.

I was so startled I nearly upset my coffee. She sat, hands folded like claws around her own cup, her pallor ghastly. When we left the shop and Eve climbed into the Lagonda and sat staring into space, I'd said quietly to Finn, "Find a hotel." He'd found an *auberge* across from Roubaix's cozy city hall, and gone off to park the Lagonda while Eve and I sat at one of the little tables in the hotel's open court. She ordered coffee in her perfect French, then ignored the disapproving glance of the waiter when she emptied her silver flask into the cup.

Now she looked up, and I almost recoiled from her sightless stare. "Shouldn't have brought you here. Waste of your m-money. I wasn't looking for your cousin, I was looking for someone else."

"That woman?"

"No." Eve knocked back a slug of her spiked coffee. "A man I've thought dead for thirty years . . . I suppose Cameron told me he *was* dead just to give me peace." A shake of her head. "Cameron was too bloody noble to understand a vicious bitch like me. What would have given me peace was seeing René's head on a spike."

She bit off the words, staring out at the bustle of hotel clerks and bellboys around the potted ferns.

"René . . . Bordelon, you said in the shop." Now we had a last name for the mysterious Monsieur René.

"He was the owner of Le Lethe. The one in Lille, anyway."

"How did you know him?"

"I worked for him during the first war."

I hesitated. This last war had so completely overshadowed the first one, I knew much less about the way things had been the first time the Germans invaded. "How terrible was it, Eve?"

"Oh, you know. German boots stamping on the necks of the starving, people shot in alleys. Bad."

So this was what fueled her nightmares. I looked at her wrecked hands, and shuddered. "Were there two Le Lethes, then?"

"Looks like it. Since your cousin worked at one in Limoges."

The echoes here were sending cold ripples through my blood. "And a second man named René? Or could René Bordelon have owned the restaurant in Limoges as well?"

Her hand slapped the table again. "No," she said. "No."

"Eve, I don't believe in this many coincidences, and neither do you. That shopkeeper said he survived the first war by fleeing Lille. He might easily have lived until 1944, when Rose got to Limoges. He could be alive now." Excitement ran through me now alongside the dread. Rose's employer, someone who had known her— even if he was a beast, he had a *name*. A name meant he was someone I could track down.

Eve shook her head stubbornly. "He would be past seventy. He—" Still her head went back and forth, a mechanical motion. "Maybe he survived the first war. But he can't be alive *now*, not a man like that, not after thirty years. Someone would have put a bullet through his black rotting brain."

I looked down at my own cold coffee, unwilling to cede hope. "Either way, his restaurant in Limoges is probably there. That's where I'm going next."

"Have fun, Yank." Her voice was hard. "This is where we part ways."

I blinked in surprise. "A moment ago you said you

wanted to see his head on a spike. How are you not on fire now to find this old enemy of yours?"

"What does that m-m-matter to you? Aren't you keen to be shut of me?"

I had been. But that was before I'd realized she had as much a stake in this search as I did. She had someone to find, just like me. I couldn't cut anyone out from something that *mattered* as much as that. I'd already scrapped the plan to continue on without Eve, had assumed she'd be champing to finish the search—and here she was, quitting?

"You do what you like. I'm not chasing wild geese anymore." Her voice was curt, her gaze stubbornly blank. "René has to be dead. So's your cousin."

My hand was the one to hit the table this time. "*Don't*," I snarled. "Don't you dare. You can put your head in the sand about your own demons if you like, but I'm going after mine."

"Head in the sand? Two years after the war's done and *you're* putting your faith in some fairy story that your cousin might still be alive."

"I know what the odds are," I shot back. "Even if it's only a sliver of hope, I'll take that over despair."

"You don't even have a sliver." Eve leaned across the table, gray eyes glittering. "The good ones never survive. They die in ditches and before firing squads and on squalid prison cots for sins they never committed. They always die. It's the wicked who go merrily on."

I set my chin. "So why are you so convinced your René Bordelon is dead, then? Why is *he* dead, if the wicked always prosper?"

"Because I'd feel it if he were alive," she said quietly. "Just like you'd feel it if your cousin were dead. Which maybe makes us both crazy, but either way it means we're done."

I looked at her, and I enunciated it carefully: "Coward."

I thought she'd explode. But she just sat, braced as if for a blow, and I saw blind panic at the back of her eyes. She didn't *want* her old enemy to be alive. So he wasn't. It was that simple.

"Fine, then. See if I care." I reached for my pocket-book and counted out the money I owed her, subtracting what I'd just paid for her hotel room. "Payment in full. Try not to drink it all in one place."

She rose, gathering up the banknotes. Without a word of farewell she took her room key and stalked off toward the stairs.

I don't know what I'd expected. Maybe for her to tell me more about Lille and the Great War. Why her hands were . . . I don't know. I sat at the little table like a helpless fool, feeling abandoned, wishing I hadn't thrown my arm around her waist in the china shop and let her lean on me. Because even after she deduced the Little Problem's presence and was tactless enough to say so, some part of me still wanted her respect. She wasn't like any woman I'd ever met; she talked to me as though I were a grown woman rather than a child—yet just now, she'd flicked me aside like a cigarette stub. *See if I care*, I'd said. Well, I did.

You don't need her, I scolded myself. *You don't need anyone.*

Finn came up, toting my traveling case over one shoulder. "Where's Gardiner?"

I rose. "She says we're done."

His smile disappeared. "You're off, then?"

"I've already paid for the rooms, so you and Eve may as well stay tonight. But I wouldn't be surprised if she wants to bolt back to London tomorrow."

"Where are you going?"

"Limoges. My cousin might be there. Or someone who knew her." I aimed a bright, nonspecific smile at Finn, ducking his gaze.

"Now?"

"Tomorrow." I felt too drained to go anywhere this afternoon, and I'd paid for my room as well as theirs.

"Well, then." He brushed the hair out of his eyes, handing over my traveling case. I wondered if he was sorry or relieved to see me go. Probably relieved. *I'm sorry,* I wanted to say. *Sorry I made you think I was a tramp. Sorry I didn't sleep with you. So I really am a tramp. Sorry about that.* But instead I blurted out the only other thing I could think of that wasn't about me climbing into his lap and gluing my lips to his.

"How *did* you end up in prison?"

"Took the *Mona Lisa* right off the wall of the British Museum," he replied, straight-faced.

"The *Mona Lisa* isn't even hanging in the British Museum," I objected.

"Not anymore it's not."

I couldn't help laughing. Even managed to meet his eyes for a split second. "Good luck, Mr. Kilgore."

"Good luck, miss." And my heart expanded a little, hearing the *miss.*

But after Finn left, I couldn't bring myself to go up to my room yet. Another wave of utter exhaustion hit me, and besides, sitting alone in a hotel room seemed sadder than sitting in a busy hotel court. I ordered another coffee and sat staring at it.

It'll be easier on your own, I told myself. *No more crazy old bat pointing a pistol at you. No more insults, no more getting slowed down by Eve's hangovers and the fact that she can't travel except in a beat-up tin can of a car. No more Scottish convicts making me act like the kind of girl who gets herself into the kind of pickle*

I'm already in. No more being called Yank. *You can go look for Rose all by yourself, free and clear.*

All by myself. It shouldn't have felt so strange—I was used to being alone. I'd been alone since I'd parted from Rose before the war, really. Alone in the middle of a bustling family who hardly knew I was there; alone in the middle of a giggling dorm with sorority sisters who didn't know I was there either.

Buck up, I told myself fiercely as a bellboy brushed past. *Just buck up. Don't be sorry for yourself, Charlie St. Clair, because that is just so goddamn* boring.

Eve had rubbed off on me. I was swearing all the time now, just like her. Even if just in my head.

You're a bad influence on me, the Little Problem said.

Be quiet, I told my own stomach. You're not real. I'm not hearing you.

Says who?

Wonderful. The Little Problem was now talking. First hallucinations, and now voices.

Then I heard an enchantingly modulated shriek behind me. "*Charlotte!* Oh, *ma p'tite,* how could you—" And I turned, sweat cold on my forehead, to see that my mother had found me.

July 1915

I t was a very organized, very tidy robbery. They arrived at noon: the German officer, a folder under his arm, two soldiers flanking him. The knock sounded, both brutal and officious, and so was the officer's tone as he snapped, "Copper inspection!" It was all plainly just an excuse. The room clearly contained no copper sheeting or piping to be seized for the German metal drive.

Eve knew what to do, well briefed by Lili and Violette. She handed over her papers and stood against the wall as they ransacked everything, not that there was much to find or take. Except, of course, Eve's Luger in the false bottom of her decrepit carpetbag. Also her latest report for Lili, statistics of the next shipment of aeroplanes to be brought to guard Lille's airspace and the arrival date of the pilots to fly them. Details eavesdropped as Eve brought *crème brûlée* and *kirschtorte* to a pair of German captains doing business over dessert. Details on the usual rice-paper slip, pinned into her hair.

How the officer and his men would love to find *those*.

So Eve looked down at her toes in an apparent agony of embarrassment as her clothes were ransacked and her mattress prodded. Her heart iced briefly as her carpet-bag was lifted and rattled, but the pistol was well padded, and the bag passed muster.

One of the soldiers yanked down Eve's curtain rod, inspecting it. "Useless," he said, tossing it aside, but not before yanking Eve's curtains off and stuffing them into a sack with a sidelong glance as if to ask if she'd protest. She didn't, just inhaled her rage and let it out again. The petty small things she saw every day drove her far closer to the brink than the large. Eve didn't mind that the Germans had the right to shoot her nearly as much as she minded having them walk into her room and steal her curtains.

"You hiding anything, *Fraulein*?" the soldier asked, dropping a hand along the back of Eve's neck. "Fresh food? Meat, maybe?"

His fingers stroked mere inches away from the coded message in Eve's hair. She met his gaze with wide, innocent eyes, not caring if he groped her as long as he didn't find the little roll of paper. "No, *monsieur*."

They swaggered out with their sack of pilfered items, Eve remembering to curtsy and murmur her thanks when the officer noted everything in his folder and issued her a *bon*—a voucher—for her curtains. *Bons* were worth nothing, but the forms must be observed. That was the lesson the invaders had taught the French.

For nearly a month now, Eve had plied her two trades in Lille. She slipped into Marguerite Le François every morning the moment she slipped out from between her sheets, putting on the new identity so easily that at times she forgot she *wasn't* Marguerite. Marguerite kept to her room unless she was out buying food, drawing as little attention to herself as possible. Marguerite murmured greetings to the family who lived across the street, a haggard mother and several skinny children, and she offered a shy smile to the baker whenever he apologized for the rocklike bread. Her silence didn't distinguish her. Most of Lille was similarly withdrawn, bemused into apathy by hunger and boredom, monotony and fear.

Such were the days, but Eve's nights made the grayness all worthwhile. Six nights a week she labored in Le Lethe—and at least once each week, she heard something worth reporting to Lili.

"I wish I knew how much g-good any of it does," she confessed to the head of the Alice Network one long July night. The fleeting visits from Lili were like splashes of champagne in an existence of weak tea—moments when she shook off Marguerite like a drab dress and turned back into Eve. "How do we know what any of it is w-w—any of it is worth?"

"We don't." Lili eased Eve's latest report into a split seam of her bag. "We report what we think helps, and then hope to God it does."

"Have you ever reported something you kn-kn-knew made a difference?" Eve persisted.

"A few times. What a feeling!" A kiss of the fingertips. "But don't fret, Uncle Edward says to tell you that you are doing *top-class work*. What is this British thing, putting everything into *classes*? It's like you never get over having gone to public school." Lili gave Eve her swift impish smile. "There, I've made you blush!"

Top-class work. Eve hugged those words at night in bed. The mattress was hard and thin; the nights hot and broken by the distant rumbling of shell fire—but in Lille, despite the danger around her, Eve slept like a baby. She never ate enough despite the nightly allotment of scraps from the restaurant; she was worked off her feet and lived cheek by jowl with fear; she'd lost weight and the glow from her cheeks, and sometimes thought she'd commit murder for a good cup of coffee—but she slept with a smile and woke each morning with the one individual thought she allowed herself before becoming Marguerite for the day.

This is where I belong.

Eve wasn't the only one to feel that way. "*Putain de merde*," Lili sighed one evening as she shuffled her handful of identity cards, trying to decide whether to become Marie the sewing girl or Rosalie the laundress when she left tomorrow. "However shall I manage when the war is over and I have to go back to being just me? How boring that will be."

"You're not b-boring." Eve smiled up at the ceiling, lying flat on her back on the bony mattress. "I'm boring. I f-f-filed letters and l-lived in a boardinghouse sharing my supper scraps with a cat." She couldn't believe she ever managed to live that way.

"That doesn't mean you were boring, *ma p'tite*. Just bored. Most women are bored, because being female is boring. We only get married because it's something to do, and then we have children and find out babies are the only thing more boring than other women."

"Will we be bored to death when this w-war is over and so are our jobs?" Eve wondered idly. The war loomed so all-encompassing, she couldn't imagine it *ever* being over. Last August everyone swore it would be done by Christmas, but being here just a few miles from the trenches, with the boom of guns in the background and the clocks permanently turned to German time, told a very different story.

"We'll have different jobs when the war is over." Lili shuffled her handful of identity cards like a fan. "I should like to do something splendid, shouldn't you? Something extraordinary."

Lili already *was* extraordinary, Eve thought. *Not like me.* The thought held no envy—it was what made them both good at what they did now. Lili's job was to be anyone, to shift with a few tricks of posture or grammar from one persona to another, whether seamstress or laundress or cheese seller. And if Lili's job was to be anyone, Eve's was to be no one, to be unobserved and unnoticed at all times.

And as the weeks passed, that became worrying. Because someone *had* taken notice of her.

René Bordelon lingered in the restaurant that night after the last guest departed. He sometimes did, lighting a cigar and enjoying it alone as his staff silently cleaned up around him. He played *bon vivant* host among the Germans, but of his own accord he seemed to swim as solitary as a shark. He lived alone, he sometimes left the restaurant to the headwaiter's charge and attended plays or concerts, he took the afternoon air in a flawless cashmere coat and swinging a silver-headed walking stick. Eve wondered what he thought about on those nights when he let the restaurant close about him, smiling at the black windows. Perhaps he simply smiled at his profit margins. Eve steered clear. Ever since he guessed her accent and forced her to give up her birthplace, she'd given him a wide berth.

But he didn't always allow that.

"Put away the record," he said as Eve came out to clear the tables. The gramophone in the corner that occasionally provided discreet background music for a German patron with a fondness for the music of his homeland was hissing at the end of a recording. "One grows tired of Schubert."

Eve crossed to the gramophone at the edge of his vision. It was past midnight; her employer sat in a pool of candlelight at the corner table with a glass of cognac. All the other tables were empty, their pristine cloths splashed with wine and tart crumbs and a few scattered glasses. The bustle of the cooks straightening the kitchens filtered in faintly, barely disturbing the silence. "Do you want another record, *monsieur*?" Eve murmured. All she wanted was to finish her shift, get home, and write down the train schedules for wounded troops coming in from the front, a nugget she'd heard just this evening . . .

He set aside his cognac. "Why don't I provide the music instead?"

"*Monsieur?*"

There was a piano in the corner, a baby grand draped in a fantastically embroidered shawl and adorned with candles, giving the impression that Le Lethe was not a restaurant at all, merely a private home with the best of chefs. Eve's employer strolled to it unhurriedly, taking a seat and running his extraordinarily long fingers across the keys. He began to play, a fragile melody that rose and fell like the sound of rain. "Satie," he said. "One of the Gymnopédies. Do you know them?"

Eve did. Marguerite would not. "No, *monsieur*," she said, whisking stray napkins and discarded forks onto her tray. "I know nothing about m-m-music."

"Shall I educate you?" He continued to play, the melody soft and lulling. "Satie is an Impressionist, but less indulgent than Debussy. He has a clarity and elegance that is uniquely French, I have always thought. He evokes melancholy without unnecessary flourishes.

Like a beautiful woman in a perfectly simple dress, who knows not to tart it up with too many scarves." His eyes drifted briefly to Eve. "I don't suppose you've ever had an elegant dress."

"No, *monsieur*." Eve moved a discarded pair of wine-glasses onto her tray, one empty, one with a few swallows of perfect golden wine inside. She kept her eyes on that wine, because anything was better than looking at her employer. In any ordinary restaurant, the cooks would swig the glass empty as soon as Eve brought it back, but not here. They'd decant those three swallows of wine back into the bottle, because even in a restaurant awash with the fruits of the black market, liquor couldn't be wasted. Unlike the leftover food, leftover wine was *not* divvied up among the staff at the end of the night. Everyone from the surliest chef to the most arrogant waiter knew René Bordelon was perfectly capable of dismissing them over three stolen swallows of white wine.

Eve's employer was still musing aloud against the rise and fall of the piano, drawing her attention again. "If the metaphor of an elegant dress without frills does not instruct you, then perhaps one could compare Satie's music to a perfect, dry Vouvray. Elegant, but spare." He inclined his head toward the glass on Eve's tray. "Try it, and see if you agree."

He was smiling faintly, perhaps just indulging an idle whim? Eve hoped so. Hoped fervently it wasn't something else. Whatever his motivation, she couldn't refuse, so she raised the glass and sipped like an uncertain little girl. She considered a splutter, but that might be overdoing it, so she merely offered a nervous smile as she replaced the empty glass. "Thank you, *monsieur*."

He nodded her out without another word, to Eve's

relief. *Do not notice me,* she wanted to beg, stealing a glance back at that solitary figure at the piano. *I am no one.* But she wasn't sure her employer believed that. He'd dismissed her carefully crafted anonymity the day he decided her vowels didn't match her identity card, and he still seemed to be looking. Wondering, perhaps, if Marguerite Le François had any more secrets to uncover.

Two nights later, Le Lethe's owner retired at the end of the evening. But the senior waiter sent Eve upstairs with the night's takings, and there was that faint smile again when she entered the lavish study.

"*Mademoiselle,*" he remarked, lowering his book and marking the page. "The nightly take?"

Eve bobbed silently and handed the ledger over. He flipped the pages, noting a smudge here and an unusual booking there, jotting a note down, and then he remarked out of nowhere, "Baudelaire."

"I'm sorry, *monsieur?*"

"The marble bust at which you are staring. It is a replica of a bust of Charles Baudelaire."

Eve was only looking at it because she'd look at anything in this room except her employer. She registered the small bust on the shelf, blinked. "Yes, *monsieur.*"

"Do you know Baudelaire?"

Marguerite, Eve thought, wouldn't be believable if she was a *complete* ignoramus—M. Bordelon had already discarded, unfortunately, the idea that she was stupid. "I've h-heard of him."

"*The Flowers of Evil* are some of the greatest poems ever penned." A checkmark went into the ledger. "Poetry is like passion—it should not be merely pretty; it should overwhelm and bruise. Baudelaire understood that. He combines the sweet with the obscene, but he does it with elegance." A smile. "It's a very French thing, making obscenity elegant. The Germans try, and they are merely vulgar."

Eve wondered if his obsession with all things *elegant* could possibly be as strong as his preference for all things *French*. "Yes, *monsieur*."

He looked amused. "You are puzzled, *mademoiselle*."

"Am I?"

"That I serve the Germans, but find them vulgar." He shrugged. "They are vulgar. There is little to do with such vulgar people but make money off them. More people should understand that. Most of Lille chooses spite and starvation over practicality and money. They embrace the motto, to quote Baudelaire, of *'I'd sooner while alive invite the ravens to drain the blood from my filthy corpse'* than serve a German. But pride like that will not leave you the victor in the field." He caressed the spine of his ledger with that long finger. "It will leave you the carcass on which the ravens dine."

Eve nodded. What else could she do? Her blood thumped cold and slow in her ears.

"The French can be practical, do not misunderstand me," he continued. "We do better, historically, with practicality than pride, when we can manage it. Practicality got the head off our king. Pride got us Napoleon. Which was the better plan, in the long run?" He looked at her, considering. "You, I think, are a practical girl. Risking a lie on an identity card for a greater potential gain—that is practicality underscored with boldness."

She didn't want him thinking about how well she could lie. "Are you f-finished with the ledger, *monsieur*?" she hedged.

He ignored that. "Your middle name is Duval, I seem to recall? Baudelaire had a Mademoiselle Duval of his own, though she was a Jeanne, not a Marguerite. A Creole girl he plucked from a gutter and turned into a beauty. He called her his Black Venus, and she inspired a good deal of obscenity and passion in these pages." Patting the volume he'd set aside as she entered. "Honing beauty is more interesting, perhaps, than acquiring beauty already polished. '*Many a gem lies hidden in darkness and oblivion, far, far away from picks and drills . . .*'"

Another direct, unblinking gaze. "What would picks and drills uncover in you, I wonder?"

He knows, Eve thought in a moment of pure, frozen panic.

He knows nothing.

She exhaled. Lowered her lashes. "Monsieur Baudelaire sounds v-very interesting," she said. "I shall try to r-read some. Will that be all, *m-m-m-m*—"

"Yes." He handed back the ledger. Eve closed the door and sagged the moment she was out of sight. She was sweating head to toe, and for the first time since arriving in Lille, she wanted to panic. Panic, cower, and *run*. Anything, just get away.

Violette was ensconced in the apartment when Eve finally returned from work, stowing her Luger beside Eve's in the false-bottomed bag. One look at Eve's white face and she said with a certain resignation, "Nerves?"

"N-no." Eve waited until they'd completed the ritual of checking window and door for loiterers, anyone who might eavesdrop on the room as insulated though it was by derelict buildings or stone walls on all sides. "My employer suspects me," she said, low-voiced.

Violette looked up sharply. "Has he been asking questions?"

"No. But he *makes conversation*. With me, someone who ought to be utterly b-b-beneath him. He kn-knows something's not right."

"Pull yourself together. He can't read minds."

I think he can. Eve knew the thought was ridiculous, but couldn't banish it.

"Lili gets good information out of you, so don't turn yellow-bellied now." Violette climbed into her makeshift pallet, plucking off her round spectacles. Eve bit her lip to stop herself from begging reassignment, anywhere in Lille where she wouldn't be under René Bordelon's unblinking eyes . . . But she couldn't face Violette's scorn, and she could *not* let Lili down. Lili needed her at Le Lethe, and so did Captain Cameron.

Top-class work.

Pull yourself together, she lashed herself. *What happened to* I am Evelyn Gardiner and this is where I belong? *You lied to René Bordelon once, and you can go on doing it.*

"Maybe he's not watching you out of suspicion." Violette's voice floated up through the dark, already filled with yawns. "Maybe it's lust."

"No." Eve laughed curtly, bending to unbutton her shoes. "I'm n-n-not elegant enough. Marguerite Le François is a c-country mouse. Too *gauche* for him."

Despite Violette's skeptical snort, she was very, very certain of that.

CHAPTER 13
CHARLIE

May 1947

There she was. My mother: lavender scented and beautiful as ever . . . only, the eyes behind the veil of her stylish blue hat were full of tears. That alone stunned me speechless as she enveloped me in a hug.

"*Ma chère,* how could you! Dashing off into a strange country!" She was scolding me, but there was the hug, her gloved hand rubbing my back as though I were a baby. She pulled back, giving me a shake. "To worry me like that, and for no reason!"

"There was a reason," I managed to say, but she was hugging me again. Two hugs in as many minutes—my mother hadn't hugged me in recent memory, at least not since before the Little Problem. Even longer. I didn't quite mean for it to happen, but my arms stole around her cinched waist.

"Oh, *chérie*—" She pulled back, dabbing at her eyes, and I found my voice.

"How did you find me?"

"Your telephone call from London, you said you were looking for Rose. What else could that mean but that you were haring off to see your Tante Jeanne in Rouen? I took the boat and telephoned her when I arrived in Calais. She said you'd been and gone already, to Roubaix."

"How did she know—" But I'd told her myself, hadn't I? *No,* Tante, *I'm not staying. I have to go to Roubaix.* I'd been trying so hard not to shriek at her for how she'd thrown Rose out, I'd given myself away.

"It's not a big place, Roubaix." My mother gestured at the hotel court. "This is only the fourth hotel I've checked."

What stinking bad luck, I thought, but some part of me was saying in a small voice, *She hugged me.*

"Tea," my mother decided, just as she'd decided in the Dolphin Hotel in Southampton not even a week ago. A handful of days seemed like too small a time to contain Eve and Finn and everything I'd learned about Rose.

My mother ordered tea and then looked me over anxiously, shaking her head. "You look a *mess*! Have you been living rough? *Mon Dieu*—"

"No, I have money. I—I pawned *Grand-maman*'s pearls." The shame of that stung me suddenly; the only thing I had of my mother's mother, and I'd traded it away for a wild goose chase. "I can get them back, I promise. I have the pawn slip. I'll pay out of my own savings."

"I am just happy to know you weren't sleeping in a ditch," my mother said, waving the thought of her mother's pearls away. That surprised me all over again. My mother, not caring about the pearls she'd always pointedly said should have been left to her? "Traveling alone across the Channel! *Chérie,* the danger!"

Not alone, I almost said, but I really didn't think *Maman* would be reassured to hear that I'd traveled with an ex-convict and a pistol-toting drunkard. I had a moment's fervent gratitude that Eve and Finn had already gone upstairs. "I'm sorry I worried you. I never meant—"

"Your hair," she clucked, and smoothed a flyaway strand back behind my ear. How did I suddenly feel so small and helpless when I'd spent my last few days breaking Eve's door down, getting a Luger pointed at my face, crossing the Channel . . . ?

I straightened in my chair, marshaling arguments. *Maman* wasn't going to hear me unless I sounded like a grown woman with a plan, not a sulky child with a temper tantrum. "This wasn't about me being ungrateful about the Appointment. It was—"

"I know." My mother lifted her teacup. "We rushed you, your father and I—"

"No, it's not that. It was about Rose."

"—with this thing in Switzerland. The Appointment." That capital letter again. "You panicked when we got off the ship in Southampton."

I shrugged. True enough, but—

"We only want what's best for you, your father and I." Reaching out to pat my hand. "All parents do. So we pushed you onto the boat before you knew what was happening."

"Did I ruin everything?" I managed to ask, meeting her eyes. "Is it too late now for . . ." I didn't know how late was too late for the procedure to be safe. I didn't know anything.

"We can get another appointment, *ma chère.* It's not too late for that."

A pang went through my chest, part disappointment and part relief. I felt the Little Problem inside me as though it were vibrating, though my stomach was perfectly still.

My mother's hand reached out to cover mine, warm and soft. "It's frightening, I know. But in these cases, earlier is *safer*. Once it's done, we'll go home and give you time to rest, reflect—"

"I don't want to rest." I looked up, a familiar thread of anger rising through all my confusion. "I don't want to go home. I want to try to find Rose, if she's still alive. *Listen* to me."

My mother sighed. "Surely you aren't still hanging on to hope for Rose."

"Yes," I stated. "Until I *know* she's dead. Because after James, I can't just write her off. Not without trying everything."

She rolled the edge of her napkin with the taut expression she always had at my brother's name.

"There's *hope, Maman*," I said, trying to reach her. "It's too late for James, but maybe we can still save Rose. She left home, and *Tante Jeanne* told me why."

A flicker. Yes, my mother had known. A tendril of anger uncoiled at the thought that she hadn't seen fit to tell me, but I pressed past it.

"Rose wouldn't have wanted to come back to her family after something like that. She might still be in Limoges. If she's there, then we have to find her."

"And you?" My mother looked at me. "You can't put your future on hold for her. Charlotte St. Clair is just as important as Rose Fournier. Rose herself would be the first to say so."

I looked across the hotel court, wondering if I'd see Rose's blond head, her outline. Nothing.

"The Appointment." *Maman*'s voice was gentle. "Let me take you to the clinic, *ma chère*."

"What if I don't want an Appointment?" The words came from nowhere. They surprised me as much as my mother.

She looked at me a moment, then sighed. "If you had a ring on your finger, that would be another matter. We'd put the wedding forward, you'd be a beautiful bride and six months later a beautiful mother. These things happen."

They did. That was a bit of math all women understood: how a wedding ring plus a premature baby still magically equaled respectability.

"But your situation is different, Charlotte. Without a fiancé . . ."

She trailed off, and I winced. I knew what happened to unmarried girls who had babies. No one talked about them, but you *knew*. Nobody wanted to marry bad girls or give them jobs, their families were ashamed of them, and their friends didn't speak to them. Their lives were ruined.

"There isn't any other option," *Maman* pressed. "One little procedure, and you'll have your life back."

I couldn't say I didn't yearn for normality again. I drew a finger around the rim of my teacup.

"Please, *chérie*." *Maman* abandoned her cooling tea, stretching both hands across the little table to clasp mine. "We'll take up the hunt for Rose again, if that's truly what you want. But won't you do what's right for your future first?"

"I'll go to the clinic," I said around the lump in my throat. "After that, we look for Rose. Promise me that, *Maman*. Please."

Her hands squeezed mine. "I promise."

———

couldn't sleep.

The Little Problem had flattened me with another wave of exhaustion, so I should have slept like a rock. My mother had upgraded the room I'd reserved for a nicer one beside her own, and I'd eaten a good dinner brought up on a silver tray rather than the usual packet of dry sandwiches. I was able to trade my much-rinsed-out nylon slip for a nightgown borrowed from my mother. I no longer had to worry about screams in the night from crazy Englishwomen or what would happen when my money ran out, because *Maman* was here to take care of everything.

But even after she retired to her own room with a kiss to my forehead, I tossed and turned in my cool hotel sheets. Finally I got up, shrugged into a borrowed bathrobe and slippers, grabbed my cigarettes, and headed for fresh air.

All I wanted was a balcony, but the French doors at the end of the hotel hall were locked. I ended up trailing down to the darkened main floor, too irritated to care about the startled look the night clerk gave me as I passed to the street outside.

A quarter moon and a few streetlights did little to break the darkness. Past two in the morning, according to the clock I'd passed in the hotel court—sleepy little Roubaix was dead to the world. I pulled out a Gauloise, patting my robe for matches, and caught sight of something a dozen feet down on the curb. A gleam of dark blue metal.

"Hello there," I told the Lagonda, strolling to pat her sleek fender. "I must admit, I'm going to miss you."

"She's flattered." A low Scots burr came from inside the backseat, and I nearly jumped out of my skin.

"What are you doing out here?" I hoped Finn couldn't

see my disheveled self too well in the dark. Why, *why* hadn't I asked my mother to take us to a different hotel? It was embarrassing, hanging about the same hotel as Eve and Finn like I was still hoping for something from them. We were like actors who had missed the cue that their scene was over. Life ought to be more like a play; the entrances and exits would be a lot cleaner.

Finn's tousled dark head leaned out the window, and I saw the ember glow of his cigarette. "Couldn't sleep."

I thrust my hands into my pockets, unlit cigarette and all, so I wouldn't start patting my hair. Is there any ensemble less glamorous and appealing in the entire world than a bathrobe and slippers? "Do you always climb into your car when you can't sleep?" I managed to say tartly.

Finn rested his bare elbow on the Lagonda's rolled-down window. "She's calming. Good cure for bad dreams."

"I thought Eve was the one who had bad dreams."

"I get my share."

I wondered what they were about. I didn't ask, just patted the fender again. Strange to think I wouldn't be driving off in her in the morning. Tomorrow it would be a train to Vevey for me, and then—what did they have in Switzerland to ferry girls to their Appointments? Cabs with cuckoo clocks? Drivers in wooden clogs? I shivered in the summer night.

Finn opened the Lagonda's door, sliding across to the far side of the seat. "Get in if you're cold."

I wasn't, but I climbed in anyway. "Can I have a light?"

He flicked a match. The brief flare gave me a shot of his profile and then left me night-blinded, wrapped in shadows. I drew in a mouthful of smoke, letting it out slowly. "How did you end up with a car like this?" I asked just to be saying something. If you weren't in the backseat of a car to make out, it seemed appropriate to make polite conversation.

"Inherited a little money from an uncle," he said, surprising me. He rarely answered direct questions, not with the truth anyway. "He wanted me to go to school, make something of myself. But a boy with engine grease under his nails has other ideas when he gets his hands on some silver."

"You mean he goes out and spends every cent on the car of his dreams." I could almost hear Finn smile.

"Aye. Couldn't quite stretch to a Bentley, but I found this girl here, being driven to scrap by a bawface idiot. I bought her, fixed her up, and she liked me right away." Finn thumped the seat, affectionate. "During the war, most of the soldiers I knew had pictures of their lasses. Maybe their mother, if they were fresh out of school. I didn't have a lass, so I had a picture of my car."

I pictured Finn in a uniform and a helmet, looking at a snap of the Lagonda on the deck of a transport ship. The thought made me smile.

He tossed his cigarette butt and lit another, match flaring in the dark. "So you're off tomorrow?"

"Yes." I nodded. "My mother found me here. We're off for Vevey in the morning."

"Not Limoges? I thought you were ready to burn Limoges down to find your cousin."

"Limoges later. This"—I waved at the Little Problem, even though he probably couldn't see the gesture—"won't wait much longer, *Maman* says. What do I know, I'm just the girl who got in trouble."

"And Vevey is where you go for—trouble?"

"You never heard of a Swiss vacation?" I stretched my lips in a smile. "It's where girls like me go."

"Thought they went down the aisle in a white dress."

"Only if they've got a boy on the hook."

He had that grim Scottish amusement in his voice. "Unless you're the Holy Virgin, you've got a lad on the hook."

I gave a harsh little laugh. "Finn, I've got half a fraternity on the hook. And I can't marry all of them."

I wondered if he'd exhale disapproval. If he'd pull away. But he just sat on the other end of the soft upholstered seat, looking at me through the dark. "What happened?"

If it had been broad daylight, I couldn't have said it. It was all so cheap and commonplace, so *stupid*. But the enveloping shadows were kind, and I turned my head so he'd only be able to see my profile and the glowing tip of my cigarette. My voice came out flat and matter-of-fact.

"If you're a girl, you're divided up into three neat parts." The fractions of dating, as I thought of it, and even the dumbest girls in my sorority knew exactly how to add those fractions up. "There are the parts boys can touch," I went on, "the parts boys can touch if you're engaged or at least pinned, and the parts they can't touch till you're married. Everybody knows the map. But boys try anyway, because that's what boys do, because we say no. Boys try, girls deny. That's the dance."

I stopped, tapping my cigarette out the window. The air smelled cooler—summer rain on the way, I thought. Finn sat silent.

"My brother was one of those soldiers who didn't adjust too well to being home. And by that I mean he ate a shotgun." *Brains and blood splattered everywhere,* a neighbor had said incautiously, not realizing I was in earshot to hear the gory details my parents had kept from me. I'd run inside and vomited, not able to shake that terrible image from my eyes. "My parents were . . . I came home from Bennington early that semester, so I could take care of them." Bringing my mother flowers, tying my father's tie for him, making burned meat loaf when it was clear no one else could manage Sunday lunch. Trying anything at all that would help fix how terribly broken they'd become.

"After the winter holidays, I finally had to go back to school, and when I didn't have anyone to take care of anymore, I just—stopped, like a broken clock. I couldn't feel anything. I was *dead* inside. I couldn't even get out of bed in the morning. I'd just lie there thinking about James and Rose and my parents, and then back to James again. Crying and crying."

It was around then that I'd started seeing Rose everywhere. Little girls with bouncing braids turned into the young Rose, tall sorority girls sauntering off to class turned into the older Rose—I saw her everywhere, superimposed on the faces of complete strangers. I imagined her so often I started thinking that I was going crazy . . . Or that maybe, just maybe, she wasn't dead.

"I lost my brother," I said hoarsely. "I *failed* him. If I'd just been able to help when he was falling to pieces, maybe he wouldn't have died like that. I wasn't going to lose my cousin too, if there was any chance she was alive. I was already blowing off all my classes—I couldn't drag myself out of bed for algebra, but I could do it for Rose. I wrote letters, telephoned people, talked to refugee bureaus. I'd worked so many summers in my father's law office, I knew what kind of overseas calls to make, what kinds of papers to ask for. What there was to find, I found." That bored English clerk, telling me that the last report on Rose Fournier had been handled by one Evelyn Gardiner, currently residing at 10 Hampson Street. Digging up the original tip about Le Lethe.

Finn was silent. My cigarette was almost done. I drew a last long drag, and flicked the glowing end out the window. "You'd think someone would have contacted my parents about my skipping so much class, but no one cared. Everyone knows girls like me aren't in college to make the dean's list, we're there to hang around Ivy League boys and find a husband. I didn't date much—mostly I was the go-to double date if someone's boyfriend had a roommate they couldn't ditch—but around this time, I got set up on a blind date. Carl, I think his name was. Dinner and a drive-through movie. He's got his hand under my sweater the minute the show starts. I know how this goes: we kiss awhile, and then I push him back when he goes too far. Only this time around, I just couldn't see the point. I was too numb to go through the whole song and dance. I wondered what it would be like if I just—went along. I didn't like Carl all that much, but I thought maybe he'd make me . . . feel something." Something that wasn't guilt or pain, anyway. It hadn't worked out that way; it had just been more numbed, empty nothing. "Carl kept giving me startled looks afterward. He couldn't believe I didn't stop him. Good girls didn't do that, and I was a *good girl*."

Nothing from Finn. I wondered if I disgusted him.

"He asked me out the next week. I said yes. It hadn't been anything special the first time, but everyone knows the first time is terrible. I hoped maybe it would get better." Still just more nothing. "He probably talked to the other boys in his fraternity, because I started getting dates all of a sudden. I went ahead and screwed them too. It didn't feel like much, but I still did it because—" I stopped, swallowed down a bone-deep lash of shame, and made myself go on. "Because I was *lonely*." Breathe. Breathe. "I was—I was tired of being numb and alone, and rolling around in a backseat with Tom or Dick or Harry was better than staying in my room weeping and telling myself I could have stopped my brother from killing himself." I drew another ragged breath. "After a while there got to be quite a few Toms, Dicks, and Harrys. Word got around that Charlie St. Clair was a cheap date. You didn't need to buy her a milk shake and a movie ticket. All you had to do was show up with a car."

My throat was thick with unreleased sobs. I put my palm out the window and let the night breeze waft over my fingers, still avoiding Finn's eyes.

"So there I was, spending all my time either huddled in bed, telephoning refugee bureaus, or screwing boys I didn't really like. By spring, I had to come home and tell my parents I was knocked up, ringless, and probably flunking out of Bennington. In the middle of all my mother's screaming, my father asked me who the boy was—almost the only thing he said through the whole thing. I had to tell him, 'There are six or seven possibilities, Dad.' He hasn't really talked to me since."

He'd have to, once I came home minus the Little Problem. Wouldn't he?

Finn cleared his throat softly. I waited in brittle misery for condemnation, maybe for an involuntary "Thank God I didn't touch you."

"Are you the one who wants to go to Vevey? Or is it your parents?"

I couldn't have been more surprised, so surprised I turned to face him for the first time. "Do I seem like I'm in any shape to be anybody's mother?"

"I'm not judging that. I'm just asking if all these arrangements are what you want, or what they want."

I don't know what I want. No one had really asked. I was underage; my parents had made the decisions for me and taken it for granted I'd do as I was told. With that nasty little voice in my head telling me I failed at everything, that I'd failed to help James and Rose and now myself, I hadn't even tried to figure out if I wanted something different. What did it matter what I wanted when I'd just fail if I tried to get it? I wanted Rose back, I wanted my future back, I wanted to save someone I loved for once instead of watching them disappear into grief or war or death, and I didn't know how to make any of those things happen.

Suddenly I was floundering, Finn's soft words lighting a flare of anger in me because they got under the brittle protective shell I'd put up. I could bounce insults off that shell all day—*tramp, whore, slut*, I'd heard them all, and I'd turn those words on myself to save anyone else the trouble. I could pretend all day that I didn't care, because *caring* left me thrashing and vulnerable. "Why are you being so nice to me, Finn? Don't you think I'm a murderer for wanting to get rid of it?"

"I'm an ex-convict," he replied quietly. "I haven't got the right to sling names at anybody."

"You're so strange," I said, close to tears, and Finn reached out to pull me against his shoulder. I turned my burning eyes into his shirt, breath hitching. Before the Little Problem I did nothing but cry—since the day I'd told my parents, I hadn't cried a drop. I couldn't start again now, or I'd never stop. Finn smelled like smoke and engine grease and a fast wind; I sat with my cheek against his chest and my shoulders heaving, and he smoked his cigarette down to the butt.

Distantly I heard bells chime the hour. Three in the morning. Finn flicked the butt out the window and I sat up, pressing at my eyes with the heel of my hand. They hadn't quite overflowed, but it had been a near thing.

He lifted his arm, and I slid across the backseat of the Lagonda toward the door. "Charlie lass," he said, and my name in his deep soft voice arrested me, made me look back over my shoulder. He was gazing at me full on, and maybe my eyes were used to the dark by now, because I could see his eyes under their straight black brows clear as day. "Do what you want," he said. "It's your life and your bairn. You might be underage, but it's still your life. Not your parents'."

"They mean well. Even when I'm furious at them, I know they mean well." Why was I talking so frankly? I hadn't talked about the Little Problem with anyone, not like this. "Finn . . ." I started to say good-bye, but we'd already said good-bye in the hotel's court. This whole late-night interlude hadn't really happened at all.

He was still waiting.

"Thank you," I said at last, my voice hoarse. And I slid out of the car and turned back toward the hotel. Finn didn't say anything at all that I could hear. I heard his voice anyway.

Do what you want.

CHAPTER 14
EVE

July 1915

The biggest secret in Lille dropped into Eve's ear like a diamond. Kommandant Hoffman and General von Heinrich had their usual table, and Eve was just gliding up to clear away the remains of the chocolate mousse when she heard it: "—private inspection at the front," the general said, sounding anxious. "The kaiser will pass through Lille in two weeks' time."

Eve continued to clear dessert plates without a flicker.

"A suitable welcome should be prepared, even if the inspection is clandestine. He must not find our attentions wanting. A small deputation to greet his train— what line will he be traveling?"

Please, Eve begged silently. *The train and the date!*

The general listed both, peering fussily at a notebook to check that he had it all correct. So German, this attention to tiny details, and Eve thanked God for

it. She withdrew before it looked like she was dawdling, feet barely touching the ground. She knew when
the kaiser—the *kaiser*!—was coming to the front. Lili
would whoop like a banshee. "*Parbleu,* little daisy, well
done! We will bomb that shit-brained bastard into bits,
and this war will be finished!"

"What are you smiling at?" the other waitress whispered. A dim-witted corn blonde named Christine
who had long since replaced the heavy-footed Amélie.
"What have we got to smile about?"

"Nothing." Eve took her place against the wall, wiping her face of emotion, but her heart was leaping like
love at first sight. This war could be over. The trenches
filled with dying men and gluelike mud; the starvation
and the humiliation of poor abused Lille; the drone of
aeroplanes and the muffled explosion of artillery over
the horizon—all ended. Eve imagined yanking down
the German street sign nailed up over the French one on
her block, and stamping it to bits as victory bells pealed.

The clock had never moved so slowly. "Can you take
up the books to Monsieur René?" Eve pleaded with
Christine as they finished their final sweep-up. "I need
to g-get home."

Christine shivered. "He scares me."

"Just look at the f-floor and say yes and no until
you're d-dismissed."

"I can't. He *scares* me!"

Eve wanted to roll her eyes. Why on earth did it matter if something scared you, when it simply had to be
done anyway? Why were so many women such timid
ninnies? She thought of Lili's lion-hearted swagger, Violette's dour and ferocious endurance. Now those were
women.

She put the ledger off on the headwaiter and was

out the door. Past midnight, the moon very high and nearly full—a bad night for sneaking across borders. Lili would be back through Lille soon . . .

"*Fraulein!*" The bark of a German voice, German boots behind her. "It is past curfew."

"I have an exemption." Eve scrabbled in her handbag for her identity cards and the various other bits of paper. "I work at Le Lethe; the shift has j-j-just ended."

The German was young, officious, his face marked with acne. "Let's see this exemption, *Fraulein.*"

Eve cursed silently, pawing through her bag. It wasn't here—she'd had to empty everything out on the bed this morning so she could unpick the bag's lining and make a better smuggling space for her coded messages. The card with her curfew exemption must be sitting on her counterpane. "I'm sorry, I don't have it. The restaurant is just there, they can c-confirm that I—"

"Do you know the penalty for breaking curfew?" the German snapped, looking pleased to have someone to write up, but a smooth metallic voice sounded from the darkness behind Eve.

"I assure you, the girl works for me. Her papers are in order."

René Bordelon came to stand beside Eve, his silver-headed cane gleaming in the moonlight. He tipped his hat at the perfect angle of courtesy and carelessness. He must have foregone tonight's look at the ledger for a walk under the summer moon.

"Herr Bordelon—"

René smiled in polite contempt, taking Eve's arm. "You may take the matter to Kommandant Hoffman if you wish. Good night."

He moved Eve along, and the breath that had stuck in her throat let out. "T-thank you, *monsieur.*"

"Not at all. I have no objection to serving Germans when they are civilized, but I enjoy putting the rude ones in their place."

Eve tugged her arm from his hand. "I would not d-dream of delaying you further, s-sir."

"Not at all." He took hold of her elbow again. "You are without papers; I will see you to your door."

He was acting the gentleman. But he wasn't one, so what did he want? It had been two nights since their last conversation which had so unnerved Eve; her pulse thrummed, but as much as she wished to avoid her employer, she knew she couldn't refuse. She fell into step beside him, preparing to ratchet up her stammer. If he wanted to probe her further, this was going to be the slowest conversation in history.

"You've had stars in your eyes all evening," he observed. "Can you be in love, Mademoiselle Le François?"

"No, *m-m-m-monsieur*. I have no t-t-time for such things." *I have a kaiser to kill.*

"Still, something has put a light in your eye."

Incipient regicide. No, don't think that. "I am g-g-grateful for all I have, *monsieur*." They made the turn away from the river. Just a few more blocks—

"You are very silent," he said. "I have met few quiet women. It makes me wonder what you are thinking. That's curious to me. I don't normally care what goes on in a woman's head, because it's usually banal. Are you banal, *mademoiselle*?"

"I'm very ordinary, *m-m-m-monsieur*."

"I wonder."

Do not wonder that. She should chatter the way thoughtless, witless Christine did. Bore him with inanities. "W-why do you call it L-L-Le Lethe, *monsieur*?" Eve asked the first thing that came to mind.

"More Baudelaire," he answered. "'*Nothing can*

*match the abyss of your bed, potent oblivion lingers on
your lips, and Lethe flows in your kisses.'"*

That was a great deal more sensuality than Eve
felt comfortable introducing into this conversation.
"P-p-pretty," she murmured, speeding up her steps. Just
a block more—

"Pretty? No. But potent." His hand at her elbow held
her back from rushing, his fingers so long they entirely
circled her arm. "Lethe is the river of forgetfulness that
runs through the underworld, so the classics tell us, and
there is nothing more potent than forgetfulness. That is
what a restaurant like mine offers in a time of war—an
oasis of civilization where one may forget the horrors
outside for a few hours. There is no horror that cannot
be forgotten, *mademoiselle*, given the right drug for the
senses. Food is one. Drink is another. The pull between
a woman's thighs is a third."

He said it so casually, the vulgarity in his perfect
toneless voice, that Eve blushed scarlet. *Good*, she managed to think. *Marguerite would blush. Dear God, get
me home!*

"Are you blushing?" He tilted his head to look down
at her, the silver threads at his temples glinting in the
moonlight. "I wondered if you would. Your eyes don't
give much away. Windows to the soul? Not so much
with you. *'My girl has eyes, deep, profound, and im-
mense,'*" he quoted to Eve's growing unease. "*'Their
flames are thoughts of love mingled with faith, which
glitter in their depths—voluptuous or chaste.'*" His own
eyes were unblinking as they held hers. "I have been
wondering about that last part, Mademoiselle Le François. Voluptuous or chaste?" He touched a fingertip to
her hot cheek. "From the blush, I would say the latter."

"A lady does not d-d-discuss such things," Eve managed to say.

"Don't be bourgeois. It doesn't suit you."

Thank God, they had reached Eve's door. She stepped into the deep overhang and fumbled for her key, feeling a trickle of sweat run the length of her spine under her dress. "G-good night, *monsieur*," she said brightly, but he stepped into the shadow of the overhang with her, crowding her unhurriedly back against the door. She couldn't see his face, but she smelled expensive cologne and hair oil as he bent his head. His narrow mouth brushed lightly, not over her lips but over the hollow at the base of her throat. His tongue was cool as he tasted her skin.

She stood pinned against the door by that feather-fine touch, too stunned to move.

"I wondered how you'd taste," he said at length, stepping back. "Cheap soap, sweetness beneath. Lily-of-the-valley soap would suit better. Something light, sweet, fragrant, young."

There was nothing in Eve's training at Folkestone, her reams of advice from Lili, or her previous lives in London *or* Nancy that suggested any kind of response. So she said nothing, standing still as an animal caught in bright light. *He will leave. He will leave, and you can sit on the bed and compile your report for Lili. The kaiser is coming to Lille.* But the glory of that golden information had left her for the moment. She didn't dare even bring it fully into her mind with René Bordelon's razor-sharp eyes so close to hers.

He hooked his silver-headed cane over his arm, tipping his hat to her. A perfect gentleman's farewell. "I would like to have you," he said conversationally. "An odd choice for me; I don't normally like raw virgins or cheap soap, but you have a certain ungroomed elegance. Consider it."

Oh, sweet God, Eve thought. And didn't move until

he replaced his hat and began his elegant saunter back down the street.

One of her neighbors must have been awake, because a window creaked open two houses down. Eve had a moment to be glad of the deep overhang—no one could have seen her getting her throat licked by a man who was known to take brandy with the *Kommandant*. Bile rose in Eve's throat, and she reached up to scrub at the moistened hollow in her collarbone.

Safely hidden by darkness, Eve's neighbor called down at René Bordelon's retreating figure. "*Collaborator*!" the hiss came, and spittle landed in the street.

He turned and raised his hat to his unseen assailant. "*Bonsoir*," he said with a small bow, and his soft chuckle sounded through the night.

*P*arbleu, little daisy, well done!" Lili grinned at Eve's report. "Two more weeks and a lucky air raid, and this war could be done!"

Eve smiled, but her triumph tonight was muted. "The kaiser's councilors, his industrialists, anyone profiting from the fight would press to continue." A machine like a war was a vast thing, not easily stopped once set in motion; Eve knew that.

"If the bastard's dead, that's the beginning of the end. I'll be off in the morning as soon as curfew lifts." Lili stowed the message in the lining of her sewing bag— she was Marie the seamstress tonight, with Marie's papers, props, and mannerisms—and began unhooking her buttoned boots. "I'm not passing this one off to a courier. I'll take it to Folkestone myself. Perhaps buy a morally questionable hat while I'm in a country where I can wear it. Though one has to wonder if you English can do morally questionable anything, even hats . . ."

"You can g-get to England?" That surprised Eve. She

already couldn't believe how fast and how effortlessly Lili passed from German-held France to Belgium and back. The distance might be small but the territory bristled with danger, yet Lili seemed to ghost right through the danger. Could she even ghost across the Channel now?

"*Bien sûr.*" Lili's voice was muffled as she changed with brisk efficiency beneath the cover of a voluminous old nightdress. "I've been three, four times this year."

Eve fought down a sudden surge of homesickness for Folkestone, its sandy English beaches and boarded English piers and Captain Cameron's English tweeds and warm eyes. Eyes that actually blinked on occasion, and didn't make her skin crawl like sharp French eyes . . . Eve gave a shake of her head, dismissing the stab of jealousy that Lili had seen Cameron more recently than she. "If you're traveling to England tomorrow, you take the bed." They had an established routine now when Lili needed to rest in Lille: she was Eve's friend, a sewing maid come to visit, staying overnight rather than violating curfew. They'd run this act past two German inspections, and seeing Lili melt into Marie who was even dimmer than the corn-blond Christine was truly fascinating.

"I won't argue." Lili dropped the folded pile of her shirtwaist and skirt and flopped down, telling some story of how she crossed over into Lille this morning. "I had a report from a source in Lens tucked into the pages of a magazine—would you believe I dropped it coming off the train?" A decidedly wicked laugh as she shook her fair hair down. "A German soldier retrieved it for me, bless him."

Eve smiled, making herself a pallet of blankets next to the narrow bed, but the smile was an effort. She hadn't been smiling very much since last night, and Lili, in the middle of another story, seemed to notice.

"All right, what's wrong with you?"

Eve looked at the leader of the Alice Network. In her old nightdress, Lili appeared far younger than her thirty-five years, her blond hair bushy and wild like that of a little girl who had been playing rough all day. But her eyes were old and knowing, and the sharp edges of her cheekbones pressed against her paper-thin skin. *Don't burden her*, Eve thought with a pang that hit straight under the breastbone. She suddenly understood Violette's grim protectiveness, because now Eve felt it too. Lili carried so much, and she made the burden look light—but it was wearing her thin as a blade.

"*Merde*," Lili said in exasperation. "Out with it!"

"It's not important—"

"Let me be the judge of that. You're no good to me if you crack up."

Eve sank down on her makeshift pallet below the edge of the bed, staring at her folded hands. "René B-Bordelon wishes to seduce me." The words fell like weights.

Lili tilted her head. "Are you certain? You don't strike me as an accomplished player in the game of seduction, if you'll pardon me for saying so."

"He licked my n-neck. Then he said he wanted to *have* me. Yes, I'm certain."

"*Quelle bête*," Lili said softly. Taking out her little silver case of cigarettes, she lit two. "Normally one discusses bad men over a stiff drink, but a smoke will have to do. Take it! Clears the mind and kills a hungry stomach."

Eve imitated Lili's two-fingered hold, then hesitated, quoting her mother. "Tobacco is a g-gentleman's vice, not a lady's."

"*Tais-toi.* We're soldiers in skirts, not ladies, and we need a damned smoke."

Eve set the cigarette to her lips, inhaling. She coughed, but she liked the taste at once. Bitter, and she'd tasted bitterness in her mouth since the moment last night when René stepped close.

"So," Lili continued, matter-of-fact. "Bordelon wants you. The question is what happens when he presses the issue. How much trouble will he make for you, if you refuse? Would he report you to the Germans?"

She was seeking Eve's professional estimation, clearly. Eve paused, taking another sip of smoke and coughing less. Her stomach rolled sickly, but more from the thought of René than the cigarette. "He wouldn't b-bother the Germans with a personal grudge; he saves his favors till he n-needs them. But he'd likely fire me. He's not used to b-being refused anything."

"We could find you a new post," Lili said, but Eve shook her head.

"Is there another place like Le Lethe? Where I could g-get good information twice a week? Where I learn the k-k-k"—striking her own knee with her fist until the word came free—"k-kaiser is coming, and on what t-train? No." Eve dragged a swallow of smoke all the way down into her lungs this time, coughing so hard tears came to her eyes. "You n-n-n-need someone in Le Lethe."

"Yes," Lili acknowledged. "Would he fire you for refusing him?"

"I have to assume he would."

"Then there is one option." Lili looked up at the ceiling, blowing a smoke ring. "Will you sleep with René Bordelon?"

Eve stared at the glowing end of her cigarette. "If I have to."

It was almost a relief to get the words out. She'd been circling them since last night, inspecting them from every angle. The idea made her sick and scared, but so what? Why did it matter if something scared you, when it simply had to be done anyway?

"A man of his age who chooses a girl he thinks is seventeen will assume he is getting a virgin." Lili sounded matter-of-fact. "Are you?"

Eve couldn't be quite so nonchalant no matter how much she wanted to be, so she just nodded, keeping her eyes on the floor.

"*Putain de merde,*" Lili swore, stubbing out her cigarette. "If you are really going to do this thing, you must please him in bed so you can continue to get more out of him. Otherwise you are buying a temporary reprieve from dismissal for a very high price."

Eve had no idea what it meant to please a man in bed—frankly, her imagination stopped the moment she imagined René Bordelon unbuttoning his perfectly tailored shirt. She felt herself blanch, and Lili noticed.

"Are you really going to do this?"

Eve nodded again. "I'll m-m-m—" The word wouldn't come out at all, even when she pounded the floor. She let it go in a hiss, and then said, "*Shit,*" loudly. The first time Eve had ever sworn in her life, and it released the tight knots in her throat.

Lili's turn to nod. "Have another cigarette, and let's talk practicalities. A man who takes a virgin for a mistress will either wish to train her to his standards, or wish her to remain passive and innocent as he does the work. You will have to pay close attention and follow his lead. But there are things one can do that will please any man . . ." She detailed a few of them, gentle but specific, and Eve took in as much as she could, cheeks burning. *Will I have to do that? And* that*?*

To keep her job at Le Lethe, yes. She would do all of it.

Seeing Eve's queasiness, Lili patted her hand. "Just notice what pleases him, and keep doing it. That's really what it's all about. Now, do you have any idea how to prevent yourself from becoming *enceinte*?"

"Yes." Eve had a sharp memory, at twelve years old, of coming on her mother in the washroom late at night rinsing herself out between the legs. There had been a tube, a rubber bag. *I don't want any more of that bastard's babies,* she'd snarled, jerking her chin toward the bedroom where Eve's father snored. Eve remained an only child; her mother's washing must have worked.

"Nothing works perfectly," Lili said as though reading Eve's mind. "So be careful. No one wants a pregnant spy. That *will* land you home in England, and quickly, given that no one in Lille will treat you well for becoming pregnant by a collaborator."

So many grim thoughts. Eve pushed them away for a practical question of her own. "Have you ever had to—do this?"

"There's been a German sentry or two who wanted to see me on my knees before I got a pass through the checkpoint."

Eve wouldn't have been sure what that meant ten minutes ago. Now, thanks to Lili's blunt tutorial, she had a much better idea. She looked at Lili, unable to imagine her kneeling down, reaching for a man's buttons, and . . . "How—was it?"

"Salty," Lili said, and smiled at Eve's blank look. "Never mind, *chérie*." Her smile faded, and they regarded each other with grim faces.

Eve tipped her head back toward the ceiling, drawing another deep lungful of smoke. She decided she liked smoking. If she ended up with another tight-mouthed landlady with boardinghouse rules about cigarettes, well, she could go to hell. "Lili, why don't they tell us it could b-be like this? All that training in Folkestone; there's n-n-n-not a hint we'd face anything like this."

"Because they don't know. And if you're clever, you won't tell them." Lili looked very serious. "Do what you must, but don't tell Captain Cameron or Major Allenton or any of the others we report to."

The thought of telling Captain Cameron she went to a collaborator's bed to get information made Eve cringe. "I wouldn't tell *any* of them!"

"Good. Because they won't trust you if they find out."

Of all the things discussed tonight, that was the one to leave Eve astonished. "W-why not?"

"Men are strange creatures." The twist on Lili's smile wasn't amusement. "If a woman surrenders her virtue to an enemy, they are confident her patriotism can't be far behind. They have very little faith in any woman's ability to resist falling in love with a man who beds her. Besides, a *horizontale* isn't respectable, and a spy's business is already disreputable enough. We can't bring shame on our country by staining our reputations—if we're to engage in espionage, we must do it as *ladies*."

"Rubbish," Eve said flatly, and Lili smiled.

"Oh, it is, little daisy. It is. But do you want to be yanked out of Lille because they believe your soft little head has been all muddled by a handsome collaborator?"

Eve tapped ash off her cigarette, stomach rolling all over again. "Would Captain Cameron really think that of me?"

"Maybe not. He's a *decent chap,* as you English like to say. But I've heard other English officers say such things before about women like us."

"Shit," Eve said again. The swearing, like the smoking, was getting easier. She looked up at Lili, who gazed down with a smile Eve couldn't interpret. Practicality, sorrow, pride?

"*C'est ainsi*," she said rather sadly. "What a bitch this business is, no?"

Yes, Eve acknowledged. But she also loved this business; it made her feel alive like nothing else, so she cloaked fear in a defiant shrug. "Someone has to do it. We're good at it. Why s-shouldn't it be us?"

Lili leaned down and kissed Eve's forehead. Eve leaned her head against Lili's knee, and the head of the Alice Network passed a hand over her hair. "Don't go rushing off to climb into that profiteer's bed," she said softly. "I know you—you're thinking to grit your teeth and get it over with. But put him off for a bit if you can. Because if we can bomb the kaiser into dust in a fortnight's time, then it's a whole new world. You might make it home without having to see Bordelon naked, after all."

Eve prayed for both those things as Lili continued to stroke her hair the way Eve's mother never had. She prayed harder than she'd ever prayed in her life—because right now she could be brave, but if she closed her eyes and remembered René's mouth tasting her flesh, all she felt was sick.

CHAPTER 15
CHARLIE

May 1947

My mother was being careful, as if I was a cat with fur raised all along its back, ready to flee if startled. She kept reaching out to touch my hand or my shoulder, as if to check that I was still within arm's reach. She kept up a light flow of chatter in the morning as we nibbled on the dry toast and coffee she'd ordered to the room, and proceeded packing up my clothes. "We'll get some new things for you in Paris, after the Appointment. This pink suit is never going to be the same . . ."

I munched my toast, irritable. I didn't like being chatty first thing in the morning, especially on next to no sleep, and I'd gotten out of the habit of having to make breakfast small talk. Eve was always too hungover to do anything more than glare until the clock hit noon, and Finn was a clam at any hour of the day. Except, apparently, at three in the morning. *Charlie lass . . .*

"Don't slouch, *ma chère*," my mother said.

I straightened. She smiled distractedly, reapplying her lipstick. Yesterday with her tear-filled eyes and her impulsive hugs she'd seemed softer than the mother I was used to. This morning, anchored by relief, she seemed to be armoring back up with every layer of lipstick into her usual glossy-shelled self. I reached out, touching her hand as she tucked her compact away. "Can we stay longer? Order more breakfast?" The Little Problem was for once making me ravenous instead of nauseated. Forget dry toast, I wanted Finn's one-pan breakfast: bacon and bread and eggs all runny. Bacon . . .

"Don't we want to watch our figures?" *Maman* patted her own waist, making a wry smile. "One must suffer to be beautiful, after all."

"I'm not going to be beautiful any way you slice it," I said. "So I want a goddamn croissant."

She looked genuinely shocked. "Where did you learn that kind of language?"

From a crazy English hag who tried to shoot me. Oddly, I missed Eve.

"We'll get croissants on the train," *Maman* said, closing her suitcase. "We don't want to be late."

She already had a bellhop at the door. I ate the last bite of my toast, rising, and my mother flicked a crumb from the corner of my mouth and straightened my collar. Why did I feel like such a child in her presence?

You are a child, the nasty voice in my head whispered. *That's why you're not fit to have a child. You don't know anything.*

Says who? the Little Problem answered.

Stop talking to me, I told my stomach. *Stop making me feel guilty. I can't do anything for you. I'm not fit to have you. Everyone says so.*

What do you *think?* the L.P. answered. I didn't have an answer, just a massive lump in my throat.

"Charlotte?"

"Coming." I followed her out into the hall, toward the elevators. "Should we telephone Dad before we catch the train?" I managed to say.

My mother shrugged.

"Isn't he worried?" I wondered if he would even *talk* to me when I came back. What if I had my Appointment and he still hated me? Still thought I was a whore? The lump in my throat doubled in size.

"If you must know, I didn't tell him you'd taken off into London like a wild thing." She caught my look. "Why would I? I didn't want to worry him."

"Well, you told him *now*, didn't you?" We stepped into the elevator. "We're days behind schedule. We won't be home when he's expecting us."

My mother waited for the bellhop to join us with our bags, and pressed the button. "We'll simply spend a week less than I planned in Paris afterward. We'll be home on time, and your father doesn't have to worry about anything."

"Go home *early*? You promised me that after Vevey, we'd talk about Rose. About going to Limoges—"

"We'll talk about that when we get home." She smiled as the elevator began to move downward. "When the time is right."

I stared at her. "When the time is right? It's right now. We're already *here*."

"*Ma chère*—" A glance toward the bellhop, listening to our English babble with uncomprehending curiosity.

I ignored him. "We can't just go home, not after *everything* I've found out."

"It's not for *us* to do, Charlotte. It's a job for your father."

"Why? I've been doing a pretty good job on my own, better than—"

"It's not suitable," my mother snapped. "You need to go home, not go off on another wild goose chase. Your father will take things up. I *will* ask him, later. When we get home."

Later. Always later. Rage pooled in my stomach. "You promised."

"I know, but—"

"*Maman,* this is *important* to me." I touched her arm, trying to make her see. "Not to give up until—"

"I'm not giving up, *chérie.*"

"That's what it looks like. How urgent is this going to be to you when we're on the other side of the Atlantic again?" My voice rose. "When it's not an easy promise you can make and then break, just to get me moving?"

The elevator chimed, doors sliding open. *Maman* glared at the curious bellhop, and he picked up our luggage and scuttled toward the hotel desk.

"Well?" I challenged.

"This is not a suitable place for such a discussion. Come along, and no more fuss, please." Gliding out into the busy hotel court.

"*Fuss?* Is that what this is about?" I stamped after her.

She turned, giving me a tight smile. "Please, Charlotte? You're already in so much trouble with your father. I will be too, if there are any more delays about this, so *please* just stop misbehaving and come along."

I stared at her. I just stared. My beautiful self-assured mother, gnawing at her perfectly painted lips, worried she might get in trouble with my father. She hadn't dared tell him I'd bolted off to France. She hadn't dared tell him we'd be so much as a week late. She'd say anything to get me on that train to Vevey, like a little girl lying her way out of a spanking. If she didn't deliver me home on time and with a flat belly, she was going to be *in trouble*.

Maman had always made me feel like a child. I looked at her now, and I felt like the adult.

"You're not going to look for Rose, are you." It wasn't a question.

"Because Rose is dead!" she snapped at last. "You *know* that, Charlotte!"

"Possibly. Maybe even probably." I tried to be fair, even in my anger. "But that isn't good enough for me, and you promised I could run it to the end. For peace of mind, if nothing else." A pause. "If Dad won't pick the search up again, can you honestly tell me you'll push him for me?"

She exhaled sharply. "I'm going to pay for our rooms. Try to compose yourself."

Off she marched in angry little steps, heels clicking. I stood with the luggage, feeling strange and brittle as glass, and when I looked across the hotel court I saw Rose. Not really, of course—it was just a sullen pimple-pocked girl leaning against the broad window waiting for her parents to finish checking in—but the French sunlight made a halo out of her blond head, shadowing her face, and for a moment I let myself believe it *was* Rose. Rose looking right at me, shaking her head a little.

You're not a child, Charlie, I imagined her saying. *Or a coward.*

She'd always been brave. Even when she was afraid of being alone, of being abandoned, like that day in the Provençal café, she was still brave. She must have been terrified when she found out she was in the fix I was in now, and yet she hadn't given in when her parents tried to "arrange things" for her. She'd had her baby and then gone off to support it alone, much as that must have scared her.

Finn's voice echoed from last night. *What do you want?*

To be brave, I thought.

Do you know what that is? asked the Little Problem. *Break it down like an equation. Solve for X. X = brave.*

I watched my mother close her pocketbook and move back toward me. I felt ill. I knew absolutely nothing about babies. They were little and helpless, greedy and breakable, and they terrified me. This one terrified me. I wasn't ready for it. Not one bit.

I took a deep breath as my mother joined me. "I'm not going to Vevey."

"What?" Her plucked brows arched. Over her shoulder, the pimply girl I'd momentarily turned into Rose went trailing off after her parents, shattering the illusion.

"I'm not going to the Appointment," I said.

"Charlotte, we are done arguing about this. *Done.* You agreed to go—"

"No." I heard my words as though they were coming out of someone else's mouth. "I'm not getting rid of it. I'm keeping it."

You'd think a decision that momentous would come with some sense of relief or catharsis. Not one bit. I felt so sick and so scared. But I was also hungry. Starving, in fact. And I told the Little Problem, rather experimentally, *I'm going to feed you up.*

It seemed to like that idea. *Bacon*, it said.

I should probably come up with a name for it other than the L.P.

"Charlotte, we both know this is the only option, so—"

"It's not the only option." I had never interrupted my

mother, but I interrupted her now. "It's the option that makes the least amount of trouble for *you*. I get taken care of, and that means Dad doesn't have to tell his partners anything embarrassing, and you don't have to tell your bridge club. I know you mean well, but this is *not* the only option. I don't have to take it."

Her face tightened with fury, and her voice sank at last to a venomous whisper. "And how are you going to live, you ungrateful little tramp? No respectable man will ever marry a girl with a bastard. How do you think you're going to manage?"

"I have money, *Maman*. Money I have *earned*, not just my trust fund. I can work. I can take care of myself. I am not helpless." I repeated it stubbornly because it was true, dammit, no matter how much the murmur of *failure failure failure* sounded in my head. I could balance a checkbook better than my mother and I could mount a search for Rose better than my father, and maybe I'd failed James but that didn't mean I'd fail at everything. "I am not. Helpless."

"Yes, you are! How do you think you are going to take care of a baby?"

"I guess I'll have to learn." There was a vast mountain of things piling up that I was going to have to learn, but just because that was terrifying didn't mean I wasn't up to it. "I don't know much about babies, but I've got six months to figure it out. And I know one other thing. I know that right here, right now, I'm going to keep looking for Rose."

I picked up my traveling case. *Maman*'s hand flashed out, seizing my wrist. "If you walk away now, don't even think about coming home."

That hit me like a kick. But I set my chin at her, and said, "You never noticed when I *was* home. I don't think this will make much of a difference."

I tugged against her grip, but her fingers tightened. "You are not going anywhere, Charlotte St. Clair, except to the train station. You are underage, and I can *make* you—" She was shouting. My very proper mother, so concerned with what people would think, shouting like a fishwife. All over the hotel court, people stared. I shouted right back.

"You just threw me out, *Maman*. I'm not going *anywhere* with you." I gave a yank, but she held fast.

"Do not take that tone with me!"

A soft, angry voice sounded behind me. The soft, angry voice of a Scotsman. "Is there trouble here, miss?"

"None at all, Finn." I yanked my arm again and this time got loose. I looked up at him. He had Eve's satchel over one shoulder and the convertible's keys in his hand—he and Eve must be checking out. "Is there room in the Lagonda for me?"

He grinned and picked up my traveling case.

My mother stared at him, taking in his rumpled shirt and rolled-up sleeves, the dark stubble of his jaw. "Who—" she began, but that was when Eve came stamping up.

"Christ, Finn," she said in her raspy pre-noon snarl. "I see you found the Yank."

"She comes or you don't," Finn said.

"You work for me!"

"It's my car."

Something warm vibrated in my stomach. I'd had some thought of going to Limoges by train, but the idea of being able to hop back into that wonderful car—! I loved that car. It comforted me more than the home I'd just been thrown out of. I looked up at Finn and my throat was thick as I said, "Thank you."

"Didn't believe we'd seen the last of you in any event." Eve, surprisingly, sounded more approving than irritated. "Americans are harder to scrape off than barnacles."

"Who is *this*?" My mother managed to get the entire question out this time.

Eve looked at her. What a pair they made: my fashionable wasp-waisted mother in her exquisite hat and spotless gloves; tattered Eve with her old dress and lobster-claw hands. Eve gave that imperious raptor gaze down her nose until *Maman*'s eyes flickered. "You must be the mother," she said at last. "I don't see any resemblance."

"How dare you—"

"Eve," I plunged in. "I'm going to look for my cousin, and somewhere in that whole mess is a man you're afraid of. I think you should find out if he's alive or dead. I think you should come with me."

I don't know why I said it. Eve and her moods and her pistol complicated everything; I'd move faster without her. But I'd made myself be brave today, no matter how much it terrified me, and I wanted Eve to be brave too—to be the unflinching, swearing woman who'd lied her head off to a pawnbroker so I could hock my pearls, and demanded answers from a china-shop clerk who hated her guts. I didn't want Eve running back to England to hide in number 10 Hampson Street. It seemed beneath her, somehow.

I wanted something for myself too. I wanted to know what had happened to Eve during the occupation of Lille, not just to her hands but to her soul.

I tried to think of an eloquent way to say all that, but I couldn't think of one. All I could say was, "I want to hear the rest of your story."

"It's not a pretty story," she said. "And it lacks an ending."

"So write the ending now." I planted hands on hips,

challenging. "You're half-cocked, but you're no coward. So what do you say? In or out?"

"Who are these people? *Charlotte!*"

I took no notice of my mother. She'd gone from directing my life to being utterly outside it. But Eve spared her a glance.

"I'm not coming if Mumsy is. I've spent all of thirty seconds in her company, and she is twice as bloody annoying as you. A day on the road and I'd probably shoot her."

"She's not coming." I looked at my mother, and a last stab of tangled anger and love rippled through me, the final dying urge to do whatever she wanted. Then it was gone. "Good-bye." I probably should have said something more. But what was there to say?

Her eyes were traveling wildly from Finn to Eve and back again. "You can't just drive off with—with—"

"Finn Kilgore," Finn spoke up unexpectedly. He reached out a hand, and automatically my mother shook it. "Lately of His Majesty's prison in Pentonville."

She dropped his hand like it had grown thorns, lips parting.

"And before you ask," Finn added in polite tones, "assault. Chucking annoying Americans in the Thames. Good day, ma'am."

He shouldered my luggage and headed for the doors. Eve lit a cigarette, turning to follow, and looked over one shoulder. "You want to hear this story of mine or not, Yank?"

One last look at my mother. She just stared at me as if she didn't know me. "I love you," I said, then walked out of the hotel onto the busy streets of Roubaix. I was light-headed. Sick. Elated. Overwhelmed. My palms were sweating, and my whole mind was a whirling roar of noise. But one thing was very clear.

"Breakfast," I said when Finn brought the Lagonda around with the top down. I gave the old girl's dashboard a pat as I climbed in. "We're aiming for Limoges, but first we get the biggest breakfast we can find in Roubaix. This baby is telling me she wants to be fed."

"It's a she?" Eve asked.

"So she tells me."

What a lot of things I was learning today. And so many still to go.

CHAPTER 16
EVE

July 1915

n ten days, the kaiser would be dead. That was what
Eve told herself.

"Hurry up!" Lili urged, quickening her pace up the
hill. Eve's hair was sticking to her neck, but Lili seemed
impervious to the summer heat, striding with her skirts
kilted up, hat slung back. "Slow-coach!"

Eve hitched the bundled blanket under her arm as she
lengthened her stride. Lili knew the countryside around
Lille like the back of her hand. "*Mon Dieu*, but it's nice
to be tramping these hills in daylight for once, and not
in the dark of the damned moon with bedraggled pilots
in tow! There, one more hill—"

She broke into an outright sprint, straight up the slope.
Eve glared, bathed in sweat and realizing how the past
six weeks of scant food had cut into her stamina, but her
spirits rose as she came out onto the brow of the hill.

The day was cloudless, the grassy slope green-gold in the sunlight. They were only a few miles outside Lille, but it was like slipping out from under a dark cloud to get away from the German signs and the German soldiers. Not that things were all roses in the countryside. Each of these small farms Eve and Lili passed had their share of hunger and hopelessness as well, pigs and butter and eggs confiscated by requisition parties. But up on this low hill, it was possible for a moment to pretend the hovering invaders were gone.

And perhaps soon they *would* be gone. If the RFC did its job.

The two women stood on the brow of the hill with identically folded arms, staring down at the train tracks stretching toward Germany. Ten days until the kaiser rattled down those tracks. Ten days, and the world could be a different place.

"There," Lili nodded down to the tracks. "I've been scouting the area, and so have Violette and Antoine." Antoine was a deceptively meek-faced local bookseller who forged identification cards and passes under the table for Lili, besides Violette the only other member of the Alice Network Eve had met—a necessary introduction, in case she ever needed new papers in an emergency. "We all agree this stretch is the best spot for the strike." Lili lifted her skirt and began unlacing her top petticoat. "God knows if the brass will take the suggestion."

"Spread a b-blanket," Eve reminded her. "We're on a picnic, remember?" Their cover story, if any German scouts found them here: Marguerite Le François and her seamstress friend, taking their meager sandwiches out to enjoy the fine weather. But when Eve spread the threadbare blanket, Lili didn't bother with sandwiches. She produced a stick of charcoal and began mapping the surrounding ground in her quick notation on the spread-out petticoat. "It's getting harder to get written papers through," she said with a touch of her usual twinkle through the fierce concentration. "But those guards have no idea how much information can be written down on a woman's petticoat."

"Why am I here? Violette knows the region better, shouldn't she be helping c-compile the report?"

"She already has. But you're the one who first heard about the kaiser's visit, little daisy. You deserve to be kept in the loop." Lili's hand darted hummingbird quick, noting the ground, the irregularities, the tracks, the trees. "When I deliver my report to Uncle Edward, he's asked me to bring you."

"M-me?"

"He wants to interview you, see if there's any more detail he can possibly milk out of your recollections. For something this big, they take no chances. We'll leave in two days."

Seeing Captain Cameron in two days. The thought should have been a balm, but it just made Eve feel strange. He seemed so far away, he might as well be in a different world. And the logistics of such a visit made her stomach flip far more than the thought of his warm eyes. "I c-can't possibly travel to Folkestone. I don't dare miss any work."

"We don't have to travel all the way to Folkestone." Lili calmly finished her jotted notations. "Uncle Edward has agreed to meet us across the border in Brussels. We'll be back within a day."

"The way I t-talk—I'll be noticed too much at a checkpoint. I'll get you c-caught." If Lili got arrested because of Eve's stammering tongue, she'd cut it out with a rusty razor.

"Je m'en fous!" Lili ruffled her hair. "Let me do the

talking! I'm used to wheedling my way in and out of train stations. You just give that look of splendid wide-eyed innocence; it'll all be right as rain. How right *is* rain, anyway? What peculiar expressions you English have."

Lili was lightening the mood deliberately, Eve knew that. All the airy chatter as she stepped back into her charcoal-mapped petticoat was intentional. "You should take more care," Eve said, collecting the picnic things. "Don't take it all as such a j-joke. You'll laugh yourself right into a f-firing squad."

"Bah." Lili gave a wave of her hand, a hand so thin it was nearly transparent in the sunlight. "I know I'll be caught one day, but who cares? I shall at least have served. So let's hurry, and do great things while there is yet time."

"There isn't m-much time," Eve groaned, following Lili down the hill. "Two d-days and we're off to Brussels. How am I supposed to get away for a day?"

"See if you can make some excuse at Le Lethe." A sidelong glance as they trailed down the slope back in the direction of town. "How is your beastly suitor?"

Eve didn't want to think about René Bordelon. She'd been trying to keep out of his way since the night he walked her home; at Le Lethe she whisked away plates, poured *schnapps,* and listened. She even managed to compile a report on this German ace pilot Max Immelmann—all while trying to keep out of her employer's sight. But he let her know he was still watching her, waiting for an answer. Sometimes it was a wordless stare at her neck, where she could still feel his tongue savoring her skin. Sometimes it was the gulp of wine he offered her from a lip-printed glass at closing time. What a world it was, when a few swallows of wine from a stranger's glass could be a courtship gesture to a girl presumed half-starved and desperate. "He's persistent," Eve said at last.

Lili pushed a strand of hair behind one ear. "Have you been able to put him off?"

"For n-now."

And really, in the life she led was there anything else besides *now*? Seeing Captain Cameron in two days— the kaiser's arrival in ten—it all existed in the same gray area. There was the past and the now. Nothing else was certain. Nothing else was real.

At Le Lethe that night, the chatter seemed brighter than usual, the bustle of the officers noisier, the laughter of the women on their arms more giddy. "Whores," Christine whispered as she and Eve stood against the wall, waiting to be summoned by a lifted finger. "That's Françoise Ponceau over there, preening in a new silk dress and pressing herself up against that captain. You know the baker makes special bread for sluts like that. He pisses on the dough before he rolls it out—"

"They d-deserve it," Eve agreed, though her stomach churned. The girl had anxious eyes over her smiles, and she'd been slipping rolls into her pocketbook all night when her captain's back was turned. She was feeding someone at home, more likely several someones, and in return she got piss-soaked bread and epithets. But it was safer to agree with Christine's whispered opinion because, frankly, most of Lille shared it.

René looked up then at his waitresses, candlelight catching a glitter from his eyes. *Look at Christine,* Eve begged inside. *Pretty and blond and dense as a post; why won't you look at Christine?* But he crooked his finger at Eve, and she came forward to pour the after-dinner drinks, and René's lips curved in appreciation for her unhurried silence, the exact arc of her arm.

"Can someone else take the l-ledger up?" Eve asked

the other waiters at the end of the night, but they just
laughed.

"That's your duty now, Marguerite! He's always in
a better mood if you take it up, and we like Monsieur
René in a good mood."

They snickered, and Eve realized that René's eyes
on her hadn't gone unnoticed. "You're all p-pigs," she
snarled, and stamped up the back stairs. A curtsy, and
his fingers whispered dryly over her own as she handed
over the nightly account.

"Are you in a hurry, Mademoiselle Le François?"
Flicking through the neat lines.

"No, *monsieur.*"

He took his time, rustling pages. In the heat of the
summer night he'd discarded his jacket and sat in
his snow-white shirtsleeves, hair as sleek as his leather
shoes with brilliantine. His cuff links were unexpected
spots of color, ruby red and flakes of gold.

"Art nouveau glass," he said, observing the direction
of her gaze. Did he notice everything? "In the style of
Klimt. You have heard of Klimt? I had the good fortune
to see some of his paintings in Vienna, before the war.
Extraordinary work. There was one called *Danaë*, the
woman of myth visited by Zeus in a shower of gold . . .
Klimt shows she is aroused by the gold as it pours between her legs."

Eve had no desire to discuss any kind of arousal in
this room, artistic or otherwise. "No, I have n-not heard
of it."

"It is abandon." He unbuttoned his cuffs, dropping
the cuff links into her hand to examine. He proceeded
to turn back his sleeves, displaying lean forearms, pale
skinned and smooth, and Eve avoided the sight by holding the little molded glass objects to the light and watching the play of colors. "Gilt-edged abandon. People

thought it obscene, but what of it? They thought Baude-laire obscene too."

Eve placed the cuff links carefully beside the bust of the poet, studying the brutal marble profile and won-dering if Baudelaire's mistress had despised him as Eve despised René. "May I ask a favor, *m-monsieur*?"

"A favor? You intrigue me."

"May I miss one night's work, in two days' time? I promised a friend I would accompany her to visit her uncle, and he lives at some distance." All perfectly true. With René, Eve did her best to confine her lies to what was unspoken.

"You wish to miss work." He measured the words. "There are many who would replace you, you know, and promise not to miss any work."

"I know, *monsieur*." Eve gave him the pleading doe-eyed look. "I hoped you were p-pleased with my ser-vice, enough to . . ."

He let her hang there for a while as he set the ledger aside. "Very well," he said at last, and Eve nearly sagged with relief. "You may have your day."

"Thank you—"

He cut her off. "It is quite late. Have you remem-bered your curfew exemption, or shall I have to walk you home again?" He unknotted his tie. "Perhaps I shall walk you home anyway. I would like to further our ac-quaintance, Marguerite."

He took possession of her name, or what he thought was her name, casually discarding *mademoiselle*. And Eve didn't think, as he removed his tie altogether, that he intended to walk out anywhere this evening. Any fur-thering of acquaintance would be happening right here. *Because I asked for a favor.*

She wanted to swallow the lump in her throat, and

she let herself, so he could see her throat move. Nervousness would please him.

He dropped his tie along the leather arm of his chair. "Have you considered my offer of the other evening?"

Eve didn't pretend to misunderstand. "Your offer s-s-surprised me, *monsieur.*"

"Did it?"

"I am not the right c-companion for a man of taste. I am a waitress. I have no beauty, no p-p-proper manners, no knowledge of the world. So yes, your offer surprised me greatly."

He rose from his deep chair, unhurried, going to the little satinwood table laden with crystal decanters. He unstoppered one and poured two fingers of something pale and sparkling into a tumbler. It glittered like a diamond, and he handed it to Eve. "Try it."

She sipped, not seeing a choice. It burned her throat: fiery sweet, faintly floral, very powerful.

"Elderflower liqueur." He rested an elbow against the ebony mantelpiece. "I get it privately from a vintner in Grasse. Beautiful country, Grasse—the air smells like that liqueur, flower scented and heady. It's unique, so I don't serve it at my restaurant. Brandy, *schnapps,* champagne, those I give to the Germans. I save the unique for myself. I think you like it?"

"I do." No point in lying to René about anything she didn't have to. "Why share it with m-me, if you do n-n-not share the unique?"

"Because you too are unique. You are in possession of good taste, Marguerite—very good taste, I would guess, but utterly untutored. Like Eve in her garden of Eden."

How Eve managed not to jump at the sound of her real name, she did not know. But she managed, sipping more elderflower fire.

"I have always appreciated good taste and elegance in my companions," he continued. "Before now I have preferred a finished product to a block of raw material, but Lille does not offer much in the way of elegant women these days. Hunger and patriotism have made shrews of all the ones I know. If I wish a suitable companion, it has struck me that I will have to play Pygmalion from the Greek myth, and sculpt one for myself." He reached up with one long finger and pushed a thread of hair off her forehead. "I had not really thought I would enjoy the process. So you see, you too have managed to surprise me."

Eve couldn't think of any reply. He didn't seem to anticipate an answer, just gestured at her glass. "More?"

"Yes."

He poured another generous measure. *He is trying to make me drunk*, Eve thought. Seventeen-year-old Marguerite would not have much of a head for strong drink. A few glasses of this would make her pliant and willing.

Eve looked into her glass and saw the train tracks that would carry the kaiser toward Lille. She saw the lazy figures of the *Kommandant* and his officers, grouped around their *schnapps,* idly spilling secrets. She saw Lili's beaming face the day Eve successfully passed on her first bit of information. She even heard Lili's voice: *What a bitch this business is.*

Maybe, Eve thought now, as she replied then. *But someone has to do it. I'm good at it. Why not me?*

She drained her glass. When she lowered the tumbler, René was standing much closer. He smelled of Paris cologne, something subtle and civilized. She wondered if now was the moment he would kiss her. She thought fleetingly of Captain Cameron, looking at her on the beach as he taught her to load a pistol. She banished the thought as René bent his head.

Don't recoil.

He leaned close, inhaling along the line of her throat, and then he straightened with a faint moue. "Perhaps a bath. You may avail yourself of my facilities."

Her lips tingled, untouched, and for a moment she didn't understand. Then she looked down at her hands, her cuffs which showed tiny splashes of *beurre blanc* and red wine no matter how careful she was throughout her shift, and realized she had a faint film of dried sweat beneath her dress from this morning's brisk walk in the countryside with Lili. *I smell*, Eve thought, and it was so humiliating she wanted to weep. *I smell like sweat and cheap soap, and before I can be deflowered I must be properly cleansed.*

"There is soap." René turned away, loosening his collar in a matter-of-fact yank. "I chose it for you."

He was waiting for gratitude. "Thank you," Eve managed to say as he indicated the door behind him. The bathroom had the same obscene luxury as his study: black-and-white tiles, a vast marble tub, a gilt-framed mirror. There was a cake of unused soap laid out, lily of the valley, undoubtedly requisitioned from some woman's bathroom on a raid, and Eve remembered René saying that scent would suit her. *Light, sweet, fragrant, young.*

Every bit of advice Lili had given her about the acts which pleased men poured through Eve's mind, and for a moment she thought she was going to be sick, but she shoved it down. *Notice what pleases him,* Lili had said. Staring at the soap, Eve knew. *Light, sweet, fragrant, young.* How he wanted her to *be*, not just smell. Thoughtful of him to have provided a script.

She filled the tub, splashing hot water with vengeful wastefulness, and sank into the heat with a shiver. For more than two months, she'd had to take her baths from a washbasin with a frayed hand towel. The heat and the two glasses of elderflower liqueur were making her head swim. She could lurk in the warm scented water forever, but she had a job to do.

Better to get it over with.

Eve left her underclothes and worn dress on the floor rather than pull them back over her clean body, wrapping herself instead in snowy towels. She looked at herself in the mirror, and didn't recognize the girl she saw. Her cheekbones pressed out, a memento of the lean rations on which she now lived, but it was more than that. Soft-faced Evelyn Gardiner surely never looked so flint hard. Marguerite Le François wasn't hard at all, so Eve practiced in the mirror—parted lips, trembling lashes—until it was perfect.

"Ah." René greeted her with a smile, inspecting her from bare feet to loosened nut-brown hair. "Much better."

"Thank you," she said. "I haven't had such a b-bath in months." Gratitude. She knew it was required.

He twined his hand in her damp hair, bringing a handful to his nose. "Lovely."

He wasn't un-handsome, lean and elegant, his suit changed for a dressing gown of figured smoke blue silk. His cool hand slipped up the length of Eve's hair and wrapped around her throat, the fingers so long he could almost circle it. He kissed her then, leisurely, open-mouthed, skillful. His eyes stayed open the whole time.

"You will stay the night," he murmured, stroking the line of her hip through the towels. "I meet with Kommandant Hoffman tomorrow morning, rather early—he wishes to discuss a celebration at the restaurant for that flying ace of theirs, Max Immelmann, now that he is to be charged with Lille's sole air defense. But I don't mind going to the *Kommandant* a trifle ill rested."

There it was—the reason Eve was here. René let his guard down enough to give her that snippet of information, which would surely be of interest to the RFC. Eve filed it away, her heartbeat slowing to a calm crawl of terror and resolve.

René smiled down at her. "So," he said, taking hold of the towel wrapped around her breasts. "Show me."

Get through it, Eve thought fiercely. *Because you can use this. Oh, yes, you can.*

She let the towels drop, tilting her face up for his next kiss. What did it matter if something scared you, when it simply had to be done?

PART III

PART II

CHAPTER 17
CHARLIE

May 1947

We were halfway to Paris, and I was surprised we hadn't ended up in a ditch. It was May, and the French countryside bloomed around us, but neither Finn nor I paid any attention because Eve sat in the backseat telling us all about being a spy.

A spy. Eve. A *spy*? I was turned all the way around in my seat, gaping at her as she talked, and even Finn kept craning over his shoulder to look.

"You'll crash the bloody car," she told him tartly. "And you, Yank, will end up with a fly in your mouth."

"Keep going," I urged. All I knew about spies was from movies, and I'd never thought any of it was true, but here was Eve, and maybe she didn't fit Hollywood's idea of a spy but there was something about her raspy, matter-of-fact voice as she talked of Folkestone and ciphering and Uncle Edward that made me believe ev-

ery word. The Lagonda ate up the miles of winding
French roads, and she kept talking. A restaurant called
Le Lethe. Its elegant owner. Line after line after line
of Baudelaire. A fellow spy with round spectacles and
a code name of Violette—"The woman in the china
shop," I exclaimed, and got a withering glare.

"No putting one over on you, is there?"

I grinned, immune to her sarcasm. I was still giddy
and unbelieving that I had walked away from my mother
at that hotel, my mother and the Appointment and my
whole planned-out life. But I'd had an absolutely enormous breakfast, and on a full stomach nervousness had
changed into a sense of adventure. I was in a car with
an ex-convict and an ex-spy, barreling down on an unknown future—if that wasn't a set of mathematical variables that equaled *adventure*, I didn't know what was.

Eve talked on and off. Wartime Lille, the shortages
and requisitions. René Bordelon, that name came and
went. Her employer, but from the hatred in her voice I
knew he'd been more than that.

"René," Finn said, arm resting along the back of the
seat as he looked over his shoulder at Eve. "Do you
think he's still alive?"

She wouldn't answer that, just grunted and started
taking nips from her flask. Finn asked something about
who she worked for, if there was anyone else in her
network besides Violette, and she sat silent for a while
and then said, "One or two."

I wanted to ask more, I was *burning* to ask more,
but I met Finn's eyes and we both quieted. This was a
tentative new triumvirate being built among the three
of us—Eve wasn't here because I was paying her; she
was here out of choice, and I no longer had the right
to pry. Besides, I had even more respect for her now

that I knew something of her true history, so I put a lid on my pot full of questions. She took another sip from her flask, manipulated so clumsily in those lobster-claw hands, and my sense of adventure sobered. Whatever made her hands look like that, it had happened in the course of her war work, as much a battle wound as the limp my brother had brought home from Tarawa. He'd been awarded a Purple Heart in a box that had been sitting next to him when he blew his head off. What kind of inner hurts did Eve carry?

She was getting hazy in the afternoon sun, talking on and off. Midsentence she began to snore. "Let her doze," said Finn. "I need to stop for petrol anyway."

"How far are we from Paris?" We'd all agreed on a night's stay in Paris on the way to Limoges.

"A few hours."

"We've already been driving for hours. It's not *that* far."

Finn grinned. "I took a wrong turn listening to her describe how to decode ciphers, and we went halfway to Rheims."

n a pearly pink twilight we stopped at a drab hotel on the outskirts of the city—no boulevard grandeur on this shrinking wallet. But shrinking wallet or no, there was something I had to buy, once Eve and Finn were checking into the hotel that smelled of day-old bouillabaisse. After a short wander down the line of shops, I found a pawnshop. It took only a few minutes to find what I needed, and I was on my way back to the hotel when I passed another shop. Secondhand clothes, and I was tired of alternating the same three sets of clothing and sleeping in my slip.

A saleswoman looked up from the counter: one of

those tiny purse-lipped Frenchwomen with perfectly tailored hems, like a chic little monkey. *"Mademoiselle—"*

"It's *Madame*." I set down my pocketbook so she could see the wedding band on my left hand. "I need a few clothes."

I gave her my budget as she evaluated my size in one sweep of her eyelids, and I tried not to twist the gold ring I'd bought from the pawnshop. It was a little too big, and so was the title *Madame*. But we were two years from the end of a war, and young widows were a common sight. I might have decided to keep the Little Problem, but I had no intention of being spit on as an unwed mother. I knew how this worked: you got a wedding ring, you made up a story about a boy who died in the war (in my case, after it) and embellished it with a few convincing details. Maybe people looked skeptical but they didn't say anything because you had the right props: a secondhand wedding ring, and a dead husband.

Donald, I decided as I stepped into a cubicle to change. Donald . . . McGowan was my nonexistent dead husband. Half Scottish and half American, dark haired. Tank corps; served with Patton. The great love of my life, Donald was, dead in a recent car accident. He always drove too fast; I'd warned him and warned him. I'd name my child after him if he was a boy . . .

I imagined Rose wrinkling her nose at me. "You don't want a son named *Donald*, Charlie. Really!"

"You're right," I told her. "But I think it's a girl, anyway. So Donald will work just fine."

"He sounds boring!"

"Don't you insult my Donald!"

"Madame?" came the saleswoman, sounding dubious, and I tamped down my laughter, trying on one set of secondhand clothes after another. Under all these airy

imaginings I was laying plans, however vague. Thinking that if I found Rose, there might be a place for the two of us together. Perhaps here in France, who knew? I had money, savings—why *couldn't* we buy ourselves a new beginning, where two false *Madames* with two false wedding rings could make some kind of honest life? I thought of the Provençal café where I'd spent the happiest day of my childhood at Rose's side. Was there a haven like that for us now that we were grown?

A café, I thought, remembering how much I'd enjoyed not just that Provençal afternoon, but my brief coffee shop job at Bennington. The waiting on customers, the rush of delicious smells, the easy pleasure of juggling orders and making change in my head. A café, somewhere here in France? I imagined a place with postcards for sale and sandwiches of soft goat cheese and marbled ham, where Edith Piaf played in the evenings and the tables were pushed back for dancing. Where two young widows kept the cash till and flirted with Frenchmen, though never without mournful glances at the photographs of our husbands. I'd have to get some good fake photographs . . .

"*Bien,*" the saleswoman said as I came out, nodding approval at the narrow black trousers and the cropped striped jersey cut high at the collarbone but nearly showing my midriff. "The New Look is not for you," she instructed me brusquely, sorting through the stack of clothes that had fit me and culling it down to the narrowest skirts, the tightest sweaters, the slimmest trousers. "You dress like Dior, but you were made for Chanel. I know her—she's little and dark and plain too."

"Well, thank you." I looked around the dim shop, nettled. "And I doubt you know Chanel."

"I worked at her *atelier* before the war! If she comes back to Paris, I will work for her again, but until then,

I get by. We all get by, but not in horrible clothes." The saleswoman glared, leveling a varnished fingernail at me. "No more ruffles! When you shop, you must think *tailored, stripes, flats.* Quit torturing that hair into waves, chop it off at the chin—"

I looked at myself in the mirror. The trousers and jersey might be secondhand, but I looked rather smart. A bit boyish. And *comfortable*, no waist cinchers or crinolines. The saleswoman perched a little straw hat over my eye at a rakish angle, and I grinned. I'd never chosen my own clothes before; *Maman* always dictated what I wore. But I was a *madame* now, a grown woman, not a helpless girl, and it was time I looked like it. "How much?"

We haggled. I had limited francs to spare, but I'd seen how covetously the saleswoman eyed my traveling suit even as she turned up her nose at the New Look. "Modeled right off the Dior collection, and I've got another at my hotel. I'll drop it by tomorrow if you give me the trousers, the two skirts, the jerseys, and that black dress."

"You may only have the black dress if you promise to wear it with pearls and very red lipstick."

"I haven't got the pearls right now, but I can do the lipstick."

"Done."

I headed back to the hotel with my parcel of clothes and a swing in my hips, and I had the pleasure of seeing Finn's eyebrows go up as I joined him and Eve where they were having drinks at the hotel café. "Happy to meet you," I said, and presented my hand with its new wedding ring. "I'm Mrs. Donald McGowan."

"Bloody hell," Eve said, and took a gulp of martini that looked like straight gin.

I patted the Little Problem. "A cover identity seemed practical."

"Donald McGowan?" Finn asked. "Who is he?"

"Dark haired, lantern jawed, Yale law school, served in the tank corps." I dabbed my eyes with an imaginary black-bordered handkerchief. "The love of my life."

"Not bad to start," Eve critiqued. "Did he like his socks folded or r-rolled?"

"Um. Folded."

"No *um*. Black coffee or cream? Did he have brothers and sisters? Did he play football at university? Details, Yank." Eve pointed a stern finger. "It's the little details that sell a cover story. Make up a biography for your Donald and study it till you can reel it off with no flubs. And wear that ring all the time, till you get that little groove in your finger that long-married w-women have. People look for that groove when they see young girls wheeling baby prams and calling themselves Mrs."

I grinned. "Yes, ma'am. Shall we go get supper?"

"Yes, and I'll c-cover this one. You've been buying till now."

A small acknowledgment that she wasn't here any-more for my money—that touched me, though I knew better than to say so. "As long as you let me check the bill," I answered instead. "You'd sign your name to any set of numbers they wrote down."

"Whatever you say." She took the bill the waiter had just put down for drinks, and pushed it over to me. "You're the banker."

"I am, aren't I?" Somehow, over the course of this week, money matters had matter-of-factly become my domain, even if I was the youngest one here. Finn and Eve automatically looked to me to haggle with hotel clerks over room rates; receipts were passed promptly to my hands for proper calculation; spare coins and cash came to me to be organized since my traveling companions would otherwise let everything float loose in a mess of pocket change and pencil stubs. "Honestly, you two," I scolded as I scribbled on the bill for the drinks. "Eve up to her neck in espionage skills and you able to keep that car running on spit and baling wire, Finn, and neither of you can calculate a tip without ten minutes' figuring and a scratch pad."

"Easier if we just let you do it," Finn said. "Wee little adding machine, you are."

I grinned again, remembering the London banker who thought me too young and stupid to manage my own money. Here I was managing money for three. It made me wonder what else I could manage.

I turned my false wedding ring around my finger, imagining myself sitting behind a well-organized till, dish towel tucked into my narrow trousers, hair chopped smartly at the chin. I imagined Rose with her blond curls and chic black dress, presiding with me as French jazz played and two babies crowed—not just Little Problems but Growing Problems with fat little feet, gabbling in both French and English . . .

I imagined Mrs. Donald McGowan and Madame Étienne Fournier, both of them doing fine. Just fine.

CHAPTER 18
EVE

July 1915

ve had never seen Lili so exasperated. "*Focus*, little daisy! Your mind is a thousand miles away."

"I'll f-focus," Eve promised, but all she could think was, *I'm sore.*

Not very sore. René Bordelon had taken some care not to hurt her. Not overwhelming care—just as much as didn't interfere with his own enjoyment—but care, yes. There had been a little blood, but not a great deal of pain. *That will be all*, Eve thought when she was permitted to dress and go home. One more night working, then the morning train with Lili to Brussels and Captain Cameron, the report on the kaiser's visit to Lille. She would not have to think about René until after that.

But he kept her the next night too, after her shift was done, which had shocked her. "I know I should give you more time to heal," he said with his faint smile. "But you are very tempting. Do you mind?"

"No," Eve said, because what else could she say? So there was a second time, and she rose from bed afterward and dressed as René watched her.

"I look forward to your return," he'd said. Sitting up in bed, extraordinarily long fingers pleating the sheet about one knee.

"As d-d-d—As do I," Eve replied, keeping an eye upon the clock, ticking toward four in the morning. She was scheduled to meet Lili at Lille Station in less than four hours. "But I'm afraid I m-must go. Thank you"—never forget the gratitude—"for the day off f-f-from work, *monsieur*."

He didn't ask her to call him René, even though he'd taken full possession of *her* name. He just smiled as she shrugged into her coat. "How little you ever really *say*, Marguerite. Most women are such cackling hens. '*Silent one, I love you all the more because you run from me . . .*'"

Eve didn't have to ask the poet. *Baudelaire*, she thought. *It's always bloody Baudelaire.* And not four hours later she had gone to meet Lili, not composed and cautious and focused on the task ahead, but short of sleep and smelling like René Bordelon.

And sore.

Eve was careful not to let that show in her walk as they hurried to the train station. Lili would have to know at some point, but not now when she was focused on getting them through a border crossing. And Captain Cameron would not know at all. Eve Gardiner was *not* trading her virginity for a trip back to England away from the fight. She was going back to René's bed because even after just two nights, she already knew that he liked to talk over a pillow. There was the bit he'd let slip about the German flier Max Immelmann; there were a few more details on the kaiser's upcoming visit. Oh yes, René talked in bed, and Eve intended to listen. As for the rest . . . Well, she would get used to it, that was all.

"Not good," Lili muttered, and Eve realized she'd gone into a daze again. *Focus*, she snapped to herself, and saw what worried Lili. The station platform swarmed with German officers, German soldiers, German officials. Eve's gloved palms began to sweat.

"Has someone been taken?" she murmured inaudibly. The great fear in the Alice Network was that one of Lili's sources would be arrested, made to tell what they knew. They were all careful to know as little as possible, but—

"No," Lili murmured back, craning discreetly through the shuffle of uniforms. "It's some stuffed shirt of a general getting a grand welcome. Of all the days . . ."

They pressed their way toward the sentry checking tickets and identity cards, but the crush was fierce, and the train already there, chuffing like a horse impatient to be off, and the sentries were meticulous with so much high brass on the platform. "Let me do the talking," Lili said. She was Vivienne the cheese seller today, with a straw boater and a high-throated blouse of worn lace, and the story was prepared: she would address the guards while Eve had an armload of packages ready to juggle and drop so they were more inclined to be impatiently waved through. But eyes were lingering fiercely on anyone not in a German uniform, and the lines inched along. *We cannot miss that train,* Eve thought, gnawing her lip until Lili got to the front of the line. She was just reaching for her identity cards when a German-accented voice called out in French.

"Mademoiselle de Bettignies! Can that be you?"

Eve saw the German first, over Lili's shoulder—mustached, perhaps forty-five, his hair combed to a point on his forehead. He glittered gold and rank: heavy epaulettes, a double row of medals, and Eve recognized him: Rupprecht, crown prince of Bavaria, *Generaloberst* of the Sixth Army and one of the best generals the Fritzes had. He had visited Lille three weeks ago, Eve remembered with frozen clarity, and dined at Le Lethe where he complimented both René Bordelon's *tarte alsacienne* and the German airfield's new Fokker Eindecker aircraft. Eve, pouring his brandy, had stored away his comments about the Fokker.

And now here he was, bearing down on them both in a crowd of German aides, his hand falling on Lili's shoulder as he exclaimed, "Louise de Bettignies, it *is* you!"

For an instant Lili still faced away from him, her hand half out of her handbag with the identity cards of Vivienne the cheese seller—and Eve saw her eyes go blank. Only for a split second, and then Lili swept Vivienne's cards back into the bag like a gambler flicking away a losing hand. Her shoulders straightened as she turned, her smile dialed from Vivienne's eager-to-please smirk up to something far more brilliant, and she dropped a curtsy Eve was fast to imitate. "Your Royal Highness! You know very well how to flatter a lady, knowing her only from the back of her neck under an exceedingly unattractive hat!"

The general kissed Lili's hand, his stars and medals flashing. "You need no stack of silk roses to dazzle, *mademoiselle*."

Lili (*Louise?*) dimpled at him, and even in the midst of dizzying shock, Eve marveled at how completely the leader of the Alice Network had altered herself. Her smile was now a flash of confidence, her chin had a proud angle, and with a tip of a finger her dismal boater sank over one eye at a dashing angle just like any of those cartwheel-size mounds of gauze she'd left in train compartments all over France. Her voice was liquid-pure French aristocrat—down-on-her-luck aristocrat, perhaps, but the court drawl was unmistakable as she said, "Such is always my luck. I meet the crown prince of Bavaria in last year's lace!" A flick for her old blouse. "Princess Elvira would never let me forget it."

"My cousin was always very fond of you. Remember that game of chess we played in her drawing room in Holleschau, the night of—"

"Yes! And you won. Encircled my knights from behind and pried my king out of his castle. I should not be surprised you command the Sixth Army now, Your Royal Highness . . ."

More chatter. No one had glanced at Eve, not the general nor his aides nor Lili. Eve clutched her armload of packages and shifted behind Lili like a maid. In a drab hat of her own, with none of Lili's sparkle, she undoubtedly resembled a servant. The train, she saw with a shiver of fear, was leaving.

"What are you doing in Lille, Mademoiselle de Bettignies?" the general asked, oblivious to the train or his hovering aides. Laugh lines grew at the corners of his eyes, and his smile was avuncular. If he weren't one of the best leaders at the kaiser's disposal, Eve would probably have liked him. "Such a dreary place!"

You made it dreary, Eve thought, and any possibility of liking disappeared.

"On my way into Belgium to see my brother. If I can even get across the border now, *mon Dieu*, my train has gone . . ." Lili made a comic face of despair, a tragic columbine clown, and the general immediately snapped for one of his hovering aides.

"A car for Mademoiselle de Bettignies and her maid. You will be escorted across by my own driver."

"If *mademoiselle* has her identity cards," the aide said, and Eve froze. The only cards Lili had were for an imaginary cheese seller named Vivienne, and if she was caught with them while claiming to be someone else—

But Lili stood laughing, perfectly at ease as she rummaged through her handbag. "I have them *somewhere*—" Upending a handkerchief, a few keys, a scatter of hairpins. "Marguerite, do you have my papers?"

Eve knew what to do then: begin laboriously opening every package in her arms, shaking her head like a slow-witted country girl, all as the general looked on amused and his aides shifted from foot to foot. "Your Royal Highness," one murmured, "the *Kommandant* awaits . . ."

"No need for papers, I know Mademoiselle de Bettignies perfectly well." The general looked sad as he kissed her hand. "From more peaceful days."

"Happier days," Lili agreed, and when the car pulled up before the station, the general handed her in himself. Eve, scarcely knowing what to think, scrambled in behind her, still juggling packages. The car's seats were richly cushioned; the smell of expensive leather overlaid motor oil. Lili fluttered her handkerchief out the window at the general, and then the doors shut and they were gliding away. In much greater luxury than a cramped train car.

Lili didn't speak. Her eyes touched on the driver, and then she made a fussy comment or two about the heat like any aristocratic lady traveling in summer. The questions rising in Eve's throat were choking her, but she looked at her lap as a lady's maid should. The car remained silent as they crossed into Belgium. In the car of a general—and a crown prince, no less—they were waved straight through the checkpoints. Though the driver offered to take them to their destination, Lili refused with a charming smile and asked to be dropped at the nearest train station. A much smaller place than the station in Lille, just a platform with a few benches.

"*Merde*," she said as they watched the gleaming car disappear back up the road. "I wouldn't mind a ride all the way to Brussels—*mon Dieu,* I'm sick of trains!—but leading a German general's aide to Uncle Edward's doorstep would probably be frowned upon, no?"

Eve was silent. She didn't even know where to begin. The platform was hot and dusty; they were alone except for an old woman dozing on the other side, well out of earshot.

Lili dropped onto the nearest bench, setting her valise beside her. "So, little daisy," she said matter-of-factly. "Are you going to accuse me of being a German spy, just because the general of the Sixth Army happens to know me by sight?"

"No." That had flashed briefly across Eve's mind at the general's first smile, she felt ashamed to admit, but now she shook her head. If she knew nothing else, she knew that Lili was no double agent.

"Well, now you know my real name." Lili smiled, tugging off her gloves. "Very few in the network do. Just Violette and Uncle Edward."

Violette, loyal lieutenant that she was, would kill Eve slowly if she ever endangered their leader by revealing her identity. Eve accepted the secret, turning it over. "Louise de Bettignies. Who is she, then?"

"The daughter of minor French nobility, who really should have been an actress, given how much she adores putting on new identities." Lili took out a handkerchief, blotting her forehead in the morning heat. "But the daughters of minor French nobility do not *become* actresses, my dear."

"What do they d-do, then?"

"When they come from families as poor as church mice? Become governesses for the children of lecherous Italian lords and Polish counts and Austrian princesses." Louise shuddered. "Bullets, let me tell you, are *quite* preferable to pounding French verbs into a lot of snobbish little heirs to crumbling castles and defunct coats of arms."

Eve felt her way, cautious but ravenously curious. "And how did Louise de Bettignies come to know the crown prince of Bavaria? Teaching his children?"

"Those of his cousin, Princess Elvira. Bitch. Face like a potato, temper like a prison wardess. Her lock-jawed children were dumb as paint and thought they owned the earth. My training turned out to be useful; governesses get plenty of practice lurking and eavesdropping. But still—" A sigh. "It was *so* dull. I'd tell myself that at least I wasn't hauling coal in a mine shaft or working eighteen hours in a laundry getting my fingers crushed by mangles. But I was so tired of it all, it was coming down to a choice: heave myself under a train like Anna Karenina, or become a nun. I did think rather seriously about a nunnery, but really, I'm far too frivolous."

The drone of summer insects rose all around them; the heat baked down and the old woman across the tracks snored on her bench.

"Anyway," Lili concluded. "That's Louise de Bettignies. But she isn't really me, anymore. I've become Lili instead, and I like her *far* better."

"I can understand why." Louise de Bettignies sounded rather grand and a little silly, a woman with a lace bertha and no skills besides pretty handwriting. It didn't match frail little Lili at all, with her darting gaze and her false-bottomed bag lined with half the secrets of the German army. "I'll never let it slip, Lili. Not to anyone."

A smile. "I trust you, little daisy."

Eve smiled back, the trust warming her to her bones.

"*Merde*," Lili sighed again. "This goddamned train, will it ever get here?" And they never mentioned it again.

The train ride was dismal but short, the excitement of their encounter with the general slowly fading to leave Eve with her brooding thoughts of René and last night. Eve didn't bother to track the streets they traversed on the way to the meeting point. She had no desire to be able to identify this house with the faded blue door where they were quickly ushered inside.

Lili had gone into Uncle Edward's study first. Eve waited in the sitting room outside, watched by a weedy young lieutenant. Lili came out, dropped a wink. "In you go. I'm going to hunt down some brandy." She leaned close, speaking in Eve's ear so the lieutenant couldn't overhear. "Our dear uncle seems *quite* eager to see you. Perhaps more than just professionally eager—"

"*Lili!*" Eve hissed, looking at the lieutenant.

"If you catch our good captain with his clothes off or his guard down, ask why he took that prison sentence for his dreary wife," Lili whispered as a parting shot. "I'm dying to know!" Eve entered her questioning session with burning ears.

"Miss Gardiner." Captain Cameron rose, and Eve stopped short. She didn't know if it was the sound of her own name, which she hadn't heard for what seemed like forever, or if it was the sight of him. *I forgot what you looked like.* She'd thought she remembered him very well: the thin English face, the sandy hair, the tapered hands. But she'd forgotten the little things, like the way he crossed his trousered legs loosely at the knee as he reseated himself, the way he interlaced those lean hands and smiled clear to the corners of his eyes. "Do sit down," he prompted, and Eve realized she was still standing in the doorway. She sat in the straight-backed chair across the table from him, taking time to settle her skirts.

"It is good to see you, Miss Gardiner." He smiled again, and Eve had a flash to their first conversation in the boardinghouse parlor. Could it really be only two months ago? What a great deal could happen in two months. Like a pair of cool French hands exploring the sides of her ribs last night, the soft hollows of her elbows and wrists, the insides of her thighs, *no*, she was not going to think about that. Not here.

Cameron looked at her over his tented fingertips, and a line appeared between his brows. "Are you well? You look . . ."

"Thinner? We d-don't eat much in Lille."

"More than that." That trace of a Scottish lilt in his voice; she'd forgotten that as well. "How are you coping, Miss Gardiner?"

Spiderlike fingers unhurriedly tracing her earlobes. "Very well."

"Are you certain?"

Narrow lips tracing the cup of her navel, the spaces between her fingers. "I do w-w-w—I do what is necessary."

"It is part of my job to evaluate our people, not just take their information." That line between Captain Cameron's eyes hadn't gone away. "Your work has been superb. Alice Dubois—what?"

"Nothing, Captain. I call her Lili. The day we m-met, she said 'Alice Dubois' sounded like a skinny schoolmistress with a face like a b-b-bin.'"

He laughed. "Yes, she would. She was unstinting

in her praise for you, just now. You've done top-class work, but"—his eyes penetrated—"the toll of that can be high."

"Not for me." *Kisses with open eyes still staring, staring, staring.* Eve met Cameron's gaze, making sure her hands didn't clench in her lap. "I was m-made for this."

Captain Cameron still stared, taking in every detail of Eve's face. He wasn't in uniform, just an old suit with the jacket thrown over the chair and shirtsleeves rolled to show lean wrists—but as much as he looked like a university professor, it would be dangerous to forget that he was an interrogator. He could slip information out of you before you even knew it was passing your lips.

So Eve gave a cheerful smile, the good-sport girl who keeps a stiff upper lip through everything. "I thought we were here to talk about the k-k-k"—a fist against her knee, to release the word—"the kaiser's visit, Captain?"

"Yours were the first set of ears to hear of it. Tell me, from the beginning."

Eve relayed the details again, crisp and concise. He listened, taking notes. He blinked now and then. So nice to see a man who could *blink*.

He sat back, surveying his notes. "Anything else?"

"The kaiser's arrival time has just changed—he'll be an hour later than planned."

"That's new. Where did you hear it?"

"W-waiting tables." *From René, after he finished but before he pulled out of me. He likes to stay there awhile, until his sweat cools, so he'll just begin . . . chatting.*

Captain Cameron caught something in her eyes. "What is it, Miss Gardiner?"

How Eve liked hearing her own name again, especially from his lips. She liked it so much, she knew it wasn't a good idea. "You had better keep calling me M-Marguerite Le François," she said. "Safer."

"Very well." The questions about the kaiser's visit continued—Captain Cameron examined it from all angles, isolating every detail Eve could offer. He extracted one or two things she hadn't thought of, and seemed pleased. "That should do it," he said, rising. "You have been a very great help."

"Thank you." Eve rose. "Tell the RFC not to miss. Tell them to b-bomb that train to *shards*."

Her intensity kindled an answering fire in his gaze. "Agreed."

As she turned for the door she heard his voice again with its faint Scottish lilt. "Be careful."

"I *am* careful." She set her hand to the doorknob.

"Are you? Lili worries. She worries for all her contacts, since she's a bit of a mother hen. But she says you're walking a very tight wire."

René's lean weight coming down in the dark. "As you say, she's a mother hen."

His voice came closer. "Eve—"

"Don't call me that." She whirled around, advancing until they stood nose to nose. "It's not my name anymore. I'm Marguerite Le François. You *made* me into Marguerite Le François. I'm not going to be Eve again until this war is over or until I am *dead*. Do you hear me?"

"There's no need for anyone to die. Be careful—"

"*Stop*." She wanted to lean forward and nail her mouth against his. It would stop him talking, and she knew his lips would be warm. *You can't. You'll like it too much.* Like hearing her name in his soft voice; it was bad for Marguerite and it was bad for her work.

She began to pull away, but Captain Cameron's hand found her waist. "It's very hard," he said softly. "What we do. It's all right to find it hard. If you want to talk to me—"

"I don't want to *talk*," she rasped.

"It might do you good, Eve."

She couldn't hear him say her name again. She could *not*. Of course that was why he was using it—she'd shown a weak point and he was pushing it, the handler seeing if his charge was close to cracking. Part of his job, *evaluating* her. Eve put her chin up, blindly turning the conversation to rock him back on his heels instead. "Either let me out of this room, Cameron, or t-take me someplace where we won't do any talking."

She had no idea where those words came from. *Idiot, idiot!* Cameron stared at her, plainly surprised, but his hand still warmed the side of her waist. Eve knew she should step away, but a hungry part of her wanted to step closer and damn the consequences. She wanted to lie down with this man, whose every word and reaction she wouldn't need to sift, measure, and weigh.

But Cameron stepped away, mutely adjusting the gold band on his left hand.

"Your wife s-sent you to prison," Eve said bluntly. "From what I heard." The unspoken words were, *What do you owe a wife like that?*

He reared back. "Who told you—"

"Major Allenton, back in Folkestone. Why did you conf-f-f—confess guilt when your wife was the one who c-c-committed fraud?" Eve had Cameron on the defensive for once, and she kept pushing.

"I suppose it's no secret." He turned away, putting his hands on the back of a chair. "I thought I could save her from prison. My wife—she has always been unhappy. She wanted a child, desperately, and she couldn't have one. She kept thinking every few weeks that *this* was the time—then the disappointment every month made her do strange things. Steal things, then make a fuss when they were missing. Fire the maids for listening at the door when they were on the other side of the house. Become obsessed with money, providing for a child's future when we didn't even have one yet, and claim her pearls had been stolen so she could cash in the insurance . . ." He rubbed at his forehead. "When that came out, she begged me to take the sentence for her. Someone had to go to prison, and she said she was too afraid. I wanted to spare her. She's so fragile."

She's a liar who was content to let you take the punishment for her crime, Eve thought. *Even if it destroyed your career and your life.* But it sounded harsh and unforgiving, and she didn't say it.

"She's to have a child in the spring." He turned around. "She's much calmer now that it's finally happened. She's . . . happier."

"You aren't."

He shook his head, a halfhearted denial, but Eve could read him like a book. He was weary and heartsick, they both were, and they might all be dead soon in this hellish place of war and blood. She stepped closer, knowing this was a very bad idea, but unable to stop, wanting so badly to banish the thoughts of René's spiderlike hands and toneless voice. *I'm here,* she thought. *Take me.*

Cameron lifted her hand, bringing it to his lips. The sad gesture of a knight-errant, one who could never take advantage of a lady. It was on the tip of Eve's tongue to tell him she was no innocent anymore, that he wouldn't be taking anything René Bordelon hadn't got first. But she couldn't tell him that. He might remove her from Lille. He might do that anyway, if she lay with him as she wanted to. *Fool,* Marguerite's voice hissed in Eve's head. *Stupid girl, what did Lili tell you? They all think a* horizontale *isn't to be trusted and you go throwing yourself at him like a whore?*

He won't think that of me, Eve thought. *He's not so narrow as that.*

But Marguerite was warier. *Risk nothing.*

Eve stepped back. Nothing too overt had been said, quite—she could deny she meant anything intimate, even if they both knew better. "Pardon me, Uncle Edward. Are we f-finished here?"

"Quite finished, *mademoiselle.* Take care of yourself in Lille."

"Lili takes care of me. She and Violette."

"Marguerite, Lili, and Violette." He smiled, and the worry in his eyes bordered on agony. "My flowers."

"Fleurs du mal," Eve heard herself saying, and shivered.

"What?"

"Baudelaire. We are not flowers to be plucked and shielded, Captain. We are flowers who flourish in evil."

CHAPTER 19
CHARLIE

May 1947

Four gin martinis sent Eve straight from supper to bed, but I was still restless. Too tired to go for a walk—the Little Problem drank my energy down like hot chocolate; I hoped *that* part of being pregnant would go away soon—but tired or not, I wasn't ready to go up to my room. Then Finn pushed back his chair from the table, pocketing the bullets Eve had given him from the Luger. "I've some work to do on the car. Come hold the torch?"

It had showered while we were eating, so the night was warm and rain scented. The pavement gleamed under the streetlamps, and cars passed by with a swish of wet tires. Finn rummaged in the car's trunk, came out with a flashlight and a toolbox. "Keep it steady," he said, handing me the flashlight and popping the hood.

"What's wrong with the old girl now?" I asked.

Finn reached down into the Lagonda's innards. "Got an old leak somewhere. I tighten things up every few days, make sure it doesn't get worse."

I stood on tiptoe, aiming the flashlight's beam as a cluster of giggling French girls blew past. "Wouldn't it be easier to find the leak and fix it?"

"You want me to take the time to break down the ruddy engine and put it back together?"

"Not really." As pleasant as today's drive had been, the warm sunshine and the new camaraderie being woven among the three of us, I was on fire to get to Limoges. *Rose.* The closer I got to the last place she'd been, the more the hope burned in me that she really might be alive and waiting for me. And once it was Rose and me again, arm in arm against the world, I could do anything.

"Come on," Finn muttered to a stubborn lug nut or screw head or whatever it was. His Scots burr got thicker, as it always did when he was trying to persuade the car to cooperate. "Rusty aud bitch . . ." He worked away with a wrench, back and forth. "Hold that torch a bit higher, miss—"

"Finn, if you call me *miss* now, you'll blow my cover. As spies like Eve would say." I tapped my fake wedding ring. "I'm Mrs. Donald McGowan, remember?"

He got the bolt to loosen or tighten or whatever. "Grand idea, that ring."

"I need a picture of my Donald," I mused. "Something I can look at mistily when I say that my heart is in the grave."

"Donald would want you to go on with your life," Finn said. "You're young. He'd tell you to marry again."

"I don't want to get married. I want to find Rose and then maybe run a café."

"A café?" Finn looked up from the Lagonda's innards, a lock of hair falling over his eyes. "Why?"

"The happiest day in my life was spent with Rose at a French café. I thought maybe, if I find her . . . It's an idea, anyway. I have to do something with my future." Now that I had the Little Problem to think about, I needed a new plan besides my mother's old one of *Get Bs at Bennington until you can hook a nice young lawyer*. Strangely, I wasn't finding my unformed future as frightening as it could have been. I could do something I liked, now. Get a job. What did math majors do, in the practical world? I didn't want to be a teacher and I couldn't be an accountant, but . . . "I could run a little business like a café," I said rather experimentally, seeing a line of orderly account books filled with my neat columns of numbers.

"Donald wouldn't like it." Finn had a faint grin as he traded out the small wrench. "His widow, waiting tables and keeping a till?"

"Donald could be a bit of a prig," I confessed.

"God rest his soul," Finn said, straight-faced.

What a difference a few days made. He used to talk like he was being charged a dollar for every word that came out of his mouth, and now here he was making jokes. "What do *you* want to do?"

"What do you mean, Mrs. McGowan?"

"Well, you're surely not going to work for Eve forever, making one-pan breakfasts to cure her hangovers and disarming her every night before bed." I sniffed the damp evening breeze—it smelled like more rain might be coming. A pair of old men in crumpled caps were hurrying home across the street, casting anxious looks at the skies. "What would you do, if you could do any-thing?"

"Before the war, I worked in a garage. Always thought maybe I'd start my own someday. Fix up other people's cars, do some restoration work . . ." Finn finished up in-side the Lagonda, and gently lowered the hood. "Don't think that'll happen now."

"Why not?"

"I wouldn't be much good at the business side of things. Besides, there are lots of former soldiers looking for work, and even more looking for bank loans. Who's going to give a good garage job or a start-up loan to an ex-soldier with a Pentonville stint on his record?" He spoke matter-of-factly.

"Is that why you're haring off to Limoges with Eve and me?" I switched off the flashlight, handing it back. There was dim veiled light from the streetlights over-head, but it seemed very dark without the flashlight's bright beam. "I know why I'm going, and I know why Eve's going. But what about you?"

"There's not much else for me to do." His soft voice had a smile. "Besides, I like both of you."

I hesitated. "Why *did* you go to prison? And don't say it's because you stole a swan from Kew Gardens or made off with the crown jewels," I rushed on, twisting my false wedding ring. "Really—what happened?"

He rubbed slowly at his oil-smeared hands with a rag. "Eve told us she was a spy in the Great War. I told you I slept with half a frat. You know *our* secrets."

He put his toolbox away in the trunk. Turned the rag over to the clean side, and began rubbing at the rain marks on the Lagonda's dark blue fender. Through the broad front window of the hotel, the night porter watched us idly.

"I saw some bad things," Finn said, "during the last year of the war."

He stopped for so long, I thought he wasn't going to say anything else.

"I have a temper," he said finally.

I smiled. "No, you don't. You're the levelest man I know—"

He brought his open hand down against the fender in a sudden slap. I jumped, voice breaking off.

"I have a temper," he repeated evenly. "The months after I left my regiment, it wasn't a braw time. I'd go out, get wrecked, start fights. Eventually I got arrested for one of them. Earned me a term in Pentonville for assault."

Assault. An ugly word. I looked at Finn and I just couldn't see it. "Who'd you get in a fight with?" I asked softly.

"I don't know. Never met him before that night."

"Why did you fight him?"

"I don't remember. I was fair smashed, walking around angry." Finn leaned his back against the Lagonda, arms folded tight across his chest. "He said something, who knows what. I hit him. Kept on hitting him. Six people pulled me off once I started bashing his head against a doorpost. Thank God they got me off him before I cracked his skull."

I stayed silent. It was misting now, very gently.

"He got better," Finn said. "Eventually. I went to Pentonville."

"Have you hit anybody since?" I asked, because I had to say something.

He stared straight ahead, not looking at anything. "No."

"Maybe your temper isn't the problem."

He laughed shortly. "I beat a man to a pulp—broke

his nose and his jaw and his eye socket and four of his fingers—and my temper isna the problem?"

"Did you get in fights like that before the war?"

"No."

"Then maybe the temper isn't really you. It's the war." Or rather, whatever he saw there. I wondered what that was, but I didn't ask.

"That's a lousy excuse, Charlie. Or every soldier who came home would be in the lockup."

"Some go to prison. Some go back to work. Some kill themselves." I thought of my brother, painfully. "Everyone's different."

"You should go in," Finn said abruptly. "Before you get all drookit."

"Yank, here. I don't know what that means."

"Before you get drenched. Not good for the bairn, Mrs. McGowan."

I ignored that, leaning up against the Lagonda beside him. "Does Eve know?"

"Yes."

"What'd she say?"

"'I have a weakness for handsome men with Scottish accents and prison records, so I'll give you a try.' And never mentioned it again." He shook his head, hair falling over his eyes again. "She's not one for judging people."

"Neither am I."

"You still shouldn't be hanging around a bad apple like me."

"Finn, I'm a former good girl, and a current unwed mother-to-be. Eve's a former spy, and a current drunk. You're a former convict, and a current mechanic and driver and cooker of English breakfasts. You know why none of us judge?" I bumped his shoulder with mine until he finally looked down at me. "Because none of us have the goddamn right to look down our noses at anyone else's sins."

He looked down at me with an invisible smile that began and ended in the corners of his eyes.

I reached behind me and hoisted myself up to sit on the Lagonda's long hood. It put me almost level with Finn when he turned to face me, as I leaned forward to fit my mouth carefully, gently, against his. His lips were soft and his jaw rough, just like the first time I'd tried to kiss him. Just like the first time, his hands rose to my waist—but this time I broke off the kiss before he could move back. I didn't think I could stand it if he pushed me away again.

But he didn't. He lowered his head back to mine, catching my lips and lingering. His hands were big and warm on either side of my waist, pulling me closer against him on the edge of the Lagonda's hood. I let my hands slide into his rumpled hair where they'd been aching to go, and his hands slipped under the edge of my new striped jersey. He didn't go lunging upward from there, just ran the backs of his fingers very slowly up and down the bare sides of my waist as we kissed. I was trembling all over by the time we pulled apart.

"I got engine grease on you," he said, looking down at his oil-stained hands. "Sorry, lass."

"It'll wash off," I managed to say. I didn't want to wash him off me, his smell or his taste or his engine grease. I wanted to keep kissing him, but it was an open street and the misty drizzle was going to be rain soon, so I slid down from the car and we turned and wandered back into the hotel. *Come up to my room,* I wanted to say, *come up with me*—but the night porter was giving us one of those very French looks, an impassive expression over knowing eyes. *"Bonsoir, Monsieur Kilgore,"* he greeted Finn, eyes flicking to the hotel register where we'd signed in. *"Madame McGowan."*

"Wonderful," I muttered as I thumped back into my solitary room. "I have not only ruined Miss Charlie St. Clair's reputation, I have officially ruined Mrs. Donald McGowan's." My Donald would have been shocked.

CHAPTER 20
EVE

René's gift, offered with a flourish shortly after Eve returned from her journey, was a silk robe. Rose red, fine enough to slip through a ring—but not new. It smelled vaguely of a woman's perfume, some woman who undoubtedly saw it seized in a requisition raid, and now it had ended up on Eve's back.

She imagined the kaiser's train blowing to bits, let it give her pleasure, let that pleasure show on her face as she rubbed her cheek against the silk. "Thank you, *m-monsieur.*"

"It suits you." He leaned back, clearly pleased that she was now suitably outfitted for her surroundings. Eve found herself darkly amused by his aesthetic relief. They were in his opulent study; he wore one of his beautiful dressing gowns, as he usually did while waiting for Eve to finish bathing away any possible food smells from a long night's shift. Now that she had come out in a silk robe rather than a towel or her black work dress, she was no longer an eyesore.

"I've a mind to take you away somewhere." He unstoppered his decanter of elderflower liqueur, pouring the usual modest measure for himself, and the generous one that would make Marguerite's head spin. "I dislike hurried nighttime trysts. I have been planning a short journey to Limoges soon. I may take you with me."

Eve sipped. "Why Limoges?"

"Lille is dreary." He made a face. "It will be pleasant to walk down a street that does not have a German name. And I am thinking of opening a second restaurant. Limoges may prove to be the place. I will take a weekend to inspect suitable locations."

A weekend with René Bordelon. It wasn't the thought of the nights that made Eve shudder, it was the *days*. Long suppers, cups of tea, afternoon walks at his side, having to sift every word and guard every reaction. She would be exhausted long before she got to the linen sheets, and what happened between them.

Half a chess game and two glasses of fragrant elderflower fire later, they retired to the bedroom. A suitable interval after things were concluded there, Eve slipped back into her work dress and prepared to go home. Watching her dress, René gave a small *tsk*. "This rushing out before the sheets grow cold," he said. "Most uncivilized."

"I don't w-want there to be talk, *monsieur*." Not to mention the fact that Eve didn't dare doze off in his presence. What if she muttered German or English in her sleep, or something else she couldn't explain away? It didn't bear thinking about. *If you spend the night with him in Limoges, you will have to think about it.* "There will be gossip in town if I don't go home at nights," she said, sliding into her stockings. "The b-baker pisses in the dough he uses to bake for the women who . . . go with the Germans."

René looked amused. "I am not a German, my dear."

You're worse. A French Judas who betrayed his own for profit—Germans were hated in Lille, but men like René Bordelon were loathed with an even brighter passion. *When the Germans lose this war, you will be the first strung up from a lamppost.* "I'll still be s-scorned," Eve hedged. "Threatened."

A shrug. "If anyone threatens you, give me their names. They will be reported to the Germans and find themselves with a ruinous fine or jail time, perhaps worse. The *Kommandant* would oblige me, being eager to reduce discord among the civilians."

The thought that someone might be hauled to a cell or fined to the point of starvation on his whisper did not seem to trouble René in the slightest. Eve had overheard him several times passing names to German officers over the dinner brandy: people who displeased him, who hoarded requisitioned supplies, who spoke out against the invaders. But to hear the suggestion tossed out as casually as this . . . She studied his expression wonderingly. It really did not stir his conscience at all.

"Are you really still so shy, my pet?" He tilted his head. "Too shy to let people know you are now mine?"

"I just don't want b-bread with piss in it," Eve whispered, as if in an agony of embarrassment. Really, it was horror.

René looked as though hovering between a chuckle or a frown at her honesty. To Eve's relief, he decided on a chuckle. "Eventually, Marguerite, I'll teach you to be indifferent to what people think. It's very freeing, to care for no one's opinion but your own." He looked urbane even when naked, his flesh pale and smooth against the linens. "Limoges soon—I'll take you with me. You may concoct some story for the staff about an aunt taken ill, if you wish. I shall be publicly displeased with you."

"Thank you, *monsieur*." But Eve had no intention of going with him to Limoges. In two more days, if all went well, the kaiser would be dead and the world would be remade.

It will not be that easy, she told herself. Wars were vast machines; they didn't grind to an instant halt when one man died, even if that man was a king. But even if the war didn't end, the world would still be a vastly different place. In that world, René Bordelon would surely be taking rapid stock of his allies and enemies, not taking leisurely weekends in Limoges.

The days before the kaiser's arrival passed at the speed of a glacier, and the nights in René's immaculate bed moved even more slowly, even if she did learn some intriguing facts and figures about the local airfields that Uncle Edward would find very interesting. At last The Day dawned, hot and sticky even in the early hours, and the *fleurs du mal* met in silence. Eve saw the same expression in Lili's darting eyes and Violette's wary ones: a hope so violent it had to be stamped down like a hydra. They hurried out of the city without speaking, making for the grassy hills. "We should not be going to watch that train," Violette said.

"*Tais-toi*," Lili said. "I for one will go mad if I have to sit inside listening for aeroplanes overhead. Besides, I can't make my report to Uncle Edward until I have results, so there's no use going back to my usual rounds."

"A bad idea," Violette muttered, but none of them went back. They made their way past the local farmhouses, small and ravaged, and the three women took their place on a long low hill overlooking the distant train tracks. The same hill where Lili and Eve had scouted terrain for the attack. Violette chewed a strand of grass in terse silence; Eve flexed and unflexed her fingers. Lili chattered as though she was at a party: "I bought the most ghastly hat on my last trip through Tournai. Blue satin roses and spotted net; I left it on the train and it's probably still there. No self-respecting streetwalker would steal that blue satin pile of—"

"Lili," Eve said, "shut up."

"Thank you," said Violette, speaking for the first time in two hours. They stared down at the train tracks as if concentration alone could make them ignite. The sun climbed higher.

Lili's eyes proved sharpest. "Is that . . ."

A tiny smear of smoke. A train.

It chugged sedately into view, too far away to hear its clacking wheels or the peals of steam from its engine. Too far away to make out details . . . But according to Eve's information, this was it. The train that carried Kaiser Wilhelm in anonymity toward the front.

Eve looked up. The blue skies stretched empty.

Lili's small hand covered hers in the grass, gripping tight. "*Nique ta mère*," she said, eyes following Eve's skyward. "You RFC buggers . . ."

The train inched closer. Lili's grip was like a vise. Eve reached for Violette's hand on the other side and squeezed that just as hard. Violette squeezed back.

When Eve heard the low drone of aeroplanes, she thought her heart would stop. For a moment it was just a buzz, like hovering bees, and then she saw them, two aeroplanes in formation like eagles. She didn't know if they were monoplanes or biplanes; she knew nothing about aviation, just the meaningless technical words she committed to memory when German officers droned over dessert. But these aeroplanes were beautiful, and she let out a gasp. Lili muttered obscenities that sounded like prayers, and Violette turned to stone.

"You know," Eve heard herself saying tautly, "I don't even know how aeroplanes bomb targets. Do they just throw the explosives over the side?"

This time Lili said, "Shut up."

The train surged along. The aeroplanes streaked through the blue sky. *Please.* They were all thinking it. *Please, make the hit.* Let it all be over now, on this summer day with the smell of warm grass and the sound of birds.

They were too far away to see any explosives drop, or the rounds, or whatever they were. They would only see the explosion, the fire, the smoke. The aeroplanes droned like lazy birds over the train. *Now,* Eve thought.

But there was no explosion.

No smoke. No fire. No crashing derailment sending the train careening from its tracks.

The kaiser chugged placidly on toward Lille.

"They failed," Eve said numbly. "They f-failed."

Violette spoke in empty rage. "Or the explosives were faulty."

Make another pass, Eve howled inside. *Try again!* But the aeroplanes disappeared, not proud eagles but failed, draggle-tailed sparrows. *Why?*

Who cared why? The kaiser lived. He would tour the front; get a view of his soldiers in the trenches; perhaps pass through Lille and nod approvingly at the clocks turned to Berlin time, the boulevards renamed with hammered German signs. Unless he came to eat at Le Lethe and gave Eve the opportunity to bury a steak knife in the back of his neck or season his chocolate mousse with rat poison, he would return to Germany alive and well, riding the machine of war as easily as he rode his untouched train through the countryside.

"It's just as well." Violette rose, sounding as though her throat were full of gravel. "The kaiser's death at Lille would focus all the German attention here. We'd likely all get caught."

"And it's n-not as though the war would have just *ended*," Eve heard herself saying emptily. "It wouldn't have changed m-m-m-m—" She couldn't make the word come and didn't care enough to force it. She just trailed off, rising and brushing off her skirt with mechanical motions.

Lili hadn't moved. She stared at the distant train, and her face was ancient.

Violette looked down, spectacles flashing. "Get up, Lili."

"Those goddamned—" Lili shook her head. "Oh, you bastards."

"*Ma p'tite,* please. Get up."

Lili rose. She looked down for a moment, kicking the grass, and when she raised her chin she was smiling. Grimly, thinly, but smiling. "I don't know about you, *mes anges,* but I feel like getting drunk tonight."

But Eve wouldn't be there sharing whatever rotgut brandy or whiskey Lili could get her hands on. *I have René tonight*, she thought. *And tomorrow night. And soon, if he takes me to Limoges, I will have him for two whole days and nights.*

All the nights had a rhythm. The bath. The quiet ten minutes or so afterward, silk robe whispering against damp skin, sipping at a very large glass of elderflower liqueur. As Eve drank, René would put on a record and tell her, maybe, about the Debussy piece they were listening to, and how Impressionism was expressed orchestrally, and who were the other Impressionists of art and literature as well as music. That was the easy part. All Eve had to do was listen admiringly.

Then the moment came when René took the glass from her hand and drew her to the bedroom next door. Then it all became difficult.

His kisses were long and slow, and he left his eyes open. His eyes remained open throughout everything, unblinking, measuring, watching for the smallest gasp or hitch in breath. He unwrapped Eve from the rose red silk at leisure, spread her unhurriedly on his pristine sheets, discarded his own robe, and then he stretched over her and took his time.

How very, very much Eve wished he would take his pleasure quickly and roll off. That would have been so easy.

"I've never trained a virgin before," he had remarked the first time. "Normally I value expertise over innocence. We shall have to see how fast you learn. I don't expect I will please you the first few times—that's the way for women, rather unfairly, I have always thought."

René liked to explore every part of Eve, tracing every crevice and corner of her body, his tongue lingering as long on the spaces behind her ears and the hollows of her knees as on the more expected places. He spun it out endlessly, content to play for hours, taking her hand and using it to explore his own pale unmarked skin. He turned her and posed her, positioned her and explored her, watching and learning through it all.

"Your eyes widen just a little whenever I surprise you," he observed one night. "Like a doe's—" And he turned to her breast and employed his teeth in a bit of sudden expert roughness. "Like that," he said, brushing her lashes with his thumb. It wasn't something Eve ever considered; how the intimacy of skin against naked skin unpeeled another layer from people besides clothes; how it was another way for people to *know* one another. *I do not want him to know me*, she thought desperately. Her work depended on him *not* knowing her, yet every night he learned more.

"It is hardest to lie to those who know us best." Captain Cameron had said that in Folkestone. Eve shoved the thought of him away, not wanting it anywhere near her nights in René's bed, but the fear persisted. If René learned her well enough, would she be able to continue fooling him?

Yes, she thought fiercely. *It will mean more and better lying, but that you can do. And remember: you are learning him too.*

Night by night, Eve learned the twitch of René's every muscle, each flare of his eyes. The man armored in his beautiful suits was easier to read now that she knew how the naked muscles moved beneath.

Once he finished toying with her, the joining was swift. He preferred to be behind or above, hand twined in her hair to tip her face back, holding her where he could see her every reaction. He liked her to look back at him—"Eyes open, pet," he ordered frequently, never missing a stroke. And when he finally allowed his own pleasure to make an end of it, he sank slowly over her, letting her body cushion his as their sweat cooled, and picked up whatever conversation they'd been having in his study, about Debussy or Klimt or Provençal wine.

Tonight it was about the kaiser.

"I'm told he was pleased by this visit. The airfield met with his approval, though one has to wonder what he thought of the trenches. Ghastly places, one hears."

"Did you m-m-meet him?" Eve lay still, her fingers twined with René's against the pillow and her legs tangled around his lean thighs. During moments like these, he was at his most incautious. "I h-hoped he would come to Le Lethe . . ."

René caught a flicker of emotion from her there, as much as she masked her face in innocence. "So you could spit in his *vichyssoise*?"

Eve made light of it, not lying. She never lied when they lay pressed together skin against skin, not if she could help it. Thoughts traveled faster skin to skin. "I wouldn't spit in his soup," she said frankly. "But I'd *t-t-think* about it."

René laughed, rolling away. His flesh slid from her, and Eve repressed the usual shiver. "One hears he is a vulgar man, kaiser or no. Still, I was hoping he'd come to the restaurant. Quite a coup that would have been, playing host to an emperor."

Eve pulled the sheet up over herself. "Has he ordered any ch-ch—any changes in orders, after seeing Lille?"

"Yes, rather interesting . . ."

And René told her.

"What good information you're getting," Lili commented on her next visit, a few days after the kaiser's departure. She stopped by as Eve was getting ready for her evening shift; Eve sat brushing out her hair as Lili copied the latest report. She held up the rice paper, shaking her head half in contempt and half in amusement. "Is the German *Kommandant* really talking about the new artillery improvements in public, over cherries jubilee and brandy?"

"No." Eve kept her eyes on the rickety washstand mirror. "René Bordelon does in private, over a pillow."

She could *feel* Lili's eyes on her back.

Eve spoke with as much dry formality as possible, but she still tripped at the first hurdle. "Just before our interview with Uncle Edward, I b-became René's . . ." What? *Mistress?* He might employ her but he didn't *keep* her. *Whore?* He didn't pay her beyond her wages, except in elderflower liqueur and a robe she was not allowed to wear except in his study. *Lover?* There was no love there.

But Lili didn't need the sentence finished. "*Pauvre petite*," she said, and crossed to take the brush from Eve's hand. "I'm sorry. Does he hurt you?"

"No." She squeezed her eyes shut. "Worse."

"How?"

"I—" Eve's throat locked. "Lili, I—I'm s-so ashamed."

The brush crackled through Eve's hair. "I know you aren't one to have your head turned easily, which is why I thought you could take such a step without compromising yourself. But such things can become more complicated than we anticipate. Are you developing a *tendresse* for him?"

"No." A bitter shake of Eve's head. "Never in this wide world."

"Good. If I thought you were becoming conflicted, I'd have to report it. And I would," Lili said evenly, continuing to stroke the brush through Eve's hair. "I'm terribly fond of you, but the work is too important to compromise. So if it's not a *tendresse*, what makes you so ashamed?"

Eve forced her burning eyes open, meeting Lili's gaze in the mirror. "The first f-few times I went to bed with him, p-p-pleasure wasn't—required." Or even expected. "Now . . ."

Now, however, Eve had had time to grow accustomed to what happened in the crisp, immaculate bed. And René Bordelon had high standards in bedmates, as he did in everything else. Pleasure was expected. Giving it *and* getting it.

That had led to something utterly unimaginable.

"Tell me." Lili sounded matter-of-fact. "Not much shocks me, you may be sure of that."

"I am starting to enjoy it," Eve said, and squeezed her eyes shut again.

The long brushstrokes never stopped.

"I despise him." Eve managed to keep her voice steady. "So how can I possibly take pleasure in what he d-d-d—in what he does to m-m—" The word wouldn't come. Eve let it die.

"He must be good at it," Lili said.

"He's the *enemy*." Eve realized she was trembling all over. Rage or shame or disgust; she didn't know. "There are collaborators in this city one can p-pity—women who sleep with officers so they can feed their families; men who work for the Germans so they can keep their children warm. But René Bordelon is nothing but a *profiteer*. He's almost as bad as the Huns."

"Maybe so," Lili said. "But lovemaking is a skill like any other, you know. A bad man can be a good carpenter or a good hatmaker or a good lover. The skill has nothing to do with the soul."

"Oh, Lili—" Eve rubbed at her temples. "You sound so F-French."

"Yes, and a Frenchwoman is *exactly* the person to talk to about such things." Lili straightened Eve's head toward the mirror. "So, Monsieur Profiteer is good at what he does between the sheets, and you are feeling guilty for enjoying yourself?"

Eve thought of René decanting a fine wine and inhaling the bouquet, René tipping an oyster down his throat in a lingering motion. "He's a sophisticate. Whether he's enjoying a glass of Bordeaux or a fine cigar or—or me, he takes his t-time getting it right."

"A physical response to skill," Lili said rather carefully, "is not a mark of what is happening in the head or the heart, you know."

"A physical response unrelated to the head or the heart is what m-marks a *whore*." Eve said it brutally.

"Oh, pish. That sounds like someone's provincial aunt talking. Never listen to people like that, little daisy. They're not only joyless drones, they usually wear chintz and think housework is a virtue."

"I still feel like a whore," Eve whispered.

Lili stopped brushing, and rested her chin atop Eve's head. "I imagine it was your mother who told you a woman who enjoys a man when he isn't her husband is a slut?"

"Something like th-that." Eve found it hard to disagree with such a statement. She looked at René with nothing but dislike—how was it that his patient, innovative, cold-skinned hands could evoke anything even remotely pleasurable? "Ordinary women wouldn't feel this," she began, but Lili waved a hand.

"If we were *ordinary,* we'd be at home reusing our tea leaves and rolling bandages to support the war effort, not carrying Lugers and smuggling coded messages around our hairpins. Steel blades such as you and I do not measure against the standards for ordinary women." Lili lifted her chin from the top of Eve's head. "Listen to me. I am older than you, and considerably wiser. Believe me when I say it is entirely possible to despise a man and still enjoy him between the sheets. *Merde,* sometimes it's even better that way. Disgust adds a certain intensity—'spasms of love, spasms of hate, it is all the same.' Puccini certainly had *that* right in *Tosca*."

Marguerite Le François wouldn't know *Tosca,* but Eve did. "*Tosca* kills the man before he can force himself on her."

"Maybe you'll kill Bordelon someday too. Think about that when he's on top of you; that'll give you a spasm of pleasure, all right."

Eve found herself giving a watery laugh. Lili's tone was light, but her warm, steady presence was a shield at Eve's back.

"So." The leader of the Alice Network stepped away, got them both cups of the horrible boiled walnut leaves and licorice that did nothing to replace tea, and then took the seat opposite Eve. "You went to Monsieur Profiteer's bed intending to please him so you could go on spying on him."

"Yes."

"The information you get from him is good, much better than you get from merely waiting tables," Lili said. "And you have now learned that part of what pleases your profiteer is letting him please *you*. You'll have to allow it, if you're to stay in his bed and keep collecting that precious information."

"I would rather f-fake the pleasure," Eve heard herself saying. What a strange conversation this was to be having in a bare little room over cups of terrible makeshift tea, as prosaically as English ladies discussed church matters over china saucers. "But I'm not a g-good enough liar, Lili. I am a very great liar, but I cannot stifle p-p—stifle pleasure and fake it at the same time. He is so v-v-very good at reading me now."

"And is he pleased with what he reads from you?"

"Yes. He's a little fond of me, I think. He's taking me for a weekend in Limoges soon."

"Then go, and take him for everything he's worth." Lili looked fierce. "Every glass of wine before bed, every *petite mort* in bed, every drop of news he leaks after bed. This job has few enough pleasures. The food is terrible, the liquor is almost nonexistent, the cigarettes are getting scarcer, and the clothes are appalling. We have nightmares and complexions like ashtrays and we live in constant expectation of getting arrested. So don't feel guilty for the little bit of pleasure you get, from whatever source. *Take it.*"

Eve sipped another swallow of sour liquid. "You aren't going to say a w-word about sin?" Lili was oddly devout despite her outer frivolity; she carried a rosary with her on every border crossing and spoke fondly of her confessor and the nuns at Anderlecht.

"We're mortals; we sin." Lili shrugged. "It's our task in life. Le Grand Seigneur forgives us—that's His."

"And what's your task? Picking us all up when we're wallowing in the m-mire?" Even stolid Violette had her black moments—Eve had seen her despondent and shaking one evening after losing a downed pilot to a German sentry halfway across the border, and it had been Lili who brought Violette out of the darkness, just as she did tonight for Eve. "Are you ever frightened and despondent?"

Lili lifted one shoulder, almost flippant. "Danger does not frighten me, but I do not like to see it. Now, haven't you got work to do? I certainly do."

She was gone ten minutes later, rice-paper report rolled inside the staff of her umbrella. Eve departed in the other direction for Le Lethe. As she entered the restaurant, already being set with linens and silver, she passed Christine, who twitched her skirts out of the way.

"Whore," she whispered, voice barely audible. Eve stopped, looking over her shoulder. She raised her eyebrows, giving them Lili's devastating arch.

"I don't know what you mean."

"I saw you." Christine's hiss was spiteful, though she kept her eyes on the candles she was lighting. "Going up the stairs to Monsieur Bordelon's rooms after shift was done. He's a profiteer and you're just a—"

Eve took a fast step forward, seizing Christine's wrist. "Say a word and I'll get you fired. One word of gossip, and you'll be out of this job where you get left-over *tartiflette* and lobster *bisque* at closing. Hear me?" She sank her nails into Christine's wrist, shifting so the waiters bustling past with trays of crystal wouldn't notice. "I can have you *fired*," Eve repeated, and didn't stutter once. "Blacklisted. You'll never get another job in this city, and then you will starve."

Christine wrenched away. "*Whore*," she hissed again.

Eve shrugged, gliding away. She'd been hitting her-self with that word for quite a few days now. But she discovered in that moment that she wasn't willing to be called *whore* by anyone else, least of all a woman stu-pider than a bowl of lobster *bisque*.

CHAPTER 21
CHARLIE

May 1947

remember this." Eve pointed to the stone-arched bridge
spanning the slow blue river that wound through
Limoges. A Roman bridge, I thought, crumbling and romantic looking, the little French cars hooting and dashing across it looking incongruously modern. "It was
twilight, not afternoon," Eve went on. "René Bordelon
stopped there, right by the river, and said he'd always
thought outside seating an abomination for any restaurant that was not a common café, but if he could have
that view, he might consider it."

She turned away, hands thrust into the pockets of
her fraying sweater, and looked along the grassy slope,
the trees, the buildings stretching away along the bank.
"The son of a bitch got his wish. He opened his second
restaurant down the bank, with this view."

She went striding off down the cobbled street. I

looked at Finn, and we both shrugged in unison, wandering after her. Eve had awakened early, and we'd made good time from Paris to Limoges. Eve had been talkative again, so each mile brought more war stories, though some of them I had trouble believing (a failed attack on the *kaiser*?). She'd directed us to a hotel near Limoges's medieval cathedral, sending Finn to park the Lagonda while she went in and interrogated the *concierge* in rapid French, waving the scribbled address I'd given her—the address of the second Le Lethe, where Rose had worked. As soon as Finn came back, Eve was setting out into the city on foot, leading us down twisting cobbled streets. Limoges was a pretty place: weeping willows drooping toward the river's surface, Gothic church spires piercing the skyline, potted geraniums hanging from balconies—and it didn't have the half-wrecked look of northern France, which had been more thoroughly overrun by Nazis.

"More peaceful here than in Paris," Finn said, echoing my thoughts. He strode along in his shirtsleeves, drawing a few disapproving looks from Frenchmen in their crisp summer suits, but the women didn't seem to mind his rumpled appearance if the glances were anything to go by. Finn looked back at all those passing faces—the bustling young mothers with their straw hats, the men frowning over their newspapers at café tables. "Pink cheeks," he noted. "Not so pinched and bleak as the people we saw up north."

"This was the Free Zone," I said, finally able to keep up with Finn's long stride now that I had flat sandals and cropped trousers rather than tottering heels. "The Vichy crew wasn't anything to write home about, but the people here still had it better than they did up north."

"Heh," Eve snorted from ahead of us. "Don't be so

sure. They had the Milice to deal with, and the Milice were nasty buggers."

"Milice?" Finn asked.

"French militia recruited to hunt their own for the Germans. I always hated those b-bastards."

"But the Milice weren't around during your war, Eve." I tilted my head, curious. "You weren't part of the last war."

"Says you, Yank."

"Wait, you did work in the second war, too? What did you—"

"Not relevant." Eve stopped suddenly, cocking her head as the sound of bells drifted down through the lazy summer air. "Those bells. I remember those b-bells." She resumed her straight-backed stride down the river-bank and I followed, shaking my head.

"When were you last here in Limoges, Gardiner?" Finn asked.

"August 1915," Eve said, not looking back. "René Bordelon brought me for a weekend."

Just a handful of words, but the suspicion I'd been nursing slid to certainty—a suspicion about the elegant owner of Le Lethe. I'd known from the sheer volume of loathing in Eve's voice that he was something special to her; you don't hate someone that much without a very personal involvement. Now I knew: he'd been her lover. Eve had climbed into bed with the enemy to spy on him.

I looked at her, her proud ravaged face and soldierly stride down the cobbled street. She hadn't been much older than me at the time. *Could you climb into bed with a Hun just to spy on him, Charlie?* Pretend I liked him, smile at his jokes, let him unbutton my blouse, all so I could rifle his desk and his conversation for useful information? Knowing I could get shot any time I was caught?

I looked at Eve, and I admired her so much. I didn't just want her to think well of me; I wanted to be more like her myself. I wanted to introduce Rose to her: "Meet the crazy cow who helped me find you when everyone else gave up." I could imagine Eve giving Rose that down-the-nose gaze, and Rose giving it right back. I could imagine the three of us tossing back drinks and talking over each other, the strangest trio of women ever to become friends.

I wondered if Eve had ever had a friend who meant to her what Rose meant to me. In all her war stories, the only woman she ever mentioned was Violette, who in Roubaix had spat in Eve's face.

"That's a serious face you've got all of a sudden," Finn said, looking down at me.

"Just musing." I couldn't manage to be sad. The sun was warm on my head, and my arm brushed Finn's every other stride or two, which filled me with a ridiculous shiver of sensation. "Every step is another step closer to Rose."

He cocked an eyebrow. "What makes you so certain she's waiting to be found?"

"I don't know." I tried to put it into words. "The hope keeps getting stronger the closer we get."

"Even though she didn't write you in, what? Three, four years?"

"Maybe she *did* write me. Letters went astray all the time, during the war. Besides, I was only eleven when she last saw me. She might have still thought I was too young to hear something as shameful as—" I patted my stomach mutely. "I'm feeling more and more strongly that she's here. Eve makes fun of me when I say I can *feel* her, but—"

Eve stopped so suddenly I nearly walked into her. "Le Lethe," she said quietly.

It must have been a lovely restaurant a few years ago. I could see the beautiful lines of the building, old beams in the half-timbered style, a wrought-iron fence enclosing a dining terrace that took full advantage of the view. But the low-hanging sign with the carved gilt letters spelling out LE LETHE had been crudely splashed with red paint, and the broad front windows were boarded over. It had been a long time since waiters served *vichyssoise* and *mille-feuilles* here.

"What happened?" I asked, but Eve had already gone to the medieval doors, padlocked and barred. She gestured to the letters carved roughly into the wood, half obscured by slops of paint: *COLLABOR*—

"*Collaborateur*," she said quietly. "Up to your old tricks, René? You should have learned the first time— the Germans always fucking lose."

"Easy to say from hindsight," Finn said mildly. "It wasn't that clear-cut on the ground."

But Eve was already moving to the next building, reaching the door and hammering on it. No one answered, and we moved on to the next house. It took four different tries and one failed interview with a housewife who knew nothing about the old restaurant, but at last we found an ancient Frenchwoman with a cigarette dangling from her first two fingers and bitter, bitter eyes.

"Le Lethe?" she answered Eve's question. "Closed at the end of '44, and good riddance."

"Why good riddance?"

A curl of the woman's lip. "The place was a nest for Germans. Every SS officer with a French whore on his arm went there on his nights off."

"The owner allowed that?" Eve's posture had changed, become softened and slump-shouldered, and her voice was conversational. She'd turned into someone else, the way I'd seen her do in a London pawnshop, and I hung back with Finn, letting her work her magic. "What was his name, the owner?"

"René du Malassis," the old woman said, and spat. "A profiteer. Some people said he was in the pocket of the Milice, and it wouldn't surprise me."

Du Malassis. I filed the name away even as Eve asked, "What happened to Monsieur du Malassis?"

"Disappeared into the night, Christmas of '44. He knew which way the wind was turning. Who knows where he went, but he hasn't showed his face here since." The old woman gave a slow, unpleasant smile. "If he did he'd get a short noose and a long struggle on a lamppost."

"For collaboration?"

"There are collaborators, *madame,* and there are men like him. In '43, you know what du Malassis did? He had a young *sous-chef* dragged out of those doors at the end of the night's shift, announcing that the lad was a thief. Searched him right there in the street with every-one watching—the restaurant's entire staff, passersby, neighbors like me who came running at the noise."

I could see it: the nighttime mist rising off the river, the wide-eyed bystanders, a boy in a *sous-chef*'s apron trembling. Eve said nothing, listening so intently she'd turned to stone. The old woman went on.

"Du Malassis dragged a handful of silver out of the boy's pockets, and said he'd telephone the police. Prom-ised he'd have the boy arrested and shipped east. Who knows if he could have done it, but everyone knew du Malassis stacked up favors with the Nazis. The boy tried to run. Du Malassis had a pistol in that elegant jacket of his, and he shot the boy in the back before he'd gone ten steps."

"Did he now," Eve said softly. I shivered.

"He did." The old woman was brusque. "And du Malassis just stood there cleaning his hands off with a handkerchief, grimacing at the smell of gunsmoke. Told his *maître d'* to telephone the authorities to have the mess cleaned up. Then turned his back on that boy's body and went inside, cool as cream. That's the kind of man he was. Not just a collaborator. An elegant killer."

Finn spoke. "Did the Nazis make any protest?"

"Not that I ever heard. He must have called in favors to avoid arrest or censure, because his restaurant kept right on prospering. Oh, there's plenty in Limoges who would have happily put a rope around that man's neck, and he knew it. That's why he ran, once it was clear the Germans would lose." The old woman took a drag off her cigarette, looking at us sharply. "Why are you so curious? Is du Malassis any relation to you?"

"To the devil, maybe," Eve said with soft venom, and the two women exchanged tight acid smiles. "Thank you for your time," Eve said, and turned away. But I stepped forward, addressing the old woman in my slangy American French.

"*Pardonnez-moi, madame.* I *am* looking for a relation—someone who might have worked at Le Lethe. Not a collaborator," I said hastily as the woman's brows came together. "You might have noticed her. People tended to notice Rose. Young, blond, a laugh like a bell." I brought out the worn photograph Rosie had sent me in one of her letters in '43. The photo of her looking over her shoulder like a Betty Grable pinup, grinning. Before the old woman said a word, I knew she'd recognized Rose.

"Yes," she said. "Pretty girl. You'd see those SS bastards pinching her on the hip when she brought their drinks, and she didn't go batting her lashes like some of those sluts du Malassis hired. She'd find a way to spill a drink on them and then go oozing apologies sweet as pie. You could see it all the way across the terrace."

That rocked me back on my heels. A new memory of Rose that wasn't mine. Rose, spilling beer on German soldiers. My eyes prickled. It sounded like her.

"When did you last see her?" My voice came out hoarse, and I realized for the first time that Finn had taken my hand and gripped it tight.

"Before the restaurant closed. She must have stopped working there." The woman spat on the ground again. "It wasn't a place for decent girls."

My heart sank. I'd so hoped Rose would be alive and *here*, living in Limoges. But I looked at the old woman and forced a smile. "Thank you for your help, *madame*."

I wasn't out of ideas yet.

Eve had another of her bad spells that night. She didn't start screaming this time, she just woke me with a series of dull thuds against the wall between our bedrooms. I poked my head out into the hotel hall. No Finn. Just me.

I pulled a sweater over my slip and padded to Eve's door, pressing my ear to the panels. Still that dull *thwack,* as though she was knocking something against the wall. *Hopefully not her head*, I thought, and rapped softly. "Eve?"

The *thwacks* kept going.

"Don't aim that pistol at me. I'm coming in."

Eve sat on the floor in the far corner, but she was clear-eyed this time, not mumbling in the grip of waking nightmares. She stared at the ceiling, the Luger in her hand, and she methodically banged its butt against the wall. *Thwack. Thwack. Thwack.*

I put my hands on my hips, glaring. "Must you?"

"Helps me think." *Thwack. Thwack.*

"It's midnight. Can't you sleep instead of think?"

"Haven't even tried. The nightmares'll be waiting. I'll wait it out till dawn." *Thwack. Thwack.*

"Well, try to bang more quietly." I turned to go, yawning. Eve's voice called me back.

"Stay. I can use your hands."

I looked over my shoulder. "For what?"

"Can you field-strip a Luger?"

"They didn't teach that at Bennington, no."

"And I thought all Americans were gun mad. Let me show you."

I found myself sitting cross-legged opposite Eve as she pointed out the various bits of the pistol and I clumsily broke it apart. "The barrel . . . The side plate . . . The firing pin . . ."

"Why am I learning this?" I asked, and yelped as she hit me across the knuckles for pushing the receiver axle the wrong way.

"Field-stripping a Luger, that *really* used to help me think. My hands are too buggered up to do it properly anymore, so I'll borrow yours. Get the oil out of my satchel."

I started spreading out the pistol's disassembled bits. "What are you pondering?" Her eyes had a thoughtful glitter that wasn't whiskey, though I saw the usual tumbler with its half measure of amber fluid at her knee.

"René du Malassis," she said. "Or rather, René Bordelon. And where he went."

"You're assuming that he's still alive, then." She'd denied it so stubbornly in Roubaix.

"He'd be seventy-two now," Eve said softly. "But yes, I'm betting he's still alive."

She couldn't stop the ripple that crossed her face, a ripple of loathing and self-loathing together. How rare it was to see an emotion she couldn't mask. She looked almost fragile, and an odd protectiveness tightened my chest. "What makes you certain du Malassis is your Bordelon?" I asked gently.

A half-smile. "Malassis is the surname of the publisher who printed Baudelaire's *Les Fleurs du mal*."

"I'm really starting to hate Baudelaire. And I've never even read him." At this point I didn't need to.

"You're lucky." Her voice was dry. "I had to listen to René quote his whole damned *oeuvre* cover to c-cover."

I paused, holding the Luger's barrel in one hand and the oiled cloth in the other. "So, you and he were . . ."

A raised eyebrow. "Are you shocked?"

"No. I'm no saint." I patted the Little Problem, which seemed happier these days. It still made me tired, but the nausea was better, and I wasn't getting any more strangely articulate thoughts from the direction of my stomach.

"René took me to this hotel." Eve looked around the room as though not quite seeing it. "Not this room. He wouldn't stand for anything this small. The best room in the hotel: fourth floor, big windows, blue velvet drapes. A huge bed . . ."

I didn't ask what had happened in that bed. There was a reason she'd decided to stay up all night rather than risk dreaming. "How does this go?" I murmured, holding out various pistol bits, and she showed me how to rub down the individual parts with the oiled cloth. "So when René Bordelon needed to flee Lille, he became René du Malassis," I said eventually. "And when he needed to flee Limoges, he disappeared again. How could that be so easy when so many collaborators were caught?" I thought of the images I'd seen in the papers of such people, male and female, humiliated or worse. The old Frenchwoman hadn't spoken idly of hanging people from lampposts.

"René was no fool." Eve put away the gun oil with clumsy hands. "He catered to those in power, but he always knew they might lose. And by the time he knew they *would* lose, he would have had a plan in place to rabbit away with his money and a new name, and start over—after Lille, and after Limoges." She paused, considering. "I think he was planning the first of those bolts when he brought me here in '15. I didn't realize it then; he said he wanted to site out spots for a second restaurant. I assumed he meant expanding his business ventures, but maybe he wasn't ever thinking about expanding. Maybe he was scoping out a spot for a new *life,* in case he needed one. And he did."

"Hmm." I laid out the last of the pistol parts, all oiled up. My hands were a greasy mess, but I'd gotten interested in the whole process. If they'd taught me to field-strip guns instead of bake biscuits in Home Ec, I might have paid more attention. "You know, there's something different between René Bordelon and René du Malassis besides the name."

"What's that, Yank?"

"Willingness to pull a trigger." I looked down at the Luger's trigger, lying innocent among the disassembled components. "The way you described him in the first war, he was too fastidious to do his own dirty work. When he caught a thief in his restaurant—your predecessor—he called the Germans in, and *they* did the shooting. The second time around, from what that old woman said, he didn't hesitate to pull the trigger himself."

"Not a small l-line to cross," Eve agreed. She sounded like she'd already done considerable pondering along these lines.

"So what changed him?" I asked. "By the end of the first war, what turned him from a profiteering aesthete into"—I remembered the old woman's words—"an elegant killer?"

Eve gave a crooked smile. "I imagine it was me."

There was a piece of this equation I didn't have yet, but before I could ask, Eve gestured for me to reassemble the Luger, lips sealing. I changed tack.

"How will we find him now? He won't still be du Malassis; he'll have taken a new name again." I slid bolt into barrel. "Where would he rabbit to from Limoges?" And what a chill it gave me to know that we weren't just hunting an old profiteer, an old enemy . . . but a murderer.

"There's an English officer I can contact," Eve said, allowing my change of direction. "Someone from the old days. He ran networks of spies like me, and he kept on doing it through the next war. Stationed in Bordeaux, currently—I telephoned from London, but he was off duck hunting. He'll be back by now. If anyone can dig up information on an old collaborator, it would be him."

I wondered if this was the Captain Cameron she'd spoken of. He didn't sound half bad in the stories she'd been telling. I wanted to get a look at him, see if he matched the internal picture I'd been building, but I had my own trail to follow.

"You contact your friend in Bordeaux," I said. "I'm going to take Finn and the car, and go look for my cousin."

Eve cocked an eyebrow, even as she was showing me how to press the Luger's barrel down to take the pressure off the spring. "Look where for your cousin? If she's alive, she might be anywhere."

"My aunt said she'd originally been sent to a village outside Limoges to have her baby. The kind of total backwater where people send disgraced girls." I was starting to get the hang of the pistol now; the parts were sliding easily in my oily fingers. "Rose stayed there to have her baby, then four months later came to work here in Limoges. But maybe she left her baby back in the village with a family to raise. Maybe she went back there when she stopped working at Le Lethe. Who knows? But it's a small town, and everyone knows everyone in small towns. Someone will recognize the picture of Rose." I shrugged. "It's a place to start, anyway."

"A good p-plan," Eve agreed, and I flushed with pride at her approval. "Take that pistol apart one more time." I field-stripped the Luger again, and Eve began another story: the weekend she and René Bordelon had spent here in the summer of 1915. "We came on the train, and he took me to buy a new dress. It was one thing for me to come to his rooms in a work dress, but he wasn't going to be seen on the promenade or at the theater with me in an old shirtwaist. It was a Poiret, almond green corded silk trimmed with black velvet, forty-three velvet-covered buttons down the back. He'd count them off as he undid them . . ."

I reassembled the firing pin, wondering what Eve planned to do when she found her old enemy. Have him arrested? Everyone knew the French dealt harshly with collaborators. Or simply trust the Luger to make an end for her? I did not at all put that out of the realm of possibility.

What did he do to you, Eve? And what did you do to him?

She was telling me how the river in Limoges had

looked gray when she was last here, not the bright blue it was now. How the leaves had fluttered around the heels of her new patent-leather shoes, bought to go with the almond green dress. "You remember it so clearly," I said, presenting her with the cleaned and oiled pistol.

"I should." Eve downed the rest of her whiskey. "That was the weekend I missed my monthly, and started fearing René had got me pregnant."

CHAPTER 22
EVE

September 1915

Autumn had barely begun, and already the cold had clamped down like a vise. Lille was a city of two worlds living side by side, the falling temperatures making a demarcation clearer than any line. On one side the Germans, who had all the coal, candles, and hot coffee they needed. On the other side the French, who had almost none of those things. The two worlds had been described as *French* and *German,* or *conquered* and *conqueror,* but now they were simply *cold* and *not cold.*

Eve didn't notice. She was pregnant, and the thought had driven every other from her mind.

It hadn't been very long, but the signs weren't difficult to read. Two monthly bloods missed—some women in Lille whispered that their courses now came irregularly due to semistarvation, but Eve didn't think she was so lucky. She'd grown thin as a wafer, but she still had enough black-market scraps from Le Lethe not to starve. Besides, other signs had been quick to follow: her breasts had begun to feel tender, she was suddenly tired at all hours, and she had to swallow down unexpected shafts of queasiness when a juicy roast passed from the kitchens, or when she had to carry a pungent slab of Morbier in for the cheese course.

Eve was certain. René Bordelon had made her pregnant.

It was a realization that should have driven her to utter despair, but there was no time for that. The Alice Network was busy. French lines in Champagne had been pushing a sustained assault; the German *Kommandant* and his generals had spoken a good many terse words about it over their coffee. Words Eve reported. She marked hours waiting tables and then marked more hours in René's bed, at work one way or another at least nineteen hours of every day. She passed information about artillery placements, about casualty lists, about train schedules and supply depots. She was so used to the knife edge she walked that it seemed almost normal; she kept her face and her voice so continuously locked that she sometimes wondered if she had a single spontaneous expression left. She could not panic and fall into despair simply because her body had decided to betray her. She could *not*.

Eve opened her door that Saturday to Violette, come to stay on her usual round through Lille, and nearly cried with relief. All week she'd had nightmares of Violette getting arrested, *now* of all times. Eve never much liked Violette, but oh, she needed her.

Violette must have seen some flash of her relief, because surprise flickered behind those round glasses. "You look glad to see me," she commented, scraping mud off her worn boots. She frowned, adding, "Is there news?"

"No news," Eve said. "But I need help, and you're the only one I can ask."

Violette took off her gloves, rubbing her chilled hands as she looked at Eve curiously. "Why me?"

Eve took a deep breath. "Lili s-s-s—she said you were a nurse."

"Red Cross, yes. Though not for long. The war had just begun."

Eve pushed down a sudden surge of doubt, but forged on anyway, because what choice was there? "I am pregnant," she said bluntly, and made herself look Violette in the eye. "Can you help me take care of it?"

Violette stared at her a moment, then let out an explosive breath. "*Merde,* are you stupid enough to mix a love affair with work like this? Don't tell me you've fallen in love with Antoine or—"

"I'm no idiot schoolgirl," Eve snapped. "I had to sleep with my employer for *information*, Violette. Didn't Lili t-tell you?"

"Of course not." Violette pushed her spectacles up her nose. "You didn't think to take some precautions?"

"I tried. They didn't w-work." Tiptoeing out of his bed at night to rinse herself out in his luxurious bathroom had felt more squalid than what took place in the bed, but Eve had never skipped doing it. If only it had worked. "And before you ask, nothing else has w-worked either. Jumping down the steps, hot baths, d-doses of brandy. Nothing."

Violette gave another sigh, less explosive, and perched on the edge of the bed. "How long?"

"Two m-months, I think." By Eve's best guess, it must have happened very early. Maybe just the second or third time.

"Not very far along, then. Good."

"Can you help me or not?" Eve's heart lodged in her throat, and her voice rasped around it.

"I saw more battle wounds than pregnant women." Violette folded her arms tight across her chest. "Why don't you tell Bordelon? A rich man like him, he might pay a real doctor."

Eve had already thought of that. "What if he wants it?" She wasn't sure he would—René was hardly a family man—but Eve suspected he had something of a dynast in him. What if he decided Eve might have a boy, and found that thought . . . interesting?

"If so, you could still get it taken care of on the sly. Tell him you miscarried."

Eve shook her head. She knew René; he hated mess and expense. To him, a mistress was something pretty that never caused trouble. Whether she miscarried a child he wanted or he had to pay to get her taken care of, she was trouble. She might easily lose her place at Le Lethe. No, her best chance to continue her work for Lili was to have things continue as they were.

"Hm." Violette didn't suggest telling Captain Cameron or the other officers who oversaw the Alice Network. "You know the procedure can be dangerous. You're sure it's what you want?"

Eve gave a single violent nod. "Yes."

"You might bleed to death, doing it this way. It's still early days; if you wait you might still miscarry, or—"

"*Do it.*"

Her voice came out in a desperate snarl. It was more than her determination to stay, to continue her work. It was the fact that behind her surface calm, Eve battled a panic bordering on madness. She'd given up so much since coming to Lille—home, safety, virginity, even her *name*—and she'd done so willingly because it was for an unseen future, a sunny clearing somewhere safely beyond war and invaders. And now the invader was inside her, claiming her as thoroughly as the Germans claimed France, and there was no more future. At a stroke she'd been rendered from a spy and a soldier, someone who battled enemies and saved lives, into just another pregnant woman to be unceremoniously bundled home and treated like a whore. Eve knew exactly what kind of future she could expect seven months from now if she did nothing: unmarried, unwanted, jobless, penniless, despised, shackled for life to an invader seeded by an enemy in the cold, starvation-racked hell of a war zone. Her body had betrayed her so completely: giving way to pleasure in a profiteer's arms, then keeping some portion of him when she tried so hard every night to wash away every trace. She was not going to let it betray her any further.

Eve had spent weeks huddled in her cold bed, fighting the wild surges of blind panic and icy dread, and she knew she would *happily* risk bleeding to death for the chance to reclaim her future from the invader.

Violette was nodding tersely. "There's a surgeon in the network who treats people for us," she said as Eve stood battling her own emotions. "He wouldn't touch something like this—he goes to mass every day—but I can borrow some instruments on a pretext tomorrow."

"Tomorrow," Eve said, dry-mouthed. "Yes."

Sunday. Holy Day, blessed day, ironic day because it was the day Eve had decided to do something most men would call her a murdering slut for even considering. It could only be Sunday, because Le Lethe was closed Sunday. It meant she had a full day free to bleed and die, or bleed and recover.

"What happens if I die?" Eve managed to ask when

Violette arrived with her bag of borrowed instruments. "During the procedure or—or after?"

"I leave you here and never come back." Violette was matter-of-fact. "I'd have to. If I tried to see you buried, I'd be arrested. Your neighbor would probably find you in a day or two, and then it would be a pauper's burial for you while Lili notified Uncle Edward."

The sordid reality of such plans hit Eve like a knife thrust. "Well. Let's g-get on with it, then." And try not to die.

"Lie quiet." Violette said it over and over that afternoon. Eve didn't know why; she lay quiescent as a marble figure on a tomb. Perhaps it was meant for reassurance. The bed was spread with a clean layer of sheets; Violette wore an apron with a crossover front surely left from her Red Cross days, and her voice had a nurse's crispness. Instruments gleamed on a folded cloth, but Eve didn't look at them too closely. She pulled off her petticoats and underclothes and stockings, everything below the waist, and lay down. Cold. She was so cold.

"Laudanum," Violette said, uncapping a tiny vial, and Eve opened her lips obediently, swallowing down the drops. "There will be pain, I warn you." Her voice was brusque, officious, and Eve thought of Lili saying, *The habit of nagging, let me assure you, goes with a nurse no matter* what *she does*. Right now, Eve found it comforting.

Violette wiped down her instruments with something astringent. She cleaned her fingers with the same harsh-smelling stuff, and warmed the metal between her hands for a moment. "Doctors," she said, "never warm their instruments. They don't realize how cold the metal is on a woman's parts."

The laudanum was already making Eve's head swim. The room blurred. Her body felt blunt and heavy. "Have you done this before?" she heard herself ask from a distance.

"Once," Violette said brusquely. "Earlier this year—Antoine's little sister, Aurélie. She works for us, escorting the couriers so the locals don't get suspicious, and she got caught at night by some German soldiers looking for fun. Only nineteen, poor thing. Her family came to me when they found out the bastards left her *enceinte*."

"Did she survive—this?" Eve looked at the instruments in Violette's hands.

"Yes, and she went right back to work for the network afterward, good stout-hearted girl that she is."

If she did it, so can I, Eve thought. But she couldn't stop herself from flinching as she felt Violette's hands part her bare knees, and heard her say, "Brace yourself, now."

Despite Violette's attempts at warming the instrument, it pierced Eve like an icicle. The pain, when it came, was sharp. "Lie quiet," the order came, though Eve didn't move. Violette did something, Eve didn't know what, it all felt very distant. The pain bloomed then faded away again, bloomed and faded. Cold. Eve closed her eyes, willing it all to go far, far away from her. *Lie quiet.*

The instruments were gone. It was done, but it wasn't done. Violette was saying something. "—will be some bleeding now. You don't panic at the sight of blood, do you?"

"I don't panic at anything," Eve said through numb lips, and Violette smiled grudgingly.

"You don't, I'll say that for you. I first saw you, and I thought you'd go screaming home to your mummy within a week."

"It hurts," Eve heard herself saying. "It hurts."

"I know," Violette said, and gave her more drops of laudanum. Bitter. Why did everything in Lille taste bitter except what came from René? He was the source of rich food and delicious wine and warm cups of *chocolat,* whereas everything shared with Lili and Violette was bitter and vile. In Lille everything was upside down; evil was delicious and good tasted like gall.

Violette was taking bloody cloths away, replacing the pads under Eve's hips and between her legs. "You're doing well," she said. "Lie still."

Church bells rang outside, sounding evening mass. Did anyone go? Who thought prayer did any good in this place? "Lille," Eve said, and heard herself quoting Baudelaire. "'*Its black enchantments, its hellish cortege of alarms, its cups of poison and its tears, its din of chains and dead men's bones . . .*'"

"You're rambling," Violette said. "Try to lie quiet."

"I know I'm rambling," Eve replied. "And I *am* lying quiet, you bossy bitch."

"That's gratitude for you," Violette commented as she piled Eve with more blankets.

"I'm cold."

"I know."

And Eve cried violently. Not from pain, not from sadness. From relief. René Bordelon had no more hold on her future, and the relief brought tears like a storm.

By morning it was over.

Violette had a list of instructions. "You might bleed more. Keep plenty of cloth on hand, *clean* cloth. And take this for pain." The little vial of laudanum was pressed into Eve's hand. "I'd stay to keep an eye on you, but I'm scheduled to travel back to Roubaix today. There are urgent reports that need carrying across the border."

"Yes." They had a job to do, after all. "Be careful, Violette. You said the Fritzes monitored your last trip too closely."

"I'll travel a different route if I must." If Violette was afraid—and no one in the network could help but be afraid now; the Germans knew there were spies in the region and the checkpoints had been hellish—she would never show her fear. Something she and Eve had in common. "Can you find a way to keep out of that profiteer's bed for a while? You need time to heal."

"I'll tell him I'm having a bad monthly. He finds all that distasteful." That would buy at least a week.

Violette pursed her lips. "How will you stop this from happening again?"

Eve shivered. "I—I don't know. What I was doing clearly didn't work." She could not possibly go through this again. Never.

"There are devices, but doctors have to fit them and mostly they won't fit unmarried girls. Take a sponge, soak it in vinegar, and push it up inside." Violette mimed wordlessly. "Not infallible, but better than nothing."

Eve nodded. "Thank you, Violette."

A quick brushing gesture, sliding away the thanks. "We won't speak of it, not ever. You know what men do to women who do this. Not just you, but me for helping."

"Never a word."

They looked at each other for a moment, and Eve thought that if they were friends there would be embraces now. They just exchanged nods as Violette pulled up her muffler and headed into the street—yet perhaps they were friends anyway. Perhaps they were friends as men so often became friends; all gruffness and no light conversation, only a shared and wordless understanding. "Good luck in Roubaix," Eve called after the trudging figure, and Violette raised a hand without turning back.

Later Eve wished she had hugged Violette. She wished that very much.

Even getting up to wave at the door left Eve exhausted and head-spinning. She crawled into her bed and stayed there, pulling her thin blankets up, stomach still cramping in long slow rolls. A dull-edged pain that came and went in waves. There was nothing to do but endure, and sometimes weep. The tears rolled over her in waves too, coming and going like the pain.

By the time night had fallen, she wasn't spotting blood anymore, but she still felt weak as a kitten. She sent a message to Le Lethe complaining of a nasty flu. René wouldn't be pleased, but there was nothing to be done about it; Eve couldn't take an entire night on her feet carrying plates back and forth from the kitchen. So she lay quiet, sweating her way through it, passing the time by field-stripping her Luger. It soothed her, the smell of gun oil and the coolness of the barrel in her hands, and she aimed it at nothing and imagined putting a bullet between René's eyes. By the third day the Luger was the cleanest pistol in France, and Eve was cautiously convinced she wouldn't die. She went back to work, avoiding the glowering Christine who clearly thought Eve should be fired for missing three shifts, but knew she wouldn't be. Eve made soft private apologies to René, knowing she looked so gaunt and ill that her story of a flu and a bad monthly were quite credible, and he did not invite her upstairs at the end of the night. Small mercies, Eve thought, wobbling home and looking forward to her room and her empty bed even though it wasn't heaped with René's down-stuffed pillows.

But the room, as Eve let herself in, was already occupied.

"Don't mind me." Lili waved, listless. "I'm just going to sit here and shiver."

"I thought you were making the crossing to Belgium." Eve locked the door. "Escorting that downed pilot."

"I did." Lili sat on the floor in the farthest corner, knees drawn up to her chest, the worn ivory beads of her rosary wound tight through her clenched fingers. "The pilot got blown up by a mine. I collected my messages in Brussels and headed straight back."

The room was freezing, and Lili trembled in her white shirtwaist and gray skirt. Eve pulled a blanket off the bed and dropped it around her shoulders. "You've got blood on your hem."

"That would be the pilot." Lili's eyes were glassy, as though she was the one on laudanum. "Or maybe the woman walking in front of him, or her husband . . . It got all three of them."

Eve sat down, drawing the blond head onto her shoulder. It seemed there were worse nights to have than nights full of cold instruments and sharp belly pains and laudanum-laced waking nightmares.

"The border searchlights light everything up like day." Lili's thumb rubbed along the rosary beads. "Once you get past the border and the shooters, there's the wooded area. The Germans mine it, you know. My pilot wouldn't stay behind me—he went running up to a couple walking in front of us. I think he thought the woman was pretty . . . They all three must have hit a land mine, because they just blew into bits not a dozen feet before me."

Eve closed her eyes. She could see the explosion, the harsh lights.

"And then I picked up my new passes from Antoine." Lili's voice was even, but her thin shoulders hitched under Eve's arm. "He reported that—"

"Sssh." Eve rested her cheek against the blond hair

that smelled like blood. "You don't have to talk. Close your eyes."

"I can't." Lili stared straight ahead, tears leaking slowly down her cheeks. "I see her."

"The woman who stepped on the mine?"

"No. Violette." Lili buried her face then in her folded arms, and began to sob. "Antoine gave me the news, little daisy. Violette was arrested. The Germans have caught her."

CHAPTER 23
CHARLIE

May 1947

ou're not invited to dinner," Eve told Finn and me. "Either of you."

The telephone call she'd put through to her English officer had borne fruit: he was coming from Bordeaux tonight for dinner at the hotel café. Eve had been wearing her fierce mask ever since the meeting was confirmed, but by now I could see behind that mask just a bit. I'd been looking at her rather wonderingly since she'd told me she'd gotten pregnant. *Pregnant.* She'd been almost my age, caught in just my predicament—only she'd been half starving in a city full of enemies who would have marched her to a firing squad if they realized who she really worked for. Suddenly my Little Problem seemed a lot smaller in comparison. I knew what I'd been taught growing up, that what she'd done was wrong, but I couldn't manage to condemn Eve.

She'd been swallowed up in a war; she did what she had to do. In truth, I admired her for carrying on after such a thing.

I knew she'd slough off my admiration, though, so I just smiled. "Just tell me one thing. Is it Captain Cameron you're meeting tonight?"

Eve shrugged, cryptic as always. "Aren't you headed for that village where your cousin went?"

"Yes." Three days we'd been in Limoges already. I'd have taken off for Rose's village sooner, but Finn had to do some more patient tinkering with the Lagonda's innards before he trusted her on the country roads. Today he'd pronounced us ready, and we were leaving Eve behind to await her mysterious dinner companion.

"What do you think?" I asked Finn, sliding into the front seat. "Is it Captain Cameron she's meeting?"

"Wouldn't be surprised."

"Think we'll be back in time to see him?"

"That depends, doesn't it?" He set the Lagonda's fuel-air mixture, advanced the timing. "On whether we find out anything about your cousin or not."

I shivered, part anticipation and part fear, as we started down the street. "Today might be the day."

Finn smiled in answer, driving us out of Limoges at a leisurely pace, one arm along the wheel. He wore his usual old shirt with the sleeves rolled up, but he'd shaved, his jaw smooth for once instead of stubbled, and I wanted to reach over and stroke my hand down his cheek. I wanted it so badly that I had to keep my hands primly folded in my lap. How was it that the Lagonda felt *more* crowded when we didn't have Eve along?

"We should be there soon," I said, just to be saying something. According to Finn's crumpled road map, our destination was only fifteen miles or so west of Limoges.

"I reckon." Finn steered the Lagonda past a fenced

meadow where cows munched grass, a gray stone farm-house in the distance. The outskirts of Limoges had quickly given way to quiet country roads and rutted lanes. It couldn't *be* more picturesque, and I sat there stiff as a board. I didn't know why I was nervous, just that I was. Finn had kissed me back when I planted one on him a few nights ago, but he hadn't made reference to it since. I wanted to move the game along, but I didn't know how. I might be a whiz with numbers but I was a dismal flirt.

"What's this village called again?" Finn asked, breaking my awkward swirl of thoughts.

"Oradour-sur-Glane." On the old road map it looked like a tiny place. Hard to imagine Rose in a French hamlet too small even to deserve the word *town*. She'd always dreamed of Paris boulevards, Hollywood lights. *New York in a pinch*, I remember her saying, *New York's chic enough for me.* And instead she'd come to Oradour-sur-Glane, a hamlet in the middle of nowhere.

The Lagonda rounded a corner, following a rough stone fence seeded with wild wallflowers, and I saw a little French girl walking barefoot along the top, arms out for balance. She had dark hair, but she instantly became Rose to my eyes, blond curls dancing over a blue summer dress I remembered my cousin wearing long ago. A wave of premonition hit me so strongly it was almost certainty. *You're at Oradour-sur-Glane, Rosie, I thought. I know you are. Lead the way, and I'll find you.*

"We won't get there faster with you pushing," Finn commented, and looking down, I realized I was press-ing my cork-sandaled feet against the floor like it was a gas pedal. "Why are you sitting like you're in church?"

"What do you mean?"

The Lagonda came to a stone bridge, a bicycle pass-ing over it in the opposite direction. Finn braked to let

the bicycle pass, then leaned down, took hold of my ankles, and swung my feet up onto the seat. "You usually
sit with your feet curled up."

I was blushing as he put the car back into motion. His
fingers could circle almost all the way around my ankle.
I wished my legs weren't so skinny. I wore a narrow
red skirt I'd bought in Paris, and a loose white buttoned
shirt like a man's that I'd pushed over my elbows and
tied up at the waist rather than tucking it in, and I knew
I looked well in it—but I still wished I didn't have such
skinny legs. Rose had nice legs, even when she was just
thirteen. First thing I'd do if I found her was hug her
till she couldn't breathe and then ask if I could have her
legs.

"We took a wrong turn somewhere," Finn said some
minutes later. "This is south, not west. All these un-
signed roads . . . Here, wait a moment."

He pulled up outside a roadside shop with a display
of postcards and a cat dozing on its step. The cat yawned
as Finn stepped over it to address the proprietor in his
rough Scots-accented French. *Rose and I could get a
cat,* I mused as the tabby washed its tail. My dearly departed Donald (God rest his soul) would never let me
get a cat, because they made him sneeze. "I've decided
I hate Donald," Rose said in my imagination. "Couldn't
you at least invent a *nice* dead husband?"

"You're smiling," Finn said, dropping back into the
still-running Lagonda.

"Just wondering what you'll think of my cousin when
you meet her. Well, not really *wondering.* Everyone
likes Rose."

"Is she much like you?"

"Not at all. Funnier, braver. Pretty."

Finn had been about to turn the car back onto the
street, but he paused, giving me a long look out of those

dark eyes. Finally he turned off the engine, reached out, and pulled me across the seat up against him. Winding his hand through my hair, he put his lips to my ear. "Charlie lass." His breath was warm, sending a spark of current through the entire surface of my skin as he kissed the beating pulse below my ear. "You." Kissing the point of my jaw. "Are." Kissing the corner of my mouth. "Brave." Kissing my lips, very lightly. "Not to mention pretty. Bonnie as a spring day."

"You know what they say about Scotsmen," I managed to say. "They're all liars."

"That's Irishmen. No blarney about a Scot."

His mouth found mine again, and he kissed me for quite a while. Dimly I heard a passing bicycle ring a bell at us, but I had my arms tight around Finn's neck, and my heart was thudding against his hard chest.

Eventually he pulled back, though he still held me tight against his side. "I could stay here all afternoon," he said. "But why don't we go find your cousin?"

"Okay," I said simply, and I had not been this happy in a long time.

"You want to take the wheel?"

I stared at him, and then I grinned. "You'd trust me with the old girl?"

"Slide over."

We traded places. I stretched my feet for the pedals, still smiling. Finn took me through the start-up—"If she was starting cold, you'd set your fuel-air mixture to slightly rich, but you can move it closer to center"— and eventually I turned the Lagonda back toward the west. She purred in my hands.

"Funny," Finn said. "The old man at the shop who gave me directions—he gave me an odd look when I said I was looking for Oradour-sur-Glane."

"What kind of look?"

"Just odd."

"Mmm." I ran my hand along the Lagonda's wheel, feeling the soft cloth of Finn's sleeve pressed against my arm. The sun was warm on my head, and as I steered the convertible along the rutted road, I started humming "*La Vie en rose*." I never wanted to leave this car.

ook." Finn pointed, but I'd already seen it. The looming shape of a church tower. "That should be it."

My blood fizzed as though it had turned to champagne. We'd traded places again as we got closer to Oradour-sur-Glane, since I was too keyed up to focus on driving. The road ahead wound toward the south end of the village, over the river Glane—I could see a church tower, low squat shapes of stone buildings around it, telephone poles. I wondered why the roofs canted at odd angles.

"It's quiet," Finn commented. No barking dogs, no rumble of tram cars, no bicycle horns sounding as we motored into the town's outskirts. Finn slowed the Lagonda, but there were no children playing in the streets. I was more puzzled than anything else, but then I noticed the nearest house had black smoke marks streaking the stone walls. And the roof had fallen in. "There must have been a fire," I said, but the marks looked old, washed by rain.

Finn eased off the gas even more, moving the car at a near idle. The Lagonda's engine whined as though she were uneasy. I looked from side to side across the street. Still no people. More marks of smoke, of fire. I saw a clock lying on a sidewalk as though it had been dropped and abandoned. The face was half melted, but I could see the hands had stopped at four.

"Not a single one of these houses has a roof." Finn pointed and I saw more blackened timbers, more destroyed shingles. No wonder the silhouettes had looked strange from a distance. It had to have been a fire, but these were stone buildings, sturdy and well spaced. How could fire jump between buildings like this?

My fizzing blood had gone very, very heavy in my veins.

The church loomed on our left, massive, built also from the heavy local stone. It too had no roof. "Why hasn't anyone rebuilt?" I whispered. "Even if there was a fire, why hasn't anyone come back?"

The thought came at me like a shrieking train: *maybe there isn't anyone left.*

"No," I said aloud as though arguing with myself. "A whole town doesn't die in a fire." People would have fled. And work had obviously been done in Oradour-sur-Glane after the fire, whenever it happened—there was no rubble, no debris. People had come to clear the buildings and the streets.

So why didn't they stay? Why didn't they rebuild?

The Lagonda crept through the center of town, past an abandoned post office, a tram station. The tracks looked as good as new, as if a tram would be rumbling around the bend at any moment. But it was so silent, not a footstep or the meow of a cat to be heard anywhere. Why were there no *birds* singing? "Stop," I said unsteadily. "I need to get out—I need to—"

Finn halted the Lagonda in the middle of the cobbled street. Who would honk a horn at him here to make him move? There was no traffic. I scrambled out, nearly falling, and Finn steadied me with a hand on my arm. "No wonder the man at the shop gave me an odd look."

"What *happened* here?" This was like a ghost ship abandoned at sea with a meal still on the table. It was like a toy village with no dolls. *Rose, where are you?*

We wandered back the way we'd come. I peered

through the window of a burned-out hotel, and saw furniture inside—small tables thick with dust, chaises for waiting guests, abandoned countertops where desk clerks must have presided. If I went in, I'd probably find the half-melted bell on the counter, waiting to summon bellboys long gone.

"Do you want to go in?" Finn asked. I gave a violent shake of my head.

An empty market square or fairground loomed to our left. A car sat abandoned, rust showing around the doors. Finn ran a hand over the peeling fender. "A Peugeot," he said. "Model 202. Someone's pride and joy."

"So why would he leave it here?"

Neither of us had any answers. But the fear inside me rose higher with every echoing footstep we took.

The church again, rising up behind the stone wall at the road and a farther steep grass slope. A trio of arched windows loomed, looking like eyeless sockets gaping at us. Finn ran a hand over the lower wall, freezing in place. "Charlie," he said. "Bullet holes."

"Bullet holes?"

He passed a hand over the set of pocked marks. "Not rounds from country hunting rifles either. Look how evenly they're spaced. Soldiers fired these rounds."

"But this is a village in the middle of *nowhere*. Who would—"

"Let's get out of here." He swung around with a white face. "We'll ask at the next village, someone can tell us what happened—"

"No." I pulled away. "Rose was here."

"She's not here now, Charlie lass." His eyes flicked up and down the empty street. "No one is. Let's get out of here."

"No . . ." But my skin was prickling all over and the silence was driving me mad, and I was already taking a step in the direction of the Lagonda. I didn't want to stay any more than he did.

That was when I saw a flicker of movement at the corner of my eye.

"Rose!" It burst out of me in a scream. I couldn't see her face, but it was unmistakably a female figure, hunched and wrapped in an old coat despite the warmth, huddled on the grassy slope below the wall of the church. I tore away from Finn, sprinting around the lower wall, up the slope and around another wall, never taking my eyes off the figure. *"Rose!"* I shouted again, hearing Finn scrambling after me, but the figure at the church wall didn't turn. "Rose," I cried a third time like an incantation, like a prayer, and my desperate pleading hand fell on her shoulder.

She turned.

She was not Rose.

Eve? I almost asked, though the woman looked nothing like Eve. She was plump, grandmotherly, with gray hair brushed into a bun—why did she make me think of tall, gaunt Eve? Then her dark eyes found me blankly and I saw the resemblance. She had the same ravaged gaze of a woman who had been harrowed and clawed to the soul. Like Eve, she could have been any age from fifty to seventy. It was all the same to her: like the melted clock, she had stopped permanently at four in the afternoon. When this town had died . . . however it died.

"Who are you?" I whispered. "What happened here?"

"I am Madame Rouffanche." Her voice was clear, no old-lady mumbling. "And they are all dead but me."

Sunlight warming my head. The rustle of grass. Small everyday things made a backdrop for the quiet horror of Madame Rouffanche's voice.

She wasn't even faintly curious as to who Finn and I were, nor did she seem surprised to see us. She was like the chorus in a Shakespeare play: the curtain went up on a set so strange and horrific the audience could not comprehend it, at least not until she walked out and in a calm, dead voice explained the scene. What had happened. When it happened. How it happened.

Not why.

She did not know why. I suppose no one could.

"It was '44," she said as we stood beneath the eyeless socket windows of the half-burned church. "June tenth. That was the day they came."

"Who?" I whispered.

"Germans. Since February, an SS Panzer Division had been stationed north of Toulouse. After the Allies landed in June, the division headed north. On June tenth they came here." Pause. "Later we learned that someone had reported Oradour-sur-Glane as sheltering resistance fighters . . . Or that Oradour-sur-Vayres was. I don't know. It wasn't ever clear."

Finn took my hand, his fingers ice cold. "Go on," I managed to say through stiff lips.

Madame Rouffanche did not need to be told. The story was begun; she would tell it until the end and then walk off the stage again. Her eyes saw past me and through me to the tenth of June 1944.

"It was about two in the afternoon. German soldiers burst into my home and ordered us—my husband, my son, my two girls, my granddaughter—to the fairground." She pointed toward the square where we had seen the abandoned Peugeot. "A number from the village were already assembled. Men and women flocking in from all directions. All the women and children were herded inside the church." She stroked the pocked smoke-streaked stone as though it were a corpse's brow. "The mothers carrying their babies in their arms, or pushing them in prams. Several hundred of us."

Not Rose, I thought sickly. Rose could *not* have been among them. She wasn't a village woman; she was living and working in Limoges. I'd been so certain I'd find her here, but not like this. She couldn't have been here on June the tenth.

"We waited for hours," Madame Rouffanche continued calmly. "Speculating, whispering, growing more afraid. Around four o'clock—"

Four. I thought of the melted clock.

"—a few soldiers entered. Just boys, really. They carried a box between them, with strings hanging out of it that trailed on the ground. They set the box in the nave, close to the choir, and they lit the strings. They retreated, and the box exploded—the church was full of black smoke. Women and children were running everywhere, shoving, screaming, choking."

She sounded flat as a printed page. I wanted to put my hands over my ears to shut out the words, but I stood frozen in horror. Finn, at my side, was not even breathing.

"We broke down the door to the sacristy and flooded in. I sat down on a step—I was trying to get low, to the good air. My daughter ran toward me, and that was when the Germans opened fire from the doors and windows. Andrée was killed where she stood." Pause. Blink. "She was eighteen." Pause. Blink. "She fell over me, and I closed my eyes and feigned death."

"Jesus," Finn said quietly.

"There were more shots, and then the Germans threw armloads of straw and firewood and broken chairs in a heap onto the bodies lying on the flagstones. There was still smoke billowing—I crawled from under my daughter and hid behind the altar. There were three windows high in the wall behind it—I went to the middle one, the biggest, and pulled up the stool the priest used to light the candles. I heaved myself up to it as best I could."

This hunched grandmotherly woman had clawed her way up a sheer stone wall, over a floor thick with bodies and a miasma of smoke and bullets. I didn't know what look Madame Rouffanche saw on my face, but she shrugged.

"I don't know how. My strength was multiplied."

"That happens." Finn was almost inaudible.

"The window had already shattered. I pulled myself up, and flung myself out. I fell about ten feet." She looked up, directly over our heads to the dark and gaping middle window in the church wall. "Here."

My throat choked with an unborn scream. *Here*, the word echoed, *here*. This woman, three years ago, had flung herself out of *this* window, down onto *this* patch of grass where we now stood in the fragrant sunshine. *Here.*

"A woman tried to follow me. The Germans opened fire as soon as they saw us." Madame Rouffanche began to walk, her steps slow and difficult. "I was hit, five times. I crawled this way." We followed her mutely, around the church wall. "I made it to the sacristy garden. The plants weren't dead then; they were growing thick." We stood among the flattened weeds, looking at the barren garden. "I hid among some rows of pea plants. I heard more shots, more screams, more shouting . . . That's when the men and the boys died, most of them. Gunned down. And then there was the rush of fire, as all the roofs were kindled. Night fell, and then came the sound of champagne corks popping . . . The Germans stayed the night, and they drank champagne."

My lips parted but no words escaped. I didn't think

there were any words. Finn turned his back abruptly, but he didn't release my hand. He gripped so hard my fingers felt like they were breaking, and I gripped him back. Madame Rouffanche looked past us serenely, her fingers working as though she were fingering nonexistent rosary beads.

"The Germans stayed a few days . . . They made some attempt to dig pits, hide the bodies. I never knew why. No one could hide it, what they'd done. Such a stench of burned flesh. Panicked dogs running everywhere, looking for their masters . . . The Germans killed most of us, but they had a soft spot for the dogs; they didn't shoot any. They dug a pit here for the dead in the presbytery garden, and it was so shallow a man's hand was still sticking up from the earth after they'd filled it in."

I looked at Finn. He was still turned away, shoulders heaving. I didn't know why I couldn't move, couldn't make a sound. I was frozen.

"By the time the Germans gave up cleaning and made their retreat, I'd been rescued. Two men who sneaked back into the village, looking to see if their sons had lived . . . I begged them to take me to the river and drown me, but they took me to a doctor. I was in hospital a year. When I came out the war was done, and the Germans were gone. But the village was still—"

Pause. Blink.

"—like this."

Pause. Blink.

"I lived," she continued matter-of-factly. "Others too. Men who'd crawled out of the burning barns after being shot; men who were in the fields or gone to neighboring towns that day; a few children who hid in the ruins or escaped the gunfire." There was something struggling to surface in her eyes—she looked as though she were rising slowly back to the present from the island of time that was June tenth, 1944. She looked at me for the first time as if she actually *saw* me. Saw Charlie St. Clair in her red skirt and cork sandals, standing in the wreckage of all the ghosts.

Finn turned back. "Why do you come here?" He gestured at the empty smoke-stained buildings around us. "Why do you *stay*?"

"It is my home," Madame Rouffanche said. "It is still my home, and I am its living witness. You are not the first people to come here, looking . . . It is easier to find me than nothing at all. So tell me who you are seeking. I will tell you if they lived." Her eyes were pitying, bottomless. "And I will tell you if they died."

For a long moment no one spoke. We stood like a trinity in that terrible place, a soft breeze ruffling Finn's hair and rippling the hem of Madame Rouffanche's coat. Then I reached into my pocketbook and took out the worn photograph of Rose. I put it into Madame Rouffanche's lined hands.

I prayed then. I prayed so hard.

She peered at the photograph, holding it closer to her old eyes. "Ahhhh . . . ," she said quietly, recognition flowering in her eyes. "Hélène."

"Hélène?" Finn said it sharply, before I could.

"Hélène Joubert, she said her name was when she came here to have her baby. A widow, very young. I think we all guessed, but . . ." A shrug. "A lovely girl. No one cared. She left her baby with the Hyvernaud family while she went to work in Limoges. She was back every weekend on the tram, Madame Hyvernaud said." A smile. "*Hélène*. A pretty name, but we never called her that. She said she'd been *Rose* as a child, for her pink cheeks, so we called her that. *La belle Rose.*"

Something in me started to shriek.

"Please," I begged, and my voice cracked. "Tell me she wasn't here. Tell me she was in Limoges. Tell me she wasn't *here*."

A long silence from Madame Rouffanche. She looked at the photograph, Rose's laughing face, and I saw her sinking again—back down to the endless loop of *JunetenthJunetenthJunetenth*. "Inside the church," she said, "there were three windows high in the wall—I went to the middle one, the biggest, and pulled up the stool the priest used to light the candles. I heaved myself up, and flung myself out. I fell about ten feet."

Almost exactly the same words she had used telling it the first time, I realized in my daze of horror. How many times had she told this story to people like me, people looking for loved ones, that her tale had hardened into such a rigid sequence, the same words in the same order? Was that how she kept herself sane while she raked over her memories every day for our benefit? "Madame, please—"

She was walking again, back the way we'd come, her steps uneven and mindless. I ran to keep up. "A woman tried to follow me out the window." Pause. Blink. Then the tale changed, as we came back to the dark broken window where Madame Rouffanche had jumped three years ago. "When I looked up—" She looked up now, and my eyes flew to follow hers. I saw what she described. I saw what she'd seen. "I'd been followed by a woman, who was holding out her baby to me from the window."

I saw a blond head, pale arms reaching down from that window. *Here.*

"I took the child—it was screaming in fear."

I saw the wailing bundle, the waving fists.

"The woman jumped, falling down next to me. She seized her baby from me and turned to run."

I saw the slim figure jump, graceful even in terror. I saw her white dress against the grass as she gathered herself up, grass stained and bloodstained, snatching the screaming bundle in her arms and darting toward safety—

"But the Germans fired at us, dozens of shots. We fell."

I saw the fusillade of bullets, the hazy drift of gun-smoke. The chips of stone flying as the church wall was hit. The drops of blood on blond hair.

"I was hit five times. I was able to crawl away." Madame Rouffanche put the photograph gently back into my shaking hand. "But your friend—*la belle Rose,* and baby Charlotte—they were killed."

I heard a rustle then, and I closed my eyes. It was the rustle of a summer dress rippled by warm wind. Rose was standing right behind me—if I turned, I would see her. I'd see her white dress stained red, I'd see the bullets that had gone through her soft throat and her sparkling eyes. I'd see her lying crumpled, legs twitching as she still tried with all her brave heart to flee. I'd see her child in her arms, the baby I'd never meet, the baby who would never grow up to be a big sister to mine. The baby she had named *Charlotte.*

Rose stood behind me, breathing. Only she wasn't breathing. She'd been dead three years. She was gone, and all my hopes were lies.

CHAPTER 24

EVE

October 1915

She died in a hail of bullets. The details blared from smuggled newspapers, and everyone read them, sickened and fascinated. She was executed by firing squad in Belgium: a Red Cross nurse and English spy, instantly famous, heroine and martyr to all. Her name was everywhere.

Edith Cavell.

Not Violette Lameron. Edith Cavell was dead, but Violette, from what the Alice Network could glean, was still alive.

"Cavell looks like Violette," Eve said, devouring the forbidden newspaper in private. Cavell had been arrested in August, but only now had the execution marched to its brutal conclusion. "It's the eyes." Most of the pictures of Edith Cavell were romanticized; she was drawn swooning before the row of guns, her photographs touched up to make her look fragile and feminine. But Eve thought the eyes were anything but fragile. Edith Cavell had helped smuggle hundreds of soldiers from Belgium—it was no job for the fragile. She had hard matter-of-fact eyes like Violette, like Lili, like Eve herself. *Another fleur du mal*, Eve thought.

"This is good. Not to be brutal, but Cavell's death is nothing but good for Violette." Lili was pacing the room—since Violette's arrest nearly three weeks ago she'd been lying low, hiding out with Eve. Hiding didn't suit her. She paced like a caged tigress, her small face tense. "The Germans are being so condemned for Cavell's execution, they won't dare march another female out before a firing squad."

What are they doing to her instead? Eve wondered, full of dread. Torture wasn't common among the Germans and their prisoners, even for spies. Interrogation, beatings, imprisonment, yes—and of course there was the looming fear of execution. But though you might be shot, you wouldn't have your fingernails pulled out first; everyone in the network knew that.

Yet what if they had made an exception for Violette?

Eve didn't voice that thought, knowing Lili was already in agony. So was Eve whenever she remembered Violette's hands tending to her so gently, trying to warm the steel instruments. Without Violette, Eve would be stuck right now with René's seed consuming her. Or she would be dead, because without Violette's expertise she'd have been mad enough to try any potion, any poison that would do the job. Eve owed Violette so much.

"They'll be questioning her." Lili's shoulders sagged as she paced. "Antoine says they have nothing definite. She wasn't caught with papers. Her name was given up when a Brussels boy in the network got taken; all he knew was her name. So the Huns will question her, but if they dig for a weak spot on Violette, all they'll find is bedrock."

Eve imagined Violette sitting across a rickety table from a German interrogator, turning her head so the light flashed, impenetrable, off her spectacles. No, Violette would not be an easy subject for questioning. *As long as they do not torture her.*

"If I could *do* something," Lili fumed. "Get out and start culling some new information—and there will be reports to collect." Her voice was steely. "I will not lose anyone else to the Huns. I'd rather be stood against a wall and shot myself than lose one more."

"Don't be foolish." Eve found herself adopting Violette's bossy sternness, taking her wayward leader in hand since their spectacled lieutenant wasn't here to do it. "Let me see what I can f-find out at Le Lethe."

You might not be at Le Lethe much longer, the thought whispered. With the network compromised, Eve and Lili might very easily find themselves recalled from Lille. It would be the logical step, but Eve couldn't stop now to fantasize about leaving Lille and never seeing René Bordelon again. *For the moment you're still here, so keep listening.*

But there was nothing about Violette to be heard in the sea of gossip. No one could talk of anything but the Cavell execution. German officers were either grim-faced or blustering over their *schnapps*. "Dammit, the woman was a *spy*!" Eve heard a captain sputter. "We're supposed to drench our handkerchiefs over a filthy spy, just because she was female?"

"War is not what it used to be," a colonel countered. "Spies in *skirts*—"

"Putting a woman in front of a firing squad, it's shame on the fatherland. This is not how we conduct war . . ."

"Spying is a craven business. There must be spies in Lille, the entire region is cursed. There was one uncovered in Brussels weeks before Cavell's execution, that one a woman too—"

Eve pricked up her ears, but nothing more was said of Violette. *Please, do not let her end up like Cavell.*

It all made René chuckle later that night as he stood naked at the sideboard before a carafe of liquid as green as a peridot. Recently, he had introduced Eve to absinthe. "What romantics Germans are, going on as if there is any honorable way to conduct a war! War merely happens. The only thing that matters at the end of a war is who is alive, and who is dead."

"Not only that," Eve said, cross-legged in the soft bed with a sheet drawn around her shoulders. "It also m-matters who comes out p-poor and who comes out rich." That earned her an approving smile, as Eve had planned. Marguerite had had to evolve from the wide-eyed country girl he first took a fancy to. She'd gained a veneer of sophistication; she no longer spluttered when she drank champagne; she'd developed a grateful appreciation for the finer things in life that her lover took such pleasure in showing her. She was supple and eager in bed, and she adopted some of René's cynicisms, which made him smile because she parroted them so earnestly. Yes, Eve had grown Marguerite up in precisely calculated stages, and René seemed pleased with what he saw as his creation. "I don't see why it's so t-terrible to want to prosper in wartime," Eve continued a bit defiantly, as if trying on René's profiteering airs and trying to justify them. "Who w-w-w—who *wants* to be hungry? Who *wants* to be dressed in rags?"

René balanced a silver-grated absinthe spoon and a sugar cube across each glass. "You're a clever girl, Marguerite. If the Germans think women are not clever enough or cunning enough to be spies, then they are dupes and fools."

Eve steered the conversation away from her own cleverness. "They say the English are f-furious over Cavell's execution."

"Furious, perhaps." René dripped ice water over the sugar, so the cubes dissolved slowly into the absinthe. "But even more grateful, I imagine."

"Why?" Eve took her glass. *La fée verte* didn't make her hallucinate or chatter, as she feared—René said that was nonsense from French vintners jealous of losing business—but she still made sure to sip sparingly.

"You haven't seen the casualty lists the English are facing, my pet. All those men dying in the trenches every month . . . Their splendid little war is into its second year now, and people are getting weary of blood. But when the Huns gun down an Englishwoman of good birth and unstained reputation—can there be anything more wholesome than a nurse?—then that's a jolt that will galvanize the home front nicely." René sipped his absinthe, sliding back beneath the sheets.

"So will the Germans execute that other s-spy?" Eve dared to ask. "The woman c-caught in Brussels."

"Not if they are clever. They won't want to feed the bad press. I wonder if this one is young and pretty?" René mused, looking at the light through the green jewel of his glass. "If she is, the English should hope the Huns shoot her. Even better than a middle-aged martyr like Cavell is a *pretty* martyr. Nothing to get public outrage fired up like a girl who's young, lovely, and dead. Swallow that down, Marguerite, and come here . . . You've never had opium, have you? We should try it sometime; coupling in an opium dream can be rather eye-opening . . ."

But the spectre of Edith Cavell wasn't finished with

them yet. When Eve returned to her own room that night, Lili sat awake at the rickety table, great purple shadows under her eyes. "Interesting news from Uncle Edward, little daisy."

"Have we been recalled?" Eve's head was still lightly buzzing from absinthe, though she'd managed to duck the prospect of opium. She wasn't taking *any* substance that might cause her to babble in front of René. "Are they pulling us from Lille?" Her head buzzed even more with hope, now that the moment had come.

"No." Lili hesitated, and Eve's heart fell. "And at the same time . . . maybe."

Exasperated, Eve unbuttoned her coat. "Talk sense."

"Antoine brought the message direct from Uncle Edward. The decision to recall us was bruited about, but his mustachioed superior"—that would be the bluff, gossip-leaking Major Allenton Eve remembered from her Folkestone days—"came down on the side of letting us continue."

"Even though the Boches will be looking to unravel the network now they have one of us?"

"Even so." Lili unwrapped a stub of cigarette from a handkerchief, fumbling for matches. "It is Mustache's opinion that our excellent placement here makes it worth the risk. So we are ordered to keep our heads low and continue our work, at least for a few weeks longer."

"Risky," Eve admitted. Even foolhardy. But wars were won by taking risks, and soldiers were the ones who shouldered the dangers. As soon as Eve agreed to take this job, she'd given the Crown her life to spend—what was the use complaining now, much as she yearned to leave Lille and René behind? She dropped down on the edge of the bed, rubbing the grit from her eyes. "So we continue," she said a trifle bitterly.

Lili lit her cigarette stub. "Perhaps not."

"Talk *sense*, Lili."

"Uncle Edward would never contradict a superior openly, but he has . . . ways of making his disagreement known. Clearly he fought the decision to keep us in place. Fought it hard. Without quite putting it into words, he makes it clear that he thinks it far too dangerous for us to continue in operation here. He fears that Violette will be executed like Cavell, and that we'll be caught and suffer the same fate."

"We might." Eve had lived with that fear so long, it seemed normal. "The Fritzes *are* cracking down. It's not as if they've failed to notice that they have dozens of kilometers of front here where they can't keep artillery functioning longer than a fortnight."

Lili let out a long sigh of smoke. "Uncle Edward thinks Mustache is an idiot, but can't countermand his direct orders. However, the hint has come very obliquely that if we were to *request* a transfer from Lille, pleading exhaustion or nerves, he could make it happen."

Eve stared. "As if soldiers can simply beg off their orders—"

"Ordinary soldiers, no. Those in our line of work are different. An asset on the verge of emotional breakdown cannot be relied upon. We'd just cause damage in place; it's far safer to yank us. So . . ."

"So." For a moment Eve let the heady vision swamp her. No more semistarvation and German clocks and cool-skinned hands on her body. No more dreams of bullets in the back. No more *danger*—but that too carried a flip-side consequence. "If we p-plead out, would they re-establish us elsewhere to work? Belgium, or—"

"Probably not." Lili flicked ash from her cigarette. "We'd be the girls who fell apart under pressure. No one puts a cracked cup back on the table and trusts it to stay in one piece."

Go home now, and the fight would be done. However long this war went on, Eve's chance to contribute would be over.

"We should probably do it." Lili's tone was objective. "Beg out. I trust Uncle Edward's instincts over Mustache's any day. If he thinks the danger is too great, he's probably right."

"Yes," Eve acknowledged. "But we have a direct order to stay, regardless. An *order*. And it's just for a few more weeks. If we keep our heads down, then once we're recalled we'll be sent somewhere new to work."

"And we have been lucky so far." Lili shrugged thin shoulders. "Better than lucky, we have been good."

Eve let out a long breath, releasing the heady vision of home. "Then I say we stick it out. At least a little l-longer."

"I'd decided that for myself already, but I didn't want to unfairly influence you. You're sure?"

"Yes."

"That's settled, then." Lili inspected her cigarette butt. "Damn. I've been saving this for a fortnight, and all I got out of it was two good puffs. I can't tell you how I love this primitive life . . ."

Eve reached out, gripping Lili's free hand. "Promise me you *will* be more careful. I worry about you."

"What's the use of worrying?" Lili wrinkled her nose. "Back in September, you know, I let the worrying get to me. I had a premonition of sorts, so strong I went to visit my family. I was convinced I had to see them while I could, one last time . . . When I left, I kept thinking, 'It's all over now; I'm going to be caught and shot.' And nothing happened, nothing at all. Worry is wasted time, little daisy."

Eve paused, choosing her words. "What if Violette is forced to give up your name?"

"Even if they force her to tell about me, they cannot *find* me. I'm a handful of water, running everywhere." Lili smiled. "I'll vary my routine, change my routes. I promise." The smile faded. "Mustache is right about one thing: this won't last much longer, of that I'm sure. There's been a big push through Champagne; they're sure to break through by the New Year. We've only to hold on a little while more." Softly. "And then Violette will be released. If they'll only give her a prison sentence—she can survive that."

"What if it isn't just a few m-months?" Eve had only been in Lille for a matter of months, but it might as well be an eternity. "What if this war lasts years?"

"Then it's years," Lili said. "What of it?"

What of it indeed? And neither of them gave any more thought to pleading their way home.

The news dropped into Eve's ear just a few days later via Kommandant Hoffman and a pair of colonels, all well into their brandies. Not quite a nugget like the news of the kaiser's visit, but important enough to make Eve's ears prick up.

"You're certain?" Lili was back on her rounds, having had new identity cards made in case her old names had been disclosed.

Eve nodded, perching on the edge of the rickety table. "The Germans mean to launch a massive assault in January or February of the new year. Confirmed."

"The target?"

"Verdun." Eve shivered slightly. There was something about the name of that place she'd never seen. A flat finality. *It sounds like a killing ground.* But it wouldn't be if the generals were forewarned. Perhaps Verdun would mark the end to the killing.

"It's a risk to you, passing this on," Lili judged. Not

all Eve's information could be passed, not if acting on it might expose a leak in Le Lethe.

"This is important," Eve answered. "It's for information like this that we didn't beg to go home."

Lili weighed that, but finally assented. "I was already scheduled to meet Uncle Edward in Tournai in two days. You'll have to come with me. For something like this, they'll question us both, as they did for the kaiser report."

Eve nodded. It would be over a Sunday; she'd miss no work. "Can you get an extra safe-conduct pass in t-time?"

"My contact hasn't let me down yet, bless him."

Eve gnawed at her thumbnail, already bitten to the quick. Perhaps it was Violette's arrest, or perhaps the vicious cold of October, but she'd been fighting a wave of superstitious dread all week. Was Christine giving her a suspicious look at work, not just a scornful one? That German lieutenant who stopped talking so suddenly when Eve came with his coffee—was he aware she'd been listening? Had René, who had been so solicitous lately, sniffed out one of her lies and decided to lull her into a false sense of security before pouncing?

Get hold of yourself.

It was a late night with René that evening. He built a fire in his chamber against the cold and read *À Rebours* aloud to Eve, occasionally putting down the book to re-enact some of Huysmans's more depraved passages. Eve was more bored by depravity than titillated by it, but Marguerite was suitably wide-eyed and uncertain, and René seemed pleased. "You're coming along nicely, pet," he murmured, running a fingertip around her earlobe. "Perhaps we should retire to the country for a while, like Huysmans's hero, eh? Somewhere warmer than Limoges where we can enjoy ourselves without all this

Teutonic dreariness. Grasse is very pleasant this time of year. The smell of flowers comes on the wind from every direction. I always thought I'd retire in Grasse, once I had my fill of the restaurant business. I have a dilapidated bit of property there already, just aching to be built up into a little jewel of a villa someday . . . Would you like to go to Grasse, Marguerite?"

"Anywhere w-w-w-warm," Eve shivered.

"You're always cold these days." René's hand slowed, tracing over her skin. "You aren't pregnant, are you?"

That came closer to surprising Eve into an unguarded reaction than anything in a long time. She barely managed not to flinch in utter revulsion. "No," she said, and added a fluttery laugh.

"Mmm. If you were, it wouldn't be a tragedy, pet." He spread his hand flat over her stomach, his long fingers spanning from hip bone to hip bone. "I've never considered myself especially paternal, but a man reaches a certain age and begins to consider his legacy. Or perhaps I've merely become pensive in this dreary weather. Turn over, will you?"

I was right not to tell him, Eve thought even as she began moving under his touch. He might have sent her off like some pampered broodmare, and where would she be now?

It was nearly dawn by the time Eve slipped away. There would be no time to sleep—she quickly wrapped up a false package to give herself something to juggle at the checkpoint, and set out for the station. Lili was late, and Eve was suppressing panic by the time she saw the familiar figure slip down from a carriage. It was a cold foggy morning, and the droplets of moisture seemed to cling to Lili's straw hat, her smoke blue coat. She looked extraordinarily small, striding through the wisps of mist. "We have a problem," she said, lowering her voice to a murmur no passerby could overhear. "Only one safe-conduct pass to be had. It gives permission to travel to Tournai, but it's just for one."

"You t-take it. I don't need to come."

"You do, for a report like this. They'll insist on questioning the source."

"I'll go alone, then—"

"You've never worked a checkpoint on your own before. The guards are very edgy these days, and they aren't used to seeing you come and go as they are me. That hitching tongue could get you looked at. If you get into trouble, I want to be there to talk you out of it." Lili hesitated, gnawing on her lip. "We can't just let it wait till next week's rounds, not something important like this. If we bluff our way through on one safe-conduct pass here, we can easily get another in Tournai to get home."

Eve eyed the German sentries at the station across the street. They looked wet and sullen. In a mood to be spiteful, perhaps, but also cold and miserable enough to be careless. "I say we do it."

"So do I. Take the pass, little daisy, and get in line—stay three people ahead, and don't look back."

A few quick instructions, then Eve moved across the street, making her way through a group of little boys playing tag around the square despite the cold mist. Eve juggled her package, managing a covert glimpse as Lili grabbed the end of a green scarf as it whisked by, reeling in one of the dashing boys. A whisper in the boy's ear—a coin in his hand too, though Lili concealed that deftly—and the child bolted off again. Lili moved to join the line, and Eve was suddenly so nervous she could hardly stand. She hammered the fear flat.

The sentry honked his nose in a vast handkerchief, clearly fighting off a cold. Eve kept herself small and deferential, handing over her safe-conduct pass without a murmur. He scanned it and waved her through—her blood leaped and she turned her back to the sentries, pretending to tuck the paper back into her pocketbook, but keeping it folded tight and small between gloved fingers. In a moment the little boy with the green scarf bumped past the Germans—they barely noticed the children, except to swat them out of the way—and ran smack into Eve, knocking himself over and the package from her arms.

"Up you go!" Eve set him back on his feet, brushing the mud off his sleeve, and the folded safe-conduct pass slid invisibly up his cuff. "Be more c-careful," she admonished, her voice sounding horribly stagy to her own ears as she picked up her package, and the child went careening off again. A sprinted circle round the square—Lili must have told him not to move too directly to his target—and then he was bumping into Lili who seized him by the wrist to administer a scolding. Eve watched through her lashes, and even when looking for it, she couldn't see Lili slip the pass out of the boy's sleeve. But she had it five minutes later, when she came to the head of the line.

Eve's heart beat again like a gong as the German sentry flicked his eyes over the safe-conduct pass. It had no identifying photograph, it was just a piece of paper allowing passage—they all looked alike; surely he wouldn't notice the same one twice . . . Violent relief pierced her as he honked his nose and waved Lili through.

"See?" Lili whispered under cover of the train's piercing whistle, coming to join Eve. "They are too stupid. Shove any bit of paper under their nose, and you can always get through!"

Eve laughed a bit too giddily in her relief. "Can you find a j-joke in absolutely everything?"

"So far," Lili said, airy. "Shall we have time to buy silly hats in Tournai, do you think? I *long* for pink satin . . ."

Eve was still laughing when it happened. Later she wondered if it was her laughter that drew their eyes, if she was too free and easy. Later she wondered, *What could I have done?* Later she thought, *If only—*

A German voice sounded behind them, cutting off Eve's laughter like a knife. "Your papers, *Frauleins.*"

Lili turned, blond brows rising. This wasn't the sneezing sentry, but a young captain with a razor-neat uniform. Beads of mist clung to the brim of his cap, and his face was hard and suspicious. Eve saw the nick in his chin where he'd cut himself shaving, saw that he had very pale lashes, and her tongue turned to stone. If she tried to speak she would not get out a single word before it stuttered like one of those Chauchat machine guns mounding up dead soldiers in the trenches . . .

But Lili spoke, and her voice was easy and impatient. "Papers?" Pointing in annoyance to the sentry. "We've already shown them there."

The captain put out his hand. "You will show me, nonetheless."

Lili bristled, an offended little French housewife. "Who are you—"

He glowered. "If you have passports, I want to see."

That's it, Eve thought, and the terror was so all-encompassing it felt almost calming. There could be no bluffing past the fact that she had no pass. *They are going to take me. They are going to take me—*

She raised her eyes as Lili handed her own safe-conduct pass over to the captain. As he bent his head to examine it, Lili's and Eve's eyes met. *When they take me, walk away,* Eve did her best to telegraph. *Walk away.*

And Lili smiled—that impish lightning flash of a smile.

"It's her pass," she said clearly. "I borrowed it illegally, you stupid Hun."

CHAPTER 25

CHARLIE

May 1947

S he was dead.

My best friend in all the world, dead.

It wasn't enough that the ravenous war had reached out with greedy fingers and stolen my brother from me. The same beast had gobbled up Rose too, taken the girl I loved like a sister and riddled her with bullets.

I think I might have stood in numbed horror forever, there on that patch of tainted grass, pinioned between the church's bullet-pocked wall and the figure of Madame Rouffanche. She might as well have been a pillar of salt like Lot's wife, made immobile and monstrous by what she should never have seen. I could feel a scream scraping up my throat like a rusty blade, but before I could release it, Finn shook me hard. I stared up at him, dazed. *Charlie,* I could see him saying. *Charlie lass—*

but I couldn't hear him. My ears felt like they'd been shelled. All I heard was a monstrous buzzing.

Madame Rouffanche was still staring at me calmly. She deserved my thanks for bearing witness. She deserved balm for her pain and medals for her courage. But I couldn't look at her. She'd been with Rose at the end, seen Rose fall. Why her and not me? Why hadn't I been here, facing the Nazis with Rose? Why hadn't I been at James's side either, listening to him rage, telling him I loved him, drowning out the terrible cacophony of his memories? I loved them both so much, and I'd failed them so utterly. I'd let my brother go out alone on a cold night, not going for a beer as he'd mumbled to me, but for a bullet. I'd thought I might redeem that mistake by finding Rose when everyone else gave up hope—but I'd redeemed nothing. In a Provençal café I'd told Rose I wouldn't leave her, but I had. I'd let an ocean and a war come between us, and now she was dead too. I'd lost them all.

Failed, the harsh voice said in my head, over and over. The litany to which I'd been living. *Failed.*

I put my hands on Madame Rouffanche's arm, giving a mute squeeze—all the thanks I could summon. Then I tore away and took off toward the street, stumbling as I ran. I fell over an abandoned flower pot, a broken earthenware thing that had probably been filled with scarlet geraniums on the doorstep of a French house-wife who got gunned down on that June tenth. I scraped my hands, but I pushed upright and kept stumbling. I saw the shape of a car through my tear-blurred eyes and veered toward it, only to realize that it wasn't the Lagonda but the abandoned Peugeot, rusting since the day its owner had been rounded up in a field and shot. I stumbled back from that innocent horrible car, looking wildly around me for the Lagonda, and that was when

Finn caught up to me, pulling me into his arms. I buried my face in his rough shirt, squeezing my eyes shut.

"Get me out of here," I said, or tried to say. What came out was a garble of harsh sobbing sounds, barely words at all, but Finn seemed to understand. He scooped me up off my feet and carried me to the Lagonda, lowering me into the seat without opening the door, then flung himself in behind the wheel. I shut my eyes tight and inhaled the comforting smells of leather and motor oil, curling against the seat as Finn roughly threw the car into gear. He drove as though a horde of ghosts was coming after us, and they *were*—oh, God, they were. In the forefront, in my mind's eye, was a baby just old enough to toddle. She was lifting her arms toward me, wanting her Tante Charlotte, but the top of her head was blown off. Rose had named her after me, and now she was dead.

She'd been dead close to three years. I made another inarticulate sound as we bumped and rattled over the river. Everything that had driven me here had been a lie.

Once we were clear of Oradour-sur-Glane, Finn pulled up crookedly at the nearest roadside *auberge* and got us a room for the night. Maybe the proprietor saw the wedding ring on my hand (Mrs. Donald McGowan, Rose was never going to laugh at my Donald), or maybe he didn't care. I stumbled into a threadbare chamber, and was stopped, swaying and tear blurred, by the sight of the bed. "I'm going to dream," I whispered as Finn came up behind me. "As soon as I go to sleep I'm going to dream. Dream of her the way she—" I stopped, squeezing my eyes shut, clutching after my old comforting numbness, but it had shattered utterly. Tears doubled me over in great waves. I couldn't breathe. I couldn't see. "Don't let me dream," I begged, and Finn took my face between his big hands.

"You won't dream tonight," he said, and I saw tears in his eyes too. "I promise."

He found a bottle of whiskey somewhere, and brought it back to the room. We didn't bother with supper; we just kicked off our shoes, climbed onto the bed, sat our backs against the wall, and started methodically drinking our way through the bottle. Sometimes I wept and sometimes I just stared at the window, which went from daylit to twilight blue to night black and star filled. Sometimes I talked, recounting memories of Rose like rosary beads, and after that it was memories of James, and soon I was weeping again for them both. Finn let me talk and cry and talk some more, sliding my boneless body down so my head was pillowed in his lap. I looked up at some point around midnight and saw silent tears sliding down his still face. "That place," he said softly. "Jesus Christ, that *place*—"

I reached up, smoothing his wet cheek. "Have you ever seen a worse one?"

He was silent for so long I didn't think he was going to answer. Then he drank the rest of his whiskey in a sharp movement and said, "Yes."

I wasn't sure I wanted to know what could be worse than Oradour-sur-Glane, but he was already talking.

"Royal Artillery, 63rd Anti-Tank Regiment." His big hand stroked my hair. "April '45. We were in northern Germany, near Celle. You heard about the death camps?"

"Yes."

"We liberated one. Belsen."

I sat up, hugging my knees to my chest. He paused. Blinked.

"C Troop, we were the first military through the gates after the medics. We saw a ghost town, like what you and I saw today. But there were living ghosts at Belsen."

He spoke as flatly as Madame Rouffanche had that afternoon, the repetitive cadence of ground-in horror. "Thousands of people, animated skeletons in striped gray uniforms just drifting through piles of bodies. Bodies stacked everywhere like heaps of rag and bone. Even the ones still walking about didn't look alive. They just—wafted. It was all so quiet." Pause. Blink. "The sun was shining. Like today . . ."

Tears were slipping out of my eyes again. Useless tears. What good do the tears do all those dead? The ones in Oradour-sur-Glane and the ones in Belsen. James, Rose. Damn the war.

"There was a Gypsy girl lying on the ground," Finn went on. "I only learned later that she was a Gypsy, because someone told me what her prisoner badge meant. For Gypsy women it was a dark triangle with a Z for *Zigeuner* . . . She's not really a woman, though, just a lass. Maybe fifteen. But she looks like she's a hundred years old, just a wee sack of bones and a bald skull and huge eyes. She's staring up at me, eyes like stones at the bottom of a well, and her hand is resting on my boot like a white spider. And she dies, right there. Her life slips away as we stare at each other. I'm here to rescue her, my regiment and me—and that's when she dies. She lives through so much, and she dies *now*."

I guessed it was always *now* whenever he thought of the Gypsy girl. Every time he thought of those hollow eyes and the white spider of a hand on his boot, she was dying in the present, in his head, over and over again.

"I've blocked out a lot of it." His voice had roughened, the Scots burr thick and blurred. "I wasna trying, it just—the details, they blurred. Grave digging, carrying bodies out of huts. Delousing people and trying to feed them. But the Gypsy lass—I remember her. She stands out."

I had no words to comfort him. Maybe there weren't any. Maybe the only solace was touch, the warmth that said *I'm here*. I reached out and took his hand between mine, gripping it tight.

"The smell—" A shudder racked the whole rangy length of his body. "Typhus and death and rot, and liquid shite lying everywhere in pools." He looked at me, dark eyes bottomless. "Be glad you got here to Oradour-sur-Glane three years after, Charlie lass. You saw the sunlight and the quiet and the ghosts—but you didna get the smell."

That seemed to be the end of anything he had to say. I poured us both more whiskey. We tossed it down, seeking oblivion as fast as possible. *Salut!* Rose said, but no, she wasn't saying anything, she was dead, and so was Finn's Gypsy girl. I laid my head back in his lap once the room started to spin, and he sat stroking my hair.

The moon slid over the window, getting brighter and brighter until I realized it was the sun and already halfway up, coming through the window in bright rays that stabbed my eyes like swords.

I blinked, trying to get my bearings. I lay tangled up with Finn on top of the sheets, both of us still fully dressed, his arm thrown loose over my waist and my face against his ribs which were moving in and out in sleep. My head was splitting. My stomach lurched as I disentangled myself, and I barely made it off the bed and over to the sink in the opposite corner.

I threw up, and then threw up again, gagging on the sour taste of half-digested whiskey. Soon, Finn was sitting up. "You look a wee bit ill," he observed.

I managed to glare between heaves.

He unfolded from the bed and came toward me, shirt half buttoned and his feet bare, and he gathered back my dangling hair as I bent over the sink again. "Any dreams?" he asked quietly.

"No." I straightened, wiping my mouth and reaching for the water glass, not quite meeting his eyes. "You?"

He shook his head. We couldn't either of us look at the other as we set about washing up. We were like a couple of unhealed stumps trying not to bump into each other, raw and hurting, and I couldn't turn my head without a jolt of pain. *Rose*, I thought, and there was another jolt of pain, dull and profoundly shocking. It hadn't been a nightmare. I had slept, I had woken, and it was real. There hadn't been any nightmares, just true horrors. My eyes burned, but I didn't have any more tears.

Just a vast, looming question.

We got ourselves washed and tidied, and Finn brought cups of black coffee wheedled from the proprietor. My roiling stomach grudgingly accepted the coffee, and soon we were back in the car, Finn turning mutely for Limoges. I sat there in my wrinkled day-old clothes, rubbing at my splitting temples, pondering the question now staring me in the face.

What now, Charlie St. Clair?

What now?

t was a quiet drive back. I found myself staring at the city's summertime loveliness as though it were a stage set: the weeping willows over the river, the half-timbered houses, and the beautiful Roman bridge Rose would have seen when she served drinks at Le Lethe. I had no reason to be in this city any longer—and yet, no destination to make me leave it.

"Wonder if Gardiner's in," Finn said. The first words he'd spoken since asking me if I'd dreamed.

I looked at him blankly. "In from where?"

"Her meeting with that English officer from Bordeaux," Finn said. "Remember?"

I'd forgotten. "Wasn't that yesterday?"

"Maybe it was." We hadn't exactly planned on staying the night in the countryside. *What now?* The question still echoed. *What now?*

Finn parked the Lagonda and we trailed inside. The *auberge*'s entryway had been freshly polished; I smelled beeswax over the fresh flowers on the desk. Roses, pink roses the color of Rose's cheeks, and my head throbbed sickly. An irritable clerk sat behind the desk, and in front of her was the kind of Englishman who thinks that if he speaks loudly enough, foreigners will automatically understand him.

"EVELYN—GARDINER? Is—she—*ICI*? *Ici*, here, *comprenez*? GARDINER—"

"*Oui, monsieur*," the clerk said, with the air of someone who had said it before. "*Elle est ici, mais elle ne veut pas vous voir.*"

"English, *anglais*? Anyone?" The man looked around: tall with a graying mustache, perhaps in his midfifties, carrying a gut before him like a badge of honor. A civilian suit, but the bearing of the man inside it was aggressively soldierly.

Finn and I looked at each other, and then Finn stepped forward. "I'm Miss Gardiner's driver."

"Good, good." The man gave an up-and-down glance of disapproval at Finn's slovenly appearance, but his tone was cordial enough. "Tell Miss Gardiner I'm here, please. She'll see me."

"She won't," Finn said.

The man stared, mustache bristling. "Of course she will! I saw her at dinner just last bloody night, we were perfectly cordial—"

Finn shrugged. "She evidently doesn't want to see you now."

"See here—"

"You don't pay my wages. She does."

The French clerk rolled her eyes behind the Englishman's back. I stepped forward, curiosity making its way through my fog of grief. "Sir—you wouldn't happen to be Captain Cameron?" He didn't match the image I'd been building of Cameron, but what other English officer would come running from Bordeaux on Eve's call?

"Cameron? That sad old fraud?" The visitor gave a snort, contemptuous. "I'm Major George Allenton, and I'm wasting valuable time here, so you scamper up those stairs, girl, and tell Miss Gardiner I'm here."

"No." It sounded like insolence, but it was just exhaustion. Quite honestly I didn't see why I should stir a finger for anyone this rude. I was glad he wasn't Captain Cameron. I'd liked Eve's stories of him.

The major looked at me, face reddening, and he opened his mouth as if to argue, but all at once he deflated. "Fine," he said, fumbling in his pocket. "You tell that sour skinny old maid the War Office owes her no more favors, regardless of what she's done for us in the past." He slapped a flat black case into my hand. "And she can throw these down the loo if she likes, but I'm done keeping them for her."

"When did you know her?" Finn asked as the major clapped his hat to his head.

"Both wars, she worked for me. And I wish she'd never been recruited for the *first* one, that hitch-tongued deceitful bitch."

Finn and I stared at each other as the major stamped away. Finally I opened the case, expecting to see— what? Jewels, documents, a ticking bomb? With Eve you never knew. But it was medals: four of them, pinned precisely across a card.

"The Médaille de Guerre, the Croix de Guerre with palm, the Croix de la Légion d'Honneur . . ." Finn let out a low whistle. "And that's the Order of the British Empire."

I released a slow breath. Eve wasn't just a former spy. She was a decorated heroine, a legend of the past for whom senior army officers still jumped even if they disliked her. I touched the O.B.E. with a fingertip. "If she'd been awarded these years ago, why wouldn't she take them?"

"I don't know."

CHAPTER 26
EVE

October 1915

L ili managed one muttered instruction as she and Eve
  were frog-marched into the station. The Germans
were shouting, alarms blared, and under the furor Lili
murmured through motionless lips, *Pretend you don't
know me. I'll get you out of this.*

Eve gave a minuscule shake of the head, not daring
to look at Lili. They were being rushed along by a pair
of hulking soldiers, Lili half-hoisted off her feet, Eve's
arms in such a tight grip her hands were going numb.
The terror hadn't quite caught up yet; Eve's thoughts
darted like mice at a sudden light. But her refusal came
reflexively: she could not walk away free, leaving Lili in
German hands. Never.

But another burst of shouting came, and Lili's lips
shaped one word.

Verdun.

Eve froze. The massive attack planned against Verdun next year. Captain Cameron in Tournai, waiting for the report. The paper slip with all the attack's details, wrapped around the inner band of a ring on Lili's right hand. Dear God, if the Germans found *that*—

But there was no more time to think, to exchange so much as a desperate glance. They were hustled inside the station, past a telephone and a cluster of German soldiers, and the German captain snapped orders. "Separate them, I will put out a warning—" Eve found herself flung into a narrow room overlooking the street. A half dozen German soldiers were there already, partially dressed, yawning through their morning routine. A young blond sergeant in his undershirt gaped at Eve, and another was shaving in a bucket of water. Eve stared back, keeping her eyes from hunting for an escape. There was none. They'd be on her like a pack of wolves if she moved an inch toward the window. To her left was another door with a glass pane, looking into an even smaller room, and Eve's throat closed as she saw Lili shoved inside. Her hat was gone and her blond hair coming down in a tangle; she looked like a child playing dress-up in her mother's skirt and blouse. But she caught herself against the room's long counter, eyes glittering and her mouth curving in a smile, and she stripped off her gloves as though preparing to sit down to tea.

"No one t-t-touch me!" Eve cried out suddenly, eyes flying among the German soldiers around her. None of them had made a move; they were all too surprised, but she gave a shrill scream anyway. She wanted them looking at her, not through the window at Lili who was swiftly prizing off the ring on her right hand and going for the slip of paper wrapped around its band. "*Don't touch me,*" Eve shrieked, and the youngest soldier stepped forward as if in reassurance. Eve stared past him at Lili, who still smiled that half smile. She watched as her companion popped the paper slip into her mouth and swallowed it.

The German captain flew screaming through the door of Lili's cell before Eve could feel any pangs of relief. *He saw, he saw . . .* Gripping Lili by the neck, the captain tried to force his fingers into her mouth. She sealed her teeth, baring them at him like a wolverine, and he flung her away in disgust. Boots stamped through the corridor outside in a rush, and Eve sank to the floor and started to sob. Not just because Lili had been caught disposing of a message, but because Marguerite *would* sob. Marguerite would be terrified and innocent and have no idea who that woman in the other room was. Eve wanted to fly at these German pigs and tear their throats out, but she had a job to do.

Verdun.

So she huddled against the floor weeping as German boots moved uneasily about her. The soldiers stared and murmured, which Eve ignored because of course Marguerite understood no German past *ja* and *nein.* Her every screaming nerve focused on the next room where there was no sound—none at all—from the leader of the Alice Network.

They won't know she's its leader, Eve thought harshly. *They don't know what a prize they have in her.* But she still saw a nightmare image of Lili shoved up against a wall like Edith Cavell. Blindfolded, her hands bound, an *X* marked on her bosom for the guns to aim at. Lili crumpling to the ground, probably still smiling.

No, Eve screamed inside, but she knew how to use her own horror, how to let the image bring another flood of tears. Tears and abject helplessness would help more than any show of courage. No one feared a helpless, weeping girl.

It wasn't long before a policeman came, and with him a grim-looking woman in green serge whom Eve recognized. She frequently assisted at German checkpoints, a merciless bitch Lili had nicknamed the Frog for her green uniform and greedy padlike fingers as she searched people's belongings. She looked down at Eve now, hard-faced, and barked out one word in French. "Undress."

"H-h-here?" Eve rose, swollen-eyed and hugging herself, shrinking away from all the curious men. "I c-c-c-c—"

"*Undress!*" the Frog snapped, but the policeman looked vaguely ashamed and ordered the soldiers out. Eve was left alone with the Frog, who started wrenching at her buttons.

"If you're carrying messages like that other bitch," she warned, "I'll find them and it'll be the firing squad for you." She stripped Eve's shirtwaist off, showing the frayed chemise underneath, and Eve loosened her own skirt with clumsy fingers. *This cannot be real.* She was just putting on this skirt a few hours ago before the dying fire in René's chamber, as he wrinkled his nose at her underclothes and said, "You look like a charity-school wretch, my pet. I'm getting you a proper chemise, something with Valenciennes lace . . ." Eve was swamped by a wave of dizziness and promptly went with it, pitching over onto the floor as though fainting. She curled up, moaning faintly as the Frog stripped the rest of her clothes away and performed a humiliatingly thorough search. *Verdun*, Eve thought, eyes squeezed shut, as the woman's hard fingers probed the undersides of her breasts and between her fingers and roughly through her hair. *Verdun*, she thought as her hairpins were yanked out one by one. Thank God she wasn't carrying information around a pin this time . . .

It didn't take long. Perhaps ten minutes, as the Frog searched first Eve's body and then her clothes—her skirt hem for lumps, her shoe heels for paper slips. At last a sharp slap stung Eve's cheek, and she opened her eyes, still leaking tears. "Get dressed," the Frog said, looking disappointed.

Eve sat up, hugging her own nakedness. "C-c-can I have a glass of w-w-w-w—"

The Frog mocked her stammer. "Glass of what, my g-g-g-girl?"

"Water," Eve cried, sniveling away, and could have kissed the bitch for her mockery. *Let them think me an idiot. Just a stupid girl who let a stranger borrow her pass.*

"Want water?" The Frog pointed to the glass of scummy liquid where the dressing soldiers had clearly dunked their toothbrushes. "Help yourself." She left with a laugh at her own wit.

Eve dressed stiffly. On the outside Marguerite Le François trembled and shivered, barely functioning, while inside Evelyn Gardiner's mind raced along like a high-speed train. She looked through to the next room, where the Frog was marching in on Lili, and was very much afraid she knew what Lili planned to do.

The Frog barked at Lili to undress.

You'll resist, Eve thought.

Lili stood still as a pillar, refusing to move. The Frog seized the much smaller woman and yanked at her skirt.

You'll keep resisting, Eve thought.

Lili struggled, but the Frog was stout and heavy-handed, and she wrenched Lili out of her clothes piece by piece. Lili stopped thrashing, but she didn't cower in nakedness as Eve had; she held herself straight and stoic as the Frog patted her down. Every rib was visible, and the bones of her sternum jutted out like a ladder. So small. The Frog moved on to the pile of clothing atop the satchel, shoving the smaller woman so hard out of the way that Lili staggered, but her contemptuous smile never faded even as she watched her satchel ransacked.

Don't find anything, Eve prayed, but the cries went up as the rifled satchel delivered Lili's identification cards, five or six of them, held in preparation for swift crossings. The Frog waved the cards in Lili's face, shrieking, but Lili just stared back, impassive.

Eventually they allowed Lili to dress, and as she did up the final buttons at her throat, a man entered with a cup in hand. Eve had angled herself so she could watch through the curtain of her loose hair even as she huddled weeping, and she recognized the newcomer: Herr Rotselaer, chief of police in nearby Tournai. Eve had seen him only at a distance in Lille, but she had compiled a report on him from comments dropped by other officers. A small dark man, dressed with care in a well-cut jacket. His eyes were piercing, and they devoured Lili. "*Mademoiselle,*" he said in French. "Are you thirsty?"

He proffered the cup in his hand. Even through the glass, Eve saw it had a curdled yellow tint. Something to make Lili vomit up that message she'd swallowed.

"Thank you, *monsieur,*" Lili said politely. "I am not thirsty, at least not for milk. Have you any brandy? It's been an absolute pisser of a day." Just as she had said when she first met Eve in Le Havre. Eve could see the two of them in that stuffy café, the rain pouring down outside, Lili in her outrageous cartwheel of a hat. The memory stabbed like a knife. *Welcome to the Alice Network.*

"Come, no fuss!" Herr Rotselaer tried to sound jocular, pushing the cup out. "Swallow, or say why!"

The Frog shook Lili by the elbow, but Lili just smiled and shook her head.

Herr Rotselaer sprang at her, trying to force the cup between her lips as the Frog yanked her head back, but Lili knocked the cup flying. Yellowed milk splatted across the floor. The Frog slapped Lili, but Herr Rotselaer held up a hand. "We'll take her for questioning," he said, and Eve's heart gave a great lurch. "Her and the other one."

"Her?" Lili snorted. "She's a stupid little shopgirl, not a spy. I chatted her up because she was the only one in line who looked half-witted enough to share her safe-conduct pass!"

Herr Rotselaer glanced through the glass where Eve huddled, crying. "Bring her here." The Frog burst through the adjoining door, seizing Eve by the elbow and bundling her into Lili's cell. Eve went to her knees before the chief of police, pushing her hiccuping sobs up to outright wails. She found hysteria surprisingly easy to muster. Inside she was ice bound, watching the blubbering mess on the outside. Through her puffy eyes she could see Lili's small bare foot not six inches away.

"*Mademoiselle*—" Herr Rotselaer tried to catch Eve's eyes, but she just cringed. "Mademoiselle Le François, if that is your true name—"

"I recognize her, sir," another German voice volunteered. The young captain had entered, the one who'd seized them in the first place. Was that why he crossed for a closer look at their papers, because he recognized Eve? *My fault, my fault*— "She lives on the Rue Saint-Cloux; I remember her from inspections. A respectable girl."

"Marguerite Le François." Herr Rotselaer fingered Eve's identity cards, jerking his chin at Lili. "Do you know this woman?"

"N—n—" It felt like betrayal, the word forming on Eve's lips. "N—" It felt like a kiss of betrayal to Lili's cheek, like thirty pieces of silver weighing her tongue down, sour and metallic. "No," Eve whispered.

"Of course she doesn't know me." Lili sounded brusque, bored. "I never saw her before today. You think I'd *try* to cross a checkpoint with a stuttering idiot?"

Herr Rotselaer looked at Eve: hair sticking to her wet cheeks, hands trembling so hard she looked like she was being run through with electrical current. "Where were you going, girl?"

"T—t—t—"

"For God's sake, can you not speak straight? *Where were you going?*"

"T—t—t—" It was no act; Eve's tongue had never hitched so badly in her life. "M—m—my niece's c—c—c—my niece's c—communion. Tour—tour—"

"Tournai?"

"Yes, H—H—H—yes, Herr R—R—"

"You have family there?"

It took Eve whole minutes to answer. Herr Rotselaer shifted from foot to foot. Lili looked impassive, but Eve could sense the tension humming through her taut as a wire. She stood an agonizing arm's length away, but her thoughts were clear as glass.

Keep blubbering, little daisy. Just keep blubbering.

Herr Rotselaer tried to ask more questions, but Eve collapsed into hysterical sobs, sinking down on the floor. The boards smelled harsh and antiseptic. She whimpered like a kicked puppy. Her pulse was slow and cold.

"Oh, for God's sake—" Herr Rotselaer made a disgusted gesture to the young captain. "Write the girl a new safe-conduct pass to Tournai and turn her loose." He turned back to Lili, eyes gleaming. "You, Mademoiselle l'Espionne, are going to answer some questions. We have other friends of yours—"

Violette, Eve thought, even as the German captain helped her up.

"—and things will go hard with them if you refuse to talk."

Lili regarded the chief of police. "You lie," she said finally. "Because you are afraid. That's good, Herr Rotselaer. I will say nothing more."

Her eyes passed across Eve's, and there was a salute in them. Then she looked at the wall and sealed her mouth like a stone.

Herr Rotselaer seized her by the arms and began to shake her then, so hard her head snapped back and forth. "You are a spy, a filthy spy, you are going to *talk*—"

But Lili said nothing. And then Eve was marched out of the room, sobbing so hard she could not speak. This time, the sobs were very real.

The captain gave her a stern lecture on the dangers of sharing official documentation, then seemed to relent in the face of her ceaseless tears. Partly in exasperation, partly in pity. "This is no place for a young girl," he said, snapping his fingers at the clerks to issue a new safe-conduct pass. "You were very foolish, *mademoiselle,* but I'm sorry about all this unpleasantness."

Eve couldn't stop weeping. *Lili*, she thought wretchedly, *oh, Lili!* She wanted to wrench her arm away, turn and sprint back into that room where she could hear Rotselaer still ranting. She wanted to tear his throat out with her teeth, but she stayed where she was, crying into her hands as the German captain fussed and fluttered.

"Go home," he said again, pressing the new safe-conduct pass into her palm, clearly wanting her out of his hair as fast as possible. "Go to Tournai, back to your parents. Go *home*."

And Eve, clutching her new pass and feeling like Judas, turned her back on her friend and walked out of German captivity.

The meeting house in Tournai was small, dingy, indistinguishable from the houses stretching off on either side. Eve wearily climbed the steps and gave the prearranged knock. Her knuckles had barely dropped when the door was wrenched open. Captain Cameron stared at her in a split second's shock, then yanked her inside the house and into his arms. "Thank God you had the sense to come," he muttered. "Even after Violette was arrested, I thought you'd be too stubborn to leave."

Eve inhaled the scents of tweed, pipe smoke, tea—he smelled so *English*. She was used to a man's embrace smelling like Paris cologne, Gauloises cigarettes, absinthe.

Cameron pulled away, remembering himself. He was tieless, his collar unbuttoned, and great shadows of exhaustion showed under his eyes. "You had a safe journey, no trouble passing?"

Eve gulped a shaky breath. "Cameron, it's Lili—"

"Where is she, delayed trying to get news of Violette? She risks too much—"

Eve almost screamed it. "Lili has been *arrested*." Agony kicked her in the gut again. "She's not coming. The Germans have her."

"Oh, Christ." Cameron said it very quietly, like a prayer. In a single breath, his face aged years. Eve began to spill explanations, but he silenced her. "Not here. This will need to be official."

Of course. Everything had to be official, even utter disaster. Eve followed Cameron numbly into a cramped parlor, its fussy little tables shoved against the wall to make room for utilitarian file cabinets bursting with papers. Two men sat going through files, one a weedy clerk in his shirtsleeves, one an aggressively military sort with a waxed mustache who looked Eve up and down as she entered. Major George Allenton, aka Mustache. He was the one who'd made sure she knew all about Cameron's prison record.

"This can't be the famous Louise de B," he said with heavy gallantry, clearly not remembering Eve from Folkestone. "Too young and pretty—"

"Not now, Major," Cameron snapped, pulling up a chair for Eve, dismissing the clerk. "The Alice Network has been compromised." Turning back as the door closed behind the clerk, Cameron sat across the table from Eve, moving like an old man. "Tell me."

Eve told him, speaking in short flat sentences. By the time she finished, Cameron's face was gray. But his eyes were full of taut anger, and he looked over at Allenton. "I argued," he said quietly, "that it was too much of a risk to keep the women in place."

Allenton shrugged. "Risks have to be taken in wartime."

Eve nearly leaned across the table and slapped him, but restrained herself as she saw Cameron biting back what were clearly hot words. Allenton picked at his thumbnail, oblivious, and Cameron scrubbed his hands over his lined face. "Lili," he said, and shook his head. "I don't know why I'm shocked. She always took too many chances. But she got away with so much . . . I suppose I thought she would keep getting away with it forever."

"She didn't get away with it this time." Eve felt so weary she didn't know how she would ever rise from this chair. "They have her now, her and Violette. I hope the Fritzes will put them together. They can take anything together."

Major Allenton shook his head. "Those Boches, letting you walk out—!"

"They th-thought I was a half-wit." All that histri-
onic crying. Eve was nothing but a long shriek of grief
inside, but she didn't think she could summon a single
tear now. She wanted to curl up in a ball like a dying
animal, but she had a job to finish, so she recited the full
report about Verdun, watching as Cameron's eyes went
from exhausted to alert. He began jotting notes, visibly
pushing aside his grief. Major Allenton kept interrupt-
ing Eve with questions, to her irritation. Cameron always let her make her report in one long recitation, then
combed back over it to expand on the particulars, but
Allenton interrupted every other sentence.

"*Verdun,* you say?"

"Verdun." Eve imagined ripping his waxed mustache
off. "Confirmed."

Allenton gave Cameron a rather down-the-nose
glance. "*This* is why I made the call to leave her in
place."

"Of course." Cameron exhaled. "I think you'll agree
Miss Gardiner should go to Folkestone now, however.
There can be no option but to dissolve the Alice Net-
work."

"Why?" Allenton looked at Eve. "I say send her back
to Lille."

Eve's heart sank, but she nodded weary assent. Cameron looked astonished, eyebrows climbing toward his
sandy hair. "You cannot be serious."

No one had addressed Eve, but she answered anyway.
"I'll go where I'm ordered. I have a job to do."

"Your job is done." Cameron turned back to her.
"You've done top-class work, but the Lille area is far
too dangerous to keep running informants. Without Lili
the entire network will come apart."

"Someone else could run it." Allenton shrugged.
"This girl's keen as mustard."

Cameron's voice was flat. "Allow me to register my disagreement in the strongest possible terms, Major."

"Oh, it won't be for long. A few more weeks."

"However long I'm needed." Eve pushed the dread away. She wasn't going to cry off when there were lives at stake, no matter how much she wanted to. "I'll catch the train back tonight."

Cameron rose. His jaw was taut with fury, and his hand as he raised Eve from her chair wasn't gentle. "Major, I'd like a word with Miss Gardiner in private. We'll discuss this upstairs, if you don't mind."

Eve let him march her out of the parlor to the sound of Allenton chuckling. Up a flight of stairs to a make-shift bedroom, nothing but a narrow iron-framed bed piled with a few blankets. Cameron came into the room with her and banged the door behind him.

"C-coming into a lady's bedroom uninvited?" Eve said. "You *are* upset."

"Upset?" He was nearly whispering, voice vibrating with tension. "Yes, I am upset. You are refusing to beg out of an order that is clearly pure idiocy. I can only conclude you want to get yourself shot."

"I'm a spy." Eve set down her bag. "Some might say it's my job to g-get shot. It's certainly my job to follow orders."

"I am telling you that order is absurd. You think there are no idiots in the intelligence business, that your superiors are all brilliant men who understand the game?" A furious hand waved in Major Allenton's direction. "This business is *rife* with idiots. They play with lives and they play badly, and when people like you die as a result, they shrug and say, 'Risks have to be taken in wartime.' You'd really march yourself into a firing squad for that kind of fool?"

"I want to plead out, believe me." Eve touched his

sleeve, halting his furious outburst. "But I won't claim to be b-broken when I am not. If I get myself transferred out of Lille due to breakdown or exhaustion, I will never find more war work elsewhere." She paused. Cameron raked a hand through his hair, but didn't contradict her. "It's just for a few more weeks," Eve continued. "I can survive a few more weeks and then—"

"You know what he said when Edith Cavell was executed?" Cameron's voice lowered, and he made another angry gesture in Allenton's direction. "That it was the best thing that could have happened, because it got everyone on the home front angry at the right time. I do not like speaking ill of a fellow officer, but you must understand me: he wouldn't care if you got caught like Violette and Lili, because dead girls mean more newspapers sold and more support for the boys in the trenches. I, however, am not in the habit of risking my people needlessly."

"I'm not doing this needlessly—"

"You want revenge for Violette and Lili, because you love them. You want revenge, and if you can't get it, you just want to die trying. Believe me, I know that feeling very well."

"If I were a man you'd be calling me patriotic for wishing to continue in my duty to my country." Eve folded her arms. "A woman wants the same thing and she's suicidal."

"An emotionally compromised asset is not an asset to her country. And your emotions are running far more wild than you let on. Anyone's would be, in a situation like this one. You keep a calm face on, but I *know* you."

"Then you know I will put emotion aside in the face of duty, just like any other soldier with orders to carry out. Like any man who takes the oath."

"Eve, *no*. I forbid it."

Calling her *Eve*—now there was a slip. She gave a wintry inner smile. He should know better than to give himself away like that.

"You will convince Allenton you're unfit to return to Lille," Cameron ordered, straightening his cuffs. "And then I'll send you to Folkestone. I do not like circumventing a superior, but I see no other way. This matter is closed."

He was turning, heading for the door. He'd go down and tell Allenton she was pleading breakdown, and that could not happen. Eve seized his hand, stopping him. "Stay with me," she whispered.

He pulled back, his anger dropping away to something shuttered, wary. "Miss Gardiner—"

She reached up and tangled her hands in his undone collar, pressing her lips to the hollow of his neck. He smelled of Lifebuoy. "*Eve*."

"I should not be here, Miss Gardiner." His hands covered hers. Eve went up on her toes, whispering into his ear with a catch in her voice.

"Don't leave me alone."

It was a low blow, and she knew it. Cameron stopped, his hands warm on hers. She pressed, knowing just what to say.

"I saw Lili dragged away by Germans this morning. I . . . Please don't leave me alone right now. I can't b-bear it."

Oh, but this was a dirty trick. It would only work because Cameron was a gentleman, a man who couldn't bear to see a woman in distress. It wouldn't work on René in a thousand years.

Cameron's voice thickened. "I've lost friends too, Eve. I know what you're feeling—"

"I want to be warm," she murmured back, her hands slipping through his hair. How long had she wanted this? "I want to lie down, and be warm, and *forget*."

"Eve—" He began to pull away again, his hand at her bare throat. The gold wedding band on his fourth finger warmed against her skin. "I can't—"

"Please." The grief stabbed her like a living thing. Even if just for a few minutes, she wanted to forget. She leaned up and kissed him, and the bed was at the back of her knees.

"I won't take advantage of you," he said, but he murmured it against her lips.

"Make me forget," Eve whispered. "Make me forget, Cameron—" And he broke. He broke like a wall collapsing, pulling Eve against him with a stifled groan, and then they were drinking each other down, open-mouthed and frantic. Eve pulled him to the bed before he could come to his senses, slipping the shirt from his shoulders. This was underhanded and wrong; she knew that. She didn't start this out of passion, but because she meant to stop him from blocking her return to Lille. But that didn't mean passion wasn't there alongside the calculation, because truth was what made the best lies real. And the truth was that Eve had wanted Cameron for a very long time, since he looked at a stuttering file girl and saw a spy.

"Christ, Eve," he said with agony in his eyes as he peeled her shirtwaist and chemise away and saw the bruises marking her bare arms from where the German guards had seized her. "Those filthy brutes—" He kissed each bruise, his hands spanning her ribs. "You're too thin," he breathed between kisses. "You poor brave girl—"

Eve pressed up to meet him, twining her legs through his, pulling him deep. She could probably fool him into thinking he was her first—she probably *should* fool him, act shy and awkward. It would be the wise thing, but she could not stand to act out another lie, not here. She didn't act for René when it was his cool-skinned marble weight moving over her, and she wouldn't act now when the man in her arms was freckle-shouldered and lanky, with a voice like a mist from Scotland, a man who actually closed his eyes when he kissed her. She wrapped herself around him, closing her own eyes and losing herself, and when it was done she found herself weeping silently in his arms.

"I know," he said in a quiet voice, fingers stroking through her loose hair. "Believe me, Eve—I know. I've seen people I cared for captured too."

She looked up at him, letting the tears fall. "Who?"

"A boy named Léon Trulin, one of my recruits. Not even nineteen . . . Arrested a few weeks ago. And there have been others." Cameron passed a hand slowly through his gray-salted hair. "I never get used to it. This is a filthy business."

It *was* a filthy business, and Eve was going right back to it, but hopefully she could distract him from that for a few hours yet. She turned in his arms, so close that her damp lashes brushed his cheek. "Is there tea?" she asked earnestly. "All I've had for months is boiled walnut leaves."

He smiled, and it made years fall away from him. Soon he'd be guilt-torn and conscience-struck, Eve knew, lashing himself for taking advantage of his subordinate's innocence and his wife's absence, but for the moment he was content. "Yes," he said with another smile. "Tea, and real sugar to put in it."

She groaned, almost pushing him out of bed. "Then *make* some!"

He pulled on his trousers and slipped out, bare feet

slapping the floorboards. So different from the way it usually was after bed: René's cigarettes, his brocade robe, his pillow talk that Eve was busy parsing and filing . . . She didn't want to think about René here, so she took the tea mug Cameron offered on returning and sipped, letting out a moan. "I could d-d-die right here."

Part of her wished for that. Die now, sitting up in bed, her back against Cameron's chest, and she wouldn't have to think about Lille or the job that still waited, crouching implacable as a troll under a bridge. She turned the thought aside, but Cameron seemed to catch it.

"What are you thinking?" He pressed a lock of hair back behind her ear.

"Nothing." Eve sipped her tea again.

Cameron hesitated, his hand stilling against her neck. "Eve . . . Who is he?"

Eve didn't pretend not to understand. She had been a very innocent girl when he sent her to Lille, not the same girl who coiled herself so fiercely around him between these sheets. "He's no one," she said matter-of-factly. "Just someone who drops useful information over a p-pillow."

Cameron said almost inaudibly, "Bordelon?"

A nod. She didn't quite dare look up at him, but her heart lodged in her throat. He would have read the reports on René, who and what he was. If Cameron recoiled from her . . .

Well, it hardly mattered. She still had a job to do.

"You don't have to go to him anymore." Cameron set his tea mug down and folded both arms tight around her. "I'll be taking you to Folkestone tomorrow morning. You don't ever have to see him again."

Clearly he assumed that since she had stopped arguing, she'd agreed to beg out of her orders to return to

Lille. For a moment Eve surrendered to that temptation. Go home, back to safety, England. Back to *tea*.

Then she sighed and let it go, putting aside her own mug and turning to rest her cheek against Cameron's shoulder. He made some noise about getting up, but she pulled him down into the sheets. They made love one more time, tender and slow, Eve stifling her cries in his shoulder, and afterward Cameron dropped into exhausted sleep. Eve waited until his breathing settled into a deep rhythm, then slipped noiselessly out of bed and into her clothes. She looked at him for a moment, and wondered with a wrench if he would ever forgive her for this. *Maybe he shouldn't,* she thought. *He can't afford to love me.* Though she certainly loved him. She smoothed his sandy hair off his forehead, which was lined even in sleep as though he worried through his dreams, and then she headed downstairs.

Major Allenton smirked as she entered the makeshift file room. He undoubtedly suspected what had happened upstairs. Eve didn't care. He was already committed to sending her back, whore or not. "I'll need a pass," she said without preamble. "I'm ready to catch the train back to Lille."

That surprised him. "I thought Cameron might be trying to talk you out of obeying that order. He can be sneaky that way. It happens, you know, when military men mess about too long in a dirty business like spying. They get underhanded."

Real dislike flickered across his face. After having to parse René's minuscule facial expressions, watching the major's thoughts work their way across his features was like watching a dog lumber around a city block on the end of a leash. Eve gave the leash just the tug it needed, dropping her lashes in doe-eyed obedience.

"You outrank Captain Cameron, sir. Of course I obey *your* orders. You want me to return, and I w-w-will."

"You really are keen as mustard, aren't you." Pleased, the major reached for a pen. The weedy clerk had gone home; it was almost nightfall. The cheap lamps showed up all the places where the wallpaper was fading. "I can see why Cameron's . . . fond of you." His eyes roved over her again. "He's been climbing the walls worrying over the network gels, but it's really you he obsesses about."

That gave Eve a lonely pang of pleasure, mixed with guilt because she was about to make him worry all over again. "My p-pass, sir?" she prompted, aware that time was ticking. Cameron might be a light sleeper—if he woke up from his doze and came downstairs now, there would be another round of arguing. Far better if he woke and simply found her gone.

The major started making out a safe-conduct pass. "I'll wager Cameron's probably never told you what his code name is." Eve suppressed the urge to roll her eyes at his air of cozy confidentiality. Thank God Allenton wasn't in the field, because getting information out of him would be like plucking candy from an infant. *You really are an idiot*, Eve wanted to say, but she gave the answer he wanted. "No, what is Cameron's code name?"

Allenton smirked, handing over her safe-conduct pass. "'Evelyn.'"

CHAPTER 27
CHARLIE

May 1947

Another night falling, the second since I'd found out Rose was dead. I still feared what I'd see in my dreams, but I didn't want to drink myself into oblivion again. My head had only just stopped throbbing.

I should already have been downstairs meeting Eve and Finn for dinner, but I was ransacking my clothes for something clean. I hadn't washed anything out after Oradour-sur-Glane, and all I had left was the black dress I'd bargained out of that little Parisian saleswoman. It was straight, angled, severe, geometric, high at the neck and slashing very low in the back, clinging to all my straight lines instead of trying to disguise them. *"Très chic,"* I could hear Rose laugh, and I squeezed my eyes tightly shut because she'd said the same thing at seven years old, when we got into her mother's closet and started trying on her evening gowns. Rose with Schiaparelli sequins slithering off the shoulders of her middy blouse, trailing yards of black taffeta hem and giggling, "*Très chic!*" as I tottered around in a pair of satin evening pumps far too big for me.

I blinked the memory away, looking at the wavery mirror in my hotel room. Rose would have liked the black dress, I thought, and went downstairs.

Eve and Finn and I had been taking our meals at the café next door: small, cozy, very French with red awnings and tables with striped cloths. Someone was turning on the radio, and it was Edith Piaf. Of course it was. *Les trois cloches,* "The Three Bells," and I wondered if the church bells had rung over Oradour-sur-Glane when the women were herded inside . . .

I saw Eve's gnarled hand waving from the farthest table, and I wended my way through the crush of tray-bearing waiters. "Hello, Yank," she greeted me. "Finn tells me you met Major Allenton. Isn't he a gem?"

"Stupid mustache."

"I came near to yanking it out by the roots once." Eve shook her head, turning an uneaten crust of baguette between her fingers. "I wish I'd done it."

Finn sat opposite Eve, elbow hooked around the back of his chair. He didn't say a word, but I saw him noticing the black dress. I remembered how we'd woken up this morning all tangled up and reeking of whiskey, and tried to catch his eye, but he avoided my gaze.

"Finn told me about Oradour-sur-Glane." Eve's stare was direct. "And your cousin."

Edith Piaf warbled behind me. *Village in the heart of the valley, as if lost* . . . I waited for Eve to say I told you so, waited for her to say she'd known all along I was on a fool's errand.

"I'm sorry," she said. "For what it's worth. Which is

nothing, when a friend's g-gone. Sorry isn't worth anything, but I still am."

I unlocked my teeth. "Rose is dead. I—I don't—" I
stopped, started over. "What happens now?"

"Well," Eve said, "I'm still looking for René Bordelon."

"I wish you luck." I pulled a hunk off the baguette.
Finn rotated his water glass between long fingers, silent.

Eve's eyebrows arched. "Thought you wanted to find
him too."

"Only because I thought he could lead me to Rose."

Eve exhaled. The drink at her elbow was only halfway down, and her eyes had a contemplative gleam.
"You might still find yourself interested in the hunt.
Allenton, arse though he is, told me some fascinating
things."

"Why do *you* want to find René?" I lashed back.
"You've told us he was a profiteer, that you spied on
him." That she'd slept with him for information, that
he'd made her pregnant and she'd had to take care of
it—but I wasn't going to bring *that* up at a café table
with waiters squeezing past on all sides. "What else is
there that's so bad an old man of seventy-three has to be
tracked down like a dog?"

Her eyes glittered. "Does there have to be anything
else?"

"Yes. Is it to do with your medals? All those Croix de
Guerres and an Order of the British Empire?" I pinned
her with my eyes. "It's time you told us everything, Eve.
Stop hinting and spill."

Finn rose abruptly, moving off toward the bar. "He's
in a mood," Eve commented, watching her driver shoulder through the throng. "Must have stirred a few things
up, seeing Oradour-sur-Glane." Then she turned back to
me, assessing. "Do you have any guts, Yank?"

"*What?*"

"I need to know. Your c-cousin's dead—are you going to go home now and knit baby booties? Or are you up for something more challenging?"

That hit too close to the question on which I'd been brooding. *What now, Charlie St. Clair?* "How do I know what I'm up for if you won't tell me what this is about?"

"It's about a friend," she said simply. "A blond woman with a sunshine laugh and the courage to light the world on fire."

Rose? I thought.

"Lili." Eve smiled. "Louise de Bettignies, Alice Dubois, who knew how many other names she had. Always Lili to me. The b-best friend anyone ever had."

Lili. So Eve had Lili, and I had Rose. "All these flowers."

"There are two kinds of flowers when it comes to women," Eve said. "The kind that sit safe in a beautiful vase, or the kind that survive in any conditions . . . even in evil. Lili was the latter. Which are you?"

I'd like to think I was the second kind too. But evil (how melodramatic that sounded) had never tested me as it had Eve or Rose or this unknown Lili. I'd never crossed paths with *evil,* just sadness and failure and bad choices. I mumbled something along those lines, and rushed ahead with a question of my own. "You've never mentioned a friend from your war years. Not once. So if Lili was the best friend you ever had, what else was she? Why is she so important?"

I sat listening as Eve talked, telling me of meeting Lili in Le Havre. The wry, warm-voiced "Welcome to the Alice Network." The tight clench of hopeful hands as they watched the botched hit against the kaiser. The tears shed, the calm advice, the arrest. I could almost *see* Eve's friend before me, the words drew her so vividly. To me she looked like Rose, if Rose had ever lived to be thirty-five.

"Your friend was something special," Finn said when Eve's voice trailed off. He'd rejoined us a little way into the recitation, sitting with his beer untouched before him—and from the surprise on his face, I could tell these stories were as new to him as to me. "She sounds like quite a soldier."

Eve finished her drink in one long swallow. "Oh, yes. Later, people called her the queen of spies. There were other intelligence networks in the first war—I learned later about the women who worked in them—but none were as fast or as precise as Lili's. She ran nearly a hundred sources covering dozens of kilometers of front, just one woman . . . The top brass all mourned when she was arrested. They knew they wouldn't be getting the same quality of information once she was in German hands." A mirthless smile. "And they didn't."

Rose and me, Finn and his Gypsy girl, Eve and Lili. Were we all three hunting ghosts from the past, women lost in a maelstrom of war? I'd lost Rose at Oradour-sur-Glane and Finn lost his girl at Belsen, but maybe Lili was still alive and well. Would seeing her again cure what ailed Eve, the guilt and the grief? I opened my mouth to ask about Lili's fate, but Eve was already speaking again, eyes fixed on me.

"I have spent more than th-th-thirty years picking things up after what happened in Lille. Which is why you shouldn't take too long to mourn your cousin, Yank. Because you'd be surprised how weeks turn into years. Do your grieving—smash a room, drink a pint, screw a sailor, whatever you need to do, but get past it. Like it or not, she's dead and you're alive." Eve rose. "Let me

know if you decide you're a *fleur du mal* after all, and
I'll tell you why you should come with me to find René
Bordelon."

"Must you always be so goddamn cryptic?" I hissed,
but Eve had already risen and stalked off, leaving her
empty glass. I stared after her, frustration and grief
boiling in me like colliding rivers. *What now, Charlie
St. Clair*?

"Louise de Bettignies," Finn said, frowning. "'Queen
of spies'—I've heard of her, now I think on it. Probably
an old headline about war heroines . . ."

He fell silent, rotating his beer between his fingers. I
could see him pulling back into the tense edginess he'd
had before Eve's stories distracted him, his usual loose-
limbed ease shifting to tight rigidity. "What's wrong,
Finn?"

"Nothing." He didn't look at me, just stared inside to
where the tables had been pulled back for dancing and
couples swayed to the music. "For me, this is normal."

"No, it isn't."

"Coming back from the 63rd, I was like this all the
time."

My brother used to get tense and foul tempered
whenever people asked him what it was really like at
Tarawa. He'd get that same closed-off expression, and
if they pushed too hard he'd explode into obscenities
and storm out. I'd always been too afraid to follow him,
afraid he'd lash out at me too, but now I wished that
just once I'd followed him and taken him by the hand.
Just—taken his hand so he knew that I was there, that I
loved him, that I understood he was hurting. But I didn't
really understand any of that until he was gone, and it
was too late.

I looked at Finn's closed face and wanted to say, *It's
not too late for you.* But I knew words wouldn't reach

him in a mood like this, any more than words reached
James, so I just reached out and touched his hand.

He shook me off. "I'll get over it."

Does anyone get over it? I looked at the chair where
Eve had sat. Three of us chasing painful memories
across the wreckage of two wars; no one appeared to be
over much of anything. I thought of what Eve had said.
Maybe you didn't have to *get* over it so much as *try*. Or
else weeks turned into months and then you looked up,
as Eve had done, and saw you'd wasted thirty years.

More Edith Piaf drifted over the radio. I stood up.
"Do you want to dance, Finn?"

"No."

I didn't either. My feet felt heavy as lead. But Rose
had loved to dance. My brother too—I remembered doing a clumsy boogie-woogie with him the night before
he left for the marines. They'd have been on the floor
by now. For them, I could drag my heavy feet out there.

I moved to the crowd of dancers, and a laughing
Frenchman pulled me in. I moved in time with his arm
at my waist, then took his friend's arm for the next song.
I didn't listen to any of their whispered French gallant-
ries, just closed my eyes and moved my feet and tried
to . . . Well, not forget my hovering cloud of grief, but
at least dance under it. My feet might be heavy now, but
maybe someday I could dance my way out from under
the cloud.

So I kept moving to the music, song after song, and
Finn nursed his single beer and watched me, and it
probably would have been all right if not for the Gypsy
woman.

I'd stepped away from the dancing to retie my sandal.
Finn rose to throw away his half-drunk beer, and both
of us saw the old woman behind a pushcart, dressed in
faded colorful shawls. Maybe she wasn't a Gypsy—she

had the nut-brown face and bright skirts, but how did I know if that was what a Gypsy really looked like?—and she mumbled something as the café proprietor came flying out. She held out a palm, supplicating, and he waved his hands as though a rat had run through his kitchens. "No begging here!" He gave the old woman a push. "Move along!"

She trudged off, obviously used to it. The café proprietor turned away, scrubbing his hands down his apron. "Gypsy bitch," he muttered. "Too bad they weren't all shipped off and locked up."

I saw the wave of dead flat anger that fell over Finn's face.

I started toward him, but he'd already dropped his beer bottle in a sharp shatter of glass. He crossed the café in three strides, buried a hand in the surprised proprietor's collar, yanked him up close, and flattened him with one brutal uppercut.

"Finn!"

My yell got lost in the shatter of china as the proprietor fell, taking a table with him. Finn shoved him over onto his back with one boot, flat fury still burning out of his eyes, then dropped a knee into the man's chest. "You—lousy—little—shite—" he said with quiet precision, punctuating each word with his fist. The short efficient blows sounded like a meat mallet falling.

"*Finn!*"

My heart thudded. I elbowed my way past fluttering women and men rising with napkins about their necks, everyone flustered and openmouthed, but a waiter got there first, catching Finn's arm. Finn hit him too, a quick explosion of fist into nose, and I saw the spray of blood, perfectly distinct, against a fallen tablecloth. The waiter reeled back and Finn went back to hitting the proprietor, who was shouting and trying to shield his face.

Six people pulled me off once I started bashing his head against a doorpost, Finn had said of the fight that landed him in prison. *Thank God they got me off him before I cracked his skull.*

I might not be six people, but no one was cracking a skull tonight. I grabbed Finn's rock-tense shoulder, hauling with all my strength. *"Finn, stop!"*

He whirled, swinging at whoever was trying to stop him. His eyes flared the instant he recognized me, and he snatched away the force behind his blow, but it was too late to stop the momentum. His knuckles hit the corner of my mouth hard enough to sting. I fell back a step, hand flying to my face.

He went dead white, fist falling to his side. "Oh, Jesus—" He rose, ignoring the man lying groaning and bloody-nosed on the ground. "Jesus, Charlie—"

I touched my lips in shock. "It's all right." To be honest I was more relieved that he was off the proprietor and didn't have that flat furious expression anymore. My heart racketed away in my chest like I'd just run a race. I took a step, reaching for him. "It's all right—"

He flinched. His eyes were horrified. "Jesus," he said again, and took off at a shambling run away from me, from the café and its crowd of murmuring customers.

The proprietor was already rising with the aid of several waiters, woozy and angry, but I didn't spare him a glance. I ran as fast as I could in the direction Finn had gone. He'd already gone past the *auberge*, slipping between buildings, and I saw him vanish into the garage behind. I followed, picking past the rows of Peugeots and Citroens to the long shape of the Lagonda. Finn was in the backseat, like he'd been that night in Roubaix when we talked at three in the morning. He sat head lowered and shoulders heaving, not seeing me until I wrenched the door open and slid in beside him.

His voice was muffled. "Go away."

I took hold of his hand. "You're hurt—" His fingers were bruised, skin split over the knuckles. I didn't have a handkerchief, so I just touched the abraded skin gently.

He yanked away, raking his fingers through his hair. "I wish I'd beat that miserable shite's skull into paste."

"Then you'd be hauled away and locked in prison again."

"I belong in prison." He still sat hunched, fists caught through his own hair. "I *hit* you, Charlie."

I touched my own lip, felt the skin unbroken. "You didn't know it was me, Finn. As soon as you saw me, you stopped yourself from—"

"I still hit you." He looked at me then, his eyes holes of guilt and anger. "You were just trying to stop me killing him, and I hit you. Why are you *here*, Charlie? Sitting in the dark with a bad man like me?"

"You're not a bad man, Finn. You're a goddamn wreck, but you're not bad."

"What do you know—"

"I know my brother wasn't bad when he punched walls and screamed curses and panicked in crowds! He wasn't bad, he was *broken*. So are you. So is Eve. So was I when I flailed my time away in school either crying in bed or sleeping with boys I didn't like." I stared at Finn, trying so hard to make him see. "What's broken does not have to stay that way."

I wanted so badly to help him. Take him between my hands and mend the cracks, like I'd failed to do for James. Like I'd even failed to do for my parents when they were grieving blindly for him.

"This is no place for you." Finn's voice was rough, clipped. I could see the angry tension coil through his shoulders again. "You should go home. Have your bairn, take up your life. Nothing good can come from hanging about with a pair of broken souls like Gardiner and me."

"I'm not going anywhere." I reached for his hand again.

He jerked away. "Don't."

"Why?" We'd sat shoulder to shoulder last night as we drank our whiskey; I'd laid my head in his lap and he'd stroked my hair, none of it with any discomfort. But now Finn prickled like a burr, and the space between us was alive with tension.

"Get out of the car, Charlie."

"Why?" I challenged again. I'd be damned if I backed down now.

"Because in moods like this, it's drink, fight, or screw." He stared ahead into the shadows, words coming angry and even. "I did the first one last night, and the second twenty minutes ago. All I want right now is to tear that black dress off you." He looked at me, and that glance seared me all over. "You really should get out of the car."

If I left him now, he'd sit here all night with his guilt and his anger and a dead Gypsy girl. "Like it or not," I said, echoing Eve's words, "she's dead and you're alive. We're both alive." And I reached up, tangled my hands into his hair, and pulled his head down to mine.

Our mouths clashed brutally, never letting go even as he lifted me up so I straddled his lap. His cheeks were wet and so were mine. He was yanking down the shoulders of my black dress and I was tearing at his shirt buttons, pushing all the layers of clothes out of the way so it was skin against hot skin, neither of us caring if anyone walked by outside the Lagonda's windows and saw us. On the road to Oradour-sur-Glane he had kissed me with exquisite tenderness, but now his mouth was rough as he devoured the soft skin between my breasts, lashes brushing my collarbone. I pressed my cheek against his hair, hands sliding down his lean chest to his belt, and for a moment he stopped, breathing in gulps, his big hands spanning my naked back. "Christ, Charlie," he said not too distinctly. "This wasn't how I was hoping to do this."

Maybe it wasn't roses and candlelight and romance. But *this,* here, now, was what we both needed. Last night had been numbness and pain and longing for oblivion— I couldn't stay there or I'd drown. I wasn't letting Finn drown either. I wasn't letting him go, not like the others I'd failed and lost. "Stay with me," I murmured against his lips, my breath coming as ragged as his. "Stay with me—" And we were tangled up along the leather seat, the important parts of my black dress all yanked out of the way, Finn's shirt and belt on the floor.

This was normally when my mind slid away from what was happening. This was when I stopped trying to feel something and instead grew distant and disappointed that I felt nothing—that the easiest equation in the world, man plus woman, always added up to zero. Not this time. The heaving scramble of limbs across the seat and the sounds of squeaking leather and heavy breathing were the same as all the other times, but now I wasn't drifting away. I was melting and burning and shaking with need. Finn was trembling too, braced above me, a shadow against more shadows, his hands tangled so tight through my hair that my scalp sparkled with pain, and his mouth drank the skin at my throat and my ears and my breasts as though he could devour me. I locked my arms and my thighs around him and clung as though I were trying to climb inside him, nails sinking deep into his back. We grappled, skin against sweating skin, and it still wasn't close enough. I clawed at him, pulling him deeper, dimly hearing the sounds I was making as we clashed in desperate, furious rhythm. It was fast and rough and good, messy and sweaty and *alive*. His face was hard against mine at the final shudder that speared us both, and I felt a tear slide between our pressed cheeks.

I didn't know which of us it had come from. But I didn't care. It hadn't come from grief, and that was enough.

CHAPTER 28
EVE

October 1915

I f there was a day of the week to be arrested, it was
Sunday. The one night out of seven that Eve didn't
work, because even decadent Le Lethe closed on the
lord's day. Eve was back in Lille by late Sunday night
without needing to miss a shift. "Small favors," she said
aloud. The room was bitterly cold, and though nothing had changed—not the narrow bed, not the false-
bottomed carpetbag in the corner where her Luger was
hidden—it had a deserted air. Violette would not come
stomping through in her heavy boots, grumping about
English pilots too rash to hide properly. Lili would not
come waltzing in with a story of how she bribed her way
past a checkpoint with a smuggled sausage. Eve looked
around the joyless little room, remembering evenings
they'd spent here smoking and laughing, and a wave of

despair hit so hard it nearly knocked the breath from her lungs. She had a job to do, and she would do it—but there would be no more moments of joy in it. There would be days at Le Lethe and nights in René's bed, and that was all. No one would use this room anymore but Eve.

Antoine will, she thought. *We can work out a new schedule.* Quiet, rock-steady Antoine knew the most about Lili's sources, since he had constructed false papers for so many of them under the counter of his bookshop—perhaps he could reconstruct Lili's rounds for someone else to take over. Somehow it had to be done. She gave in to a wave of weariness, and lay down without even taking her coat off. She should have been hungry, but somehow she was imagining the smell of René's expensive cologne—dreading the moment she would go back to him tomorrow, no doubt—and even the imagined whiff turned her stomach. She buried her nose in her thin pillow, imagining the smell of tea and English tweed instead. "Cameron," she whispered, and a soft tactile memory flashed of his hair under her hand and his lips lingering in the space behind her ear. She wondered if he regretted their time this afternoon. She wondered if he hated her for seducing him and then sneaking off. She wondered . . .

But she was exhausted from terror and arrest, from anguish and love, and sleep descended in a black wave.

The next day was brilliant and cold, and Eve trudged toward Le Lethe bundled to the tip of her nose. Normally in late afternoon the restaurant was bustling: waiters laying silver and linen for the first diners, cooks cursing as they prepared their stations. Today Le Lethe was dark, the kitchens shut up. Eve paused, puzzled, then unbuttoned her coat. There was no sign on the door or on the bar to say the restaurant was closed for the evening, and René was too fond of his own profits to ever shut his doors if he did not have to.

A voice floated down the stairs from René's apartments. "Marguerite, is that you?"

Eve hesitated, tempted to pretend she'd heard nothing and slip back out into the cold. Her nerves were taut with alarm, but she would cause more suspicion now by darting out. "Yes, it's me," she called.

"Come up."

René's study blazed with light, though the shades were drawn. The fireplace spilled warmth across the patterned Aubusson rug, and the multicolored Tiffany shade threw patterns of sapphire and amethyst onto the green silk wall. René sat reading in his usual chair, a glass of Bordeaux at hand.

"Ah," he greeted Eve. "There you are, pet."

Eve permitted herself to look puzzled. "Is the restaurant not to open?"

"Not today." He marked his book with a strip of embroidered silk and laid it aside. Eve felt a chill, though his smile was pleasant. "I intended it as a surprise for you."

Run, a quiet voice in Eve's head told her. "A surprise?" She linked her hands behind her back, touching the doorknob. It turned silently. "Another w-weekend away? You did say you wished to go to G-Grasse . . ."

"No, a different kind of surprise." René sipped his Bordeaux, unhurried. "One you're going to give *me.*"

Eve's fingers tightened around the doorknob. One yank and she could be gone. "Am I?"

"Yes." René reached under the cushion on the armrest of his chair, and brought out a pistol. He leveled it at Eve: a Luger nine-millimeter P08, just like her own. At this distance, Eve knew it would drill her between the eyes long before she could wrench the door open.

"Sit down, pet." René gestured at the chair opposite, and as Eve sat, she saw the tiny scratch on the barrel. She knew that scratch; she buffed it every time she field-stripped her weapon. It wasn't just *a* Luger René was holding, it was *her* Luger. Suddenly Eve remembered that faint whiff of René's cologne she'd smelled in her room last night, and fear hit like a shrieking freight train.

René Bordelon had searched her room. He had her pistol. Who knew what else he knew?

"Marguerite Le François," René said as though he were about to start one of his pet discourses on the arts, "tell me who you really are."

Why is it so hard to b-believe?" Eve was playing up the stammer, letting her hands flutter and tremble, running up every flag of innocence and confusion that she could fly. "It's my f-father's pistol. I kept it because I was afraid, the w-w-way the German officers swagger about looking at the local g-girls—"

René's suspicious eyes bored into her. "You were arrested in the company of a woman who had *six* different forms of identification. She was undoubtedly a spy, so what were you doing with her?"

"I d-didn't know her! We began talking at the station, and she'd forgotten her p-p-p—her pass. I offered to let her get by on m-mine." Eve's thoughts careened ahead of her tongue, wildly stitching together a defense—any defense—that he might swallow. She'd never imagined he would hear of her arrest. It was all just sheerest blind chance: some German friend of René's had enthused over Lili's capture, mentioning in passing the stuttering girl taken along with her. A girl named Marguerite something, released because anyone could see she was innocent.

If only they hadn't mentioned the name. René would never have known. But they had, and the implications must have crashed on him like a tidal wave because he'd gone at once to her room. The Luger was all he'd found; Eve kept no ciphers or coded messages. But for him it was suspicious enough, so here they sat in opposing chairs.

"You would not be stupid enough to let a stranger use your safe-conduct pass, pet," he said.

"I d-didn't see the harm!" Eve tried to let her eyes fill with tears, but she was utterly cried out. She'd wept herself into hysterics yesterday morning for Herr Rotselaer; she'd wept afterward for Lili. Her eyes now were dry as stone, just when she needed them dewy and pathetic. She lowered her eyelids instead. *You can get out of this,* she told herself. *You can.*

But René had not once yet allowed the Luger or his attention to sag. "Where were you yesterday? Why were you getting on a train at all?"

"My n-niece's c-c-c-communion in T-T-Tournai."

"You've never mentioned any family in Tournai."

"You n-never asked!"

"Is your stammer even real? Or do you fake it to make people think you simpleminded? That would be very clever of you."

"Of c-course it's real! You think I like speaking this way?" Eve cried. "I'm n-not a spy! Did you find anything suspicious in m-my room?"

"This." Tapping the Luger's barrel against the carved arm of his chair. "Why didn't you turn this weapon in when the Germans forbade civilians to own weapons?"

"I c-couldn't part with it, it was my f-f-f—"

"*Stop stuttering!*" he roared so suddenly her flinch was entirely real. "*Do you think I'm stupid?*"

There was his real fear, Eve thought. That he had

been made a fool of. Was he remembering all the pillow talk, all the gossip he had dropped in her ear? Or wondering what would happen to his favored status if the Germans found out his mistress had been feeding secrets to England?

The former, Eve thought, more than the latter. It wasn't German trust and German favors he most feared losing, but his pride. René Bordelon had to be the cleverest man in the room, always. What an unbearable thought, the possibility that a know-nothing girl half his age could have been so much cleverer.

Too bad Eve didn't feel clever at the moment. All she felt was terrified.

You can get out of this, she thought, because thinking the alternative was unbearable. *But what then?* Even if she convinced René she was innocent, her time at Le Lethe would be over. She was finished in Lille, regardless of any orders from Allenton, and that failure stabbed—but if she could just get away, perhaps she could be stationed somewhere else.

And a sweeter thought yet drifted through her head: *I will never have to share a bed with René Bordelon again.*

Perhaps her eyes sparked, because he sat forward sharply. "What are you thinking? Why are you—"

He was just close enough. Eve hadn't planned it, but she snapped her foot out like a whip, catching the Luger's barrel. Just a glancing blow, but it spun the pistol out of René's hand toward the fireplace. No time to grab for it; Eve lunged the other way, toward the door. If she could get through while he scrabbled for the pistol, get to the stairs, then she had a chance to escape into the streets of Lille. She wouldn't risk the trains; she'd walk across the border to Belgium. All of that went through her mind like a splinter of ice as she lunged across the sumptuous carpet. She got one hand on the doorknob, silver polished diamond bright, and thought, *I can make it.*

But René didn't scramble for the gun. He came straight after her, and as Eve's fingers tightened on the study's doorknob, his arm descended in a short, brutal arc. The miniature bust of Baudelaire smashed down on Eve's hand.

The impact lanced up her right arm in a bolt of white-hot pain. She heard a distinct *crunch* as three knuckles in her first two fingers shattered, crushed between the bust and the doorknob. She found herself on her knees before the door, gasping as wave after wave of agony coursed through her. She saw René's shining shoes approach, saw the small marble bust swinging rather casually from his hand as he came to stand, breathing hard, between her and the door.

"Well," she managed to say through pain-clenched teeth, clutching her trembling hand. "Goddammit."

She said it unthinkingly in English, not French, and she heard René's sharp intake of breath. He squatted down beside her so their eyes could meet at the same level, and his gaze was alight with—what? Fear, doubt. Above all, fury. "You are a spy," he breathed, and there was no more doubt in his voice.

There it was. Eve had given herself away. After fearing such a moment for so long, it fell curiously flat. Perhaps because she knew there was nothing she could have said to convince him she was innocent. Why not admit guilt?

He wrapped his free hand around her throat, those extraordinarily long fingers pressing almost to the back of her neck. He never released the bust in his other hand, and she knew how easily he could bring it around to crush her temple. "Who *are* you?"

Her hand hurt so badly, Eve could barely breathe. She sank her teeth into the scream rising in her throat until it died unborn. She managed a crooked little smile, not pulling against his grip, just nailing her eyes to his. Giving him her own gaze for once, and not his demure little pet's.

She might very well die here in this warm, luxurious room. But just once, she wanted to throw it in his face how badly he had been duped. She could curse herself for such a rash, prideful impulse, but she had no power to resist it.

"My name is Eve," she breathed, every word smooth as silk. "*Eve*, not fucking Marguerite. And yes: I am a spy."

He stared, transfixed. Eve switched to German.

"I speak perfect German, you profiteering coward, and I've been eavesdropping on your precious customers for months."

She watched the horror, the disbelief, the rage crowd his eyes. She managed another smile and added one more thing in French, just for good measure.

"I will not tell you one single solitary fact about my work, my friends, or the woman I was arrested with. But I will tell you this, René Bordelon. You're a gullible fool. You're a terrible lover. And I *hate* Baudelaire."

CHAPTER 29
CHARLIE

May 1947

"Go back to the hotel, Charlie. Get some sleep." Finn sat half buried in the car's shadows, buttoning his shirt. Avoiding my eyes. My whole body still thrummed from what had just happened, and I sat for a moment trying to find the words to tell him how different this had been from anything else I'd ever had. But Finn looked at me, and I could see him back behind his walls again, impossible to reach. "Get to bed, lass."

"I'm not leaving you here to brood," I answered quietly. I wasn't ever doing it again—leaving someone I cared for to fight their demons alone.

"I'm not," he said. "I'm going next door, back to the café. I have some apologies to make."

It sounded like a start, something to make him feel more himself again, so I nodded. We slid out of the car on opposite sides, stood for a moment looking at each other over the Lagonda's roof. I thought for a moment Finn was going to say something, and then his eyes dropped to my bruised mouth and he flinched. "Good night."

"Good night."

And now I was alone in my empty hotel room, lying on the bed, unable to sleep. Yellow light filtered through the shutters from the streetlamps, and the muted sounds of nighttime traffic. Over and over, I ran my fingertips back and forth across my belly. The Little Problem had been quiet ever since I decided not to go to Vevey. Probably figured she could take her ease and just grow, grow, grow until it came time for her to be born. Only then would she realize that the world was a cold place, and her mother had very little idea of how to give her a good life. Before Oradour-sur-Glane I'd at least had a fantasy idea, a magical equation where Charlie plus Rose magically guaranteed a happy future for everyone. Now I didn't even have that.

"Sorry," I said softly to the stomach that was still flat under my exploring fingers. "Your mama's every bit as helpless as you, baby girl." I don't know why I thought it was a girl, but I did. *Baby Rose*, I thought, and just like that, she had a name. Of course she did. Another Rose. A Rose of my own.

A church bell chimed midnight. My stomach rumbled, the newly named Little Problem complaining that she hadn't had dinner. Strange how bodies kept stubbornly functioning in the middle of grief or guilt or shock. "That's one thing I *do* notice about you, Rosebud," I told my stomach. "You might not be showing yet, but I already need the lavatory twice as much."

I got out of bed, pulled a sweater around me, used the lavatory, then found myself padding down the corridor. No light under Finn's door. I hoped he'd managed his apologies next door and come back to dreamless sleep. I wondered if he regretted what we'd done in the backseat. I didn't. I hesitated outside his door, then tiptoed past to Eve's. Light showed in a yellow strip—she was awake. I struck the door open without knocking, striding inside.

Eve sat at her windowsill looking down at the dark street. The dim light hid the ravages of her face—she could have been any age, tall and lean with a stark profile and long bare feet curled beneath her. She could have been the girl who went to Lille in 1915 . . . except for those maimed and terrible hands lying in her lap. It all came back to those hands. It had all *started* with those hands. I remembered how the gorge had risen in my throat when I'd first seen them, that night in London.

"Don't you Yanks know how to knock?" Eve's cigarette glowed at the tip as she raised it for a long drag.

I folded my arms. "The thing is," I began, as though we were continuing a discussion already begun, "I don't know what comes next."

Eve finally looked at me. She raised her eyebrows.

"I had a plan, all broken down like a simple geometry problem. Find Rose if she was still alive, have my baby, learn to cope. I don't have a plan, now. But I'm not ready to go home. I'm not ready to go back to my mother and start arguing all over again about how I'm going to live. I'm not ready to sit on a couch knitting booties."

Above all, I wasn't ready to lose this little trio that had molded itself around Eve and Finn and me in a dark blue car. Part of me had had enough pain for a lifetime, and that part wanted to pull up stakes and run home rather than take the risk that Finn would reject me tomorrow morning. But another part of me—small but increasingly demanding, just like the Rosebud—wanted to stick this out, whatever *this* was. I wasn't sure exactly what had pulled the three of us together, or why it had turned out we were all chasing some variant of the same thing: legacies left by lost women in past wars. I didn't have a destination anymore, or a goal at the end of this road, but we were headed somewhere and I wasn't ready to abandon the journey.

"I know what I want, Eve. I want time to figure out what comes next." I groped my way through this thicket as Eve sat giving me no clue if my words were sinking in. I looked at her hands, taking a deep breath. "And I want to hear the rest of your story."

Eve exhaled smoke. I heard the honk of a horn outside, some late-night driver.

"You asked me at the café tonight if I had guts." I heard my own heart pounding. "I don't know if I do or not. At around my age you were racking up medals in a war zone; I haven't done anything even remotely in your class. But I've got the guts not to go crawling home. I've got the guts to hear what happened to you, no matter how bad it was." I sat down opposite those steady eyes that were afire with remembered pain and savage self-loathing. "Finish the story. Give me a reason to stay."

"You want a reason?" She passed me her cigarettes. "Revenge."

The pack was slippery in my hand. "Revenge for who?"

"For Lili's arrest." Eve's voice in the dark was low, graveled, ferocious. "And for what happened to me, the night I was caught."

And as dark wore on to dawn, Eve told me the rest of it.

CHAPTER 30

EVE

October 1915

It didn't matter what she said or didn't say. Whether Eve insulted René, answered him civilly, or refused to answer at all, he brought down the bust of Baudelaire in a sharp, precise movement and broke another finger joint. Even in the throes of agony, Eve could look down at her hands and count.

She had twenty-eight finger joints in total.

René had so far gone through nine of them.

"I am going to give you to the Germans." His metallic voice was level, but she could hear the emotions running taut below the surface. "First, however, you are going to talk to me. You are going to tell me everything I want to know."

He sat opposite, one finger tapping the dome of Baudelaire's head. The once-pristine marble was now flecked with blood. He'd broken her first few joints without skill, clumsy at it, flinching at the noise of shattering bone. He was getting better at it now, though the blood still made his nostrils flare in distaste. *You're as new to this torture business as I am,* Eve thought. She had no idea how much time might have passed. Time had turned elastic, molding itself around the pulse of her agony. The fire flickered, and the two of them sat in leather armchairs with the table drawn between them, as they used to sit playing chess before retiring to bed. Only now Eve's hands were tied flat to that table's surface with the silk cord from one of René's robes. Tied so tightly it hurt, so tightly she had no hope of pulling free.

She didn't try. Escape wasn't a possibility now. The only things possible were to remain silent, and show no fear. So she kept her back straight, much as she wished she could curl over her hands and shriek, and she managed a smile for René. He would not know what that smile cost her.

"You wouldn't rather play chess?" she suggested. "I let you teach me how to play, because Marguerite was t-too ignorant to know chess, but I'm actually rather good. I'd love to play a real match instead of always losing on p-purpose so you can feel superior."

Rage tightened his face. Eve barely had time to brace herself before the bust descended, and with it the now-familiar sound of crunching bone.

She screamed through clenched teeth, making René's chin jerk. She had told herself at first that she wouldn't scream, but she'd broken down by the fifth knuckle. This was the tenth. She couldn't pretend it didn't hurt. She couldn't look directly at her hand anymore either. From the corner of her eye, she saw a mess of blood and black bruising and grotesquely twisted joints. All the damage so far was to her right hand—the left still sat beside it, undamaged, curled into a fist.

"Who is the woman with whom you were arrested?" René's voice was taut. "She can't be the head of the local network, but she might know him."

Inside, Eve smiled. Even now, René and the Huns had underestimated Lili. They underestimated anything female. "Her name is Alice Dubois, and she's a nobody."

"I don't believe you."

He hadn't believed anything out of her mouth so far. After the sixth knuckle went in a burst of blood, Eve had tried giving him false information, anything her imagination could make up. Hoping it would make him stop. But he had not stopped, even when she pretended to acquiesce and started talking. He might be new to the business of torture, but he was keen.

"What is the woman's real name? Tell me!"

"Why?" Eve managed to spit. "You won't believe anything I say. Give me to the G-Germans and let them ask the questions." At this point she *wanted* a German cell. The Huns might interrogate her, they might kick her about the floor, but they did not hate her personally as betrayed, outwitted René did. *Just turn me in,* Eve prayed, biting the inside of her lip to stifle a moan, tasting her own blood.

"I will not turn you in until I've drained you of information," René said as though reading her mind. "If I'm to overcome the distrust the Germans will harbor knowing I took a spy for a mistress, I must give them something valuable. If I can't, I may as well spare myself the suspicion altogether and just shoot you." A pause. "It's not as though anyone will inquire about a disappeared waitress."

"You can't kill me. You'd never get away with it." Of course he could, but Eve began flinging doubts at him anyway. She'd already thought of this, the moment he pointed the pistol at her. "You think you could march me out of this study on my own two feet, off to some lonely spot where you can shoot me and leave me in the bushes to rot? I'd scream and struggle every step of the way. Someone would see."

"I could kill you here in this room—"

"And then have to dispose of me somewhere, all by yourself. Your German friends may owe you favors, but they won't dispose of a corpse for you. You think you can lug a body out of your restaurant and get rid of it, all without someone noticing? This is a *city* of spies, René, German and French and English alike. Everyone sees everything. You'd never get away with it—"

Oh, yes, he could. Money, luck, and a good scheme could always make murder possible. But Eve kept flinging up objections anyway, and she could see the doubts being sowed in René's eyes. He had no firm plan and he was floundering here, for all his taut control. *You make brilliant plans,* Eve thought, *but unlike me, you can't improvise worth a damn.* René was so rarely surprised by other people; when he *was* knocked back onto his heels he had no idea how to proceed. Eve filed that away. God only knew if she would ever be able to use it against him, but she still filed it away.

"I could kill you," he said at last, "but I'd rather drain you of information. If I can give the Germans the network of agents that has done so much damage in this area, they will be *exceedingly* grateful. Because as it stands, they don't have the evidence to sentence the two women they are holding to death."

Eve filed that away too.

René smiled, fingers tapping Baudelaire's marble head, and she couldn't help the ice-cold shiver that flashed through her body, everywhere except her destroyed hand. "So—who was the woman, Eve?"

"She's no one."

"Liar."

"*Yes*," Eve spat. "I'm a liar and you kn-know it, and you won't trust anything out of my mouth. You have no idea how to c-conduct this interrogation. This isn't about getting information from me; this is about you being outsmarted. You're destroying me because I was *cleverer* than you."

He stared at her, mouth tight, two spots of color gleaming high in his cheeks. "You are just a lying bitch."

"Here's something you can believe." Eve leaned forward over her own mangled hand. "Every moan I ever made in your bed was faked."

He brought the bust down. The first knuckle in her right thumb shattered and Eve couldn't catch the scream in her teeth this time. Even as she screamed, she wondered if the neighbors would hear through the windows, the muffling brocade drapes, the thick walls. *No one can help you, even if they hear.* The darkened city outside might as well be on the other side of the world. *Let me faint,* Eve prayed, *let me faint*—but René picked up the glass of water at his elbow and tossed it in her face, and the world cleared with a jolt.

"Were you aiming from the start to seduce me?" His voice was tight.

"You walked yourself into that trap, you g-gutless French pansy." Eve managed a cough of a laugh, water sliding down her chin. "I was glad you did, though. The way you spilled your g-guts over a pillow, it was worth the four minutes of panting and moaning first—"

She had only three knuckles still whole on her right hand, and René broke them all in a flurry of now-expert blows. Eve shrieked. A sharp stench rose into the air of the rich study. Dimly, through the agony, she realized she had soiled herself. Urine and worse ran down the butter-soft leather of René's expensive armchair to the

Aubusson carpet below, and even through the torture engulfing her hand, she was ground down by a bone-deep wave of shame.

"What a dirty slut you are," he said. "No wonder I insisted you take a bath before I ever fucked you."

Another wash of shame, but the fear was stronger. She was more terrified than she even knew was possible. *Trapped*—the word kept running through her brain like a mouse skittering before a stalking cat. *Trapped—trapped*. No one was coming to help her. She was very possibly going to die here, the moment he tired of giving her pain and decided it was less trouble to shoot her than to turn her in. Her mouth was so dry with terror, it felt like gravel.

"That's one hand," René said casually, setting down the bust. His eyes glittered, perhaps with arousal, perhaps with his own brand of shame—the shame of being made a dupe. Either way, there were no more flinches or flared nostrils for the mess of the scene, the blood, the sounds and smells. "You still have your left hand, and that's enough to get along. I'll spare the rest of your fingers if you start talking. Tell me who the woman arrested at the station is. Tell me who ran the network. Tell me why you returned to Lille when you had already escaped to Tournai."

Verdun, Eve thought. At least the message got out. She had to hope it would be worth it, that the message for which she and Lili were captured would save lives.

"Tell me those things, and I will bandage your hand, give you laudanum for the pain, and take you to the Germans. I'll even request a surgeon to set your fingers." René reached out, stroking the side of her face. The path of his fingertips carried its own agony, a shiver of revulsion so deep Eve's bones quivered. "Just talk to me."

"You won't believe me even if I—"

"I will, pet, I will. Because I think I've broken you. I think you're finally willing to speak the truth."

Eve's eyes blurred. She wanted to tell him, that was the terrible part. The words were on her tongue: *I worked for Louise de Bettignies, code name Alice Dubois, and she ran the entire network.* Lili, whose name Eve wouldn't know if they hadn't run into that German general on the train platform. If only that had never happened.

I worked for Louise de Bettignies, and she ran the network—a woman not five feet tall and brave as a lioness. And if she were here in my place, she would not say a word no matter how many fingers she lost.

Or would she? How did one know what anyone would do when they had fourteen joints systematically smashed?

But Lili wasn't here in this chair with her hands bound in front of her. Eve was. Who knew what Lili would do; all Eve could be sure of was what Eve Gardiner would do.

"Who is the woman?" René whispered. "Who?"

Eve wished she could smile mockingly. She had no more smiles to give. She wished she could summon a cutting phrase. She had no insults left. So she just spit blood in his face, spattering his immaculately shaved cheek. "Go to hell, you cut-price collaborating cunt."

His eyes were all fire. "Oh, pet," he breathed, "thank you."

He reached tenderly for Eve's left hand. She curled her fingers into a fist, fighting him, but he wrenched her hand open and flattened it on the table, holding her like a vise as he reached for the little marble bust. *Fucking Baudelaire,* Eve thought, baring her blood-laced teeth at René. The terror was overwhelming.

"Who is the woman?" René asked, enjoying himself now, bust poised over the little finger of her left hand.

"Even if you would believe me," Eve said, "I won't tell you."

"You have fourteen chances to change your mind," René replied, and brought the bust down.

Time splintered, after that. There was scarlet-edged pain, and then velvet-black unconsciousness. René's metallic voice slid through both like a steel needle, stitching together the waking nightmare and the fainting relief. When a cup of water dashed in her face no longer brought her up from unconsciousness, he pressed a thumb precisely against one of her ruined knuckles until Eve woke screaming. Then he took his time wiping his fingertips on a clean handkerchief, and the questions would start again. So would the sound of breaking bones.

The pain came and went, but the terror was constant. Sometimes she cowered with tears sliding down her face, and sometimes she was able to sit upright in her soiled chair and meet René's eyes. In either state, she had stopped answering his questions. The agony stole her ability to form words, or even a token laugh.

There was a kind of relief when the last of her finger joints shattered. Eve looked down at the carnage that used to be her hands, and it felt like crossing a finish line. *I suppose he might move on to my toes,* she thought, remote inside her own shaking, sobbing shell. *Or my knees . . .* But the pain was already so enormous, the thought of more no longer had the power to frighten her. She had come this far; she could continue her silence.

Because René couldn't hold her here forever, bleeding all over his Aubusson rug as his restaurant remained closed, as his profits died, and as his neighbors began to wonder about the noise coming from his apartments. At some point he had to give up this game. He would either give her to the Germans, or kill her. Eve barely cared which anymore. Either meant that the pain would stop.

Endure, the whisper came. In Lili's voice; Lili would never leave her. *Endure him, little daisy.* Enduring the Germans, once they got hold of her, would be a different game—unlike René, they would have the power to cross-check her lies, verify her truths. But she had no strength to worry about what agonies were to come, only the agonies that were here.

Endure. It was simple, really. No more need to pretend, to keep up a cover, to walk the razor's edge. Eve was off the razor and in among the teeth now, but at least there was no more need to lie. Just endure.

So she did.

She came out of one of her black faints—they were becoming more frequent—not with a shriek of pain but with a trickle of fire down her throat. René stood behind her, tipping her chin back as he held a glass of brandy to her lips. Eve coughed as a trickle went down, then tried to seal her mouth, but he rammed the glass against her teeth. "Drink this, or I will dig your eye out with an absinthe spoon."

Eve had thought the terror was at its peak, but there were always new summits, new levels of fear, and she went flying up them. She opened her lips and swallowed the brandy down, a hefty dose that burned her stomach. René sat back down opposite, eyes devouring her.

"Eve," he said, tasting her real name. "Aptly named. What a temptation you were. You never even needed to hand me an apple; I took you empty-handed and made a muse of you. Look at you now. *'I see reflected in your face horror and madness, icy and silent . . .'"*

"More goddamn Baudelaire?" Eve managed to say.

"From 'The Sick Muse.' Also apt."

They sat in silence. Eve waited for more questions, but René seemed content to gaze at her. She slipped down into the black pool, and this time woke slowly, swimming back to consciousness, the pain strangely blurred. René's chair was empty. The sinuous, sliding texture of the jade green silk walls swam as Eve searched for him. She blinked as the walls expanded and contracted like the eye of a kaleidoscope. She shook her head to clear it, fastening her gaze on the Tiffany lampshade. There was a peacock in the shade, tail fanned out in a thousand hues of blue and green glass, and Eve cried out as the peacock turned its head. Its glittering eyes found hers, and every eye in its tail feathers turned to look at her too. Evil eyes, wasn't that what they called the eyes in peacock feathers? They reared up toward Eve, rippling out of the lampshade with a tinkling sound of moving glass.

You're imagining it, Eve thought blurrily. But when she blinked again, the glass peacock was still there, perched on top of the lamp, tail arrayed in a poisonous fan, all those accusing eyes staring. She was suddenly pouring sweat.

The peacock spoke, its voice brittle as the glass it was made of. "Who is the woman you were arrested with?"

She cried out again. Her mind had snapped; she'd gone utterly mad. *Or René gave me something,* she thought, *something in the brandy—* But that thought flew away, gone before she could grasp it or make truth of it.

The peacock spoke again. "Who is the woman, Eve?"

"I—I don't know." She didn't know anything anymore; she'd fallen sideways into a world of nightmares and nothing was certain. The bust of Baudelaire sat on the table, his marble eyes open and filled with blood. Red drops slid down his marble cheeks. "Who is the woman?" he asked, words grinding harsh from his marble throat. "You *do* know."

There were lilies in a slender fluted vase on the mantel, long-stemmed and graceful. Evil-eyed lilies, *fleurs du mal,* kept forever in glass. Eve's mouth burned, looking at the cool water around their green stems. "Thirsty," she murmured. Her tongue had turned to dusty stone.

"You shall have water when you tell me who the woman is."

Eve was still staring at the lilies, which stared back with bloody eyes. *"To quench the terrible thirst that torments me, I'd have to swallow all the wine it would take to fill her grave."* Lilies' grave. Lili's grave. Eve cried out. The pit was opening at her feet in the middle of the Aubusson carpet, yawing black earth—

"Le vin de l'assassin," the marble statue said, naming the poem. "'The murderer's wine.' Very good, Eve. Who is the woman?"

The chuckle sounded like René, but Eve couldn't see him. He was gone. She could see only the swimming green walls that breathed in rhythm with her hammering pulse, the peacock fanning its glass tail, and the bust with its bloody cheeks. The yaw of the pit at her feet. There was something down there at its bottom, some great ravenous beast. She pulled against the rope about her wrists and it wakened the pain in her hands. The beast was out of the pit and it was eating her hands, chewing its way up her wrists. If she opened her eyes, she would see its gleaming teeth slowly devouring her broken fingers. She screamed again, pulling frantically against the ropes, and the agony roared. She was going to die of this pain, eaten alive and conscious to the end. She wept, head moving mindlessly back and forth as the teeth of some rough slouching beast chewed languorously up her wrists.

"Who is the woman, Eve?"

Lili, she thought. *Did the beast already kill you?* She didn't know. She couldn't remember. Drops of sweat slid down her neck from her sodden hair.

"Who is the woman?"

Eve forced herself to open her eyes. She would look the beast in the face as it killed her. She looked down at her hands, expecting to see them clamped in a fanged maw, and then she shrieked. Her hands were not gone— they had *changed* somehow, the shattered fingers trying to regrow themselves. She had twice as many fingers, every one painted in blood and tipped not with a nail, but with an eye. All the eyes blinked at her in unison, accusing and blind.

The beast is me, she thought in utter agony. *The beast is me. Did I kill Lili? Did I kill her?*

"Who is the woman, Eve?"

Did I kill her?

Eve's lips parted blindly, and the mad, pulsing world went dark. Waves and waves of blackness and pain, terror and teeth.

Time to wake up, pet."

Light stabbed Eve's eyes as she peeled them open, but nothing stabbed like the silver needle of René's voice. She sat upright, a jolt of agony coursing through her hands. She was still roped to her chair, mouth dry as cotton and her skull splitting. René smiled, leaning against the window overlooking the street. He wore a gray morning suit, his hair was combed and oiled, and he had a teacup in hand. The light came through the window strong and bright. It was *morning*, though Eve couldn't tell which morning, if a night or two nights or a month's worth of nights had passed in that storm of pain and—

Teeth. Pulsing walls, evil eyes, *teeth*. Eve's gaze flew wildly about the study, but it looked the same as it ever had. The green silk walls were not breathing, the peacock on the Tiffany lampshade stayed confined in glass, the lilies in their fluted vase were just flowers.

Lilies. *Lili*. Eve's heart skittered, and she looked back at René. He smiled, taking a sip of steaming tea.

"I trust you are more comfortable."

Eve looked down at her hands for the first time. They had been bandaged in clean cloth, bulky anonymous mitts that hid the horror underneath. She still wore her soiled clothes, but her face and hair had been sponged. René had expended some effort to make her presentable.

"Herr Rotselaer is bringing his men to arrest you," René explained, glancing out the window to the street below. "They should be arriving—oh, perhaps in half an hour. I thought you should look at least a trifle tidy for your captors. Some of these young officers are still squeamish when it comes to hurting women. Even English spies."

The relief crashed over Eve like an avalanche. *The Fritzes are coming for me.* She was not going to die here in this room. She was going to a German cell. Perhaps she would only come out of that cell to face a firing squad, but right now, it was enough that the cell would not have René in it. He had given up tormenting her. Given up.

I held out, she thought in a kind of numb wonder. *I endured.*

In her mind, Lili smiled. Perhaps she would see Lili

in prison, and Violette. If they could stand together, they could face anything that came. Even a line of guns.

"Your friend," René said as though reading her mind. "Give her a hello from me if you should see her in the adjoining cell. She sounds like a rather extraordinary woman, your Louise de Bettignies. I'm sorry never to have met her."

He sipped his tea, standing there in the sunlight. Eve stared at him, the marks of a comb in his hair, the fresh shave of his jaw.

"You told me," he said. "If you're wondering."

"I told you n-n—" she tried to say through numbed lips. "*N-N*—I told you n—" *Nothing. Rien.* Such a small word, and it would not come out. Her tongue had frozen fast.

"Louise de Bettignies, alias Alice Dubois, alias a dozen other names. You listed them all. The German *Kommandant* will be very happy to realize just who it is Herr Rotselaer has in custody. The head, in fact, of the local network. Astounding to think it was a woman."

Eve just repeated, "I told you n-n—" Her faulty tongue was failing on the most important word she ever had to speak, stuttering in a panic so far past ordinary terror that she barely felt it at all. It wasn't a reaction her body was big enough to contain; it just hovered over her like a floating mountain, ready to flatten her utterly. *I told him nothing.*

But she thought of the inexplicable fever dreams, the bust of Baudelaire coming to life—

René nodded, doubtless seeing the expressions chasing across her face. For so long she'd kept her face locked against him like a vault. Now it had broken open, and he was flipping through her every thought and emotion like pages of a book. "You were right in one thing you told me yesterday: I had no way to parse truth from

lie in anything you told me. But opium"—swirling the
tea in his cup—"induces strange visions when admin-
istered in quantity. It also reduces resistance. You certainly seemed to see some strange things last night . . .
It made you very pliable in the end."

Eve could only repeat like a broken record. "I told
you n-n-n—"

"N-n-n-no, my pet. You babbled like a brook. You
gave me your friend Louise, for which I am duly thank-
ful." He toasted her with the teacup. "And so are the
Germans."

Betrayed. The word howled through Eve's head. *Be-*
trayed. No, she would never have betrayed Lili.

He knows her name. Where did he learn it but you?
No.

Betrayer.
No . . .

"Really," René went on idly, ignoring Eve's silence,
"if I'd known opium was the way to make you so agree-
able, you might still have your hands in one piece, and
I'd have a study that didn't smell like piss. How I'm going to get the stains out of my Aubusson, I don't know."
His smile deepened; there was something edged and
restless about it. "But perhaps a ruined rug is worth it. I
enjoyed smashing you up, Marguerite. Eve. You know, I
don't think either of those names suits you."

Lili in front of a wall, blindfolded, as rifles were
leveled—

Betrayer. Betrayer. *Evelyn Gardiner, you weak foul*
coward.

"I have a better name for you." René put down his
cup, drifted closer. He leaned down to press his cheek
against Eve's, and she inhaled the scent of his cologne.
"My dear little Judas."

Eve's head darted like a snake. She was roped to the

chair and her hands swathed in mitts, but she caught René's lower lip with her teeth and bit deep. She tasted the coppery tang of his blood, bitter as her own failure. Sawed her teeth harder and harder, even as he shouted and began wrenching at her hair. It was the last, savage kiss between source and spy, captor and captive, collaborator and betrayer, their mouths locked together by teeth and blood. René had to tear himself loose. Eve's chair crashed over, and her head hit the floor with a force that blurred the world in sickly pulses. "You vicious bitch," René hissed, his collar blood spattered, his eyes black with fury, his metallic voice finally rising out of its smug inflectionless calm. "You spying English cunt, you half-breed shopgirl, you shrewish thieving whore—" He went on, his elegant vocabulary broken down to the most obscene gutter slang that could be dredged out of the French language, his mouth scarlet with his own blood as though he'd been eating souls, and so he had. He had been eating souls and hearts and lives these past months, anything for profit, and René Bordelon now looked like the ravening beast he was, but Eve felt no flicker of triumph for breaking him. She too had broken, with a snap far more audible and final than the wet crunch of her destroyed knuckles. She lay there roped to her fallen chair, weeping and weeping, but there were not enough tears in the world for her shame and her horror. She was a Judas; she had betrayed her best friend in all the world to her worst enemy in all the world.

I want to die, Eve thought as René pulled himself together, retreated to the window angrily stuffing a wad of cloth against his mouth. *I want to die.*

She was still thinking it, still weeping, when the Germans came. When they untied the ropes and hauled her away.

CHAPTER 31
CHARLIE

May 1947

esus," Finn said softly. I'd been too frozen by Eve's recitation to realize he'd come in.

"No," Eve said in her low, graveled voice. "Jesus wasn't anywhere near that green-walled study. Only Judas." She reached for her packet of cigarettes but it was long empty. "It's the s-s-study I dream about. Not René's face, not the sound of my fingers breaking. The study. Those breathing walls, and the Tiffany peacock, and that bust of B-Baudelaire . . ."

She trailed off, her averted profile harsh. Somewhere in the distance I heard a church bell chime, and we all listened to the doleful sound: Finn with his shoulder jammed against the wall, arms folded across his chest; me curled up on the window seat; Eve across from me motionless as a statue, hands folded in her lap.

Those hands. From the beginning I'd wanted to know

what had happened to her hands, and now I knew. They were the price she'd paid for serving her country, the war wounds that reminded her every day of how she'd broken. An uncompromising heart like hers wouldn't accept that she wasn't to blame for succumbing. She just saw cowardice, and it shamed her enough to make her refuse the medals she'd earned. I looked at my own un-marked hands, imagining a marble bust smashing down over and over until my fingers looked like Eve's, and a bone-deep shudder went through me. "Eve," I heard myself say low-voiced. "You are the bravest soul I have ever met."

She brushed that aside. "I broke. A little opium in a brandy glass, and I spilled my guts."

Something about that bothered me. It didn't entirely add up, and I opened my mouth to say why, but Finn was already speaking, his voice soft and angry.

"Don't be a dobber, Gardiner. Everybody breaks. Hit people in the right place, find the thing they care for, hurt them long enough—we all crack. There's no shame in that."

"Yes, there is, you soft-headed Scot. Lili was con-demned at trial because of it, and so were Violette and I."

"So blame René Bordelon for torturing it out of you. Blame the Germans for handing down the sentence—"

"Oh, there's enough blame in this withered heart for all of us." Her voice was ruthless in its condemnation, and she still didn't look at us. "René and the Germans played their part, but so did I. Violette never forgave me, and I don't blame her."

"What happened to Lili?" I asked. "Was—was it the firing squad after all?" I could see her standing up against a wall, small and gallant under her blindfold, and my gorge rose. Eve had made Lili every bit as real and precious to me as Rose.

"No," said Eve. "It was too soon after Cavell's execution. Too much outcry for the Germans to shoot another woman p-point blank. It was quite another fate for the three of us." Eve shivered as if a rat had run across her nerves.

"But you survived," I said, dry-mouthed. "Violette survived. Did Lili—"

"Enough about the trial and the rest of it. It's not a tale for dark nights, and anyway, it's not important at the moment." Eve pushed it away almost visibly, whatever it was, and fixed her eyes on mine. "What's important now is René Bordelon. You know now what he did to me, what kind of man he was. When the war ended and I came home, I had every intention of returning to Lille and blowing his foul head off. I'd been dreaming about it for years. Captain Cameron scuttled that—lied to my face the day I arrived in England, saying René was dead." Her voice was sliding back from hoarse emotion into her usual crispness the further she got from the recitation of her own torture. "Cameron probably thought I'd have *peace* that way. That man was too damned noble to understand vengeance. How it keeps you up night after night shaking with hatred, dreaming that if you can only taste blood in your mouth, you'll sleep without d-d-d-dreams."

Finn gave a single fierce nod. He understood. So did I. I thought of the German soldiers who had shot Rose and her daughter, and my hatred was violent and instant.

"Well, I may be nearly thirty years l-l-l"—Eve's gnarled fist struck hard against her own knee, and she jerked the halted word free—"thirty years late, but I am going to settle accounts. René owes me." Eve's eyes never left mine. "He owes *you* too."

I blinked. "Me?"

"You say you want a reason to stay on this search,

Yank, and I'll give it to you, but you have to ask. Do you really want to hear this?"

I just blinked again. We'd all been so thoroughly entrenched in Eve's past, I felt like an actor being dragged onstage into the wrong play. "Yes. I want to hear. But I don't understand, I've never *met* René Bordelon."

"He still owes you. He did a lot more than just employ that cousin of yours." Eve sounded concise as a field officer now. "I needed to f-find out what René's been up to since coming to Limoges as René du Malassis, so I asked Major Allenton. He's an idiot, so of c-course he advanced right up the ranks over the years. Did quite a bit of work during the second war—I might have been involved in some of it, and that gave me a way to start the conversation that finally worked itself around to René du Malassis. With a generous application of wine and flattery, Allenton positively *dripped* information over dinner, some of it public knowledge, some of it very private. Thank God for loose-lipped idiots.

"Allenton coordinated with a number of French Resistance networks in the second war, arranging the drop of supplies, collecting information. It was widely known that Monsieur du Malassis was a profiteer in Limoges. For political favors, he passed information to the Nazis and to the Milice working for those scum in Vichy." Eve reached for her satchel, and fished out something which she proffered by the tips of two misshapen fingers. "That's René in 1944. He was a person of interest, so Allenton had a photograph."

I took it, a photograph taken at some elegant dinner with local worthies and Nazi officials lined up for the flash. A man on the far left had been circled, and I peered close. At last Eve's nemesis had a face—but not the elegant wolflike one I had envisioned from her stories. An old man in a dark suit stared back at me, lean

faced, his silver hair swept back from a high forehead.
Age had turned him stalk boned rather than stout, but
he wasn't frail; the silver-headed cane hooked over one
arm swung like an accessory. I examined the faint smile
on that line-bracketed face, the way he held the stem of
his wineglass between two fingers, and wondered if I
was simply projecting the past when I thought his pho-
tographed gaze looked cold, cold, cold.

Finn leaned over my shoulder for a look, and let out
a soft curse. I knew what he was thinking. This old
man had destroyed Eve in his green-walled study. She'd
turned into a bitter crone crouched in the wreckage of
nightmares and whiskey while he had gone on to make
more money, befriend more German invaders, destroy
more lives. Shoot a young *sous-chef* in the back for
thieving. Sit at banquet tables glittering with crystal and
swastikas, and smile as he got his picture taken . . .

I looked at his face, and I hated him.

"He was widely known in the second war as a
profiteer," Eve continued quietly. "But what *isn't*
widely known is that he was partially responsible for
a m-m-m—for a massacre. It filtered up to Major Allenton, through sources in the Milice, that a civilian
informer in Limoges passed information about French
Resistance activity in a small town nearby. Specifically,
he gave the Milice a girl's name, and stated that she
and others in the Resistance had kidnapped and killed
a German officer. That officer was a close friend of SS
Sturmbannführer Diekmann of the Der Führer Regiment, the Das Reich Division. When the Milice passed
this tip on and the captured officer was confirmed
killed, everyone probably expected Diekmann to arrest
and hang the girl. But he decided to make an example
not just of her, but her entire town." Eve's eyes never left
me. "The girl was going by the name of Hélène Jou-

bert. The town was Oradour-sur-Glane. René was the informer who reported both."

Dread swept over me. I remembered Madame Rouffanche's voice, saying, *Hélène Joubert, she said her name was . . . we called her Rose.*

"It's not clear if your cousin actually was Resistance," Eve went on. "She certainly had connections if the man who fathered her child was involved. She wasn't listed as active in any of the networks Allenton knew, though that's not proof. Maybe she had nothing more to do with them after bearing her child, or maybe she passed on information from her workplace in Limoges. Who knows? Whether she spied on the Nazis who came to Le Lethe or not, I think René decided your Rose was suspicious. He would have been rather fearful at that point about eavesdropping waitresses." A tight, bitter smile. "Even if she *was* Resistance, your cousin wouldn't have been involved in the kidnapping and killing of any German officers, that would have been an operation for more experienced fighters. But René wanted her gone, so—"

"So he made sure *hers* was the name to be reported?" I whispered. "Why wouldn't he just fire her if he wanted her away from his restaurant?"

"He probably viewed it as safer to have her permanently disposed of. He could have shot her himself— certainly by then, he had no qualms about pulling a trigger. But he might not have felt he could do such a thing again, not after the public incident with the *sous-chef.* That might have cost him too many Nazi favors. So he just passed on your cousin's name, and the town where he already knew she went on weekends, and took care of her that way." Eve tilted her head. "In fairness, he couldn't have known the entire town would be massacred. But even had the Germans been merciful to the rest of Oradour-sur-Glane, your cousin would undoubtedly still have been rounded up and executed by the SS. Because of René Bordelon."

My skin was crawling. The photograph in my hand burned me. I looked again at that smug old face.

"There is no vengeance to be had against the Germans who actually ended your cousin's life," Eve said. "Sturmbannführer Diekmann, the man who ordered the massacre, died a matter of weeks afterward in the Allied assault—that's a matter of military record, confirmed by Allenton. The soldiers who carried out his orders would have either died with him, been disseminated back to Germany after the war, or still linger on in prisoner of war camps. None were named and brought to trial for what happened at Oradour-sur-Glane, either at Nuremberg or afterward, and without another mass trial, it's unlikely you'd ever find out which man fired the shots that killed your cousin. Those men are probably beyond your reach. René is not. He didn't pull the trigger, but he certainly did his best to arrange your cousin's death."

I couldn't move. I couldn't speak. I couldn't even breathe. I sat staring down at that smug face. *Oh, Rose . . .*

"I am going to track down René Bordelon, Charlie St. Clair, and make him pay for what he's done." Eve flexed her destroyed hands. "Are you coming with me?"

PART IV

CHAPTER 32
EVE

March 1916
Brussels

The trial was over in a single day.

For Eve, those grinding hours in the imposing room passed in a blur. Violette stared straight ahead when they were all marched in under guard, and Lili cast her mobile gaze all around the high glass ceiling and curule chairs and proud Belgian lions—but Eve focused downward on her mottle-skinned, half-healed fingers clenched together in front of her. They still hurt savagely despite the passage of the intervening months; the pain seemed far more important than the drone of German words overhead.

More formalities as the other officials filed in. Eve's eyes traveled from face to face. German soldiers, German officials, German clerks . . . But no Frenchmen, no civilians allowed in to view the spectacle. René Bordelon was not here to crane his gaze at the ruin he had made of her, and for that Eve was grateful. She dreaded seeing his face more than she dreaded hearing her sentence. Had she seen him, she knew she would have collapsed, shivering, to the thick carpet.

I did not use to be so small and fearful, she thought as one of the judges harangued them. She had been this broken thing for months now, lying in her cell trembling and weeping at any provocation, and she still wasn't used to it. The only thing fierce about Eve anymore was her self-loathing.

Betrayer. The whisper was a part of her blood now; it pulsed with every heartbeat, poisonous and matter-of-fact. *Betrayer.*

Lili knew of her betrayal. They'd barely been allowed to speak to each other, these past months in their separate prison cells in Saint-Gilles, but Eve had bribed one of the guards to tell Lili what she'd done. She couldn't have carried the weight of that betrayal as a lie. Eve's heart hammered now as she gazed across the room, forcing herself to look past Violette's stolid profile to where Lili sat. *Spit on me*, Eve begged silently. *I have earned it.*

But all Lili did was smile. Her small face flashed one of its mischievous looks as though she didn't sit ringed about by hostile guards, as if she was still a free woman—and she put two fingers to her lips and blew Eve a kiss.

Eve flinched as though the kiss were a blow.

They were questioned one at a time, not allowed to hear each other's testimony. Violette first, her real name of Léonie van Houtte spoken for the first time in Eve's hearing, though she still couldn't think of Lili's lieutenant by any name but Violette. She at least viewed Eve as the traitor she was; the other woman's stare was hate filled as Eve filed out under guard. Eve was brought in to be questioned next, and she didn't bother with a defense. *Everyone here knows what the outcome will be.* She stood silent under the harangue of German, feeling her hands throb, breathing the stale smells of hair oil and shoe polish, and soon enough she was led out again. Lili was the one they wanted most; she could sense the liquid ripple that went over the room in anticipation, almost savage, and wondered if such a ripple had gone over the viewers in the Colosseum before the lions were released. The lions in this room were gold and carved, but they could still levy death.

The judges disappeared; half an hour ticked past measured by a deliberate clock—and it was over. Eve, Lili, Violette, and several lesser defendants were all arrayed before the court, and a vast silence fell. Eve's mouth went dry as paper, and she could feel herself trembling. At the corner of her eye, she saw Violette's fingers twitch as though she wanted to reach for Lili's hand. Lili stood like a statue.

The words rolled out in nasal German.

"For Louise de Bettignies, death."

"For Léonie van Houtte, death."

"For Evelyn Gardiner, death."

Ripples crossed the room, and Eve felt as though she had been kicked in the chest. Not by dread.

Relief.

She looked down at her mangled hands with blurring eyes and thought, as she'd thought while weeping on the floor of René's green-walled study, *I want to die.*

No more months of cells and monotony, pain and morphine and guilt. Just the mouths of the guns, arrayed before her. The imagined sight was beautiful. A ripple of gunfire and then—nothing.

But before her heart could squeeze in relief, Lili stepped forward. She spoke in soft, perfect German, the only time in the entire trial she spoke in the language of the enemy.

"Gentlemen, I ask you not to shoot my friends. They are young, and I implore your mercy for them." Her blond head tilted. "Me, I want to die well."

"I accept my sentence." Violette spoke in clear, contemptuous tones, cutting her leader off. "You can shoot me. But I ask you before I die, and you cannot refuse me: do not part me from Lil—from Louise de Bettignies."

Eve heard her own voice. "Or me."

A row of German faces looked down at them, and Eve saw blank confusion there. She'd seen the same expression from their guards at Saint-Gilles: bewilderment, looking at tiny Lili and stuttering Eve and Violette with her glasses like a schoolteacher, wondering how any of them could possibly be spies.

The Boches have held us for months, Eve thought, *and they still don't know what to make of the* fleurs du mal. The thought gave her a flicker of savage pride for a moment, something to straighten her shoulders before the guilt flattened them again.

The three women of the Alice Network were allowed to stand as further discussion carried on in whispers among the German officials. Another hour crept past. Eve's hands throbbed. Another announcement. Another kick resounding dully through her chest, only this was not relief. This was despair.

The trial was done.

"So," Lili said. "They will not shoot us."

Violette was still shivering in reaction as they waited in the courtyard between their guards. Eve stood numb and upright, but the news seemed to have nearly shattered Violette, who had looked braced for a bullet right then and there in the courtroom. "They will send us to *Germany* . . . ," she muttered.

The sentence had been amended: they were all to suffer fifteen years' hard labor in Siegburg Prison.

"Fifteen years?" Lili wrinkled her nose. "No. We labor until the victory of France, that is all."

"I w-w-wish it was the line of guns," Eve heard herself saying.

Violette's red-rimmed eyes bored into her, bitter and accusing. "You deserve the guns," she said, and spat full into Eve's face. "*Judas.*"

The guards intervened, dragging Violette a few paces away. Eve stood unmoving, letting the warm spittle trickle down her cheek, and the other guards let Lili approach, drawing back a little. Only a tiny oasis of privacy, but it was the most a prisoner could expect.

"Sorry, little daisy." The touch of a worn cuff against Eve's cheek, wiping her clean. She almost flinched at the sensation. She hadn't been touched kindly in so long. "Violette takes it hard."

"She hates me." Eve said it without rancor. "For b-betraying you."

"Pah, who knows how the Boches got my name or found out I ran the network? You don't remember giving it up, opium or no opium." Lili shrugged in complete indifference. "I was identified. *How* that happened doesn't matter."

"It does," Eve stated.

A smile. "Not to me."

Eve nearly wept. *Do not forgive me,* she wanted to cry. *Please, do not forgive me!* Forgiveness hurt so much more than hatred.

Violette was allowed to rejoin them, glaring but quiescent, and Eve welcomed her silent loathing. They all stood in silence, waiting for the car that would take them back to their cells. From there, it would probably be a matter of days until they were transported to Siegburg Prison.

Siegburg. Eve had heard horror stories of that place. She looked east toward Germany, and saw the other women looking too, as though the prison's dank walls were already in sight.

"Do not think about it, *mes anges*." Lili came up between Eve and Violette, putting an arm around each and squeezing hard. "Enjoy the present. You are both here, and I am close to you."

Eve leaned her head on Lili's shoulder and they all stood in the pale March sunlight, waiting to be taken away.

CHAPTER 33
CHARLIE

June 1947

Through the remainder of the night, I stared at the photograph of a monster and tried to make sense of what he'd done. *You got Rose killed*, I thought, over and over. *You got Rose killed*. An SS officer had given the order to fire, and a German soldier had pulled the trigger—but my cousin would never have been targeted at all if not for this man in his elegant suit and silver-headed cane.

I hadn't been able to answer Eve's question. I was too shocked, taking the photograph and stumbling back to my room in complete silence. I felt as though I'd been hit by a boulder, lying across my bed limp and crushed under the weight.

René Bordelon. The name echoed. *You got Rose killed*.

He had always been the link between Eve and me.

Rose had worked for him, Eve had worked for him—
two women out of probably thousands who had labored
in his employ over the decades—and because of that
unremarkable fact, his name on a piece of paper had led
me to Eve, and then here. But I had never thought the
link more than a paper one.

By dawn I was dressed, packed, and headed out to
the front steps of the *auberge*. It didn't surprise me
to see Eve already there with her satchel at her feet,
straight and fierce and smoking her first cigarette of the
day. She turned, and I saw that her eyes were as red and
grained as mine.

"I'll do it," I said. "I'll help you track him down."

"Good," Eve said as matter-of-factly as if I'd agreed
to help her get a cup of coffee. "Finn's getting the car."

We stood and waited in the pink morning light.
"Why do you even want my help?" I couldn't help asking. Another question I'd turned over last night. "You've
wanted to bring this man to justice for more than thirty
years. Wouldn't it be easier without some pregnant college girl in tow? You don't *need* me." Though a large
part of me wished she did. I wanted to take care of her,
even if she was prickly as a handful of needles.

"No, I don't need you," she said briskly. "But the bastard's wronged both of us, not just me, and that means
you have a right to revenge if you want it. I believe in
revenge." Eve looked at me, inscrutable. "I've lost faith
in much over the years, but not that."

She stood there tall and stony as an obelisk, and I
wondered just what form her revenge was going to take.
It gave me a disquieting pang, as the Lagonda came
around the corner.

"Besides," Eve said in an undertone as Finn loaded
the bags into the trunk. "I may not need you, but I defi-

nitely need him. And I put the odds at fifty-fifty that wherever you go, he goes."

I blinked. "What makes you say that?"

She touched a red mark on my throat that I'd seen in the mirror this morning and tried to cover with my loosened hair—a mark Finn's mouth had left last night. "I know the difference between a mosquito bite and a love bite, Yank."

"Done with your blethering, ladies?" Finn came around the driver's side. "It's a braw morning for a drive."

"Yes," I mumbled, ears burning. Eve grinned as she climbed into the backseat. Finn missed the grin, but he saw my red flush and paused after he slid behind the wheel.

"All right, lass?" he asked quietly.

There wasn't really a word for what I was after the past day and night together. Grieving and hopeful, profoundly shocked and profoundly angry—angrier every time I looked at the photograph of the old man we had all agreed to track down. And if I looked at Finn my skin tingled with an all-over flash of what had passed between us not twelve hours ago. "I'm all right," I said finally. He nodded, and I couldn't tell how things stood between us, if he was sorry or not for what had happened. So I left him to put the car in gear, and turned to Eve in the backseat.

"One thing you haven't told us: *how* do we find René Bordelon? He's not going by that name anymore, or René du Malassis either. And we don't know where he went when he fled Limoges. So how do we pick up his trail from here?"

Eve took a last drag off her cigarette and flicked the end into the street. "I have an idea about th-th—about that. He told me more than once that he intended to retire in Grasse, that he even had some dilapidated property there, an old villa he might restore someday. He's seventy-three now; he won't be starting another restaurant. Sounds like *retired* to me. I'll wager he went to rebuild that villa, read his books, play his music, and enjoy the southern sunshine. I say we go to G-G-Grasse."

"And do what?" I raised my eyebrows. "Drive around looking out the window?"

"Give me some credit, Yank. René never told me where his property in Grasse was, but I've got some good ideas of how to find it."

"But what if he isn't there at all?" Finn sounded doubtful. "All we have is a few chance remarks made more than thirty years ago."

"Has anyone h-h-here got a better idea of where to start?"

Admittedly, I didn't. I shrugged. Finn reached for the set of maps crumpled at my feet. "At an easy pace, we make Grasse in two days. Stop in Grenoble tonight . . ."

"Grenoble it is." Eve tilted her head back, closing her eyes to the sky. "Step on it, Scotsman."

The Lagonda hummed along southeast, the three of us each lost in our own thoughts. I found myself looking at the photograph of René again. I wondered what that SS officer had looked like, the one who gave the orders to massacre the village. I wondered what the German soldiers had looked like, the ones who could look at a girl fleeing a burning church with a baby in her arms, and be willing to pull a trigger. Anger flushed through me, slow and burning, and I thought of what Eve had said about those men, that I'd likely never find out which soldiers killed Rose.

Maybe I could, someday. Names had to exist, records. Maybe the German soldiers who survived could be brought to trial, not just for Rose but for Madame Rouffanche and her murdered village. Oradour-sur-Glane deserved justice for its dead as much as any of the atrocities investigated at Nuremberg.

But that was a problem for another day. Here, now, aimed for Grasse, the Nazis who had a hand in Rose's death were out of my reach. But René Bordelon might not be.

As the car rolled through ever-rising hills and the gorgeous expanse of lakes and pastures, I pondered a new equation: Rose plus Lili, divided by Eve plus me, equaling René Bordelon. Four women with one man among us all. I stared at his face in the grainy photograph, looking for remorse, guilt, cruelty. But you couldn't see those things in a picture. He was just an old man out to dinner.

I tried to tuck the photograph back into Eve's satchel, but her gnarled hand lashed out like a whip and knocked mine away. "Keep it."

The photograph went into my pocketbook, and I could feel that man's empty eyes staring at me through the leather, so I turned around and looked back at Eve. She looked steadier, lighter than the hunched guilt-consumed figure in the windowsill last night, reciting her tale of torture and self-loathing. I reached out and touched her hand gently.

"You wouldn't tell us about your trial last night," I said, "or what happened to you and Lili and Violette afterward."

"Not a tale for dark nights."

I tilted my head up at the hot sun above. "No shadows now."

She let out a long breath. "I suppose not."

Finn and I listened as she told us of the trial: the Belgian lions, the hammering questions in German, the reduced sentences. Violette spitting in her face. I remembered the older Violette in Roubaix doing the same, and shivered at the echo. Violette . . . an idea pricked me there, an insistent little thought I'd had last night as well—an equation that didn't balance out—but I pushed that aside for now as Eve said, "Then we came to Siegburg."

CHAPTER 34
EVE

March 1916

After the war ended, Eve was surprised by how little impression Siegburg's endless flow of days had made in her memory. Her time as a spy in Lille had stretched not even six months, yet she remembered it all in diamond-edged clarity. Two and a half years in Siegburg passed like a foul gray dream, every day the same as the one before.

"Take her to her cell."

That was her welcome to Siegburg, in the spring of '16—a brusque order and then a heavy hand in the middle of her back, shoving her down a dark corridor after Lili and Violette. None of them had had a look at the prison's outside; it was far too dark by the time the rattling van pulled into the courtyard. "Never mind," Lili whispered. "We shall have a good look at it over our shoulders, the day we're released."

But it was hard to think of release when being shoved along a corridor that smelled of piss and sweat and despair. Eve found herself shivering, pressing her teeth together so they would not rattle. The creak of a key being turned, hinges squealing, and then a massive door yawned. "Gardiner," the guard barked, and that same brusque hand shoved Eve forward.

"Wait—" She turned, frantic for a glimpse of Lili and Violette, but the door had already slammed. The blackness was absolute, a pool of stifling, freezing darkness.

Everyone breaks down the first night. Eve would hear that later from her fellow prisoners. But Eve came to Siegburg already broken. The blackness was not nearly as terrible as the inside of her own mind, so she merely unlocked her chattering teeth and felt her way around the cell with misshapen fingers. Stone walls, smaller in dimension than her cell at Saint-Gilles. A foul bed, hard as wood and stinking of old sweat, old vomit, old terror. Eve wondered how many women had slept and cried and stifled their screams in that bed. Dimly through the door she heard cries, once a burst of shrill laughter, but no guard answered the calls. Once the cells were locked for the night at Siegburg, Eve learned soon enough, they weren't opened until morning. A woman might be dying slowly of fever or blood poisoning, shrieking with pain over a broken bone, writhing in the agony of giving birth—the door still wouldn't open until dawn. A good many died that way. That was, Eve supposed dully, the entire point.

She couldn't lie down on that foul bed. She curled in the corner on the stones, shaking with cold, waiting for morning. Dawn arrived in the company of a hard-faced guard marching in with a stack of clothes—rough blue stockings, dirty white frock with a great prisoners' cross on the chest—and the endless string of captive days began.

H|unger. Cold. Lice. Slaps from the guards. The daily labor: rough sewing with pricked fingers, polishing latches with abrasive cleansers, pushing together little caps of metal. Whispered conversations with the other women: Was it true there had been a battle at Mont Sorrel? The Somme? Was it true the British had captured La Boisselle? Contalmaison? Even more than food, the prisoners craved news. All they heard from the guards was that the Germans were winning.

"Liars," Lili snorted. "Such liars! They're losing and they know it. All we need do is endure."

Endure, Eve thought. A year slipped by—more foul gray days, more slaps, more lice, more screams in the night. Lili's serene confidence, burning brighter even as her body whittled down to stark bone. Black dreamless nights on that foul-smelling cot. Seeing women sweat to death from yellowing fevers, waste away under the twin grinding stones of cold and hunger. Seeing them stagger to the infirmary, that huge room with its ugly green shades that stank of shit and blood—some called it the Lazaretto, some just called it *hell*. You didn't go to the infirmary to be treated; you went there to die. The Germans didn't need to waste bullets killing their female prisoners when neglect and disease could do it for them. A sound strategy, Eve thought remotely. Women dying in hospital beds resulted in far less international outcry than women dying before firing squads.

And what women these were. Identical skeletons wearing the same prisoners' cross, dirty-haired, hollow-eyed *fleurs du mal* every one: fiery Louise Thuliez who had smuggled soldiers across borders for Edith Cavell;

Belgian-born Madame Ramet whose son had been shot and whose two daughters had accompanied her to prison; the stoic Princesse de Croy who had organized a spy network in Belgium . . . Before Siegburg, Eve had never known just how many women there were who had risked all for the war. Even now, in their way, they continued to fight.

"Madame Blankaert says those little steel caps we have been given to assemble are grenade heads," Lili whispered. "Shall we do something about it?"

"Lili," Violette said wearily, "don't provoke them."

"*Ta gueule.* It's inconceivable that we be put to work on ammunition to be used against our countrymen." And the following day the words were shouted out: *In the name of England, of France, of Belgium, and of all Allied countries, I implore my companions to adamantly refuse to work on munitions. Germany does not have the right to demand from us this work of death against our homelands, to force us to ourselves make the engines which, in battle, will strike our fathers, our brothers, our husbands, our sons. We all here continue to fight and suffer courageously for king, for our flags, for our homelands—*

And all over Siegburg, the gray-faced female skeletons were suddenly alight, screaming like Valkyries, even as guards ran back and forth shoving, slapping, shouting. Eve screamed until her throat stung, even when she got a clenched fist across the cheekbone that snapped her head back like a whip. The world for a moment was bright, screaming color rather than soul-leaching gray. Eve screamed until she was bundled back into her cell, and Lili laughed even as the guards hauled her and Mme. Blankaert away to solitary confinement for inciting the strike. "Well worth it," she said when they finally let her out a month later.

Eve wasn't sure—Lili was just a handful of bones, insubstantial as a shadow. Eve dropped her own blanket around the other woman's shoulders. *Endure. All we need do is endure.*

Another endless gray year. A freezing spring coming late in 1918, and with it a cautious hope feathering its way through the prisoners. "The Boches are losing," the whisper went around as the year advanced. "They're beaten, falling back everywhere along the front—" It wasn't just the whispered rumors that made their way inside prison walls, rumors of English victories and French encroachments on German territory. Everyone could see the slump in the shoulders of the guards, hear the increasing shrillness in the assertions of German victory. It hovered in the air: the bloody slog of war might finally be coming to an end.

If it had ended sooner, Eve later thought on the long nights when she was staring down the barrel of a Luger. If it had ended just a few short months sooner.

September 1918

"Thank you for coming, little daisy."

Lili lay in the cold infirmary, her body hardly making an impression below the grubby blankets. Eve perched on the cot's edge, shivering in her prison smock. She should have been with the other women working, but there had been a typhus epidemic not long ago and when Eve reported feeling feverish and headachy, they were quick to send her to the infirmary. Easy then to sneak from her own cot to Lili's. "How are you feeling?" she managed to ask.

"Not so terrible." Lili patted her side: for a while now she'd suffered from a pleural abscess between two

of her ribs, but had made light of it. "The surgeon will
lance the thing, and it will be done." The surgery was
scheduled for four in the afternoon. Not long now.

"They're bringing a surgeon from Bonn?" Eve tried
to quell her apprehension. Lancing an abscess was
surely minor surgery. But in this understaffed hellhole,
on a half-starved woman . . .

Lili is not afraid, Eve reminded herself. *Don't you
be either.*

But perhaps Lili *was* afraid, because she fixed Eve
with an unusually sober gaze. Her lively eyes were sunk
into a face that was little more than a skull. "Take care
of Violette for me, if . . ." An expressive shrug.

"You're going to be fine." Eve cut her off before she
could go further. "You have to be."

It was what she'd clung to for more than two years.
Evelyn Gardiner had betrayed her friends, had broken
down and brought them to this foul place. If she could
bring them out again safely, some part of that betrayal
could be forgotten, if not ever forgiven. It was what she
thought every day when she pushed half her bread ra-
tion into Lili's hands, when she tried to give her blankets to Violette even though Violette still looked at her
with stony eyes. *Bring them out safely, and you will
have atoned.*

And she'd almost done it—surely the war could not
go on much longer. *We are almost there. Almost home.*

Perhaps Lili saw some of that desperation in Eve's
eyes, because she reached out and laid her emaci-
ated fingers over Eve's misshapen ones. "Take care of
yourself, little daisy. If I'm not here to haul you out of
trouble—"

"Don't say that." Eve gripped Lili's hand, panic
choking her. She was not going to lose Lili, not over
an *abscess*. Not now. Not after more than two years of

imprisonment, not so close to the end. "It's just a lance-and-drain operation. Of course you'll survive!"

Lili's voice was steady. "But the Germans have no interest in my survival, *ma petite*."

Eve's eyes welled, because she couldn't deny it: the officials of Siegburg hated every bone in Lili's trouble-making body, and made no secret of it. "You shouldn't have led that strike, or—"

Or what? Caused strife from the day she walked through Siegburg's doors? Planned elaborate escapes, kept spirits high with jokes and stories? If Lili had been the sort to keep her head low, she would not have led the most efficient spy network in France.

"You are going to be *fine*," Eve repeated stubbornly, and would have said more, but two orderlies appeared.

"Up, Bettignies. The surgeon has arrived."

Lili could barely stand. Eve slid an arm around her shoulder, lifting her to her feet. She wore a shape-less dishrag-colored smock, and she made a face at it. "*Quelle horreur.* What I'd give for something in pink moiré!"

"And a morally questionable hat?" Eve managed to say.

"I'd settle for some morally questionable soap. My hair is *filthy*."

Eve's throat caught. "Lili—"

"Pray for me when I go in there?" Gesturing with her sharp little chin in the direction of the surgery. "I need people praying for me. I wrote a letter to my old Mother Prioress in Anderlecht, but I'll take your prayers any day, Evelyn Gardiner."

It was the first time Lili used Eve's real name. Even after the trial, they went on using the old code names. The ones that felt true. "I cannot pray for you," Eve whispered. "I do not believe in God anymore."

"But I do." Lili kissed the rosary knotted through her fingers, even as the orderlies took her by the elbows.

So Eve jerked out a nod. "Then I'll pray," she said. "And I'll see you in a few hours. I *will*."

They hauled Lili out of the infirmary, Eve following behind. A nurse came out of the surgery at the end of the corridor, and for a moment Eve had a glimpse of the surgeon from Bonn smoking a cigarette. There was no bustle, Eve saw—no one was sterilizing instruments, no one was making preparations with ether or chloroform . . .

Lili, she thought in a wash of dread. *Lili, don't go in there—*

Ahead she heard Lili's clear voice reciting her rosary. "Pray for us sinners, now and at the hour of our deaths . . ."

The corridor outside was thronged with women. Louise Thuliez, the Princesse de Croy, Violette—as many of the *fleurs du mal* who could steal away from their work shifts, all anxious glances and murmured prayers for the queen of spies. The two orderlies picked up their feet, hastening Lili along, and her voice faltered in its calm recitation. For a moment Eve thought Lili would finally break—that she would collapse and weep, have to be carried off prostrate to her operating table.

No. She straightened between the orderlies, lifting her chin in the old impish gesture, eyes darting along the line of her friends. The dull light struck her hair, coiled around her head in matted blond braids, and it had the look of a crown. "*Mes amies,*" she said softly, and as she passed Violette, she reached out and pressed her rosary into those trembling hands. "*Je vous aime—*"

And she was gone past them, tiny as a child between the two orderlies, almost floating as she went light-footed, lighthearted, down the long corridor toward the operating room. Eve felt her own heart beating sickly, somber as a drum. *Lili . . .*

Just before she disappeared, Lili turned her head back one final time and gave her swift mischievous glance. She blew a kiss to the *fleurs du mal,* and it hit Eve like a physical blow. Then Lili disappeared into the operating room, but her voice still floated out, merry and serene.

"You must be the surgeon. I wonder if I can have some chloroform? Because it's been an absolute *pisser* of a day."

That was when Eve's knees buckled. That was when she knew.

"She'll be fine," Louise Thuliez was saying. "It would take more than a lung abscess to bring down our Lili—"

"Nothing at all . . ."

More murmurs of agreement, assurances spoken over eyes full of worry. Violette clutched the rosary so hard its looped beads cut into her fingers. "She'll be out of bed within a week. Less than a week . . ."

But Violette wasn't there in the infirmary for the next four hours, as Eve was. The guards shooed the prisoners away, but Eve was still under observation for typhus symptoms. She was just a corridor and a locked door away when the moans came, and the whimpers, and the strangled screams. The sounds of a woman being operated upon without ether, without chloroform, without morphine. Eve sat huddled on her cot as all her stubborn hope drained away, sobbing so hard she almost drowned out the noise of Lili's agony—but not quite. Eve heard it all, start to finish. By morning she had sobbed herself mute; her voice was gone.

And so was Lili.

———

Excerpt from *La Guerre des Femmes*, memoir of Louise de Bettignies's war work by Antoine Redier, as told to him by his wife Léonie van Houtte, code name Violette Lameron:

She finished as she had lived, a soldier.

CHAPTER 35
CHARLIE

June 1947

My heart hurt.

I'd so hoped that the queen of spies was still alive, that we might meet her on this journey as we'd met Violette. A white-haired woman now, but still small and gallant and merry. Someone I'd ached to know—but she'd never had the chance to grow old.

Eve, I wanted to say to the figure hunched in the backseat, *I'm so sorry*—but words were just air, useless after a tale like that. Finn had pulled the Lagonda over to the side of the road twenty minutes before as we listened, and now we sat in the summer silence, utterly still.

I reached out for Eve's knobbed hands as she lowered them from her face, but she was speaking again, looking pale and ravaged in the merciless sunlight. "There it is. You know it all. Lili died the ugliest death a b-brave woman ever suffered. And it was all thanks to me. I sent her inside those walls, and I failed to bring her out again."

Denial boiled in me furiously. *No. No, you were not to blame. You cannot think that.* But she did think that, and all the words in the world from me would not shift her self-loathing. I knew that much about Evelyn Gardiner. As much as I was always yearning to fix what was broken, I could do nothing to fix Eve.

Or could I?

She passed a gnarled hand across her mouth; both were trembling. "Get this car moving, Scotsman," she said hoarsely. "We aren't getting to Grenoble by sitting on a roadside."

Finn steered the Lagonda back onto the road, and we finished the long drive in silence, worn out from the stark, ugly end of Eve's confession. Eve sat in back with her eyes closed. Finn drove like a chauffeur, looking front and center, only speaking up to ask for a map. As for me, I sat turning over an idea.

A lovely city, Grenoble: compact houses and pretty little churches, the lazy blue meandering of the rivers Drac and Isère, framed all around by the distant cloud-wrapped Alps. Another *auberge*, and Finn helped Eve up the stairs with the baggage, casting a glance back at me.

"I have to make a telephone call," I said, and he probably thought I meant to my family. But the call I put through at the hotel desk, after a long wrangle with the French operator, wasn't to the United States. It was to a china shop in Roubaix, whose name I fortunately remembered.

"*Allo?*" I'd only met her once, but I knew her voice immediately. I imagined her turning her head, spectacles reflecting the light.

"Violette Lameron," I greeted her.

A long pause. "Who are you?"

"Charlotte St. Clair, *madame*. You saw me not long ago; I came into the shop with Eve Gardiner—Marguerite Le François, as you knew her. Please don't hang up." Because she was on the verge; I could tell from the controlled rasp of breathing on the other end of the line.

"What do you want?" Her voice came noticeably colder. "I wouldn't help that Judas bitch out of a burning house, so if it's a favor for her—"

I fought down a swell of anger, the urge to snap that *nothing* was Eve's fault. The urge to ask how well *she* would have held out against a glass of opium and ten broken fingers. But Violette was as invested in Eve's guilt as Eve was herself, and nothing I could say would shift either of them. Only facts would do that, and for the facts, I needed Violette.

"Someone needs to look into the trial records where you and Eve and Lili were sentenced." I lowered my voice, turning my back on the curious hotel clerk. "I believe there's a lie hiding in there."

I'd thought it from the first, hearing about the exchange of information that condemned Lili. Something there did not add up correctly. *Solve for X.*

Violette sounded rather contemptuous. "You're just a little American. What could you possibly know about records for a European trial thirty years past?"

I could surmise a lot more than she thought. All those summers working in my father's office specializing in international law: I'd indexed and notated French and German legal books, I'd filed trial paperwork, I'd heard my father expound over dinner as he compared European and American law . . . "The trial of three female spies in the heart of wartime would have been very well documented," I told Violette. "You three were heroines, famous. German officers, French newspapers, Belgian clerks, English diplomats, all paying attention that day—*everything* about your trial would have been filed away, if only so it could be produced as proof of no wrongdoing later. If there's a lie in there, it can be found—it's just a matter of getting a look at the records. Will you help?"

"What lie?" Violette asked, curiosity sharpening her voice despite herself.

Got you, I thought. And told her.

An even longer silence fell. "Why ask me? You don't know me, *mademoiselle.*"

"I know what you're capable of, because Eve's told me all about you. You won't stop until you get the truth. I don't know if the trial records are public or sealed after all this time, but if they're sealed, I imagine you could get access much more easily than me. Because *you* were on trial that day, and you can argue your right to know the full story. And you don't have the full story, you or Eve, because you didn't hear all the deliberations." I laid out a little honey, thinking it couldn't hurt. "You're a war heroine, Violette. Surely there are powerful people who still respect you, who owe you favors, who will pull strings for you. You'll find a way to get the information if it's there."

"And if it is?"

"Just tell me. Tell me if I'm right. Please."

She was silent so long I feared the connection had dropped. I stood there dry-mouthed at the desk. *Please,* I begged silently.

Violette sounded bemused when she spoke. But she sounded *honed* as well, as if the spy inside the respectable shopkeeper had opened her eyes for the first time in years. I didn't think that part ever died, not in women like Eve and Violette. "Where would I contact you, Mademoiselle St. Clair, if I found anything?"

I promised to telephone her from Grasse tomorrow with the name of our hotel, and hung up feeling shaky. I'd cast a fishing line into the water; now all I could do was wait and see if anything came up on the other end. I wondered, going upstairs, if I should tell Eve what I'd done, but answered myself with a resounding *No.* She'd looked so fragile in the car, frail enough to crumble at the slightest blow. I wasn't raising her hope about anything until I had something in hand to warrant it.

Entering the silence of my pretty little room, I flung open the shutters and looked out into the fast-falling twilight. Couples promenaded below, arm in arm, and I remembered Rose and me laughing about someday being old enough to go on double dates. I saw a tall blonde hand in hand with a laughing boy, but my memory didn't stubbornly try to give her Rose's face. She was just a girl, no one I knew. My hallucinatory flashes of seeing Rose everywhere I looked seemed to have stopped since Oradour-sur-Glane. *Come back,* I thought, looking at the throng. *Come back, Rosie*—but of course, she wasn't coming back. Like my brother, she was dead.

A knock sounded. I thought it might be Eve, come to tell me what she had planned once we arrived in Grasse, but it was Finn. He looked different, and it took me a moment to put my finger on it. He'd shaved, put on a jacket (worn at the elbows but a handsome dark blue), and his shoes had been shined to a gleam.

"Come to dinner with me," he said without preamble.

"I didn't think Eve would come down to eat tonight. She looked like she wanted a whiskey supper." Whatever got her to oblivion fastest. Knowing now how Lili had died and how it haunted her, I could understand that better.

"Gardiner's done for the night." Finn patted his pocket, jingling with Eve's nightly haul of bullets. "It'll just be us. Come to dinner with me, Charlie."

Something in his tone made me straighten. From the way he'd dressed up, I didn't think he meant one of our usual quick refueling stops at the nearest café. "Is this—is this a date?" I asked, keeping my hand from going to my mussed hair.

"Yes." His eyes were steady. "It's what a man does when he likes a lass. Puts on a jacket. Puts a shine on his shoes. Asks her to dinner."

"I don't know any men who do that. Not after we already . . ." I got a flash of what we'd done in the car last night, the windows fogged up and our breath coming ragged.

"Your trouble is, your experience is all with boys. Not men."

I raised my eyebrows. "Is that the gray-bearded voice of wisdom, coming from a man not quite thirty?"

"What I mean is, it's not a matter of age. There are boys aged fifty, and men aged fifteen. It's all in what they *do,* not how old they are." He paused. "A boy messes up with a lass, and he slinks off without fixing anything. A man makes a mistake, he fixes it. He apologizes."

"You're sorry for what happened, then." I remembered him last night, his hands spanning my naked back as he said not too distinctly, *This wasn't how I wanted to do this.* My heart squeezed. I wasn't sorry at all.

"I don't regret it one bit." His voice was even. "I'm just sorry it wasn't—slower. Done after dinner and a date, not a fistfight and a bruised lip. That's not how you start things with a lass you like, and I like you, Charlie. You're smarter than any woman I know, a wee little adding machine in a black dress, and I like that. You've got a sharp tongue, and I like that too. You try to save everyone you meet, from your cousin and your brother to hopeless cock-ups like Gardiner and me, and I like that most of all. So I'm here to apologize. I'm here to take you to dinner. I'm here in a jacket." Pause. "I hate jackets."

I fought the smile spreading over my face, but I failed. He gave a smile back that was all in the crinkles around his eyes, and it made me positively weak in the knees. I cleared my throat, tugging at my striped jersey, and said, "Give me ten minutes to change."

"Done." He pulled the door closed. An instant later his voice floated through.

"Can you wear that black dress again?"

didn't say it would be much of a dinner," he said. We leaned on the stone balustrade of an old bridge over the river Isère, a packet of sandwiches between us. Finn had bought them from a café near the Place Saint-André, and we were eating them right out of the paper wrappings. "I'm a bit skint."

"We wouldn't get a better view in a fancy restaurant." A dark night full of stars, the flow of water scattered with broken moonlight, and the murmur and rush of the city around us.

"Your favorite food," Finn said suddenly. "What is it?"

I laughed. "Why?"

"It's something I don't know about you. There's a lot I don't know about you, Miss St. Clair." He reached out and touched a crumb on my lip, dabbing it away. "That's what a first date is for. So: favorite food?"

"Used to be a hamburger. Onion, lettuce, dab of mustard, no cheese. But since the Rosebud here"—patting my stomach—"it's bacon. Crispy, burned just a little. The way I'm eating, there won't be a pig left in France by the time this baby's born. What's *your* favorite food, Mr. Kilgore?"

"Fish and chips from a proper chippy, lots of malt vinegar. Favorite color?"

I eyed his jacket, which made his hair look darker and his shoulders broader. "Blue."

"Same here. Last book you read?"

We traded back and forth, both of us a little silly and enjoying it. Finn asked me about college and I told him about Bennington and algebra classes. I asked him how he'd gotten so good with cars and he told me about working in his uncle's garage at age eleven. The little things, the getting-to-know-you things. Normally those conversations happened early on, before anyone got half naked in the backseat of a convertible, but we'd done it all backward.

"First thing you'd buy if you had ten thousand pounds sterling?"

"My grandmother's pearls back. I love those pearls. You?"

"A '46 Bentley Mark VI," Finn said promptly. "First car made by Bentley and Rolls; it's a beauty. Though if it's ten thousand sterling I've got, maybe I could go all the way to the Ferrari 125 S. It just debuted, took six of thirteen races on the Piacenza circuit . . ."

He started telling me about the V12 engine, and it was utterly adorable. I couldn't have told you *why* it was adorable—when Trevor Preston-Greene bought me a milk shake after English Lit and droned for an hour about his Chevrolet Stylemaster coupe, I wanted to up-end my chocolate malt over his hair. But now I stood utterly charmed as Finn told me all about the De Dion type rear suspension. "Listen to me blethering on," he broke off finally, seeing me smile.

"Yes," I said. "Bored to tears, here. Tell me more about the five-speed gearbox."

"Makes car go zoom," he said straight-faced. "Your turn to blether about something boring."

"The Pythagorean equation," I said, picking something easy. "A-squared plus B-squared equals C-squared. That means that for all right-angled triangles, the square on the hypotenuse is equal to the sum of the squares on the other two sides . . ." Finn mimed clutching his hair. "Really, now. Simple Euclidean geometry is no reason for despair!"

We both laughed, tossing our sandwich crusts down for the geese honking noisily below. Afterward we just leaned against the stones, gazing out at the water in comfortable silence. I wasn't used to silence on dates. Girls weren't supposed to let silence fall; you had to keep the conversation going so he wouldn't think you were a sad sack. *Be interesting! Be sparkling! Or he won't ask you out again!* But the silence now was as comfortable as the chatter.

He was the one to break it, voice thoughtful. "You think Gardiner's right about Bordelon being in Grasse somewhere, retired and waiting to be found? Or is she half cracked?"

I hesitated, not wanting to disrupt this gentle peace with reality. "It seems like an awful long shot, but she's been right more often than she's been wrong." A question of my own burst out. "What happens if we *do* find him? What is Eve going to do?"

"If she can prove he's René du Malassis from Limoges who collaborated with the Nazis, informed for the Milice, and shot an employee in the back merely for petty theft, she can turn him in." Finn dusted the last sandwich crumbs off his hands. "De Gaulle isn't kind to profiteering killers, even elderly ones. Bordelon would face prison, especially if it can be proved his collaboration resulted in the—in what happened at Oradour-sur-Glane. He'd lose his reputation, his freedom . . ."

"Is that going to be enough for Eve?"

Finn looked at me. I looked at him.

"No," we said at the same time, and his hand covered mine on the stone parapet of the bridge.

"We need to stop her from doing anything irrevocable, Finn." Real life wasn't a movie—in the real world there were consequences for revenge. Consequences like prison, and Eve might have endured Siegburg as a girl, but I didn't think she'd survive now if she went to prison for assault or whatever they called it in France. "I'm not letting her burn up the rest of her life just to take that old bastard out."

"But it's her life, isn't it?" Finn's fingers slid inside mine, so our hands slowly interlaced. "I've been with Gardiner awhile now. I can understand her wanting to risk it all to make something right."

"Killing an old man is making things *right*? I can't be a party to that, even if he is a back-shooting murderer." I shivered, partly from the terrible thought and partly because Finn's thumb was passing back and forth along the back of my hand, leaving tingles. "We'll have to make sure she doesn't go off the rails." Wasn't *that* going to be a job.

"A job for tomorrow." Finn tugged me away from the balustrade. "Promise me something, Charlie?"

"What?"

"Don't look at that photograph tomorrow. Just enjoy the drive."

We meandered back to the hotel hand in hand, largely silent. Finn opened the door to guide me through, fingertips resting on my bare back above the black dress's low *V* slash, and my skin rippled. He walked me down the corridor to my room, formally, as if I had a father who cared about my curfew glaring at the clock.

"I had a lovely time," he said, very solemn. "I'll ring you tomorrow."

"Boys never call."

"Men call."

We lingered inside our fragile bubble of happiness, the kind of happiness that sits on top of melancholy as easily as icing on a cake. I didn't want to leave it. "I'm no good at this, Finn," I said at last. A Yank in a black dress plus a Scotsman in a jacket, multiplied by a summer night and a packet of sandwiches, divided by an awkward silence and the fact that the Yank had a pregnant belly—I didn't know how that equation came out, what it equaled. "What happens now?"

He sounded hoarse. "What happens now is entirely up to you."

"Oh." I stood a moment, looking at him, and then I went up on tiptoe. Our lips met, soft as drifting feathers, and I melted into him as his arms circled my waist. We kissed, slow and endless, Finn pressing me soft and yielding between the hard door and his hard chest, and I fumbled blindly behind me for the handle. The door burst open and we spilled through it, kissing and stumbling, my shoes landing on top of his discarded jacket. Finn got a hand loose from my hair and batted the door shut. He picked me up then, holding me in the air for another kiss, and then he made me shriek as he dropped me on the bed from what seemed like a very long height. He stood for a moment looking down at me, and I couldn't believe I was this nervous. We'd already done this, but not in a *bed*, not with lights on . . .

He dropped down with a groan, stretching himself, long and luxuriant, over me. "Beds," he said, dropping slow kisses along my neck, the Scots burr coming thicker, "are a verra big improvement on backseats."

"I fit just fine in both—" as I tugged at his shirt.

"Because you're a midget." He submitted to my tugging, letting me pull his shirt over his head, then flipped me back down, grinning. "Quit rushing! It's not supposed to be a sprint—"

"Thought you liked fast," I managed to say. In the light he was lean and brown and beautiful. "You and your five-speed gearboxes . . ."

"Cars should be fast. Beds should be slow."

I tangled my hands in his hair, feeling my back arch as he dragged the zipper of my dress down inch by inch. "How slow?"

"Verra . . . verra . . . slow . . . ," he murmured against my lips. "Takes all night, where we're going."

"All night?" I hooked my legs around him, looked at the dark eyes so close to mine our lashes brushed. *I am falling for you,* I thought bemusedly, *I am falling so hard.* "You've got to drive all the way to Grasse tomorrow," I whispered instead. "What about sleep?"

"Sleep?" His hands twined through my hair so tight it hurt as he growled into my ear. "Quit your blethering."

CHAPTER 36
EVE

March 1919

I t was Eve's first step back in England since her career as a spy began. Folkestone, where Cameron had stood waving good-bye as Eve sailed to Le Havre. Where he stood now, coat rippling about his knees, waiting for her on the pier.

"Miss Gardiner," he said when she stepped off the ferry. It had been some months since her release—she'd lived that time in a bathtub, scrubbing obsessively as arrangements were made to bring her back from her temporary lodgings in Louvain to England.

"Captain Cameron," she answered. "No, it's Major Cameron now, isn't it?" Eyeing his new insignia. In addition to his majority was the blue and red ribbon of the DSO on the left breast of his uniform coat. "I've missed a few th-th—a few things, being away."

"I was hoping to bring you back to England sooner."

Eve shrugged. The women of Siegburg had been released before the Armistice was even signed, let loose
from their cells by defeated-looking prison officials,
stampeding in a weeping, joyous flood for the trains
that would take them home. Eve would have been weeping with joy too, had Lili been arm in arm with her to
take that train. After Lili died, it had not mattered in the
slightest how fast she could get away from Siegburg.

Cameron's eyes were going over her now, registering
the changes. Eve knew she was still thin as a rack, her
hair straw dry from lice treatments and hacked close
to her skull. She kept her hands thrust into her pockets
so he couldn't see the misshapen knuckles, but there was
nothing she could do to hide her eyes, which never sat
still anymore. Eve took in the world in constant darting
glances now, looking for danger on all sides. Even here
on the open pier, she angled her back against the nearest
piling, seeking protection. Eve registered the shock in
Cameron's own steady eyes as he saw how deeply the
past few years had marked her.

They hadn't been kind to him either; deep lines
graven about his mouth, broken veins at his forehead,
streaks of gray at his temples. *I used to love you*, Eve
thought, but it was a blank thought, almost meaningless. She used to feel a lot of things before Lili died.
Now what she mainly felt was grief and rage and guilt,
devouring each other like tail-eating serpents. And the
never-ending whisper of her blood, saying, *Betrayer*.

"I thought there would be some three-ring c-c-circus,"
Eve said at last, nodding at the empty pier. She had been
almost the only person to disembark—Folkestone, now
that the war was over, had reverted to a much sleepier
place—and there were no aides or military attachés
anywhere in sight. "Major Allenton was in touch, k-kept
going on about a welcome ceremony."

Apparently, Evelyn Gardiner was now a heroine. So were many of the other female prisoners—Violette, Eve heard, was feted all over Roubaix when she returned home. Eve would be feted too, if she'd allow it. Which she wouldn't.

"I talked Allenton out of the public welcome," Cameron said. "He wanted a few generals to greet you, some newspapermen and so on. A brass band."

"Fortunate you discouraged him. Though I'd have enjoyed hammering a bloody tuba over his ears." Eve hitched her satchel over her shoulder, and set off down the pier.

"I thought I'd see you in France." Cameron fell in beside her. "At Louise de Bettignies's funeral."

"I meant to go." Eve had got as far as Cologne, where Lili's original grave was to be opened so her body could be repatriated back to her homeland, but never made it out of the hotel room. She'd ended up getting drunk instead, and nearly shooting the maid who came with her supper—the girl was squat, square faced, and for a horrific moment Eve had thought she was the Frog, that horrible woman in Lille who had strip-searched Eve and Lili. The memory dizzied Eve now, momentarily, and she gulped a deep breath of sea air.

Cameron's voice was low. "Why didn't you come?"

"C-C-Couldn't face it." She'd said her good-bye to Lili in a corridor that stank of typhus and blood. She didn't need a graveside with droning plaudits and French generals. But she didn't say that to Cameron, just quickened her steps, suddenly needing to be away from him.

Cameron's long legs kept up. "Do you have anyone to meet you? A place to stay?"

"I'll find something."

His hand caught her elbow. "*Eve.* Stop. Let me help you, for God's sake."

She wrenched free. He didn't mean any harm, but she couldn't bear to be touched. There were a lot of things she was finding she couldn't bear, now that she was out of prison. Open windows. Crowds. Wide spaces without corners to set her back against. Sleep . . .

"Keep it *Miss Gardiner*, Cameron. Far better that way." She looked out at the ocean rather than meet his gaze. His soft eyes might swallow her whole, and Eve couldn't be soft. Not now. "Tell me," she said instead. "We d-d-didn't get much news about the war, inside p-prison, and now no one wants to go over old battles. Lili's last message, the one about the Verdun assault." Over and over, Eve had wondered how that assault went. What they changed by getting that message through. "How did things go down?"

"The French commander received your information." Cameron looked as if he wanted to stop there, but Eve's gaze pierced him, and he continued reluctantly. "The report about the coming assault was given, but it wasn't believed. Losses were—well. Very bad."

Eve squeezed her eyes shut, feeling something rise in her throat. It was either a laugh or a scream. "So it was all worth nothing." Lili giving up her freedom so that report could get through. Eve leaving Cameron's sleeping arms and walking back into mortal danger because such reports were worth risking her life for. All of it rendered useless. Nothing Eve or Lili or Violette had done had avoided the bloodbath. "Nothing I did in France ever amounted to anything."

His voice was fierce. "*No.* Do not think that." He would have seized her shoulders but he sensed her recoil. "The Alice Network saved *hundreds,* Eve. Perhaps thousands. You were the best network in the war. None of the others in France or Belgium ever equaled it."

Eve smiled, mirthless. Who cared about praise when

the failures were so much bigger than the victories? That miracle chance in '15 to kill the kaiser—failed. Stopping the assault on Verdun—failed. Keeping the network together after Lili's arrest—failed.

Cameron had gone on. "I don't know if you've read Major Allenton's communications. He says you never responded. But you've been awarded these. He meant to award them to you at Louise's funeral. She received the same, posthumously."

Eve refused to take the case, so after an awkward pause, Cameron opened it for her. Four medals glittered in Eve's blurring vision.

"The Médaille de Guerre. The Croix de Guerre with palm. The Croix de la Légion d'Honneur. And the Order of the British Empire. Awarded in honor of your war efforts."

Tin toys. Eve took a hand from her pocket at last and knocked them to the ground, trembling. "I don't want any medals."

"Then Major Allenton will hold them for you—"

"Cram them up his arse!"

Cameron gathered up Eve's medals and dropped them back into the case. "I didn't want mine either, believe me."

"But you had to take them, because you're still in the army." Eve gave a one-note bark of a laugh. "The army doesn't want *me* anymore. I did my part and the war's over, so now they'll pin some b-bits of tin on me and tell me to bugger off back to the file room. Well, they can keep their damned tin scraps."

Cameron flinched this time at her language. His eyes dropped, and Eve realized she hadn't put her hand back in her pocket. His eyes went from her fingers to her face and back, as though he were seeing the demure quiet-voiced girl he'd sent away to France with her carpetbag and her soft hands and her innocence. War and torture and prison and René Bordelon had happened, and now she was nothing like that girl. She was a damaged wreck of a woman with a foul mouth and destroyed hands and no innocence at all. *Not your fault*, Eve wanted to say to the guilty sorrow in his eyes, but he wouldn't believe her. She sighed, flexing her ruined fingers.

"You had to kn-kn-kn—to know about these," she said. "There was a report."

"Knowing's not the same as seeing." He reached out for the crippled hand, but stopped himself. She was glad. She didn't want to keep shoving him away; he hadn't earned that. He gave a sigh of his own instead. "Let's get a drink."

It was a horrible pub on the docks, the kind of place where gravel-voiced women slopped gin into grimy glasses for men who were already drunk at ten in the morning, but it was just what Eve needed: anonymous, cheap, windowless so she didn't worry about people sneaking up behind her. Two shots of gin followed by a pint of bitter steadied her jumping pulse. She used to be proud of that slow pulse that got her through danger, but it had been a long time since she'd held up that coolly under pressure. Maybe the last time was in René Bordelon's green-walled study.

René. She took another draught of beer, tasting hatred along with it. In Siegburg her hate had tasted bitter; now it was a sweet thing. Because now, she could do something about it. The satchel at her feet held a Luger. Not her old Luger with the scratch on the barrel, the one René had taken from her—but it would do.

Cameron, for all his gentlemanly air, knocked the gin back as fast as Eve, giving a murmured toast of "*Gabrielle*." When Eve raised her eyebrows, he explained, "Another of my recruits. Shot in April of '16. I rotate them, the ones I lost." He raised his beer and said "*Léon*" before downing a swallow.

"Was I in your rotation?"

"No, only those confirmed dead." Cameron's eyes had that terrible drowning softness again. "Every week following your trial, I expected to get the news you'd died in Siegburg."

"After Lili, I almost did."

They looked at each other a long time, and then they ordered another round of gin. "*Lili.*"

They were both silent, until Cameron abruptly started saying something about a pension for Eve. "You'll find it more useful than the medals. I knew you didn't have any family, so I pushed a pension for you through the War Office. It's not much, but it'll keep you afloat. Maybe help you buy a house somewhere in London."

"Thank you." Eve didn't want the medals, but she'd take the pension. It wasn't like she'd be going back to typewriting with hands like hers; she needed something to live on.

Cameron studied her. "Your stammer's better."

"Go to prison, and you find there are worse things than a halting tongue." She took another draught of beer. "And *this* helps."

He set down his glass. "Eve, if I can—"

"So, what are you going to do now?" She cut him off fast, before he could say anything he'd regret.

"I was sent to Russia for a while, during their bit of upheaval. Siberia. The things I saw . . ." He sat blank-faced for a moment, and Eve wondered what he was seeing through the curtain of remembered Russian snows. She didn't ask. "It's Ireland next for me," he resumed. "To run a training school."

"School for what?"

"People like you."

"Who n-needs people like me anymore? The war's over."

He laughed bitterly. "There's always another war, Eve."

Eve didn't even want to think about the next war, or a generation of new, fresh-faced spies who would be fed into its gaping mouth. At least they'd have a good teacher. "When do you leave?"

"Soon."

"Is your wife going?"

"Yes. And our child."

"I'm glad you had—that is, I know your wife wanted a ch-child." How wearying these courtesies were; Eve felt like she was struggling under a boulder. "What did you decide to name—"

He spoke softly. "Evelyn."

Eve stared down at the sticky tabletop. "Why not Lili?" she heard herself ask. "Why not Gabrielle, or any of your others? Why was it *me*, Cameron?"

"If you could see yourself, you wouldn't ask."

"I can see myself. I'm a w-wreck."

"Nothing could wreck you, Eve. You've got a core of steel."

Eve took a shaky breath. "I'm sorry I d-deceived you. Ran out when you were sleeping and went back to Lille when you didn't want me to return." Her voice was thick. "I'm so sorry."

"I know."

Eve looked down at the table where his hand lay next to her maimed one. His shifted a little so that his thumb grazed the tip of her nearest finger.

"I wish—" Eve began, and stopped. Wished what? That he wasn't married? Eve was too much of a mess to step into the place at his side even if that place *was* empty. That they could find a bed and curl up together anyway? Eve couldn't bear to share a room with anyone; the nightmares were too bad. That they could go back a few years, to before? Before what, Siegburg? Lili? The war? "I wish you were happy," she said at last.

Cameron didn't lift her hand to his lips in the old gesture. He lowered his head to the tabletop instead, and pressed his worn mouth to her abused knuckles. "I'm a broken-down army officer with a lot of dead recruits on my hands, Eve. I don't have it in me to be happy."

"You could resign from the army."

"I can't, really. Because as many dead as I've got behind me, there are more in front, waiting in Ireland to be trained . . . And I know I'll do better by them than asses like Allenton."

He was more than halfway drunk, Eve realized. He'd never insulted a superior aloud before.

"I'm still useful," Cameron said, pronouncing his words carefully. "I can go to Ireland and train up the next generation of cannon fodder, so that's what I'll do. I'll go on working until I can't anymore. Then I suppose I'll die."

"Or retire."

"Retirement kills people like us, Eve. It's how we die if the bullets don't get there first." He smiled bitterly. "Bullets, boredom, or brandy—that's how people like us go, because God knows we aren't made for peace."

"No. We aren't." Eve leaned down and pressed her own lips against his hand. And then they drank until it was time for Cameron's train. He held his liquor like an Englishman, glassy-eyed but still ramrod straight as they headed up the pier.

"I go to Ireland in a week." His voice was as bleak as if he were going to hell. "Where are you going?"

"Back to France. As soon as possible."

"What's in France?"

"An enemy." Eve looked up, brushing the dry wisps of hair out of her eyes, feeling the weight of the pistol in her satchel. "René Bordelon, Cameron. I am going to kill him if it's the last thing I do in this life."

That was Eve's *use*, now that the war was done.

Cameron's eyes puzzled her, a study in agony and indecision. Later, Eve would go over that look very carefully and realize just how well he'd pulled the wool over her eyes. "Eve," he said at last. "Didn't you know? René Bordelon is dead."

CHAPTER 37
CHARLIE

June 1947

braced myself the next day for Eve's sarcasm, because absolutely no one could have looked at Finn and me and not known exactly what had happened. Both of us were heavy-eyed from lack of sleep, I couldn't keep a smile off my face, and Finn cast so many sideways glances at me, I was surprised he didn't tip the car in a ditch before we even got out of Grenoble.

But Eve was silent from the moment she climbed into the Lagonda. When I looked back at her she was gazing off over the hills, and I liked that better than having her make trenchant comments about the way Finn and I covertly held hands in the front seat. "What happens when we get to Grasse?" I tried asking her.

An enigmatic smile.

I groaned. "You are so infuriating, you know that?" But I couldn't stay cross. Finn's fingers twined through mine were rough and warm, and I was so happy it nearly stunned me. I'd felt nothing but numbness for so long, and then felt the numbness shattered by grief and guilt and anger—those things were still there, but they were overlaid now by this rich, quiet glow. It wasn't just the sleepless night we'd shared. It was the way Finn had gone downstairs for coffee while I sat combing my hair, and come back with not just coffee but a plate of crisp bacon charmed out of the hotel cook, all because he knew I was craving it. It was the way I'd looked at myself in the mirror and seen not the angry girl setting her chin at an angle that told the world *I don't care*, but a happy young woman with a French tan and a scatter of freckles. It was the face of someone who *did* care, and was cared for in return.

I shook my head slightly to disrupt my own thoughts. I didn't want to examine the happiness too closely; I was too afraid it would fall apart. I was content to let it be, never releasing Finn's hand, but turning around in my seat again as we drew nearer Grasse and having another go at Eve. "Let's have it. How are we going to find Bordelon?"

"I'm still turning my plan over for weak points, Yank," she replied. "I know perfectly well I'm not entirely level on the subject of René—"

"You mean not entirely *sane*," Finn muttered.

"I heard that, Scotsman." She didn't sound angry. "I'm not all there, and we all know it, so I'm making sure this plan hasn't got holes. Because this could easily get cocked up, and I have no intention of letting that happen."

"How can I help with this plan of yours?" I asked, but Finn muttered something as Eve began to answer. "What is it?"

"That oil leak." He dropped my hand, pointing at a dial. "Need to tighten a few things . . ."

"We're only an hour from Grasse." I gave the convertible's dashboard a thump. "This old bucket!"

"Watch your tone, miss. She's an old lady, and she deserves a rest if she wants one."

"This car is not actually *alive,* Finn."

"Says you, lass." Finn eased the car off onto one of the side roads as we bickered. Who knew bickering could be so enjoyable? Green hills rose in the distance on all sides, and the air had some heady fragrance I didn't recognize. Not far south was the sea, I thought. The lazy influence of the Mediterranean was rising fast in the air.

Then I gave a breathless "Oh . . ." as the Lagonda finished the turn on the off-road and coasted to a stop. For a moment all three of us stared. The slope below was a dazzling carpet of blue-purple spires, and the smell rose into the wind, intoxicatingly sweet. Hyacinths— thousands upon thousands of hyacinths.

I leaned so far over the door I nearly fell out, inhaling deeply. "We must have driven onto one of the flower farms." Grasse was a capital for perfume makers, I already knew that, but I'd never seen the local flower fields that supplied the trade. I scrambled out of the car, leaving the door gaping, and leaned down to bury my nose in the nearest bank of blooms. The scent dizzied me. Farther down the slope I could see swells of pink, rolling masses of roses. From even farther came the rich waft of jasmine. I looked back and saw Eve sitting very still, breathing in the scents, saw Finn smiling as he fetched his toolbox. I couldn't resist plunging into the waves of blue, running my fingertips along the spires. It was like wading into a fragrant sapphire lake.

Finn was closing up the hood by the time I came running back. "Eve!" I called, and leaning over, I deposited an armload of hyacinths into her lap. "For you."

Eve looked at the mass of flowers, her tortured hands moving gently through the soft petals, and I felt my eyes prickle. *You testy, stubborn, goddamn old bat, I do love you,* I thought.

She looked up at me, smiling a rather rusty smile, and I wondered if she was about to say something similarly affectionate. "Here's the plan once we g-get to Grasse," she said instead.

I laughed. Should have known better than to expect a sentimental moment from Eve. Finn came up beside me, and she nodded at him. "You'll need a sharp suit, Scotsman, and some business cards. You, Yank, will need to play my devoted granddaughter. And we'll all need patience, because this is going to take time."

She outlined the rest in a few sentences. The two of us listened, nodding. "Could work," Finn said. "If Bordelon is in Grasse to begin with."

"And if we find him?" I asked.

Eve smiled, blandly. "Why do you ask?"

"Humor me." I was thinking of the conversation on the bridge last night, my gnawing fear that Eve wanted blood. I was not going to be a party to a murder. "What are you going to do when you find him?"

Eve quoted in French. "'*I shall come back to your bedroom and silently glide toward you with the shadows of the night . . . I shall give you kisses frigid as the moon and the caresses of a serpent that slithers around a grave.*'"

I groaned. "Let me guess. Baudelaire?"

"My f-favorite poem, '*Le Revenant,*' 'The Ghost,' but it sounds better in French. *Revenant* comes from the verb *revenir.*"

To come back.

"He never thought I'd come back. He's going to be very wrong." Finn and I exchanged glances, and Eve turned brisk again. "Back in the car, children. We can't gawp at the flowers all day."

We motored into Grasse at twilight: a place of square towers, narrow twisting roads, apricot roofs and Mediterranean colors, and over everything the scent of the flower fields. Eve strode up to the hotel clerk and opened her mouth, but I forestalled her. "Two rooms," I said, looking up at Finn. "One for *Grand-maman* and one for us, don't you think, dear?"

I said it without a hitch, laying a casual hand on his arm so the clerk would see my wedding ring. As Eve had said, selling a story is done by reciting the little details without any flubs.

"Two rooms," Finn confirmed, slightly strangled. The clerk didn't bat an eye. Later I put in a telephone call to Violette in Roubaix, letting her know where to reach me. We were in Grasse, and the hunt was on.

Finn's new cards were embossed and expensive-looking. "Pass them over with a patronizing air," Eve instructed. "And for God's sake, will you two quit giggling?"

But Finn and I went on howling with laughter. The cards, in their impressive-looking script, read:

Donald McGowan, Solicitor

"My Donald!" I managed to say at last. "Well, my mother always did want me to catch a lawyer."

"Solicitor," Eve corrected. "Limeys have solicitors, and very supercilious they are too. You'll have to work up a good frown, Finn." He had an impressive frown indeed as he handed his card across the *maître d*'s desk about four days later. By then he'd had some practice. "I am making inquiries on behalf of a lady," he murmured. "A matter of some delicacy."

The *maître d'* appraised him in a glance. Finn Kilgore in his rumpled shirt and tousled hair wouldn't have gotten the time of day in Les Trois Cloches, one of Grasse's finest restaurants—but Donald McGowan in his charcoal gray suit and narrow striped tie rated a subtle straightening in posture. "How may I be of assistance, *monsieur*?"

It was the slow hour between lunch and dinner when diners were few; Eve always timed our arrival carefully so the staff had time to gossip. Or answer questions.

"My client, Mrs. Knight." Finn glanced back to where Eve stood in a black silk dress and broad-brimmed hat, her hands hidden by kid gloves, leaning on my arm, looking frail as she dabbed her eyes with a black-bordered handkerchief. "She emigrated to New York years ago, but much of her family remained in France," Finn explained. "And with so many dead in the war . . ."

The *maître d'* crossed himself. "So many."

"I have found death records for her father, her aunt, two uncles. But a cousin is still missing."

If you can traipse all over France looking for your missing cousin, then so can I, Eve had said when she told us where she got the idea. *Who in Europe* doesn't *have a missing cousin or two these days?*

"We discovered he fled Limoges for Grasse in '44, just ahead of the Gestapo . . ." Finn lowered his voice, dropping a few vague hints about Resistance activity and enemies in Vichy. Painting a vision of Eve's childhood companion (brave patriot narrowly escaping arrest), now yearned for by Eve (lonely survivor of a massacred family).

"Will anyone fall for that?" I'd asked back in the hya-cinth field. "It's very Hollywood."

"They'll fall for it *because* it's Hollywood. After a war like this one, everyone w-wants a happy ending, even if it's not their own."

Sure enough, this *maître d'*, like the ones before him, was nodding, clearly sympathetic.

"René du Malassis," Finn said, winding up. "But he may have taken a different name. The Milice were looking for him"—a trade of grimaces; even two years after the war, everybody bristled at the mention of the Milice—"and this has made Mrs. Knight's inquiries very difficult. But we do have a photograph . . ."

The photograph of René, folded and clipped so all his swastika-wearing dinner partners would not show, was pushed discreetly across the table. The *maître d'* stud-ied it. Eve allowed her shoulders to shake, and I patted her back, looking worried. "*Grand-maman,* don't upset yourself." My role here: to ramp up the sympathy fac-tor. I chafed Eve's gloved hand between my own, heart thudding as the *maître d'* hesitated.

"No," he said, shaking his head, and my heart thud-ded again more leadenly. "No, I'm afraid I don't recog-nize the gentleman."

I crossed Les Trois Cloches off the list as Finn slid a discreet banknote across the table with a murmured, *If you see the gentleman, do contact me . . .* Only a few hundred more places to go.

"Don't look dejected," Eve said once we were out-side. "I said this would take legwork and luck, d-didn't I? This is the part that *isn't* Hollywood. You don't just go looking for someone and have him pop up like a rab-bit out of a magician's hat."

"You're certain this is the best way to locate him?" Finn asked, donning his fedora. No more striding about hatless for him; Donald McGowan (solicitor) was a good deal more businesslike.

"One of these places"—Eve gave a whack to the crumpled list in her bag—"will know him."

Her argument was simple: René Bordelon prized the finer things of life. Whatever else had changed, that wouldn't have. He'd still patronize the best clubs, drink at the best cafés, attend the best theaters, and he was the kind of patron the staff noticed, because he tipped and dressed well, and could talk wine with the *sommelier* and Klimt with the museum guide. We had a relatively recent photograph—if we canvassed the best culture spots in Grasse, Eve argued, someone would recognize that face. Then we'd have a name.

Standing on that sunny day among the flowers, I'd wondered, "How long is this going to take?"

"If it were Paris, forever. But Grasse isn't enormous."

Finn had worried about something more sinister. "What if he finds out a woman is looking for him? A woman with mangled hands, about the age his little Marguerite would be now?"

Eve glowered. "I'm a professional, Finn. Give me some credit. You think I'm going to march all over Grasse with a horn announcing my presence?" Hence *Mrs. Knight* and *Mr. McGowan,* and the gloves concealing Eve's hands.

"One condition, Gardiner," Finn replied. "You leave that Luger in the hotel room."

"You think if I saw René Bordelon on the streets of Grasse, I'd walk up and put a bullet into his brain?"

"I'm no dunderhead. I won't take the chance."

Four days now we'd been at it. We were barely unpacked in our hotel before Eve was gathering information, compiling lists. And as soon as Finn had his business cards and his suit, and Eve had a good pair of

gloves and a dowager hat that hid her face without looking like it was trying to hide her face, out we'd sallied.

I was almost too nervous to speak the first time we
sailed into a high-end café with our prepared story.
Now, six restaurants, three museums, one theater, five
clubs, and four days later, it was almost boring. Except
for the moment of liquid anticipation every time a new
concierge or waiter leaned over René's photograph and
I thought maybe, this time . . .

"Welcome to real spy work," Eve said outside Les
Trois Cloches, transforming before my eyes as she
straightened from her old-lady hobble. "Mostly tedious,
occasionally exhilarating."

Her eyes sparkled, and I thought how much better
she looked than the day I met her. Then she could have
been sixty or seventy, harrowed and lined and pale.
Now she'd shaken off the slump of grief and inactiv-
ity that made her seem old and fragile, and I was as-
tounded at the change. Her face had healthy color again
even if there were still harsh lines graven about eyes and
mouth; she moved with swift efficiency rather than a
defensive hunch; her graying hair had a gleam to it like
her sharp eyes. She looked her age again, fifty-four, with
plenty of vigor left.

"She hasn't had one of her screaming nightmares
since we got here," I commented to Finn after dinner that night, watching Eve head upstairs. "And she's
not slamming back as much whiskey."

"The chase is good for her." Finn finished his after-
dinner coffee. "She's a hunter at heart. The past thirty
years, she's been standing still. Dying slowly with nothing to pursue. Maybe it's not a bad thing if this hunt lasts
awhile."

"Well," I said. "*I* certainly wouldn't mind that."

He gave me that invisible smile that turned my knees

to water. "I'm pure done in from all this tramping about. You?"

"Exhausted. We should make it an early night."

But there wasn't much sleeping being done in our little room with its blue shutters and wide soft bed. Neither Finn nor I objected when Eve's search expanded to a week, ten days. The mornings were for the three of us: flaky croissants and cups of ink-dark espresso at a table so small our knees jammed together. Then the hunt, the repetition of our now-seamless play: stopping at a shop for handmade shoes off the Place aux Aires, then an atelier for expensive cologne. Strolling through the narrow twisting streets of the *vieille ville* headed for clubs and theaters that might recognize a favorite patron, and finally during the sleepy hour before dinner, visiting restaurants full of shaded lamps and heavy silver cutlery. Finally back to the hotel and supper, passing a bottle of Provençal *rosé* over plates of heaped *frites*. Those were the days, and Finn and I were content to let Eve direct them, because the nights were ours.

"Have I mentioned," I asked one night, my head against Finn's arm, "that you look absolutely jaw dropping in a three-piece suit?"

"Aye, you have."

"It seemed worth repeating." I leaned over to tip out the last of the wine we'd brought up to bed. I was completely naked, no longer even slightly self-conscious in front of him as he lay with his hands clasped behind his head, admiring me. "When do we get the Lagonda back?"

"Maybe another week." Upon learning we'd be in Grasse awhile, Finn made arrangements to have that elusive leak repaired. He telephoned every other day to check on his precious car like an anxious mother.

"You need a new car, Finn."

"You know what a new car costs these days, what with the wartime metal drive?"

"Here's to the Lagonda's health, then." I passed him the mug we were using for a wineglass. "I wouldn't mind driving around Grasse instead of walking everywhere. My feet hurt, and I was counting on a few more months before I get enormous enough for aching feet." As soon as we'd arrived in Grasse, my morning sickness had dropped away, and so had my perpetual draining tiredness. I didn't know if it was the flower-scented breezes or all the lovemaking or just that the Rosebud was into her fourth month now, but suddenly I felt marvelous, full of boundless energy and ready for anything—even the endless walking all over Grasse. But I still missed the car.

Finn drained the last of the *rosé*, then wriggled around so he was sitting with his back against the footboard. He started massaging my toes under the sheet, and I wriggled pleasurably. The night was warm, we had all the shutters open and the smell of jasmine and roses drifted in. The lamplight encircled the bed, turning it into a ship adrift on a dark sea. By agreement we didn't talk about René here, or the war, or any of the terrible things that had happened because of either. The nighttime hours belonged to happier conversations.

"Wait till you're eight months in," Finn predicted, massaging my arches. "That's when the feet really start to hurt."

"What would you know about eight months in, Mr. Kilgore?"

"Watching all my friends' wives. I'm about the only one not hitched—first thing most of my mates in the 63rd did once they got home was knock up some girl and marry her. I'm a godfather at least three times over."

"I can just see you standing over a font with a screaming armful of lace!"

"Screaming? Never. Babies like me. Go right to sleep the minute I pick them up." A pause. "I like bairns. Always wanted a few."

We let that hang in the air a moment before tiptoeing around it. "What else do you like?" I asked, giving him my other foot. "Besides Bentleys." Last night he'd read aloud out of his motoring magazine the entire mechanical rundown of the Bentley Mark VI, aping my American accent outrageously as I pummeled him with a pillow.

"A man with a Bentley has everything he needs, lass. Except maybe a good garage to keep her in fighting trim. The one that's got the Lagonda now, they're good."

I tickled his chest with my toes. "You could run a place like that, you know."

"Got to be good with more than cars to run a garage." He made a rueful face. "You know me. The bankbook would end up under an oil can and you'd never read the check stubs for engine grease, and soon the banks would own it all."

Not if I were the one keeping the books . . . I didn't finish the thought even to myself, just released it gently and told him instead about the Provençal café I remembered so well, how that long-ago day had made striped awnings and Edith Piaf and goat cheese sandwiches my idea of heaven on earth. "Though an English breakfast should be featured. In the ideal café, that is."

"Well, I do a braw one-pan fry-up . . ."

We both knew what we were doing here, during these lazy nighttime conversations. We were outlining a future and tentatively, almost fearfully, starting to sketch each other into it, then backing away from the unspoken with half smiles. Sometimes the night brought bad dreams for one of us, but nightmares were easier to bear when there were warm arms in the dark to burrow into. When grief came for either of us, it wound its way through the night and became part of the sweetness.

I haven't known you long enough to be this crazy about you, I thought, watching Finn's profile in the soft light. *But I am.*

One afternoon, two and a half weeks into our stay, Eve said over a post-lunch espresso, "Maybe René isn't here."

Finn and I traded glances, both doubtless thinking of all the heads shaken no over the photograph since we'd arrived. Three restaurant managers and an expensive tailor had thought they recognized the face, but couldn't remember the name that went with it. Otherwise, nothing.

"Maybe I should g-give it up. Let Charlie here go back home to knit booties, and have you"—Eve nodded at Finn—"take me back to the land of fish and chips."

"Can't say I'm ready to go home yet." I kept my voice light, but Finn squeezed my hand and I squeezed back.

"Let's give it another week or two," Finn said. Eve nodded. "But let's take the afternoon off. I want to amble over to the garage and check on the Lagonda."

"He's going to harangue those poor mechanics to death," Eve chuckled as he walked away.

"Or apologize to the car for not visiting more often," I agreed.

We sat for a while, finishing our espressos, and then Eve looked at me. "I'm no good at afternoons off. Let's pick a few restaurants. I reckon the two of us can b-brace the waiters without our solicitor in tow."

I looked at her, gray eyes gleaming in her tanned face as she clapped her big hat over her brow at a rakish angle. "Maybe you should introduce me as your daughter this time. You're not so plausible as my old granny anymore."

"Pshaw."

"I'm serious! It's this flowery air in Grasse; it's like the elixir of youth." As we strolled through the oldest part of the city, where the buildings arched overhead, leaning on each other like friendly shoulders, I realized I loved Grasse. All the other cities we'd passed through— Lille, Roubaix, Limoges—had been blurred for me by the search for Rose. But here in Grasse we'd finally stopped to breathe, and the city was unfolding to me like the jasmine blossoms in the fields. *I never want to leave this place,* I thought, before pulling myself back to the search at hand.

Two unsuccessful restaurant stops later, Eve pulled out her map to search for a third. I munched a concoction of fried courgette flowers to which the Rosebud had become almost as addicted as bacon, eyeing a nearby shop window. The display was all children's clothes: sailor suits, ruffled skirts, and laid out across a display pram a tiny lacy baby dress embroidered in rose vines. I looked at that dress and had an attack of utter lust. I could see the Rosebud wearing it at her christening. I could *feel* her now—in what felt like a matter of days, I'd gone from utterly flat in front to just a little rounded. You couldn't see it through my clothes, but it was there, that tiny bump. Finn didn't say anything, but he kept running his fingertips over my abdomen at night, butterfly touches like kisses.

"Buy it," Eve said, noticing my stare. "That armload of lace you're drooling over—just b-buy it."

"I doubt I can afford it." Wistfully, I swallowed my last fried flower. "I'll bet it costs more than all my secondhand clothes put together."

Eve crammed her map into her handbag, marched into the shop, and emerged minutes later with a brown paper package that she tossed me unceremoniously. "Maybe now you'll pick up the pace."

"You didn't have to—"

"I hate being thanked. March, Yank!"

I marched. "You're spending a lot lately, Eve." The money from my pawned pearls had run out, and Eve was now covering all our expenses, though I'd sworn to repay her as soon as I could crack my bank account open in London.

"What have I got to spend it on? Whiskey, vengeance, and baby dresses."

I grinned, hugging the package. "Would you be her godmother?"

"Keep saying *her* and it'll come out a boy just to spite you."

"His godmother, then." I paused, suddenly serious though I'd said it flippantly. "Really, Eve—would you?"

"I don't behave well in church."

"I'm counting on it."

"All right." She gave me a rusty smile, then stalked on like a heron through deep water. "If you insist."

"I do insist," I said, and the words came out thick with emotion.

The restaurant was just off the Place du Petit Puy with its white-fronted cathedral. It was long past the lunch hour; diners would be trickling in soon for early evening drinks. I blinked at the dimness inside after the dazzling sun, mentally shifting back to my role of devoted family attendant just as Eve was already drooping against me as though too frail to walk unsupported.

I stepped to the *maître d'* and went into Finn's spiel, which I could have recited in my sleep. Eve dabbed at her eyes, and soon I was pushing the photograph across the table. My mind was on the baby dress; I wasn't really thinking of our quarry.

And then I was, because the *maître d'* nodded in recognition. That nod hit me like a hammer blow.

"*Bien sûr, mademoiselle.* I know the gentleman well, one of our favored patrons. Monsieur René Gautier."

For an instant I froze. *René Gautier.* The name reverberated around my skull like a ricocheting bullet. *René Gautier—*

Eve stepped up beside me. How she hung on to her quivery fragility, I had no idea, but she *had* won four medals for spying. I saw why as she quavered, without stammering or batting an eye, "Oh, *monsieur,* how happy you've made me! My René, it's been so many years since I've seen him! René Gautier, that's the name he's taken?"

"Yes, *madame.*" The *maître d'* smiled, clearly savoring his chance to be the bearer of good news. Eve was right—after a war, everyone wanted a happy ending. "He has a charming little villa outside Grasse, but he comes here frequently. For the *rillettes de canard,* we serve the finest *rillettes* on the Riviera, if I do say so myself—"

I didn't care about the goddamn *rillettes.* I leaned in closer, pulse racketing. "His villa, would you have an address?"

"Just past the mimosa fields off the Rue des Papillons, *mademoiselle.* We sometimes deliver a crate of wine, a Vouvray one can get nowhere else in Grasse—"

Eve was already straightening her hat. "Thank you, *monsieur,* you have made us very happy," I gabbled, reaching for Eve's arm, but the *maître d'* looked past us and beamed.

"Ah, what luck! Here is *monsieur* now."

CHAPTER 38
EVE

As she turned to face her enemy, time folded in on itself. It was both 1915 and 1947; she was twenty-two, bloodied, and broken, and she was fifty-four, shaking, and still broken; René Bordelon was a suave dark-haired *bon vivant*, and he was this stiff-shouldered old man with silver hair and an exquisitely tailored suit. At that instant while time crashed together, both versions were true.

Then past and present merged with a click, and it was only 1947, a beautiful summer evening in Grasse, and an old spy stood separated from her old enemy by nothing more than a few feet of tiled floor. As Eve looked at him, tall and stalk boned, the same silver-headed cane hooked over one arm, terror opened like a trapdoor in her stomach and all her patched-together courage shattered in one long silent shriek.

He did not recognize her. He rotated his black homburg in his hands, raising an eyebrow at the *maître d'*'s eager expression. "I am expected, I see?"

A shudder racked Eve at the sound of the inflection-less voice of her nightmares. Her hands ached inside her gloves as she gazed, numb with disbelief, at the man who had broken them. She had never imagined she might encounter him before she was ready. She'd thought she could manage their first meeting on her own terms, surprise him when she was well prepared. Instead fate had surprised her, and she was not prepared at all.

He had not changed. The hair gone silver, the lines at the forehead—those were just window dressing. The spiderous fingers, the even voice, the cheap soul of a torturer peeping out from behind the expensive suit of a sophisticate, that was all the same.

Except the scar on his lip. Eve's mark, she realized, left when she'd bitten him in their last venomous kiss.

The *maître d'* was chattering explanations, and dimly Eve felt Charlie touching her elbow, murmuring something she couldn't hear through the buzzing in her ears. She knew she should say something, do something, but she could only stand frozen.

René's dark eyes returned to her face, and he stepped forward. "Mrs. Knight? I don't recognize the name, *madame* . . . ?"

Eve had no idea how she managed it, but she stepped to meet him, holding out her hand. He took it, and the old revulsion swamped her at his familiar long-fingered grip. She wanted to fling his hand away and flee like a coward, keening her old terror and agony.

Too late. He was here; so was she. And Evelyn Gardiner was done running.

She squeezed his hand hard, and saw his face change as he felt the deformities covered by her glove. She leaned forward so only he could hear her voice. The words came low, calm, perfectly even.

"Perhaps you'll recognize the name Marguerite Le

François, René Bordelon. Or should I say, Evelyn Gardiner?"

The restaurant was suddenly making a great fuss. They had a happy reunion under their roof—waiters beamed and the *maître d'* offered the best table in the house. And in the middle of all the hubbub, Eve and René held each other in a gaze like an exchange of swords.

Finally, the bastard dropped her hand and gestured toward the table the waiters were so cheerfully preparing. "Shall we?"

Eve managed to incline her head. She turned, wondering how she was able to walk without stumbling. Charlie came to her side like a knight's squire, her face white as she took Eve's elbow. That fierce little hand was wonderfully steadying. "Eve," she murmured, eyes darting at the man behind them. "What can I do?"

"Keep out of the way," Eve managed to mutter back. This dueling ground was no place for Charlie St. Clair; René would swat her as casually as he had swatted and maimed so many others in passing. Eve would claw him to pieces before she allowed him to hurt anyone else she cared for.

Claw him to pieces? her mind sneered. *You can barely look him in the eye.* But she shoved that aside along with her terror and sat down opposite him, an expanse of snowy linen stretching between them. Charlie perched on a chair at Eve's side, uncharacteristically mute. The waiters were well trained, hovering out of earshot to give this happy reunion its privacy.

René leaned back and steepled his fingertips. Eve had a sick flash, seeing those fingers curled around a blood-stained bust of Baudelaire—seeing them trace her naked breasts in bed.

"Well," he said softly in French. "Marguerite."

Her pulse nearly stopped, hearing that name from his lips. But her old coolness came back with her old identity, sweeping over her in a wave. Her blood beat slow and cold, and for the first time since she turned to find him standing in the restaurant entryway she looked at the poisonous old man with some semblance of calm.

"René Gautier," she replied. "After Théophile Gautier, I p-presume? The poet to whom Baudelaire dedicated *The Flowers of Evil*? In Limoges you were du Malassis after Baudelaire's publisher, so I see you still haven't found another poet."

René shrugged as casually as though this were any ordinary dinner conversation. "Why not stay with the best once one has found it?"

"A fancy way of saying you have a stagnant mind."

A waiter gushed up and presented a bottle of champagne. "Since it is a reunion worthy of celebration, *monsieur*?"

"It is at that," René murmured. "Why not?"

"I could use a drink," Eve agreed. A whiskey the size of a bucket would have been better, but she'd take champagne. She knotted her hands into fists in her lap, realizing—as the champagne cork popped and René twitched—that he was not as cool inside as he pretended. Good.

In unison they reached for their glasses as the waiter retreated. No one suggested a toast. "So many lines on that face," he said. "What have you been doing with yourself all these years?"

"Living hard. I don't need to ask what you've been doing. Pretty much what you were doing the last time we met: living well, aiding Germans, getting your countrymen shot. Though now you're not opposed to doing the shooting yourself. Lost your squeamishness in your old age?"

"It's thanks to you I lost my squeamishness, pet."

The word ran over her skin like a rat. "I was never your pet."

"Does *Judas* suit you better?"

That hit hard, but Eve managed—barely—not to flinch. "About as well as *dupe* suits you."

He gave a tight smile. As Eve watched him lounging in his expensive suit, his long nose appreciating the fizz of his perfectly chilled champagne, fury began to build. So many had died—Lili in her squalid prison, Charlie's cousin and her baby in a hail of bullets, a young *sous-chef* with a pocket full of stolen silver—and this man had spent those years doing what? Drinking champagne and sleeping without nightmares.

Eve's nightmares had not begun until after Siegburg. In her prison cell, shivering in an agony of cold on an unwashed pallet, there were no dreams, but afterward there were horror images of the green-walled study, the evil-eyed lilies, the descending bust. The room, never the man. Dreaming of that room where he'd broken her had graven the lines around her eyes that he studied so contemptuously. He looked like he'd spent the last thirty years sleeping very well.

Eve caught a glimpse of Charlie's face, pale and immobile when she was usually so animated, and wondered if the Yank was thinking the same thing. She remembered Charlie saying that she'd never faced evil as Eve had.

You are facing it now.

René took another sip, made a small sound of appreciation, and patted his lips with a napkin. "I confess I'm surprised to see you, Marguerite. May I call you

Marguerite? I never really managed to think of you any other way."

"I'm surprised you thought of me at all. You never were one to look back at the wreckage in your wake."

"Well, you were unique. I thought you might turn up in Limoges looking for me, after the first war."

If not for Cameron's lie . . . "You covered your tracks rather well when you left Lille for Limoges."

"New identification papers aren't difficult to manage when one already has black-market connections." A wave of his hand. "You might still have found me once they let you out of Siegburg. I did keep an eye out for news of your release. Why such a delay tracking me down?"

"Does it matter?" Eve slugged half her champagne in a single swallow. She was finding her words faster, the old back-and-forth rhythm she used to play so well against René in their conversations. "I'm here now."

"To shoot me between the eyes? I believe you'd have done that in the doorway if you had a weapon."

May God damn Finn Kilgore to hell, Eve thought. If not for him, she'd have been carrying her Luger.

"If that broken mess you call a hand can still fire a pistol, that is." René summoned a waiter with a lifted finger. "The *rillettes de canard*. I find myself hungry."

"Certainly, *monsieur*. And for *madame*?"

"No, thank you."

"Your stammer's improved," René said once the waiter retreated. "Does it go away when you're afraid?"

"When I'm angry." Eve smiled. "When you get angry, you get a tiny tic at the corner of your eye. I can see it now."

"I think you're the only woman who has ever made me lose my temper, Marguerite."

"Small victories. Do you still have that bust of Baude-laire?"

"I treasure it. At night sometimes I hear the sound of your fingers breaking, and I go to sleep with a smile."

A flash of the green-walled study, the smell of blood and fear, but Eve shoved it aside. "When I need to sleep, I think of your face the moment you realized you were being fucked by a spy."

He never blinked, but something behind his eyes tightened. Eve's scalp shrank, but she smiled again, bolting the rest of her champagne and pouring more. *I still know how to get to you, you old bastard.*

"I suppose you want revenge," René said abruptly. "Revenge is the consolation prize of the losing side."

"My side won."

"But *you* lost. So how do you intend to get your revenge, Marguerite? I don't believe you have the nerve for murder. That broken piss-stained little thing I last saw sobbing her heart out on my Aubusson couldn't so much as lift her head, much less a pistol."

Eve flinched deep in her bones. She had been that broken piss-stained little thing for more than thirty years, in many ways. Until a knock on her door one damp London night barely a month ago. Until the au-dible *click* in the front of the restaurant today, where past and present united. Until now.

She would not be that broken piss-stained little thing again. Ever.

René was still talking. "Perhaps you think you can disgrace me, turn me in as a profiteer? I'm a respected man in Grasse, with powerful friends. You're a half-mad crone gone crazed from grief. Who do you think will be believed?"

"You're the man who informed against Oradour-sur-Glane." Charlie's voice dropped into the conversation like a chunk of ice. Eve looked at her, startled. *Don't speak, don't draw his notice*—but Charlie went on, eyes burning like coals. "You're responsible for the massacre of six hundred souls. I don't care how many powerful friends you have, you old bastard. France will not forgive that."

René's eyes went over Charlie's face, lingering, but he still spoke to Eve. "Who's this little thing, then, Marguerite? Not a daughter or granddaughter, I think. That shriveled old cunt of yours surely never produced anything this pretty."

Eve didn't respond. She looked at Charlie instead, feeling the squeeze of an unfamiliar emotion inside. Perhaps love. "Call her Mercury, René. The winged messenger who came knocking at my door. She's the reason I'm sitting here. She's the reason you won't get away this time. She's your downfall." Eve raised her champagne in salute. "Meet Charlotte St. Clair."

His brow creased. "I don't know the name."

"You know my cousin's." Charlie's fingers tightened so hard around her champagne flute, Eve was surprised it didn't shatter. "Rose Fournier, also going by the name of Hélène Joubert. She was blond and lovely and she worked for you in Limoges, and you got her killed, you son of a bitch. You gave her name to the Milice because you were afraid she might be spying on you, and she died with nearly every other soul in Oradour-sur-Glane."

The waiter chose that moment to arrive with the *rillettes de canard*. René continued to look at Charlie thoughtfully as he unfolded his napkin, smeared a toast point with duck-fat pâté, and consumed it with another small sound of appreciation. "I remember her," he said at last when the waiter glided away. "The little bitch who liked to eavesdrop. I take a dim view of nosy wait-resses." A glance at Eve. "Never let it be said I don't learn from the past."

"Why didn't you just fire her?" The words rasped as if they were scraping out of Charlie's throat. "Why did you turn her in?"

"Just to be safe. And to be blunt, because it pleased me. I have a great antipathy now for spying women." A shrug. "But I hope you aren't blaming me for the death of the entire village? That would be astoundingly poor logic. I am hardly at fault for some German general choosing to so thoroughly exceed protocol."

"I blame you for *her* death," Charlie whispered. "You didn't know if she was Resistance or not, and you still reported her. She could have been innocent, and you didn't care. You bastard—"

"Quiet, child. The adults are speaking." René reached for another toast point. "More champagne, Marguerite?"

"I believe we're done here." Eve drained her flute and rose. "Come along, Charlie."

The girl froze. Eve could see her trembling, knew the kind of rage that gripped her, how she wanted to hurl herself across the table and saw that old throat open with a butter knife. Eve understood that feeling very well.

Not yet, Yank. Not just yet.

"*Charlie.*" Eve's voice cracked like a whip.

The girl rose, visibly shaking. She looked at René, calmly sitting there with duck fat glistening on his lips, and she whispered, "We're not done yet."

"Yes, we are." He talked past her, to Eve. "If I see you again, you raddled bitch, or hear you are trying to find my home or blacken my reputation, I will have you arrested for harassment. I'll consign you to oblivion and go back to a life where I never have to think of you."

"You think of me constantly," Eve said. "The thought

of me gnaws at you every day. Because I'm walking proof you never were as clever as you thought you were."

His eyes flared. "You're a turncoat who betrayed her own thanks to a spoonful of opium."

"But I still fooled you blind. And that's been eating you alive for thirty years."

The mask fell at last, and Eve saw raw fury. His eyes burned as though he could fell her dead on the spot, and she gave a slow, contemptuous smile. They did not move, just exchanged their dueling gazes in venomous stillness as waiters exchanged puzzled looks. This was clearly not the happy reunion they had thought to see.

"Au revoir." Eve reached over to his plate, picked up a toast point, ate it slowly. "'I must lie down where all the ladders start, in the foul rag and bone shop of the heart.'"

"That's not Baudelaire," he said.

"Yeats. I told you to find another poet." Eve picked up her hat. "In that foul rag and bone shop *you* call a heart, René, take the time to admit you are afraid. Because your *fleur du mal* has come back." She took Charlie's arm in a grip like steel and turned for the door. "Sleep on that."

CHAPTER 39
CHARLIE

stopped outside the restaurant and stood gulping for air, as though I'd just stumbled out of a poison cloud. I could still hear that flat metallic voice telling me he'd reported Rose to her death *just to be safe*. That it had pleased him.

Eve had described him so often. The unwavering eyes, the long fingers, the elegant surface. But she had not done him justice. That hadn't been a man sitting across the table from me. It had been a human viper.

I wanted to be sick. But Eve moved past me, heading down the street nearly at a run, and I forced myself into motion.

"Eve, we don't have to run." Dashing to catch up. "He's not coming after you."

"No." Eve never stopped. "I'm going after him."

For an instant my heart howled agreement. I thought of that man, and I didn't feel any of the queasiness I'd experienced when I first realized Eve's revenge might be murderous. Half a glass of champagne in René Bordelon's company would be enough to convince anyone that sometimes even old men deserved to die.

But common sense struggled through the red haze of fury, and my heart lurched. "Eve, wait. You can't risk it, you—"

"Hurry up!" She kept striding, blazing eyed, through the twisting streets. A tall Frenchman took one look at her expression and stepped out of her way. My mind raced, pulled in two directions. *Stop her,* common sense argued, even as rage screamed, *Why?*

Turning the last corner, I saw the Lagonda in front of our hotel, blue and gleaming. I sagged in relief. I needed Finn: his calm, his quiet logic, and if all else failed his implacable arms keeping Eve from charging into disaster. But he wasn't beside his beloved car, and inside, the desk clerk passed me a note covered in his back-slanting scrawl. "He went out to have drinks with the garage mechanic," I said, replying to Eve's look of brusque inquiry. "They're offering him a job, something about engine restoration—"

"Good." Eve took the stairs two at a time. I crammed the note in my pocket and followed.

The desk clerk called after me. "*Madame,* a telegram for you from Roubaix—"

"I'll come back for it," I flung over my shoulder. By the time I burst into Eve's room, she already had the Luger out of the bedside drawer. The sight of it stopped me dead. "*Shit,*" I said for the first time in my life.

Eve gave a grim smile as she peeled off her gloves. "You cannot possibly be surprised."

I pressed my fingers against my pounding temples. Fury was definitely giving way to fear. "You'll go to his house and kill him, then? Just wait till he comes home from slurping up *rillettes,* walk up to his door, and put seven shots into his skull?"

"Yes." She pushed the first bullet home. "'A charming little villa,' the waiter said. Just p-p-past the mimosa fields off the Rue des Papillons. It shouldn't be hard to find."

I folded my arms across my chest. "Put that pistol down and listen to me. Whether you succeed or fail, you'd go to prison. Don't you understand that?"

"I don't care."

"I do." I seized her by the arm. "I want my daughter to have a godmother."

She slid the last bullet into place. "And I want to see that man dead."

Part of me agreed. But his life wasn't worth trading for Eve's future—he'd already eaten too much of her past. And I wasn't going to risk ruining my own future, just as it was starting to be patched together, by assisting in a murder. "Eve, stop and think."

"I have." Eve checked the Luger's barrel. "If I kill René at his home, there shouldn't be any witnesses. He hasn't got a wedding ring, so there's no wife or children to get in the way. I intend to leave his rotten body on the floor and walk out free as a bird."

"The restaurant knows you were looking for him, asking where he lived. Not just the restaurant today either. We've been making inquiries all over Grasse for weeks." Maybe logic would reach her; I scrambled to marshal my arguments. "If he turns up dead now—"

"The police might look for us, but how? We all gave false names, to the hotel here and everyone else. Besides, I d-don't intend to stay in Grasse long enough for people to come looking for me."

"And how are you getting out of Grasse, with Finn not here to drive? How are you even getting to René's *house* first?"

"Cab, if necessary." She sounded so calm, as though

she were planning tea. In the restaurant I'd sensed the
fear behind the ice, seen her hands trembling in her lap
under the table. Now she soared in some place far above
fear, remote and relentless as a gliding eagle. Tossing
the pistol into her satchel, Eve kicked out of the pumps
she was wearing as respectable Mrs. Knight, and thrust
her feet into her old sandals. "Come help me kill him, if
you like. You have a right to want him dead too."

"No. I won't help you murder that man."

"You don't think he deserves to die?"

"He does, but I want something worse than death for
him. I want to see him exposed, humiliated, imprisoned.
I want him held up to the world so they can see what
he really is. That will kill him slowly, Eve. The worst
punishment in the world for a man as proud as that." I
took a deep breath, willing her to hear me. "Let's go to
the police. We have the photograph of him surrounded
by Nazis, we have your testimony, we can call on the
woman in Limoges who saw him shoot that *sous-chef* in
cold blood. René Bordelon might have powerful friends,
but so do you. You are a *war heroine*; people *will* believe you. So turn him in and make his life a living hell."

For me that would be good enough. To see that man
in a cell, knowing he'd been put there by Eve and me,
suffering the public abuse of De Gaulle's France that
held collaborators and profiteers in as much contempt as
vermin. No more chilled champagne and *rillettes,* just
humiliation and the kind of gray prison days Eve had
suffered.

"He'll never sit in a cell, Yank." Eve's voice was implacable. "René Bordelon has made a career of avoiding
c-c-consequences. If we accuse a respected local man
with money and powerful friends, it will take time to
prove those accusations. He'll use that time to rabbit,

because he *always* runs. He's outrun the bad decisions of two wars, and he'll run now because he knows I won't stop coming for him. If I rely on an arrest warrant, he'll be gone before it comes to his door, and he'll resettle somewhere I'll never find him." She picked up the satchel with her Luger. "So I'll rely on a bullet."

I wanted to throttle her. "Don't you see how many ways that could go wrong? He could easily shoot *you,* or call the police and see you carried off in handcuffs—"

"I'll take the risk." She looked down at me as I stepped between her and the door. "Out of my way, Charlie St. Clair."

I looked her right in the eye. "No."

She started toward me. I didn't try to push her back. I wrapped my arms around her and held fast. "Are you going to drag me down the stairs screaming every step of the way?" I said, and realized I was near tears. "I won't let go, Eve. I won't."

I'd lost my brother. I'd lost Rose. I wasn't losing anyone else I loved.

Eve went stiff in my arms, as though she was about to fight—but then she sagged. I heard the glottal sound of a sob tearing loose from her throat, and then the satchel slid to the floor. We stood there a long time as Eve wept, as the sky in the open window behind her turned purple with twilight. I just held her, relief shuddering inside my chest.

She wouldn't say anything at all when the tears dried up. She let me persuade her to lie down, took the whiskey I poured, shivering now and then under the blanket I laid over her. I sat by the bed nibbling my thumbnail, wishing silently for Finn. He knew better than I how to take care of her in these moods. I heard her breathing deepen and tiptoed downstairs to the hotel front desk, but they had no idea where Finn had gone with his mechanic friend. "Your telegram, *madame*," the clerk reminded me. "From Roubaix."

I'd completely forgotten. It had to be from Violette. My heart was suddenly pounding for entirely new reasons as I snatched the paper. The words were terse, even for a telegram.

Lie confirmed. A Mlle Tellier responsible.

Golden choirs erupted in my head. I felt ten feet tall. I'd been right in my suspicions; I'd been *right*. For once I had it in my hands, the power to fix what was broken. This—*this*—was what Eve needed.

I sprinted back to her room, heart pounding. "Eve, look—"

The door gaped open. The bed stood empty. The satchel with the Luger was gone.

I hadn't even been gone five minutes. She must have been up and moving the minute I tiptoed out, as cool and collected as she'd been shaking and crying just moments before. Fear roared through me again, hammering at my temples like spikes of ice. I ran to the open window, searching the street below, but I saw no tall gaunt figure. *You sneaky bitch,* I thought in a wave of fury, at her for tricking me and at myself for being tricked.

I knew where she was going. I couldn't telephone the police, and I couldn't wait for Finn. The Lagonda sat at the curb below.

I stuffed Violette's telegram into my pocket, snatched the car keys from the bedside table in my room, and ran.

t was, Eve supposed, a dirty trick.

"Faster," she told the cabdriver, tossing a handful of francs into the front seat. She didn't care if she spent every coin she had. She wouldn't need any for a journey back.

The cab sped along as Eve sat relishing the comforting weight of the Luger in her lap, her eyes dry. All those crocodile tears, easily shed and just as easily wiped away. Underhanded and unscrupulous, but she'd seen no other option as she looked at Charlie standing implacably between her and the door, soft mouth set in a firm line. Eve smiled. What a different girl from the truculent, uncertain little thing she'd first found on her doorstep.

I'm sorry I won't ever see you again, she thought. *I am so sorry for that.*

"You look very serious this evening, *madame*," the cabdriver said, jocular. "Didn't you say you were going to visit a friend?"

"Yes."

"A long visit?"

"Very." Eternal, in fact. Eve had no intention of leaving René Bordelon's house once she entered it. *That* was the reason she didn't fear prison. A dead woman couldn't be put behind bars.

The Luger held seven shots. Six were for René, and it might take all six—evil men clung hard to life. The last shot, Eve was saving for herself.

"Just like you, Cameron," she murmured aloud, not seeing the darkening streets of Grasse slipping by. Instead she saw a grainy headline from a newspaper clipping: "Soldier's Death." When had that been, '22? No, '24. The words had stabbed Eve through a massive hangover. *Concerning the death of Major C. A. Cameron—*

The world had disconnected. Eventually Eve had managed to pick up the clipping again—from an overseas paper, mailed to her by a solicitor—and read through dry, burning eyes. There was a strangled sound, and it took her a moment to realize it was coming from her own throat.

—death of Major C. A. Cameron of the Royal Field Artillery, who died at Sheffield Barracks as the result of a revolver wound; the coroner returned a verdict of suicide.

Cameron, dead. Cameron with his warm eyes and his Scottish lilt. Cameron kissing her bruises away, murmuring, *You poor brave girl . . .*

By '24 they hadn't seen each other in what, five years? Not since that day in Folkestone. But they'd telephoned sometimes, generally in the small hours of the night when one of them was drunk. Eve had known he was back from Ireland; he'd talked a little of his training school, talked with more excitement of being made military attaché to Riga . . .

But instead, he'd blown his brains out.

The evidence shows that the deceased had brooded over his nonappointment as an attaché at Riga, the newspaper announcement read, *canceled due to his having undergone a sentence of penal servitude.*

The army had punished him for the old sin, Eve had thought bitterly. They didn't mind an officer with a soiled reputation if there was a war on, but afterward he was just an embarrassment.

I'll go on working until I can't anymore. His voice rang in her ears once again, so loud and clear he might as well have been sitting in the cab with her. *Then I suppose I'll die. Bullets, boredom, or brandy—that's how people like us go, because God knows we aren't made for peace.*

"That we aren't," Eve murmured.

It wasn't until the solicitor arrived on her doorstep the following day that she fell apart completely. The solicitor who had mailed her the announcement of Cameron's death in the first place, now bringing legal papers and assuring her of his complete discretion . . . telling her that the pension paid to her account for the last five years had not come from the War Office after all, but from Cameron. That he had ensured it to continue after his death, tied it up in his will in a private bequest without his family's knowledge and separate from his widow's funds. That it was well-invested, the earnest solicitor intoned, and should continue for Eve's life.

She chased the solicitor out, shrieking, and then she collapsed utterly, crawling into her bed like a wounded animal and hiding there for months. *How did you do it, Cameron?* she'd wondered, staring at her own Luger. Barrel to the temple? Under the chin? Or between the teeth, the kiss of cold steel and gun oil the last sensation on earth? Eve had played those games often in the years

that followed, on dark nights when the guilt wouldn't
let her sleep. Putting the Luger through the paces of
suicide . . . but she had never quite pulled the trigger.

Too much of a stubborn bitch, she used to think.
No fatal streak of romanticism or nobility in *her* soul,
not like Cameron's. But now, as the cab streaked out
of Grasse and past the mimosa fields, Eve wondered
if it had been not stubbornness but fate. Maybe guilt
and grief could not be sated until justice had its turn
first. Maybe it was the cold spy-trained part of her brain
whispering that despite Cameron's decades-long lie, an
enemy *was* still out there to be dealt with. And until he
was, the bullet between the teeth could not be fired.

Well, tonight the enemy would die. For Lili, for Rose,
for Charlie, for Eve. Tonight, Evelyn Gardiner's fight
would be finished. More than thirty goddamned years
past due, but better late than never.

She thought of the last bullet, knowing Charlie would
hate her for firing it and so would Finn—but it was
partly for them, as they'd realize later. A murderer dead
next to her victim left them utterly in the clear. No one
would be punished for this but the guilty. They could
swan off into the sunset together, bless them.

"*Madame,* we have arrived."

The cab halted at the end of an access path that led
perhaps a quarter mile toward a gracious little jewel of a
villa. Its white walls shone in the moonlight, and its roof
peaked against the dark sky. Several windows showed
light through the curtains. He was home. Eve wondered
how long René had sat in that restaurant nibbling his toast
points after she and Charlie left. Not long, she suspected.
That told her something: he was still frightened of her.

You should be, she thought.

"Shall I drive you to the doorstep, *madame*?"

"I'll walk," she said, and swung out of the cab.

CHAPTER 41
CHARLIE

I'm sorry, Finn, I thought every time I heard the Lagonda's gears grind. I hadn't driven much in the last year, it was now full dark, and I could hardly reach the pedals—the car was groaning at me as I steered her through the narrow French roads. *I swear if there is so much as a scratch on your baby when this is done, I will make it up to you.* The brakes gave a resentful squeal, and I winced.

I didn't drive particularly well, but I drove fast. I was outside Grasse in no time, and then the fun started. "Just past the mimosa fields" wasn't exactly a pinpoint instruction in a city surrounded by acres of flowers. A half-moon climbed as I hunted, aware that Eve was ahead of me and time was ticking by. I thought of her facing me in the hotel, telling me to get out of her way. She'd looked like a worn-out knight lowering his visor for one last charge, haggard, gaunt, composed, serene.

My brother had had that expression the last time I

saw him alive, I realized. The expression that said "I am ready to die."

Not Eve, I thought. *Please not Eve!* If I failed her, lost her, I was never going to forgive myself.

The Rue des Papillons sported several private paths leading to country villas for the rich. The first I tried led to a house with a prominent for sale sign, the second to a family home where about six children were trooping inside for supper, clearly not René's domicile. Now I leaned forward, and against the dark sky saw the dim peak of another house. Heart hammering, I pulled as much to the side as I could and scrambled out. There was a mailbox, and just enough moonlight to read the curling script: GAUTIER.

This was the house. I saw no cab, no sign of Eve. *Let me not be too late,* I prayed, and began running toward the house. The scent of mimosa hung faint and sweet in the air, smelling as I imagined a baby's hair would smell. My hand went to the tiny bump of my stomach as I ran, and I had a moment's stark terror not for Eve's safety but for my own, because it wasn't just me who could be hurt tonight.

No one will be hurt tonight. I would make sure of that. Somehow.

I rounded the corner of the house, heading toward the back door.

CHAPTER 42
EVE

Most country kitchens would be unlocked, at least in a time of peace. René Bordelon's was not. Eve had anticipated that; she set down her satchel and plucked two hairpins from the knot of her hair. It had been a very long time since her lock-picking lessons in Folkestone, but it wasn't difficult: all you needed was one pin to brace and the other to gently work at the tumblers.

Even so, manipulating the pins with her destroyed fingers took long, agonizing minutes. If it hadn't been a very old, very simple lock, Eve might not have managed it. When the *click* came, she took another moment on the threshold to steady herself, letting her breathing slow. She had only one chance at this, and she would not shoot straight with a galloping heart and an unsteady hand. At last Eve trusted herself to step inside, taking her Luger out and leaving the satchel on the threshold.

A large country kitchen, empty. Nothing but trestle tables and hanging pots lit by moonlight. Eve padded through the shadows, turning the handle of the door at the other end of the kitchen. A tiny creak, and she froze for another agonizing moment, listening.

Nothing.

She eased out into a corridor lined with oil paintings, candle sconces. A strip of rich carpet made her steps noiseless, René's lavish taste helping her on the way to kill him. A faint thread of music drifted on the air. Eve cocked her head, listening a moment, then ghosted down a branching hall to the right. The music grew louder, something lush and involved. *Debussy,* she thought, and smiled.

CHAPTER 43
CHARLIE

N o," I whispered, "no—"

The villa's kitchen door gaped open. Eve's satchel lay on the step. I rifled through it. No Luger. I was too late.

But I heard no shots, no voices. The house was silent as an unexploded grenade.

I wanted to rush in screaming her name, but I was in René Bordelon's territory now, and I would not rouse that viper if he was still unaware of what had come for him. If. Perhaps he was beyond defending. Had Eve already killed him? My blood screamed in my veins, telling me to run, to protect myself and the Rosebud, not to walk any farther into this nest of danger. But my friend was here, and I kept moving.

A dark kitchen. A door ajar. A long hall, rich and quiet. My heart thundered. The faint sound of music. Were those footsteps? The dimness seemed to pulsate. I followed the music, and as I turned a corner I saw them, framed in the broad door arch like a painting.

Eve in silhouette, a dark shape against the brilliant light flooding from the study. It looked exactly the same as the one in Lille she'd described to me: green silk-hung walls, a gramophone spinning its music, a Tiffany lamp throwing peacock colors. René stood in his immaculate shirtsleeves before an open traveling case, oblivious, turned away from the door. Eve was raising the Luger. Too late for me to dare intervene. I froze, pulse pounding.

Neither Eve nor I made a sound, but the lifelong instincts of a snake must have hissed a subliminal warning, because René jerked around. His sudden motion seemed to startle Eve. She squeezed her trigger before the Luger's barrel had fully leveled. The shot ricocheted off the marble mantel, and my ears rang. René was scrabbling in his traveling case. There was no surprise on his face, no fear—only a poisonous leap of hatred as he raised something toward Eve, as Eve's arm straightened again. It happened as slowly as if trapped in amber: two Lugers leveling, two triggers pulling, two shots firing.

One body falling.

Eve's.

After that endless moment, everything happened at once. Eve's Luger clattered to the floor, and her gaunt body sagged against the carpet. I lunged down the corridor, but not fast enough. René had already stepped forward and kicked Eve's pistol away, into the corner of the study. I'd meant to rush at him before he could shoot again, but he was backing away out of my reach, his own pistol leveled at me.

"Down on your knees," he said.

So fast. It had all happened so fast. Eve made a faint sound at my feet, her crippled hands clamped over her left shoulder, and I knelt beside her. I felt the hot slide of blood as I gripped her fingers. "Eve, no, no—" Her eyes were open, colorless, blinking slowly.

"Well," she said in a high, flat voice. "Goddammit."

The record on the gramophone came to a hissing end. I could hear the rasping chorus of our breathing, mine in hitching gasps, Eve's in shallow halts, René Bordelon's fast and deep as he stared at us through a study that reeked of gunsmoke. A ribbon of dark blood coursed slowly down his pristine collar. Half his ear dangled from a shred of flesh, and a silent howl tore through me.

Close. Eve was so close. The thought flashed through my mind as I stared into the infinite black hole of the Luger aimed right between my eyes.

"Move that way, girl." The barrel gestured. "Away from the old bitch."

"No." My hands were pressed on top of Eve's, over her wound. I was no nurse, but I knew she needed bandaging, pressure. *He will not let her have any of those things, he will see her dead first*—but I still said, "No."

He fired another shot, making me scream as the doorjamb beside me splintered. "Let her go, and slide along the wall that way."

Eve's voice was ragged, but clear. "Do it, Yank."

My fingers were clenched so tight over Eve's I had to force them open. Her hands were gloved in blood, and more blood oozed down her torso, slow and implacable. René's pistol followed me as I inched away and set my back against a tall bookshelf, but his eyes stayed riveted to Eve as she managed to pull herself half sitting against the door frame. Her eyes were flat stones full of agony, but I didn't think it was the pain of her own wound. It was the pain of seeing him still on his feet.

Failed, her gaze screamed, filled with self-loathing. *Failed*.

I was the one who'd failed. I couldn't keep her safe.

"Hands off that wound, Marguerite." René's voice was rattled out of the toneless calm he'd maintained at the restaurant. "I'm going to watch you die, and I don't want anything slowing that down."

"Might be a while." Eve looked down at her own shoulder. "Nothing too v-v-vital in a shoulder for a bullet to hit."

"You'll still b-b-b-bleed to death, pet. I like that better; it's slower."

Eve peeled her crimson hands away from the dark, spreading stain. My throat closed as I saw it. Just a shoulder wound, and yet it was going to kill her. We were going to sit in this elegant study, the home of all Eve's nightmares, and watch her bleed out.

René ignored Eve's wound, his eyes mesmerized by her knobbed, bloody hands. "You wore gloves this afternoon," he remarked. "I wanted to see how they looked, after all this time."

"Not too pretty."

"Oh, I think they're lovely. I made a masterpiece there."

"Gloat all you want." Eve nodded toward me. "But let the girl go. She has n-nothing to do with this; she wasn't supposed to be here—"

"But she is here," René cut her off. "And as I have no way of knowing what you've told her, and what kind of trouble she could make, she dies here too. Once you're dead, I'll take care of her. Do think on that as you bleed out, Marguerite. I can see she means something to you."

I sat in an ice-water drench of terror with my arms folded tight around my budding belly. I was not even twenty years old and I was going to die. And my Rosebud would never live at all.

"You can't afford to shoot her, René." Eve's voice was

even, conversational, at what cost I couldn't imagine. "I may be a raddled crone with no friends and f-f-family to look for me, but she's got both, and they've got money. Kill her, you'll have more trouble than even you can ooze your way out of."

René paused, and my heart nearly stopped in my chest. "No," he said at last, touching a hand to his mangled ear and wincing. "You broke into my home and attempted to rob me, a frail old man living alone. I managed to fire back; naturally I had no idea in the dark that you were women, much less the women who accosted me at the restaurant today. I had to sit down with heart palpitations after firing, and by the time I managed to telephone the police, both of you were sadly dead. Simple country people like those here do not look kindly on intruders."

My hopes crashed. I wasn't entirely sure he'd get away with it as easily as that; the restaurant's staff could surely testify that he'd known us . . . but he could muddle things long enough to flee if it proved necessary. He'd clearly already been preparing to run; the traveling case told that story. Eve had been right: René Bordelon always ran from consequences. He'd outrun the consequences of two wars, and with money and luck—two things he'd seemingly never been short on—he could in all probability outrun this too.

Over my dead goddamn body, I thought, and nearly burst out in hysterical laughter because that was exactly how it would happen. Eve would die, and then I would, and then he'd step out over our bodies. He probably would have shot me already if he'd thought about it more clearly; I was young and strong and still a physical threat. But he wasn't thinking clearly. The woman who had humiliated and outwitted him lay dying before his eyes. Until she had gone, she was his whole world and I was an afterthought. His eyes devoured her.

"You th-th-think you can shoot a strange girl between the eyes as she stares at you, René?" Eve was still arguing, still staring him down, but the pulse of blood from her shoulder was coming faster. "The only time you ever pulled a trigger, it was to shoot a man in the back—"

I had no doubt at all that he would be able to kill me in cold blood. None. He might have been too fastidious to do his own dirty work when Eve first met him, but he was a different man now. "Eve, don't talk." My voice came out tinny. "Save your strength—"

"For what?" René looked contemptuous. "Rescue? I assure you, no one heard our shots. The nearest neighbor is at least three miles away."

Rescue. My thoughts leaped another way, toward Finn for whom I'd left a hasty message at the hotel desk telling him where we'd gone and why, in case things went wrong. Well, things had certainly gone wrong. I had a brief delirious image of him roaring out of the night to rescue us, but I didn't think fate would be so helpful.

"I assure you, I have no qualms about shooting your little American here." René fished a handkerchief one-handed from his breast pocket, clapping it to his shredded ear. "My study is already ruined. A trifle more blood on the walls makes no difference to me—"

Rose, I thought in a stab of anguish, *Rose, what do I do?* I didn't know if I was asking my cousin or my daughter. My eyes hunted everywhere for a weapon, but Eve's pistol lay halfway across the room. My gaze traveled up the bookcase behind me—a pair of silver candlesticks on top, too far away, he'd shoot me before I could get to my feet. But closer, on the middle shelf—

"Leave her alive, René. I am begging you."

I barely heard Eve pleading. On the middle shelf

above my head was a white shape. A miniature bust staring blank eyed across the room. I'd never seen that bust before, but I was fairly sure I recognized it.

Baudelaire.

"I confess I didn't think you'd be this quick to find my home." René paced, moving stiffly, as if his age was settling back into his stalky bones after this jolt of action. "Who gave you my address, Marguerite?"

"I can wheedle information out of anyone, René. Didn't I p-prove that with you?"

The ripple of rage across his face was instantaneous. How ridiculous he was, eaten up with fury over a decades-old mistake. But his rage was useful. It could be turned against him. I gave the bust over my seated head a last measuring glance. One lunge, one good swipe, and I could get a hand on it.

"'The hidden Enemy who chews at our hearts grows by taking strength from the blood we lose,'" René quoted. "Turns out the hidden enemy isn't as dangerous as she thought she was."

"Yes, she is," I said. "Your hidden enemy isn't Eve, you old bastard. The hidden enemy is me."

His eyes snapped to me, and he looked surprised. As though he'd forgotten I was even in the room. Part of me wanted to shriek and cower from his eyes, from the pistol that jerked in my direction, but I set my chin at its most contemptuous *I don't care* angle. Never had I cared so much.

"Shut up, Yank," Eve growled. She was sweating, color gone from her face. How long did she have? I had no idea.

Get him closer. Eve had once said René planned brilliantly, but improvised badly. I had to goad him into something rash, and I knew I could. I might never have met the man before today, but I knew him through Eve. Knew him right down to the bone.

I gave him the most scornful look I could manage. "The enemy here is me," I said again. "I'm the one who found your restaurant in Limoges. I'm the one who hunted Eve up. I'm the one who dragged her all the way from London. *Me.* You thought you were so clever, starting a new life, and all it took to find you was a college girl making a few telephone calls."

His voice was arctic. "Shut up."

Oh, I wanted to. But that wouldn't save me or the Rosebud. It was either take a chance and provoke him now, or wait passively to die right after Eve. "I don't take orders from an idiot like you," I said, feeling sweat slide down my spine. "This Baudelaire obsession of yours, it isn't just really, *really* boring, it makes you easy to find. You're not clever, you're predictable. If you hadn't named your restaurant after the same damn poem twice in a row, you'd still be sipping champagne over dinner right now, not packing a bag and running. For the *third* time in your miserable cliché of a life."

"I said, shut up."

"Why, so you can talk? You do love to talk. All those things you told Eve, just because she looked at you with her big doe eyes. You're a big talker, René." I'd never called an old man by his first name in my life, not without a Mr. or *Monsieur* attached, but I thought we were on first-name terms by now. Bullets plus blood plus threats of imminent death equaled a certain intimacy. "Don't even think about shooting me," I added as his mouth tightened and the Luger twitched. "My husband's back in Grasse right now, and if you kill me he'll bury you alive. I left him a note; he's on his way already. You might get away with letting Eve die here, but you can't murder me in cold blood."

Of course he could. I was just trying to muddy the water, get him flustered. His pistol twitched again, and fear froze me until I realized he was looking at my wedding ring, searching my face. Trying to see if I was telling the truth.

"It's true," Eve said, and bleeding out or not, she could still lie like a rug. "Her husband's a Scotsman with a temper, a solicitor with colleagues on both sides of the Atlantic—"

"This is getting out of hand," I pressed. "Look at you standing there like you've won the game. You've lost. You can't control all of this. Let me go, let me bandage Eve—"

His eyes slid back to her. "I've waited thirty years to watch her die, you little American cow. I'm not passing that pleasure up for any price on earth. When she's dead I'll drink champagne over the corpse and take my time remembering how she wept on my carpet after spilling her secrets—"

"She didn't spill any secrets, you filthy liar."

"You know nothing," René Bordelon said coolly. "That sniveling bitch was a tattling coward."

From the corner of my eye I saw Eve's chin jerk. The oldest, deepest wound: her betrayal of Lili. I felt Violette's telegram burning in my pocket. If only it had arrived a day earlier, perhaps I could have averted all of this.

She might be bleeding out, but it wasn't too late for her to know the truth.

"You lied to her," I said. "Eve never gave you anything, not even under the opium. The convicting information about Louise de Bettignies came from another source, a Mademoiselle Tellier." Violette's search of the trial records, the portions unheard by the defendants at the time, must have uncovered that. Who knew who this Mlle Tellier was—if we survived this night, we could find out. "You learned from your German friends that they already had what they needed for a conviction against Louise de Bettignies, so you knew there was no point in torturing Eve further. But before you turned her in, you made sure she thought *she* was the informer." I took a deep breath. "Admit it, René. Eve beat you. She won. You lied to make her think she'd lost."

His drilling gaze flickered. Under my shrieking fear, I was pierced by a flash of silver-bright triumph. Eve was struggling to sit up straighter against the wall. I couldn't tell how much my words had sunk in. René's Luger moved back in her direction. *No, no. Me, you look at me.*

"How does it feel?" I taunted. "You tried to break her, and it didn't work. Nothing has worked for you since the day she outsmarted you. She ended up a decorated war heroine, and you ended up restarting your life twice because you were too goddamn *dumb* to pick the right side in two successive wars—"

He broke. Too angry to shoot me from a safe distance, he came at me: the man who killed Rose, raising the Luger as he advanced. But I was lunging up from the floor, my hand sweeping the shelf above me, and the seconds stretched agonizingly as I fumbled—fumbled—and finally seized hold of the bust of Baudelaire. I brought it around in a wild swing, knocking René's arm away before he could fire. He stumbled back, off balance, toward the desk, and my heart lodged in my throat. *Drop the pistol, drop it*—but though he fell back on one elbow beside the lamp, that aged hand on the edge of the desk still stubbornly gripped the Luger.

"Charlie," Eve said, clear and crisp. I knew what she wanted and I was already surging forward with a howl of hatred, swinging the marble bust in a brutal descending arc. He raised his other arm, protecting his head, but I wasn't aiming for his head. The bust of Baudelaire came down with a sickening crunch on those long spider-thin fingers clenched around the Luger. I heard bones shatter under the marble, and he screamed— screamed like Eve had screamed when he crushed her knuckles one by one, screamed like Lili had screamed on a surgeon's table in Siegburg, screamed like Rose had screamed when the first German bullets came ripping through her baby's body into her own. I screamed too as I hammered the bust down again, hearing another crunch of bones as I flattened those long, long fingers into red ruin.

He let go of the Luger.

It fell to the floor, and I lunged for it, but René reached out with his undamaged hand and seized hold of my hair, still howling in agony, trying to wrench me back. So I kicked the pistol instead, sending it skittering across the floor to Eve.

She lifted her blood-soaked hands and raised René's Luger from the reddened floor. Brought it level with an effort that skinned her lips back from her teeth, as I wrenched my hair away from that vengeful grip and dove to the ground—

As Eve calmly buried a shot between René Bordelon's eyes.

His face disappeared in a red mist. The pistol cracked again as Eve spaced three more shots into his chest.

He toppled back, sliding to the floor with his ruined hand flung out in surprise. Surprised to the end that there was pain he couldn't outrun, vengeance he couldn't escape, consequences he couldn't evade. Women who couldn't be beaten.

The air stank, acrid with gunsmoke and the sharper tang of gore. The silence fell like a lead weight. I struggled up from the floor, still clutching the bust of Baudelaire. I couldn't look away from René's crumpled body.

He should have looked small and old in death, pitiable. All I saw was an aged viper with its head cut off, venomous to the end. My stomach lurched and suddenly I wanted to vomit. I turned away, folding one arm around my belly, lurching back toward Eve who still had the Luger in her ruined hand. She looked tattered and blood splashed, splendid and terrible, and she gave a slow pitiless smile like a Valkyrie riding in howling triumph over a horde of dead enemies.

"One shot left," she said quite clearly, still looking at René's corpse, and before my suddenly horrified eyes she lifted the Luger to her own temple.

CHAPTER 44

EVE

ve's finger was tightening on the trigger when pain split the world apart. Not the dull pain in her shoulder, slowly pulsing blood, but a hot agony sharp and bright as silver, lancing through her fingers. Charlie St. Clair, keening that berserker cry that had torn out of her throat as she lunged for René, had swung the bust of Baudelaire straight at Eve's hand. The shot went off, deafening Eve's already ringing ears, deflected into the wall as Eve's arm jerked off target. Eve strangled a cry of her own as she cradled hand and empty pistol alike to her chest.

"You Yank bitch," she managed through clenched teeth, tears starting in her eyes. "My goddamn *hand* is broken. *Again.*"

"The way you tricked me and ran out at the hotel, you deserve it." Charlie dropped to her knees, and with quick strength wrested the Luger from Eve's hooked fingers and tossed it aside. "I'm not letting you shoot yourself."

"I don't have to shoot myself to d-die." The Luger would have been the better way, poetic justice: when Eve sighted down the scratched barrel at René's suddenly widening eyes, she'd seen it was her own Luger that he'd taken from her so many years ago. The one Cameron gave her. But Eve didn't need a bullet to die. She could bleed out right here; all she had to do was—nothing.

"Get off me," she snapped at Charlie, who was trying to get a better look at Eve's shoulder. The pain chewed like an animal, slow and steady. "Let it go, girl. Just let it go."

"I will *not*," Charlie roared. She lunged around the room looking for supplies, completely ignoring the corpse on the floor. She came back with an armload of clean linen shirts from René's half-packed traveling case, and a decanter of brandy. "Let me clean this, it'll be disinfectant enough until we can get a doctor—"

Eve struck her away with the broken hand. The agony was excruciating. Once again the sensation of red-hot sand crunching in her knuckles. Eve wanted to curl up and weep, curl up and die. She was weak and shaken and done. She had no more enemies to kill. Hatred was the steel strut that had kept her upright; she felt now like a snail without a shell, soft and helpless. It was time to *go*, didn't the girl see that?

Of course she didn't. Charlie was moving like quicksilver, refusing to give up. That moment when she spat in René's face that he was too goddamn dumb to pick the right side in two wars—Eve had wanted to cheer. It was as though Charlie had turned into Lili right before her eyes, little and fierce as a wolverine, dancing on her wits just a hair's breadth ahead of disaster, improvising her way out of death. Lili had been defeated in the end, but not Charlie.

"You don't have to die." Charlie pressed a wad of linen around Eve's shoulder, stanching the blood. "Eve, you don't have to."

Have to? Eve *wanted* to. She was a whiskey-soaked cripple with a stutter and no future. Most of her life had been wrecked because of guilt and grief and one bad man. And Eve knew enough about justice to know that killing René wasn't enough to make life sweet again.

She must have muttered some of this, because Charlie was arguing. "Didn't you hear what I said to him? You didn't betray Lili. The Germans got their information about her from someone else. The moment you told me how you'd been drugged into giving it up, I wondered—"

Eve shook her head, feeling tears tremble. "No. It was me." It had to be. Charlie's accusation spat at René had passed over her ears in a blur. She had lived with the guilt so long, it was part of her soul. A few words had no power to shift it.

"—opium isn't a truth drug, Eve! It made you hallucinate, but that doesn't mean it made you talk! I asked Violette to look into the trial, the things said when the defendants weren't present, and I was *right*. It was this Tellier woman, whoever she was, another prisoner—"

Eve went on shaking her head back and forth.

"Isn't it worth trying to find out more? Looking at those trial records yourself? You're a *spy*, you have an O.B.E. and people like Major Allenton owe you favors! Telephone Violette, get more details—"

"No." Back and forth, back and forth.

"You goddamn bitch, don't you even want to get out from under all that guilt? Or will you just lie under it like a donkey in a harness?" Charlie thrust her sharp little face right into Eve's and bellowed, *"You didn't do it!"*

The tears spilled over Eve's cheeks. This afternoon

she had cried crocodile tears to get away from this girl, but these tears were real. She wept and wept, and for a moment Charlie held her, Eve sobbing into her sharp little shoulder.

But then Charlie was pushing and prodding, urging Eve up. "We can't stay here. Lean on me, keep that pad pressed *tight*."

Eve wanted to let it fall, let the blood fall out after it. Let the police find two curled corpses in the morning: source and spy, captor and captive, collaborator and betrayer, locked together till the bitter end. But—

You didn't do it.

Blood trickled down Eve's side as Charlie half-supported and half-dragged her down the corridor, back to the shadowy kitchen, out to the warm French night. Eve was still shaking with sobs, and the pain in her hand was shattering. "Stay here while I bring the car up," Charlie said. "You can't walk that quarter mile—"

But another set of headlights was showing down on the road, next to the Lagonda's shadowy shape. Head-lights bright enough to cut through even Eve's pain-blurred, tear-blind vision. The police? "P—P—P—P—" Her tongue broke down completely; she couldn't get out a single word. Clumsily, she wrenched at the linen pads over her wound. She'd bleed out before she went into another prison.

But Charlie cried, "*Finn!*" and soon a familiar Scot-tish burr was rattling furious words. A strong arm went around Eve's waist, taking her weight. Eve slid toward unconsciousness, hoping it was death, hoping to be done.

But still thinking, in some reawakened part of her examining, questioning brain, *You didn't do it.*

CHAPTER 45
CHARLIE

Twenty-four hours later, we were in Paris.

"Eve needs a doctor." It was the first thing I'd said to Finn outside René's villa, after the initial frenzy of explanations. "But if we take her to a hospital, she'll be caught. Anyone with a gunshot wound will be looked at when they find—" A glance back at the house.

"I think I can patch her up long enough to get out of Grasse." Finn soaked the makeshift bandages in more brandy and wrapped them tight around Eve, limp and unconscious in the Lagonda's backseat. "The bullet doesn't seem to have broken anything. She's lost a lot of blood, but with enough strapping . . ."

Caught. It kept echoing through my head. *We'll be caught.* As Finn worked on Eve, I'd run back into the blood-stinking study and, wrapping my shirttail around my hand and avoiding the blood so no one would see a woman's small footprints, tipped the peacock-tail lamp and the gramophone over and yanked the drawers open like someone had ransacked for a cash box. Maybe it would look like a robbery gone bad. Maybe . . . Still using my shirttail, I fumbled in my pocket and found the photograph of René we had been showing all over Grasse, folded and clipped to show just his face. I unclipped it to show the line of swastika-wearing Nazis at his side, and dropped the photograph on the bullet-riddled corpse on the floor.

I'd felt a wave of sickness then, but Finn was shouting for me and there was no more time, so I stuffed both Lugers and the little bust of Baudelaire into Eve's satchel, quickly wiped the door handles and anything else we might have touched, and ran. I drove the Lagonda back to the hotel with Eve stretched out in the backseat, and Finn followed in the car he had borrowed from the hotel manager to get here.

That first night was the worst. Eve revived long enough to get into the hotel with Finn's coat hiding her bloodied shoulder, right past the yawning night clerk, but she fainted on the upper stairs. Finn put her to bed, washed and dressed the wound with some sheets swiped from the hotel linen closet, and then all we could do was watch through the night as she lay frighteningly still. I stared at her through blurring eyes, and Finn wrapped me in his arms.

"I could kill her," he whispered. "Pulling you into danger—"

"I'm the one who followed her," I whispered back. "I was trying to *stop* her. It went all wrong. Finn, she could be arrested—"

His arms tightened around me. "We won't let that happen."

No. We would not. God knows I'd tried to keep Eve from killing René, but now that it was done, I had no intention of letting the police get their hands on her. She had suffered enough.

I looked at her, frail and unconscious in the bed, and suddenly I was shaking with sobs. "Finn, she tried to k-kill herself."

He kissed the top of my head. "We won't let that happen either."

We checked out at first light, my arm about Eve's waist keeping her steady. The clerk was yawning, incurious, and we were out of Grasse in an hour, Finn pushing the Lagonda far past her usual pace. "Gardiner," he muttered as the gears protested, "you owe me a new car. I'm never getting those bloodstains out of the seats, and this engine is *never* going to be the same."

All through that long day of driving, Eve never spoke, just huddled in the backseat like a collection of gaunt bones. Even as we drove into Paris, motoring over the dark waters of the Seine, and she watched as I tossed the bust of Baudelaire out the window into the river, she did not say a word. But I saw her shudder convulsively.

God only knew how, but Finn found a doctor willing to give Eve's wound a look without asking questions. "You can always find men like that," he said after the man disinfected, stitched, and left. "Disqualified doctors, old army lads. How do you think ex-convicts get patched up if they don't want a record that they've been getting into brawls?"

Now that Eve had her fingers splinted and her shoulder dressed, had pills for pain and pills to keep infection away, we decided to lay low. "She needs time to heal," I said, because she was still alarmingly apathetic when she wasn't being foul tempered. "And Paris is big enough to hide in, if anyone . . ."

If anyone comes sniffing after us when René is found, Finn and I both thought. But we didn't mention René to Eve, or each other. We found cheap rooms in the Montmartre and let Eve sleep and take her pills and call us names for not getting her whiskey. It was a full five days before Finn saw the announcement in the paper.

Former restauranteur dead outside Grasse.

I snatched the paper, devouring the details. René Bordelon's housekeeper had come for her weekly cleaning, and discovered the corpse. The deceased was a wealthy man living alone; the room had been ransacked. The passage of days made evidence difficult to collect . . .

I rested my head on the paper, feeling suddenly dizzy. No mention that an old woman and her lawyer had been asking all over Grasse after him. Maybe the police knew about that, maybe they didn't, but no one mentioned inquiries being made. No one was looking to connect a rich American widow and her imposing solicitor with a bed-bound Englishwoman and her disreputable driver in Paris.

"Five days to find him," Finn said, thoughtful. "If he'd had family or friends, it would have been sooner. Someone would have telephoned, got worried about him. But he didn't make friends. He didn't care about anyone, he wasn't close to anyone."

"And I left the photograph on his chest. The one with him and his Nazi acquaintances." I exhaled slowly, reading the short notice again. "I thought if the police saw he'd been a collaborator, they might not look too hard for whoever had killed him. Robbery or retribution, they'd just . . . let it be."

Finn kissed the back of my neck. "Cunning lassie."

I shoved the paper away. There was a photograph of René, courtly, smiling—it made my stomach writhe. "I know you didn't meet him, but please believe me. He was monstrous." I was the one who dreamed now about green silk rooms filled with screams.

"I'm glad I didn't meet him," Finn answered quietly.

"I've seen enough monstrous things. But I still wish I could have been there. Protected you both."

I was glad he hadn't been. He was the one with a prison record; he'd have been in even more dire danger of ending up behind bars if we'd been caught. Eve and I had been enough, in the end, to take care of René—but I didn't say so. Finn had his pride, after all. "Shall we go tell Eve she's probably safe?" I said instead.

"Might stop her hurling insults at us."

Eve listened without comment. Instead of calming her, the news seemed to redouble her restlessness, as she picked at the splints around her broken knuckles and complained about her shoulder bandages. I thought she'd be pestering me with questions about her trial in 1916, the evidence Violette had dug up on my urging, but she never touched the subject.

And ten days after she'd been shot, I knocked on the door with a breakfast croissant and found nothing but a note on the pillow.

Finn let loose with every curse in the book, but I just stared at the terse words. *Gone home. Don't worry.*

"'Don't *worry*.'" Finn tore a hand through his hair. "Where in hell would that dunderheaded battle-ax take off to? Violette, you think? Trying to find out more about the trial?"

He sprinted downstairs to put a telephone call through to Roubaix, but I stood staring at Eve's note with a different suspicion mounting. I ransacked the room, but both Lugers were gone.

Finn was back quickly. "Violette's seen or heard nothing from Eve, she swears."

"I don't think she went to Lille or Roubaix," I whispered. "I think she's going home to die. Gone where we can't stop her from pulling a trigger."

I'd had such foolish faith that if Eve knew she hadn't betrayed Lili, it would fix the old wound she'd carried for so long. She'd learned she wasn't a betrayer, and her enemy lay dead by her own hand—I'd hoped all that would be enough. I'd hoped she would now look to her future, not her tainted past. But maybe Eve had looked in the mirror and still seen nothing to live for, once hatred and guilt were gone. Nothing but the barrel of a gun.

Just like my brother.

My breath began to hitch in my throat. "We need to go, Finn. We need to get back to London *now*."

"She might not be headed for London, lass. If she wants to kill herself, she could have rented another room two streets down; we'd never know where. Or she could have gone to Lili's grave, or—"

"Her note said *home*. She's had no home but London for more than thirty years. If she wants to die there . . ."

Please, no. No.

That second drive across France was very different from the first. The car seemed empty with no acerbic presence in the backseat, and there were no detours to Rouen or Lille. Just a straight, fast drive in a matter of hours from Paris to Calais, then the ferry carrying us back into a bank of English fog. By the following morning, the Lagonda was chugging toward London. My throat closed, and I realized in sudden shock that today was my twentieth birthday. I'd forgotten all about it.

Twenty.

At nineteen, not even two months ago, I'd gotten off the train in the rainy dark with my photograph of Rose and my impossible hopes. *Evelyn Gardiner* had just been a name on a piece of paper. I hadn't known Eve or Finn or René Bordelon. I hadn't even known myself.

Not even two months. How much had changed in

such a short time. I rubbed my just-rounding stomach,
and wondered when the Rosebud would start to move.

"Number 10 Hampson Street," Finn muttered, steer-
ing the Lagonda through the pitted streets. London still
had its scars of war, but the people strolling along those
pocked streets had more swing in their steps and cheer
on their faces on this warm summer day than they had
when I'd first arrived. Finn and I had the only grim faces
to be seen. "Gardiner, you'd better be home."

Home and safe, I prayed, because if I came through
the door of Eve's house and saw her lying there with a
pistol in her stiffened hand, I was never going to forgive
myself. *I won't let go,* I'd told her in Grasse. *I can't lose
you.* If I did—

But number 10 Hampson Street was empty. Not just
empty; there was a new sign posted. FOR SALE.

Six weeks later

"Ready?" Finn asked.

"Not really." I turned for his inspection. "Do I
look grand enough for Park Lane?"

"You look like a bonny wee thing."

"Not that wee anymore." I was very obviously pregnant now, rounding stomach hugged tight by my black
dress. It wouldn't fit me much longer, but I'd squeezed
into it today for luck. It made me look very elegant and
adult, and I needed that this afternoon. Because my
mother and father had come to London, and they were
waiting for me at the Dorchester on Park Lane.

My mother and I had been telephoning a good deal
since I'd come back to London. No matter what she'd
said to me when we were last together, she was my
mother and I knew she worried about me. "*Chérie,* you

must have some kind of *plan*," she'd ventured a few weeks ago. "We'll meet, we'll all talk—"

"I'm sorry, but I don't want to come back to New York."

It was a sign of just how nervous my mother was that she didn't argue. "Then we'll come to London. Your father has business there very soon, anyway. I'll come with him, and we'll all sit down and make some plans."

I already had plans. I'd been refining them these past weeks while sharing Finn's little bed-sit. We worried about Eve, going almost every day to her house to knock, but it wasn't just Eve we talked about over our one-pan breakfasts. It was the Rosebud, for whom I was slowly acquiring a proper layette. It was the future and how we could manage it, Finn outlining ideas and me scribbling figures on my bank statements to see how those ideas could be made a reality (and the bankers had no trouble allowing me to withdraw my own money, once I came in with my false wedding ring on). But I wasn't sure how interested my parents were going to be in my plans. So I prepared for them to tell me what course of action *they* had decided on, and prepared to say no. Whether I was still underage or not, they were going to find out I was not nearly as easy to push around as I used to be. Facing a pistol-wielding murderer does tend to put *parents* further down the list of things to be intimidated by.

Still, I was afraid this meeting would go awry once I put my foot down, and I didn't want it to go awry. In spite of everything, I missed my parents. I wanted to tell them I was sorry I'd caused so much trouble, that I understood better now how losing James had wrecked them so utterly. I wanted to say how much I wanted them back.

"You're sure you want me to come?" Finn wore the charcoal gray suit he'd worn in Grasse as Donald Mc-

Gowan, solicitor. (My Donald!) "Your mother didn't have a very good first impression of me in Roubaix."

"You're not getting out of it that easy, Finn Kilgore. Let's go."

He grinned. "I'll hail a cab." The Lagonda was back in the shop, where Finn, when he wasn't repairing other peoples' cars, was at work rebuilding her engine. The final dash from Paris really had been too much for the old girl, more's the pity. It would have given me a great dose of confidence, gliding up to the Dorchester in the Lagonda. She might be scrap metal under the hood, but she was still all style.

I picked up my hat, a really stunning black confection I'd splurged on because I remembered Eve shaking her head over the queen of spies's passion for morally questionable hats. This little puff of black gauze and feathers was definitely morally questionable, and I smiled as I tilted it over one eye. "Very nice, Yank," I imagined Eve saying, and felt the usual lurch in my stomach. The company that had put her house up for sale couldn't tell us anything; they'd received their instructions by telegram. All we could do was leave a note with Finn's address, begging her to contact us, and go by the house whenever possible to see if we might catch sight of her. All we'd sighted, a week ago, was a notice on the door that the house had been sold.

Where are you? It was something Eve seemed content to let us wonder. On the days I wasn't terrified she was dead, I wanted to kill her myself for making me so afraid.

"Charlie lass." Finn's voice from the open door sounded strange. "Come look at this."

I took my pocketbook and joined him at the doorstep. Anything I was about to say died in my throat as I looked out. Sitting low and rakish at the curb outside was an absolute stunner of a car. It gleamed in the morning sun: a convertible in glittering, patrician silver.

"The '46 Bentley Mark VI," Finn whispered, moving toward it like a sleepwalker. "Four and a half liter engine . . . independent front suspension by helical springs . . . divided propeller shaft . . ." He ran an unbelieving hand down the fender.

But it wasn't the car, lovely as she was, that started my heart pounding. Tucked under the windshield wiper was a big white envelope with our names in a familiar black scrawl. My mouth went dry as I ripped the envelope open. There was something bulky at the bottom, but it was the single sheet of paper I yanked out first. The note began with no apology, no salutation, no greeting. Of course it didn't.

> *You started the process with Violette, Yank, but I had to find and see the details for myself to believe it. Lili's name and involvement in the Alice Network were given by a former cellmate, Mlle Tellier, who, in return for a relaxed sentence, passed the Germans five letters and a confession during the time I was being questioned by René Bordelon. Confirmed with difficulty through trial records, classified documents, and other back-room sources—but confirmed. Also confirmed: Tellier poisoned herself after the Armistice.*
>
> *René lied. It wasn't me.*
> *You were right.*

I realized I was crying like a helpless thing. But I wasn't helpless at all. For so long I'd listened to the nasty inner voice telling me I was, that I'd failed my brother, my parents, Rose, myself. But I hadn't failed Eve. And maybe I hadn't failed the others as badly as I'd always thought. I'd done what I could for Rose and James—I couldn't save them, but it wasn't my fault they died. And I could still fix things with my parents.

As for Charlotte St. Clair, I could take care of her. She had taken the hopeless mess around her, pared away the meaningless variables, the Y's and Z's that didn't matter, solved for X. She had things broken down to a very simple equation—herself plus Finn plus the Rosebud, and she knew exactly how that equation came out. Eve's note read on:

> *Violette has written me. I'm on my way to France, where the two of us will visit Lili's grave. After that, I'm going traveling. Will be back in time for the christening. In the meantime, I owe you some pearls and Finn a car.*

Finn took the envelope, upending it. A tangle slid into his big hand: the keys to the Bentley, all tangled up with a string of perfect milky pearls—*my* pearls. I'd gone back to the pawnshop as soon as I returned to London, but my ticket had expired and they were gone. Yet here they were. I could hardly see them, the tears were dripping so fast. One last line in the note.

> *Call it a wedding gift.*
> *—EVE*

We brought traffic in and out of the Dorchester to a standstill. Porters, bellboys, elegantly hatted men and their white-gloved wives—everyone turned to look as the Bentley came to a halt before the hotel's facade. She purred like a kitten and ran like a dream, and her pearl gray upholstery cradled me like a hug. Finn could hardly bear to hand the keys to the valet.

"Take her round," he said, coming around the fenders toward the passenger side to let me out. "The missus and I are staying for lunch."

Under the hotel awning, I saw my mother in a frilly blue dress, my father looking up and down the street. Saw my mother's gaze linger rather appreciatively on Finn in his handsome suit, saw my father run his eyes over the superb lines of the car—and then saw their lips part in surprise as Finn handed me out in my dashing hat and French pearls.

"*Maman*," I said, linking my arm through Finn's and smiling. "Dad. I would like to introduce you to Mr. Finn Kilgore. We haven't made it official yet"—seeing my mother's eyes dart to my left hand—"but we're planning on it, very soon. We've got a great many plans for the future, and I want you both to be part of them."

My mother began to flutter and my father fluttered too in his more reserved way as Finn offered a hand and I made further introductions. Then as the four of us turned toward the doors of the Dorchester opening into its incredibly elegant inner court, I looked over my shoulder and saw her one last time. Rose stood under the hotel awning in a white summer dress, blond hair ruffling in the breeze. She gave me her impish look, the one I remembered so well, and she waved.

I waved back, swallowing the thickness in my throat. Smiled. And led the way inside.

EPILOGUE

Summer 1949

The flower fields outside Grasse were in bloom, waves and waves of roses, jasmine, hyacinth. The air was heady, and the café made a beautiful place to sit. Those striped awnings invited you not to hurry on your way to Cannes or Nice, but to put your feet up, order another bottle of *rosé*, and while away another hour looking over the hills. The lean woman with the silver-touched plait had been there long enough to stack up several empty bottles over the afternoon. Her face was very brown, she wore boots and khaki trousers and a stack of boar-tusk ivory bracelets on one wrist, and she had the seat in the corner that put her back to the wall and her eyes on all possible lines of fire. But she wasn't thinking about lines of fire at the moment—she watched the cars come and go on the road below.

"You'll be waiting awhile," the café girls had warned

when she first came stalking in asking for the owners. "*Monsieur* and *madame* drive up to the flower fields every Sunday to picnic. They'll be hours."

"I'll wait," Eve said. She was used to waiting. She'd waited more than thirty years to shoot René Bordelon, after all, and ever since then she had spent a good deal of time waiting under a killing sun for game. Shooting René had taught Eve just how much she liked to stalk, hunt, and kill dangerous things. She didn't care for targeting shy gazelles or graceful giraffes, but the huge wild boars of Poland or the pride of man-eating lions stalking a village in east Africa had proved fair targets for the pair of Lugers sitting oiled and immaculate in the satchel under her chair. And no one on a hunting party cared if she still swore too much, drank too much, and occasionally woke shuddering from nightmares, because it wasn't uncommon for her fellow hunters to show similar scars. Not on the hands, maybe, but in the eyes—eyes that had seen terrible things and now looked for respite in the world's more remote and dangerous far corners. There had been a tense, graying English colonel on the last safari who never said a word about Eve's mangled knuckles as long as she never inquired why he'd left his regiment after El Alamein, who had sat up late over a good many bottles of Scotch and asked if Eve fancied traveling with him this winter to see the pyramids. Perhaps she would. He had long-fingered hands a little like Cameron's.

A car rumbled past the café-garage—a Bugatti with the top down, full of whooping Italian boys on their way to the coast. This place saw good business from the fast-living drivers racing along the Riviera roads, Eve judged from the expanded garage. Finn's silver Bentley was there, the one she'd given him, and next to it a Peugeot with its hood raised and an Aston Martin up on blocks. She could well imagine people coming to the garage for repairs and waiting at the adjoining café, nibbling biscuits with rose jam, drinking too much wine, crooning along to the radio. Edith Piaf was playing now—*"Mon légionnaire,"* an old favorite.

It was late afternoon by the time the car chuffed up the slope: the Lagonda, rolling along at a dignified pace, her dark blue sides still buffed shiny as a dime. It pulled into the garage, and Eve waited, smiling. A moment later out came Charlie in slim black pants and a white blouse, tanned golden-brown, her hair cropped in a sleek bob. She swung a picnic basket in one hand and with the other kept firm hold on a little girl's dusty smock. Eve wondered how old her goddaughter was, and had no idea. Eighteen months? Eve hadn't seen her since the christening, and this sharp-chinned blond creature with the furious scowl was very different from the gurgling armful in rose-vine-embroidered frills whom Eve had held over the font. She'd donned her medals for the occasion, worn straight and proud on her shoulder where they belonged, and tiny Evelyn Rose Kilgore had nearly tugged off the Croix de Guerre in her baby fist.

"Finn," Charlie was calling over her shoulder. "Stop tinkering. It's Sunday. You are not allowed to tinker on Sunday."

His voice floated out. "Almost done. That old oil leak . . ."

"Good thing we don't use the Lagonda for anything but picnics. She's practically scrap."

"Have a little respect, Charlie lass." Finn came out then, tousled and rangy, collar unbuttoned to show his brown throat. All the café girls were eying that triangle of skin at his neck like they wanted to eat it, but he had one arm around his wife and the other reaching down to pick up the baby. "Och, Evie Rose," he said in his broadest Scots. "You're a braw handful, you wee bairn you."

"She's horrible," Charlie said as her daughter let out a yell that could cut sheet iron. "One cranky baby minus one afternoon nap equals tantrums to the power of ten. Let's put her down to bed early tonight . . ."

They hadn't seen Eve yet, tucked at the farthest table under the shade of the awning. She waved one gnarled hand overhead. Her hands still got their share of stares, and they still weren't too good at anything but pulling a trigger, but that was all right. Any *fleur du mal* who lived to be old was entitled to a little wear and tear.

Seeing the figure waving under the awning, Charlie shaded her eyes and then let out a shout, pelting toward Eve. "You're g-going to hug me, aren't you," Eve said to no one in particular. She sighed, and rose, and went grinning to be hugged. "Goddamn Yanks."

Author's Note

Louise de Bettignies is a historical figure little known today—and undeservedly so, for the courage, ingenuity, and resourcefulness of the woman christened the queen of spies needs no exaggeration to make for thrilling reading. Recruited by one Captain Cecil Aylmer Cameron, who had already set up intelligence operations in Folkestone and who had an eye for talent, former governess Louise de Bettignies took the code name of Alice Dubois (among several, though the nickname of *Lili* was my own invention) and turned her facility with languages and her organizational flair to the intelligence business. The result was one of the war's most spectacularly successful spy rings.

The Alice Network was supplied by Louise's many sources based in the Lille area, and reported on the local stretch of German front with a speed and accuracy that made British intelligence and military men gush. "The services Louise de Bettignies rendered are inestimable." "A regular modern day Joan of Arc." "If anything happened to her, it would be nothing less than a calamity." The Germans were equally impressed (if incensed) by the uncanny accuracy of the underground information flow, so efficient that new artillery placements were often bombed within days of being set up. Bigger intelligence prizes were unearthed by the Alice Network as well: the kaiser's visit where his train narrowly escaped being bombed, and the Verdun objective, which was one of Louise's last reports (which, tragically, went unbelieved at the command level).

The leader of the Alice Network was constantly on the move between German-occupied France, free France, Belgium, England, and the Netherlands as she passed reports, collected information, and checked on her agents, and her methods of information smuggling (coded messages wrapped around rings or hairpins, tucked below cakes in cake boxes, slipped between the pages of magazines) are all true as recorded here. Her physical courage was remarkable—she routinely sneaked across the hostile border under German searchlights and armed sentries, the ground littered with the bodies of refugees who had been spotted and shot, and she remained undeterred even after seeing a pair of escapees blown up by a mine scant yards ahead. Perhaps even more remarkable was her ability to think on her feet: Louise de Bettignies had an uncanny ability to bluff her way past checkpoints, whether by juggling packages until an exasperated sentry waved her through, or by utilizing local children in a game of tag to smuggle her a pass (both true incidents). Also true is the remarkable occasion when she was recognized on the way to a rendezvous by a German general who knew her from a chess match played during her governess days, and who gallantly put his car at her disposal.

Eve Gardiner is a fictional character, but two things about her are very real. One is her stammer—my husband has struggled with a stutter all his life, and his struggles are Eve's: the periodic difficulty with ordinary conversation, the moments of anger or high emotion that smooth out speech, the frustration and fury at being interrupted, talked over, or automatically assumed to be less intelligent. It was my husband's idea to give my young WWI spy a stutter and to see her turn it into an asset, to weaponize a weakness and use it against those who would underestimate her. The other real-life influence on Eve's character is her code name. When Louise de Bettignies's luck finally ran out in the autumn of 1915, a young woman named Marguerite Le François was arrested with her. In the interrogation that followed over the next few hours, the Germans quickly determined that the terrified young Marguerite was no spy, merely a local girl who had foolishly allowed a friendly stranger to borrow her pass at a checkpoint. She was released, scolded, and told to go home, even as Louise was arrested and transported to prison. The historical Marguerite Le François was very probably just an innocent dupe . . . but what if she wasn't? As I read a historical account of the arrest where the two women were stripped, searched, and terrorized, where young Marguerite moved the Germans to pity by sobbing and fainting, and Louise incensed them by eating a coded message and then asking for a brandy, I couldn't help but wonder if the two imprisoned women pulled off their last and best bluff while in German handcuffs. Thus was Eve Gardiner born, and I slid her as a mostly fictional third party into the existing historical duology of Louise and her chief lieutenant.

The bespectacled Léonie van Houtte was very real to history, working under the code name of Charlotte Lameron (changed to Violette Lameron, as I already had a Charlotte). Léonie first joined the war effort as a Red Cross nurse, and soon afterward was recruited as

Louise de Bettignies's staunch aide and loyal friend. "I was ready to follow her anywhere," Léonie later wrote, "for I knew instinctively that she was a girl capable of great things." Though Léonie was arrested shortly before Louise, the two were tried together, sentenced together, and served their prison time at Siegburg together. Louise died in Siegburg of a pleural abscess, but Léonie survived, a be-medalled veteran spy who married a journalist after the war and managed a china shop in Roubaix. Her husband later wrote *La Guerre des Femmes*, a memoir of Louise de Bettignies's war work as related to him by his wife. Léonie's precise first-hand accounts were invaluable, including detailed descriptions of the network's operations, Louise's arrest, the trial, and the years in Siegburg filled with horrendous abuses and rare triumphant moments—like the occasion when Louise incited her fellow inmates to strike rather than make munitions. Many of Louise's sparkling *bon mots* are also quoted direct from *La Guerre des Femmes*.

Another historical figure on the network's roster is Antoine, briefly mentioned in this book as Lili's document forger. The real Antoine le Four was a bookseller with the soul of a poet, an expert in forged antiques— and as his modern-day descendants are only now learning from his archived letters, he very possibly turned his skill at forgery detection in the other direction, and made fake papers for the Alice Network. Several of his family may also have been involved in the network, including his young sister Aurélie le Four, who acted as courier escort and was raped and impregnated by German soldiers as described by Violette in chapter 22. Her subsequent abortion, also verified by family archives, was performed by a nurse friend of Louise de Bettignies, though it is not known for certain if that nurse was Violette/Léonie. Both Aurélie and Antoine appear to have continued their resistance work even after Louise's imprisonment, fortunately escaping arrest themselves. Their letters provide a poignant, powerful look into the depth of French suffering, and the power of French patriotism.

English patriotism is no less powerfully represented in the person of real-life historical figure Captain (later Major) Cecil Aylmer Cameron. The man known to his sources as Uncle Edward recruited not only Louise de Bettignies, but Léon Trulin, another French spy who became a martyr after being arrested and shot by the Germans. Cameron's unusual past—his arrest on charges of insurance fraud, the prison term he served supposedly trying to protect his wife, his reinstatement to intelligence work during the war, and his post-war suicide—is all true, though any speculation on my part about motivations for the fraud, the state of his marriage, or the character of his wife are purely fictionalized for the sake of the story. One of Cameron's code names during the war, however, was "Evelyn," and that is the name he gave to his only child.

René Bordelon, like Eve, is a fictional character based on a tiny scrap of historical truth. Profiteers like him certainly existed, and he became my bridge between the two wars and the two timelines. He also became the historically nameless informer who passed the name of Oradour-sur-Glane to the Milice, and thus to the Nazis during World War II.

The massacre of Oradour-sur-Glane's inhabitants remains a mystery as well as a tragedy. Confusion and conflicting reports abound: an informant apparently reported to the Milice that French Resistance activity centered in the area had resulted in the kidnapping and execution of a German officer, but it isn't known if the Resistance activity was centered in Oradour-sur-Glane or in nearby Oradour-sur-Vayres, or if it existed at all. It will probably never be known why the SS officer who handled the matter decided to massacre an entire village in reprisal (he received considerable censure from his German superiors afterward), or if a complete massacre was even his intent in the first place—there is some conjecture that Resistance explosives were already being stored in the Oradour-sur-Glane church, resulting in the explosion and fire that killed so many. The only thing certain in the fog of war is that the men of Oradour-sur-Glane were mostly rounded up and shot in barns and surrounding village buildings, while the women and children were herded into the church and killed. The outlying execution sites had some survivors, but only one survived the inferno at the church: Madame Rouffanche. I lifted the story of her escape almost word for word from her testimony at the 1953 trial where the surviving known SS officers who took part in the massacre were tried and condemned for their crimes. It is true that a young mother and her baby attempted to climb through the church window after Madame Rouffanche, and that they were killed by gunfire—it was, however, a local woman named Henriette Joyeux and her infant son, not the fictional Rose Fournier. The town of Oradour-sur-Glane stands empty to this day as an eerie ghost-town memorial: roofless bullet-scarred buildings, burned clocks permanently stopped at four in the afternoon, the rusted-out Peugeot permanently parked by the fairground. Madame Rouffanche lived nearby for the rest of her long life.

Finn Kilgore is fictional, though his experiences liberating the concentration camp at Belsen are lifted directly from the testimony of soldiers of the 63rd Anti-Tank Regiment of the Royal Artillery who took part in the liberation. Charlie St. Clair and her family are also fictional, though the bleak situation faced by unmarried pregnant girls was nearly as dire in her day as it was in Eve's. Abortions were illegal, but obtainable for women who were rich enough (like Charlie) to pay for a safe operation, or desperate enough (like Eve) to risk death rather than pregnancy. Many women in German-occupied territory faced such harsh choices in World War I—Aurélie le Four's letters, begging God and her family to forgive her for choosing not to bear the child of her rapists, are heart-breaking. Eve would have faced even more disastrous consequences than unwed motherhood, given the historical double standard for women in the intelligence world. Spying at that time did not have the glamorous gloss it later achieved thanks to James Bond and Hollywood; it was not seen as a gentleman's profession, much less a lady's. If a woman had to dirty herself in spying she must keep her reputation intact, and great pains were taken to emphasize that female sources like Louise de Bettignies were still virtuous. "Coquettes they may have been, but prostitutes never," a biographer of Louise wrote earnestly of the women in the Alice Network. "[They] never resorted to the customary feminine wiles to obtain information." Women like Eve and Louise lived with harsher realities, but would have known very well that female spies were seen either as Madonnas or whores: stainless visions of purity like the martyred Edith Cavell, or sultry untrustworthy harlots like Mata Hari.

As always, I have taken some liberties with historical record, shifting some events and compressing others to serve the story. Car ferries like the one that transported Finn's precious Lagonda to France existed in 1947, though I wasn't able to verify there was such a ferry from Folkestone to Le Havre. Louise de Bettignies and Marguerite Le François were driven to Tournai for their interrogation before Marguerite's release and Louise's official arrest. There was a lapse of a few days after the trial in Brussels before the women were told their death sentences had been commuted to prison terms.

The matter of Louise's conviction and what evidence the Germans had on her remains debatable. She refused to give away anything during her months of imprisonment; the Germans finally got her cellmate Mlle Tellier to pass on some letters Louise had written, but it's difficult to say if they got anything incriminating from those letters. I have arranged the existing conflicting reports to make a clearer climax, but Louise de Bettignies may have been convicted on very little hard evidence at all besides being caught with multiple identification cards while trying to sneak past a checkpoint on a borrowed pass.

The sequence of events around Louise's death is another place I have condensed the narrative. Her operation for pleural abscesses happened somewhat earlier that year, as she did not die immediately after surgery but managed to survive for some months as an invalid—another example of her remarkable toughness, since according to *La Guerre des Femmes,* Louise's operation lasted four agonizing hours in an unheated and inadequately disinfected room of the notorious Siegburg infirmary that had recently housed a typhus epidemic. It's impossible to say if the Siegburg officials intended for that surgery to kill her; the infirmary's lack of hygiene and proper medical care killed many patients even without extra malice intended. But Louise was certainly a problem prisoner for the Germans, and they had little compassion for her dying days, refusing her final request to be sent to die in her mother's care, and ultimately sending her from Siegburg to a lonely deathbed in Cologne, away from her loyal friends and fellow prisoners. I dearly wished I could have changed history and given Louise a better fate; I confess I condensed her post-operation suffering. Louise's grand funeral took place in 1920 rather than 1919, when her body was finally repatriated.

The female spies of World War I are largely forgotten today. As much as their contributions during the war were appreciated, there was a certain unease with how to treat them afterward. Women who entered the active zone of combat were generally viewed by the public in one of two ways: as females who shed all womanliness and became hardened and mannish thanks to the dangers of war, or as gallant little women forced by duty to take up dangerous burdens, but still fragile flowers at heart. Louise de Bettignies was admired, praised, and heaped with medals, but her contemporaries focused far less on her toughness and bravery than on her tiny stature, her femininity, her patriotism. "Louise was the most womanly woman one could imagine . . . There was nothing of the Amazon about her." Matters were no different after World War II, when Charlie St. Clair would have been seeing the calls for Rosie the Riveter to put down the burdens of war and return to hearth and home where she belonged. Clearly, women in active fighting zones unsettled their contemporaries, but they still left a legacy behind. Girls of the '30s and '40s joined the SOE to train as spies against the Nazis because they had been inspired by books and stories about women like Louise de Bettignies—and they weren't inspired by her feminine graces. They were inspired by her courage, her toughness, and her unflinching drive, just as I imagined Charlie being inspired by Eve's. Such women were *fleurs du mal* indeed—with steel, with endurance, and with flair, they thrived in evil and inspired others in doing so.

Acknowledgments

I owe heartfelt thanks to many people who helped in the writing of this book. My mother, who hashed out countless plot tangles with me over long walks and even longer phone conversations. My husband, who fine-tuned Eve's stammer in every scene and frequently told me, "You keep writing, I'll make dinner." My wonderful critique partners, Stephanie Dray and Sophie Perinot, whose red pencils and insights proved absolutely invaluable. My agent, Kevan Lyon, and editors, Amanda Bergeron and Tessa Woodward, cheerleaders par excellence. My MRW chapter mate, Lisa Christie, and her husband, Eric, for answering my questions about classic cars, fact-checking my mechanical details, and providing me with a tour of the wonderful Henry Petronis car collection. And finally, Annalori Ferrell, whose bilingual talents aided immeasurably in translating French research documents and teaching me suitably colorful French curses, and who provided an insider's look at the World War I occupation of northern France under which past generations of her family lived. It is with the permission of Anna and her family that her great-great uncle Antoine le Four, along with his stalwart sister Aurélie, are named in the book as members of the Alice Network.

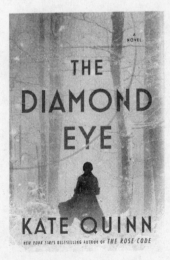

In the summer of 1942, as the world was locked in war against Hitler,

a woman crossed the sea from the Soviet Union to the United States.

She was a single mother, a graduate student, a library researcher.

She was a soldier, a war hero, a sniper with 309 kills to her name.

She was Russia's envoy, America's sweetheart, and Eleanor Roosevelt's dear friend.

Her story is incredible. Her story is true.

Meet Lady Death.

PROLOGUE

27 August, 1942
Washington, D.C.

He stood with a pocketful of diamonds and a heart full of death, watching a Russian sniper shake hands with the First Lady of the United States.

"Whoever heard of a girl sniper?" the marksman heard a photographer behind him grumble, craning for a look at the young woman who had just disembarked from the embassy limousine. She'd seemed to flinch at the barrage of camera flashes like muzzle fire, averting her gaze and walking in a phalanx of Soviet minders up the steps of the White House. "I say she's a fake," the photographer snorted.

Yet we couldn't resist coming here for a look at her, thought the marksman, idly flipping his falsified press badge. A delegation from the Soviet Union arriving for the international student conference that was Eleanor Roosevelt's latest goodwill project—it wouldn't have merited more than a few lines of newsprint, much less rousted a lot of hungover journalists and photographers out of their beds before dawn and sent them scurrying to the White House gates with pens in hand, if not for that girl in her crisp olive-green uniform.

"Did they say she had seventy-five kills on the Russian front?" a *Washington Post* journalist wondered, rummaging his notes. "I thought it was over a hundred . . ."

"Higher," said the marksman in the Tidewater Virginia drawl he'd grown up with. He'd long since ironed his soft southern vowels out into a flat mid-Atlantic cadence that could belong anywhere and nowhere, but he often let Virginia creep back into his tone, depending on who he was talking to. People trusted a southern accent, and they found themselves trusting the marksman: a loose-jointed man of medium height, medium hair between brown and blond, a bony face and mud-colored eyes, usually jingling a clutter of uncut diamonds and loose bullets in his trouser pocket. Bullets and diamonds; the job and its payment. He didn't like banks; anyone who hired him paid in cash, which he then promptly converted to jewels. Lighter than cash, easy to hide—just like bullets. He always kept a handful of both on hand. You never knew when you'd have to shoot or run.

"How does a girl like that kill over a hundred Nazis?" a photographer at his side was speculating, still watching the Russian woman on the front steps of the White House, standing to one side in a cluster of dark-suited embassy men as the First Lady welcomed the rest of the Soviet delegation. "Wasn't she a librarian or a schoolteacher or something?"

"Russkies let women in their army, though . . ."

Their medical battalions, maybe, the marksman thought. *But even the Reds don't make women into snipers.*

Yet he was here to see for himself, wasn't he? Wanting a look at the woman whose sparse biography he had already committed to memory: Lyudmila Pavlichenko; twenty-six years old; fourth-year history student at the Kiev State University and senior research assistant at the Odessa Public Library—before the war. Then war was declared, followed by thirteen months of continuous fighting against Hitler's forces on the Russian front.

Nickname: Lady Death.

"Dammit, how many kills *was* it on her tally?" The *Washington Post* journalist was still searching his notes. "Was it more than two hundred?"

Three hundred and nine, the marksman thought, but he didn't believe a word of it. He was thirty-eight years old and had been operating for nineteen of those years, and he'd barely hit thirty marks. Was he supposed to believe that this little junior librarian/schoolteacher had racked up over ten times that number in barely more than a year?

No. Lady Death was a trick pony stuffed with Soviet propaganda, handpicked for this student delegation, and the marksman could see why. A pretty brunette with lively dark eyes and a neat, photogenic face above her bemedalled uniform, nothing like the sort of mannish freak Americans would expect of a Russian female soldier. The Soviets needed American aid; they needed good press coverage on this delegation to American shores, so they'd handpicked the most winsome candidates they could find. Front and center, this girl sniper who looked so small and appealing beside that tall bony bitch, Eleanor Roosevelt.

"Congratulations on your safe arrival in America." The press corps clustered close enough to hear the First Lady's cultured, silver-spoon voice easily as she addressed the Soviet delegation, see the flash of her horse teeth. "On behalf of my husband the President, welcome to the White House. He looks forward to meeting you all at a later time, and invites you to spend your first days on American soil under our roof. You are some of the first Soviet guests to be hosted in the White House, a historic moment in the friendship between our nations."

She began ushering the Russians inside, and that was that. It wasn't even six-thirty yet, the skies above the capitol barely flushed with sunlight as the pack of journalists, photographers, and one lone innocuous assassin began to disperse. "Never thought I'd see the day a Russian sniper got welcomed to the White House," a grizzled columnist grumbled. "FDR will rue the day."

He won't be alive to do it, the marksman thought, eyes still on Mila Pavlichenko's neat dark head as she followed the First Lady toward the doors of the White House. *In nine days—the last day of the international conference—President Roosevelt will be dead.*

"I can see the headlines now," the *Washington Post* reporter muttered, scribbling in his pad. "'Russian Female Sniper Receives Warm White House Welcome.'"

The marksman smiled, jingling his pocketful of diamonds and bullets again. Ten days from now, the headlines would scream, "Russian Female Sniper Murders FDR."

CHAPTER 1

was not a soldier yet. We were not at war yet. I could not conceive of taking a life yet. I was just a mother, twenty-one and terrified. When you're a mother, panic can engulf you in the blink of an eyelash. All it takes is that instant when your eye sweeps a room for your child and doesn't find him.

"Now, Mila," my mother began. "Don't be angry—"

"Where's Slavka?" I hadn't even pulled off my patched gloves and snow-dusted coat yet, but my heart was already thudding. There was my son's half-constructed block factory on the floor of the apartment, there was the small worn pile of his books, but no sturdy dark-haired five-year-old.

"His father dropped in. He knew he had missed the appointment—"

"Nice of Alexei to acknowledge that," I gritted. The second appointment I had set up to have our divorce finalized; the second appointment my husband had missed. Each time it had taken me months to scrape up the required fifty-ruble fee; weeks to get an appointment with the backlogged office; then hours waiting in a cold, stuffy corridor craning my eyes for a sight of my husband's golden head . . . all to lead to nothing. Anger smoldered in the pit of my stomach. Any Soviet citizen already spent entirely too much time waiting in lines as it was!

My mother wiped her hands on her apron, her big dark eyes pleading. "He was very sorry, *malyshka*. He wanted to take Slavka out for a treat. He's hardly seen the boy these past few years, his own son—"

Whose fault is that? I wanted to retort. I wasn't the one keeping our son out of Alexei's life. My husband was the one who decided only a month or two after giving our son the name of Rostislav Pavlichenko that marriage and fatherhood weren't really to his liking. But my mother's kind, pretty face looked hopeful, and I bit back my hot words.

Mama's voice was soft. "Maybe there's a reason he keeps missing these appointments."

"Yes, there is," I stated. "To make me dance on his string."

"Maybe what he's really hoping for is to reconcile."

"Mama, not again—"

"A *doctor*, Mila. The best surgeon in Ukraine, you said—"

"He is, but—"

"A man on his way up. Rooms of his own rather than a communal apartment, a good salary, a Party member. Not things to throw away." My mother launched into the old argument. She hadn't approved of how Alexei and I had come together; she'd said it happened too fast and he was too old for me and she was right—but she also wanted me safe and warm and fed. "You always said he's no drunk and never once hit you," she went on now. "Maybe he's not the man you dreamed of, but a surgeon's wife won't ever stand in a bread queue, and neither will his children. You don't remember the hungry years, you were just a little thing . . . but there's nothing a woman won't put up with to keep her babies fed."

I looked down at my worn gloves. None of what she said was wrong, I knew that.

I also knew that a part of me was afraid to let my little boy be alone with his father.

"Mama. Where are they?"

The shooting range wasn't much, just a converted storage space: bars on the windows, a small armory, a line of wooden shields with targets, men on a firing line standing with braced feet and pistols raised or lying on their bellies to fire rifles . . . and in the middle, a tall blond man with a small boy. My stomach flipped in relief.

"Every man should know how to shoot," I could hear Alexei telling our son as I came closer. He was showing Slavka how to hold a rifle far too large for him, and his voice had that expansive cadence I remembered so well. There was nothing my husband liked better than explaining things to people who knew less than him. "Though inborn abilities are required to be a true expert, of course."

"What kind of abilities, Papa?" Slavka was round-eyed, looking up at this golden stranger he hardly knew. A man who had walked out of his life without a backward glance when he was just six weeks old.

"Patience. A good eye. A steady hand, and a precise feel for the tool in your grip. That's why your Papa's such a good shot—he has a surgeon's touch." Alexei flashed a smile downward, and Slavka's eyes got even rounder. "Now, you try—"

"Rostislav Alexeivich," I called, striding down the

firing line, careful to keep down-range. "Give that rifle back. You're too young to be handling weapons that large."

Slavka started guiltily, but Alexei didn't look surprised to see me or my thunderous face. "Hello there," he said easily, brushing a lock of fair hair off his tall forehead. He loomed a head above me: thirty-six, leanly built and golden, his teeth showing white in his easy smile. "You're looking lovely, *kroshka*."

I didn't bother asking him not to call me that—he already knew it made my hackles rise. For about one week during our marriage I had found it adorable when he called me his *breadcrumb*—"Because you're such a little bit of a thing, Mila!"—but it hadn't take me long to realize a crumb was something that could be flicked away into a dustbin. A piece of trash.

"You shouldn't have taken Slavka out without me," I said instead, as evenly as possible. The pulse of fear was still beating through me, even at the sight of my son here and safe. I didn't really think Alexei would try to steal our son away from me, but such things weren't unheard of. At the factory where I'd worked when Slavka was a baby, one of the lathe operators had wept and raged when her former husband swooped their daughter out of school and took her off to Leningrad without any warning. She never got the girl back; her husband had too many Party friends in his pocket. These things *happened*.

"Relax, Mila." Alexei's smile broadened, and that was when the fear in my stomach started curling back into anger. He knew I'd been afraid; he knew, and he rather enjoyed it. "Who's going to teach a boy to shoot if his father doesn't do it?"

"I know how to shoot, I can—"

"Anyway, it doesn't matter." Another amused glance. "You're here now. Here to spoil the fun!"

I saw him throw a wink over my head to some friend behind me. *Women!* that wink said. *Always spoiling a man's fun, am I right?* I busied myself pulling off my gloves and disentangling from my winter coat, aware I was the only woman standing on the firing line. Females stood at the back, applauding when their brothers or boyfriends or husbands sank a shot. From Lenin on down, Soviet men talk a good game about women standing shoulder to shoulder to their men in every field society had to offer, but when it came to children being tended, dishes being scrubbed, or applause being given, my eyes had always observed that it was still female hands doing most of the tending, scrubbing, and clapping. Not that I questioned such a thing overly much: it was simply the way of the world, and always had been.

"*Mamochka?*" Slavka looked up at me anxiously.

"Give that weapon back, please," I said quietly, brushing a hand over his hair to make it plain I wasn't angry at him. "You're too little for a rifle that large."

"No, he's not," Alexei scoffed, taking the weapon. "Baby him like that and you'll never make a man of him. Watch me load, Slavka . . ."

Alexei's hands moved swiftly, loading the TOZ-8. It was his hands I'd noticed first, when I saw him at that dance—a surgeon's hands, long-fingered and precise, working with absolute skill and focus. *What, you can't say no when a tall blond man smiles at you?* my mother scolded when she learned I was pregnant—but it wasn't Alexei Pavlichenko's height or his charm or even his hands that had tumbled me into his arms. It was his skill, his focus, his drive—so different from the boys my age, all horseplay and careless talk. Alexei hadn't been a boy, he'd been a man over thirty who knew what he wanted—and what he wanted, he trained for; aimed for; *got*. I'd seen that in him that first night, young and laughing as I was in my flimsy violet-printed dress. Barely fifteen years old.

A mother nine months later.

I sent Slavka to hang up my coat at the back of the room, then turned back to Alexei. "You missed the appointment." Fighting to keep my voice even. I was not going to sound shrill; it would just amuse him. "I waited nearly three hours."

He shrugged. "It slipped my mind. I'm a busy man, *kroshka*."

"You know they require us both to be there in order to finalize the divorce. You don't want to be married to me, Alexei, so why won't you show up?"

"I'll make it up to you," he said, breezy, and one of his friends farther down the line laughed, seeing my face.

"She doesn't want you to make it up to her!" Laughter rippled behind me, and someone muttering, *I'll let her make it up to me!* Alexei grinned over my head.

"I'll set another appointment to finalize the divorce," I said as coolly as I could manage. "If you can just be there, it will all be over in a matter of minutes." I didn't like the mess I'd made of my own life, a mother at fifteen, estranged within months, and potentially divorced at twenty-one—but better to be divorced than to be stranded in this limbo of the last six years, neither married nor unmarried.

"Ah, don't poker up, Mila. You know I like to tease." Alexei gave me a playful dig in the ribs. Only it was a dig that hurt through my wool blouse. "You're looking well, you know. Glowing, almost . . . Maybe there's a reason you want this divorce? A man?"

He was still teasing, still playful, but there was an

edge behind the words. He didn't really want me any-more, but he didn't like the idea of anyone else wanting me, either. Much less having me.

"There's no one," I said. Even if there had been some-one else, I wouldn't have told him—but there wasn't. Between university classes and studies, Komsomol meetings and caring for Slavka, I was getting by on about five hours of sleep a night. Where was there the *time* for a new man in my life?

Alexei turned the rifle over between his hands, still looking at me. "You're in your third year of studies now?"

"My second." The history department at Kiev Uni-versity, and my student card had been hard-won after a year of studying at night while working shifts as a turner lathe operator at the arsenal factory. Back then I'd been operating on about four hours of sleep, but it was all worth it. All for Slavka, for his future and mine. "Alexei, if I can get another appointment—"

"Alexei!" someone called further down the firing line, looking me over. "This the little wife?"

My husband brought me under his arm with a quick squeeze. "Tell her what a good shot I am, Seryosha. She's not impressed with me anymore. Just like a wife, eh?" Alexei saw the look on my face and leaned down to nuzzle my ear. "Just teasing, *kroshka,* don't bristle."

"Your man's good, watch him with the TOZ-8!"

"Just a simple single-shot rifle," Alexei told me as I wriggled out from under his arm. "We call it the Melkashka."

"I know what it's called." I was no expert, but I'd been to the range before with the factory shooting club; I knew something about firearms. "TOZ-8, good 120 through 180 meters—"

"TOZ-8, muzzle velocity 320 meters a second, good

from 120 to 180 meters," Alexei said, not listening. "Sliding bolt here—"

"I know. I've handled—"

He raised the rifle, fast and sure, and the crack of the shot sounded. "See? Dead center."

I bit my tongue hard enough to hurt. I wanted to turn my back, gather up my son, and storm out of here, but Slavka was dawdling by the coat hooks listening to two men having some loud political discussion—and I didn't want to depart without some kind of guarantee. A guarantee that the next appointment I set to finalize our divorce, Alexei would *be there*.

"You never used to spend much time at the range. What made you want to get so good at it?" I pushed out a note of grudging admiration for his marksmanship. "You're a surgeon; you know what happens to muscles and organs when they take a bullet. You used to tell me about patching wounds like that."

"Soon there will be war, don't you know that?" Reloading the Melkashka. "When that day comes, they'll need a gun in every hand."

"Not yours." As long as I could remember, my father had been shaking his head and saying, *One day there will be war,* but it hadn't happened yet. "If war comes, *you* won't be a soldier."

My husband frowned. "You think I'm not capable?"

"I mean a surgeon like you is too valuable to waste on the front line," I said quickly, recognizing my mistake. I hadn't lived with Alexei in so long, I'd forgot how to flatter his pride. "You'll be running a battlefield hospital, not pulling a trigger on command like a blind monkey."

His frown disappeared, and he raised the rifle. "A man sees chances in war, Mila. Chances he doesn't get in ordinary life. I intend to be ready."

He fired off another shot, not quite hitting the bull's-eye. "Good shot, Papa," Slavka said breathlessly, running back up.

Alexei ruffled his hair. Two young girls at the back were watching, winding their curls around their fingers, and maybe my husband saw their admiration, because he squatted down beside his son and said, "Let me show you."

That was the very first thing he'd said to *me*. To little Mila Belova, just past her fifteenth birthday and careening happily through a drafty dance hall, entranced by the music and the laughter and the violet dress swirling about my legs. I was dancing with a girlfriend, both of us eyeing the boys showing off across the room, and then the song changed to something slower, more formal . . . and a toweringly tall man with fair hair pulled me neatly away from my girlfriend and into the curve of his arm, saying "Let me show you . . ." Later he spread his coat on the grass for me to sit outside the dance hall and told me he meant to be a great man someday. *I'll make the name Pavlichenko resound from Moscow to Vladivostok.* He'd grinned, to show he was joking, but I knew he wasn't. Not really.

I can see it now, I'd laughed in reply. *Alexei Pavlichenko, Hero of the Soviet Union!* He burned bright with ambition, so bright he'd dazzled me. Looking at him now in the winter dimness of the shooting range, remembering how he'd taken my hand soon afterward and guided it as he whispered *Let me show you* in quite a different way . . . well. I could still admire the fire of ambition in him, much as I disliked him, but I couldn't feel even a flicker of the old bedazzlement.